D0638846

THE CASTRO GENE

Nonfiction by Todd Buchholz

New Ideas from Dead CEOs
New Ideas from Dead Economists
From Here to Economy
Market Shock
Bringing the Jobs Home

THE CASTRO GENE

A Novel

TODD BUCHHOLZ

IPSWICH, MASSACHUSETTS

Copyright © 2007 by Todd Buchholz

FIRST EDITION

All rights reserved. No part of this book may be reproduced in any form or by
any electronic or mechanical means, including information storage and
retrieval systems, without permission in writing from the publisher,
except by a reviewer who may quote brief passages in a review.

This book is a work of fiction. Names, characters, places, and incidents either
are the products of the author's imagination or are used fictitiously.
Any resemblance to actual events or locales or persons, living or dead,
is entirely coincidental.

ISBN-13: 978-1-933515-06-9
ISBN-10: 1-933515-06-6

Published in the United States by Oceanview Publishing,
Ipswich, Massachusetts
www.oceanviewpub.com

2 4 6 8 10 9 7 5 3 1

PRINTED IN THE UNITED STATES OF AMERICA

To my mother, Joan, and grandparents, Samuel and
Pauline Lewis, the greatest storytellers of my life.

THE CASTRO GENE

PROLOGUE

NOVEMBER 22, 1963

Oriana screamed at her chauffeur. *"Get me home! Get me home!"*

The Bentley raced through the barren streets of Palm Springs, ripping through the dusty roads lined with date palms. Oriana rocked back and forth in the back seat of the car and wept into a silk scarf.

She hadn't felt so lonely since packing her bags and fleeing the Havana Hilton in '59. Back then, she didn't even have a chance to kiss her lover good-bye. Too many bayonets waving in the streets, too many Americans targeted by the commandos of Fidel Castro.

But this was worse. Even before the Bentley finished braking in front of her estate, she sprung out of the vehicle, kicked off her Chanel heels, and ran. She flung open the doors, nearly knocked the Rodin off its pedestal in the foyer, and rushed to her television—the first color television in Palm Springs. As it warmed up she wondered how her careful plans could have been shredded so thoroughly.

The vacuum tube finally yielded a picture, and she saw a young reporter from Texas on CBS describing the gunshots that tore apart the president. And the country.

Oriana collapsed onto her sofa and sobbed. "It's all wrong, it's all wrong."

But for the next forty-two years, through the Warren Commission, Watergate, and Whitewater, she kept quiet about what she knew.

CHAPTER 1

2005

Ten thousand boxing fans screamed for bloody murder, their panting and shouting shaking the molded plastic seats at the Taj Mahal Hotel and Casino in Atlantic City.

"He's dying out there!" shouted "Fight Doctor" Hank Robbins, a Philadelphia podiatrist who provided overheated commentary for HBO Sports. "Perez can hardly hold up his gloves. But will ya take a look at Braden! This twenty-four-year-old kid is snorting and charging like a young bull chasing a red cape."

"The Braden boy shows stamina, but can he put Perez away?" replied Carl Mann, who'd already been sprayed with blood from Perez's nose. "Lots of kids can hit hard, but it takes real skill to close the door on a fight."

Lucas Braden was wondering the same thing. Did he have the killer instinct? Though he looked a hell of a lot better than Perez, after seven rounds his arms hurt, and his ten-ounce gloves felt as heavy as metal anvils. As he watched referee Dickie Mill check out Perez's dilated pupils to ensure the half-Cuban/half-Puerto Rican middleweight could continue, Luke tried to take inventory of his own body. His left eye felt puffed up from an elbow smashing his face in the second round. Perez had a vicious right jab. With a swollen left eye, Luke worried that he wouldn't see the jab coming. Legs? Numb. Luke had bounced and danced through round three, but after that his legs lost their spring. So much for jogging five miles and stair-stepping for an hour each day. All that sweat bought him just three rounds worth of stamina.

"Braden looks fresh!" the *Sports Illustrated* photographer yelled to his partner. With his floppy brown hair and wide blue-green eyes, Luke didn't have the classic mug of a boxer. Though his nose had been smashed numerous times, somehow it didn't look like the Kentucky Fried biscuit of most boxers. His neighbor, an elderly Chinese herbalist, fed Luke shark-fin soup and shark cartilage. "For my joints?" he asked the old man. "No, so your nose bounce back."

Luke heard the photographer's "fresh" comment and almost smiled through his mouthpiece. The photographers did not know that he was on the verge of collapse. None of them had ever been in a ring. You don't know the game—hell, you don't know yourself—until you've felt a left hook crawl across your jaw, crushing skin cells, collapsing a chin artery, and chopping off the blood flow to the brain. You blink, without really knowing whether your eyes will open again. You smell your own sweat, nostrils flare as Mother Nature prepares you for a battle that most men left behind in the Neanderthal era. Your body reaches back to some frightening prehistoric yesteryear and prepares you for a battle to the death. Sure, the cornerman may throw in the towel after four rounds, but your DNA, your sperm count, your testosterone, your very essence do not believe in the rules of the Marquis of Queensbury. You're not facing off against another athlete. You're fighting a saber-toothed tiger, a raging wild boar, a desperate, diseased hairy anthropod from one million B.C.

What the hell was he doing in the ring with these beasts?

"That ring was made for Dante not for a Braden," his father had warned him three years earlier when Luke disclosed his plans to enter professional boxing. He didn't know what his father was talking about, but that wasn't surprising. A professor of English literature at Columbia University, Dr. Francis Braden usually called up literary references when he scolded his son. The professor called his son a "Yahoo" so often during his childhood that Luke thought it was a sports team somewhere. Only later did he realize his father was comparing him to the smelly humanoids in *Gulliver's Travels*. And so Luke fled the Upper West Side of New York City at the age of seventeen, right out of high school, and enrolled in the College of Pugilistic Arts, that is, Delancy's Gym on West 28th Street.

Sure, he could have gone to college. No doubt some local college would have taken him with his C average. Every week Professor Braden would come home with brochures and applications—from schools no one had ever heard of—tucked deep into his leather briefcase embossed with the seal of Columbia University. The seal shows a woman seated on a throne, with the motto *In Lumine Tuo Videbimus Lumen*, "In Thy Light Shall We See Light." The light must have been blinding because his father couldn't see Luke's humiliation.

Luke was not dumb, but his father's "tweedier-than-thou" manner drove him away from teachers. He liked high school math and, of course, gym class, but history, English, and Spanish were for the pigeons in Central Park, not for young, horny boys.

Finally when his high school guidance counselor urged his father to put him on Ritalin, Luke exploded at both of them. "I don't have A.D.D. I'll tell you what I've got. I've got a case of being a normal seventeen-year-old boy. You know what that means? I just want to play sports and get laid."

That's the day Luke stuffed his clothes in a duffel bag, marched past his puzzled father, and took the subway to his new home, Delancy's gym. At Delancy's Gym he learned to box from an old white guy named Buck Roberts, who had earned his Golden Gloves championship back when Franklin Roosevelt was still a governor.

Taking one peek at the one-hundred-forty pound Luke, Buck told him to get a night job.

"Where?" Luke asked.

The old man with the broken nose picked up the cracked plastic telephone and called his buddy, a waiter at Smith & Wollensky's steakhouse on Third Avenue. Two hours later Luke was unloading ribs and chops, and was invited to eat a pound of aged top sirloin every night. At first, he just got heavier, but within eight weeks, Buck's weightlifting regimen turned the beef to beefcake. Luke started looking tougher, his punches backed by his prime ribs and powerful legs.

He didn't make close friends at the gym. The guys he sparred with didn't have fathers who taught at Columbia. Most of them couldn't identify their fathers in a police lineup. Luke kept quiet about his family. Even told one guy that his parents and two imaginary sisters had been killed in a train derailment next to a slag heap in Scranton, Pennsylvania. The street toughs sweating in the boxing rings knew he wasn't like them. His sparring partners, some of whom dealt drugs on the side, felt more comfortable with the drug lords from the country called Colombia than from a son of a professor in the university English department on West 116th Street. Roberts even nicknamed Luke "the professor."

Now as the bell rang for round eight, the twenty-four-year-old "professor" faced his most challenging test. Luke stared at the crowd and heard a loud thumping. It was his own heart. A group of Cuban-Americans sitting behind Perez's corner were waving flags and shouting "Perez *Ganara!* Perez *Ganara!*" A gray-haired man stood up and pumped his fists to encourage the spectators in the rafters. Luke could read "Papa" on his T-shirt. Luke could not tell the color of Papa Perez's shirt. Maybe being color blind was not such a bad thing for a boxer. The blood on the mat looked less vivid, rather greenish-gray, in fact.

None of Luke's relatives made it to Atlantic City for the fight. Perhaps his father's friends would read about it in the Sunday *Times* while enjoying brunch at Sarabeth's.

Luke glanced back at his corner. Not even Buck Roberts had made it. His cardiologist had slammed him on a low-fat, low-salt, low-stress diet. No travel. No excitement. Not even ESPN. Instead, old Buck sent Henry Beetle, a skinny, spectacled black kid even younger than Luke, to work the corner stool. Henry was a boxing savant. He looked like the class nerd of P.S. 80 in Harlem, but could tell you that in June 1930 "Slapsie Maxie" Rosenbloom knocked out Jimmy Slattery to nab the light heavyweight championship. He could tell you about Count Basie playing the Apollo in 1938, and he could curse you in Yiddish, Italian, and Cantonese. Most important, Henry knew how to stop a cut over the eye from bleeding into the socket.

"You got it, Prof!" Henry yelled. "It's a lock! Three more rounds to go! Ahead on points. Just like Ali-Frazier I. Let's keep scorin' the points. The knockout will follow!"

Luke couldn't hear Henry.

In a skybox suite high above the ring, protected from view by glass so dark that it would block even Clark Kent's vision, Paul Tremont watched three televisions. Cufflinks flashing, he paced the suite with graceful strides. One of Tremont's televisions showed the HBO broadcast of the fight. Another displayed a split-screen, closed-circuit camera aimed at Luke's and Perez's corners. A third television glittered with the Reuters financial trading screen, flashing red and green numbers representing Tokyo stocks and the foreign exchange action. The stylish, seventyish gent had wagered about half a billion dollars that the yen would fall against the U.S. dollar that evening. He also had bet $50,000 on Perez to win the bout against Braden.

Paul Tremont ignored the Reuters screen. Not only had he bet on Perez flattening Luke Braden, he was also channeling money to Perez's aunts and uncles in Miami Beach to keep Perez on the team, part of the Tremont stable of fighters. Just a few hundred thousand, chump change, a rounding error in his daily profit and loss statement.

Don King, Donald Trump, and some other showboats were trying to steal away Perez, tantalizing him with ridiculous promises, including a made-for-TV bio-pic starring Ricky Martin as Frederico Perez. But Tremont held the trump card. He had promised a small gift to Fidel Castro, a deed to an oil well off the coast of Venezuela. In exchange, Castro agreed to allow Tremont's private plane to fly Perez's mother from Havana to Miami after the fight. King and Trump couldn't pull off that kind of deal. To prepare for it, Tremont's security guards had placed Castro's telephone number on speed-dial in the skybox so the two barons could chat after the match.

Down on the canvas, the referee gently slapped Perez across the cheek and then clapped his hands together loudly. "Get it on, fellas!" Dickie Mill shouted. Mill was a bony-faced, jut-jawed ex-cop who enjoyed a good brawl. The networks loved him because he didn't shrink from blood and didn't censor or stop a violent rumble. In their battles for the attention of testosterone-charged seventeen-year-old males, Dickie Mill was their man.

With his ten-ounce left glove, Luke clumsily shoved the clear plastic mouth guard past his lips. He had been worried about the gloves, manufactured by a Mexican company. Buck Roberts called them "cripplers" because most of the padding is stuffed into the back of the glove, exposing the opponent's face, kidneys, and cervical discs to raw knuckles. Perez's corner had insisted on the lethal gloves.

Now Perez charged forward, his nose smeared with an oozing combination of blood and Vaseline. Luke glided toward the center of the ring. The cameras flashed around him in a 360-degree laser show, and the halogen television lights cast a savage heat. Luke stared at Perez's fists, which the Cuban-Puerto Rican held in front of his face. Perez had a roadkill face that looked like the treads on Goodyear snow tires. His record was forty-two wins and thirteen losses. Even the victories etched deep scars into his skin. Luke's punches had already added to the count. But Perez was tough, and his bulging, tatooed biceps kept Luke on edge.

Luke tapped Perez on the forehead with a jab, just to gauge his distance. He followed with a right cross to the shoulder, knocking Perez off balance. Or so Luke thought. Luke stepped in closer to follow with another right. That's when Perez unleashed his own right, which came out of nowhere, to smash into Luke's damaged eye. Luke quickly backed up and tried to cover his face. Perez glared with hunger and took another step forward.

"Cover up, Prof! Go to the ropes!" Henry advised.

The crowd leapt up roaring.

Luke worried that he was losing total vision in the left eye while the salivating Perez seemed revived. Perez unloaded another right, catching Luke on the ear. Suddenly Luke thought the crowd went silent. But it was just an eardrum that had quit on him.

Perez moved left, then right in front of Luke, testing Luke's reflexes. He fired a left into Luke's side and Luke winced. He knew he was in trouble. He dipped his knee, deliberately inviting Perez in closer. Perez took the bait, and delivered a left hook. Luke ducked. Perez's wild swing left his pockmarked face open. Luke bounced off the ropes, channeled all his energy and crashed his left fist into Perez's chin. Perez looked startled. His eyes rolled into his head. Luke lunged forward, driving into Perez's face a brutal combination of jabs and hooks. As blood and sweat sprayed across the ring, Perez fell toward his corner, sliding on his side. The moment his body hit the mat, the crowd turned silent, stunned by the quick reversal.

Luke immediately ran towards Henry. "Is it over?" he asked through his mouthpiece. "Can't hear. Left ear is blank. Can't see too good either."

"You bet. He's gone, man," Henry replied. Then Henry gave a thumbs-up to make sure Luke got the message.

They saw a different story in Perez's corner. Perez climbed to one knee and begged his trainer, "Stop the fight. *No mas*," he said, using the infamous expression of Roberto Duran, who quit fighting Sugar Ray Leonard in a humiliating bout in 1980.

Dickie Mill heard the plea. Disappointed, he looked at Perez's manager to overrule his fighter's surrender. He glanced up at Tremont's skybox too.

The manager, a beefy Hispanic, shouted to Perez: "C'mon! You're gonna fight! You get out there, you fucker. You can beat this guy!"

Perez shook his head and pointed to his neck.

In his skybox, Paul Tremont picked up his telephone and called down to the ring. He didn't care that the Reuters screen was beeping to alert him that the yen was spiking in Hong Kong and that he had just bled $25 million. "Christ, stop the fight," he yelled to Perez's trainer.

The cornerman was already pushing Perez out to the middle as Perez's father rushed to ringside, his Puerto Rican flag in hand. The cornerman and Dickie Mill appealed to Papa for support. Perez looked for the stool, but his team had hurled it out of the ring. Then Papa grabbed his son by the shoulders, ignoring the jiggling flesh that used to be hard muscle.

"You will go, boy!" he said shoving his son into the ring.

"Yes! Let's go!" screamed Dickie Mill.

"What kind of father is he?" Tremont asked behind the smoky glass. "He's selling his son like meat."

As Perez stumbled to his feet, his lips blue, Luke felt sick himself. Perez could no longer defend himself, but the crowd was cheering for a knockout. Luke didn't want to hit him, so he merely pushed Perez in the chest, and the weakened fighter tripped backwards to the rope. Dickie Mill rushed over and penalized Luke two points for dodging the fighter.

"You fight or you lose, Chicken Little!" Mill shouted.

Luke shoved Perez once more. Dickie Mill again deducted points from Luke's score.

"That's four points, Prof. Now the score's even," Henry shouted. "You gotta take this guy out or we'll lose on points."

It started in the upper deck. An avalanche of Fritos, Milk Duds, and programs flew into the ring.

"You're a wuss, Braden!" yelled a reporter.

A beer can crashed at his feet. From Perez's side he heard the cackling sounds of chickens, as Perez's fans flapped their arms in mockery.

In his opponent's eyes Luke saw a true picture, a picture of a damaged man. Unfortunately, Perez's eyes did not show up on the big-screen television that hovered forty feet above the ring. The pixels did not show his fear.

And so Dickie Mill grabbed Luke's ten-ounce gloves and pulled him toward Perez for the final thirty seconds of the round. Perez leaned forward and Luke retreated. The chicken clucks grew louder, and beer kept splashing. A battalion of yellow-shirted security guards streamed down the aisles to tame the disgusted crowd.

A Perez fan swiped an arena microphone, flipped the switch and yelled, "No *cajones*, Braden!" Like a fast-moving virus, the chant broke out, "No *cajones*! No *cajones*!"

Dickie Mill grabbed Luke by the gloves again. "No *cajones*, no points, boy! I'm deducting two more points." He held up two fingers to the judges.

Luke closed his eyes for a moment. He'd had the balls to stand up to his father. As a boy he'd been man enough to get through his mother's funeral without crying. As Mill backed away and clapped his hands together to resume the round, Luke drew back his left arm. Perez was staring at the right, as Luke fired a left hook to his temple that cracked like a thunderbolt. His opponent's head snapped to the right, his body stiffened as he dropped on his side like a heavy door knocked off its hinges.

The crowd stopped shouting. The avalanche of trash ceased. Perez's father dropped his Puerto Rican flag and ran to the center of the ring, along with the trainer. Dickie Mill rushed over to the judges and waved for a doctor. Luke tore across the ring shouting at Henry to cut off the laces of his bloody boxing gloves.

With that last punch, Luke got back his *cajones*. But he paid for them with the life of Frederico Perez.

"His own father murdered him," Paul Tremont muttered, picking up his phone and punching in the speed dial number for Fidel Castro to give him the bad news. He saw no reason to give away an oil well to a cold-hearted dictator.

CHAPTER 2

The doctors said that Luke's punches, delivered through those crippling Mexican gloves, flooded the subarachnoid spaces of Perez's brain with blood. Luke wasn't certain what the diagnosis meant, but he did know that he had committed murder. Oh sure, he knew it wasn't legally murder, though the Atlantic City police department did interrogate him. But his hands felt bloody. Just twenty-four years old, he felt banished from the ring, "Dante's ring," as his father called it. Though he had not spoken with his father in three years, he was now thankful that Professor Francis Braden never read the sports section of the paper.

For the next six weeks, Luke hung out in his cramped New York apartment, tucked in between the old Meatpacking District and the human meat market that was Greenwich Village. His street had become yuppified and gayified since he first remembered going down to the Village in the late 1980s. But his apartment was locked in a time warp, circa 1967. He had furnished it himself, and it had all the class and sophistication of a *Brady Bunch* special on television. Above his bed hung a photo of Muhammad Ali posing underwater for *Life* magazine in the 1960s, but the picture frame had two sides. Whenever Luke felt surly, he flipped over Ali to look at Sonny Liston, that bear of a boxer who threatened to crush his opponents' brains with his fists. We can't float like a butterfly, sting like a bee, and smile at the world all the time, Luke knew. We've all got gremlins struggling to burst out and do evil. Most of the time Luke kept Ali's face on display. But these past six weeks had been Sonny time.

What do you do after you've killed a man? Luke wondered as he peered out his window with its sliver of a view of the old Woolworth Building, in 1913 the world's tallest skyscraper at fifty-five stories. He was alive, though he still couldn't hear much from his left ear. It felt like he was permanently wearing an earmuff. He leaned against a pillow, turned on the television, and tried to teach himself to read lips.

He couldn't go back to Delancy's. Buck had shouted several encouraging messages into the answering machine, using every foul word he'd heard in seventy years of fighting. Luke did not return the calls. After a talent scout from the William Morris Agency called about starring in some professional wrestling battle to the death, Luke yanked out the phone cord. Though he thought about twisting the wires around his own neck, he figured that he shouldn't add to his body count. Frederico Perez was enough. Luke reached for the bottle of Glenlivet that he kept in the drawer next to the Gideon's Bible he had swiped from some hotel room. His father introduced him to single-malt Scotch when Luke told him that the guys at school drank Colt 45. Now, he felt trapped in Greenwich Village between the Gideons and the untouched gift of his father. He twisted open the Glenlivet, didn't bother to find a glass, and lost the rest of the evening.

But he couldn't afford to stay drunk. After paying his manager, agent, and publicist, he had little of his winnings left. Six weeks after the Perez fight, he was down to the few thousand dollars he had saved from butchering beef at Smith & Wollensky's. He didn't look much better than his bank account. His six-pack abs now blended into one slight bulge at the belly, a victim of Chinese takeout and Ray's Famous Pizza.

His apartment did not have much closet space, but he didn't need a lot of room. Most of his clothes consisted of gym shorts, jockstraps, and sweatshirts crammed into a locker at Delancy's. He owned one blue suit, and it was clean. With that blue suit and a buzz haircut, he got a job as a security guard at Gresham Bros. Investments, one of the oldest and most prestigious names in Wall Street money making. He was a "street man," according to Gresham lingo, that is, he hung out in the lobby, accepted packages from messengers, and occasionally shooed bums from dragging their loaded shopping carts into the Broad Street building. Luke usually walked to work from the Village. The other guards were "bridge-and-tunnel" people, riding the subway in from Brooklyn and Queens, often complaining about the stench of urine in the Broad Street station. None of them had fathers who were English professors at Columbia. They were like the guys punching the bags at Delancy's, only without criminal records. Also, most of them still had teeth.

In fact, his fellow guards thought Luke sounded like the young MBAs riding the elevators, who cranked out millions of dollars for the Brothers Gresham. One security guard, Lenny Baggio, actually accused Luke of being a spy for the partners.

"Why do you talk so good?" Lenny asked, through a twisted set of yellowish teeth that looked like the crowd jammed on the F train to Astoria, Queens.

"I'm an idiot savant, like *Rain Man*," Luke replied. "I speak perfect English, but everything else I do is shit."

Each morning he would watch the twenty-something girls in their cool black suits and bobbing ponytails flirt with their blue-suited male colleagues on their way up to the trading floor, that giant ATM machine on the thirtieth floor. A lot more than thirty floors separated Luke from their turf. These young Olympians didn't gather around the watercooler. They clutched Evian bottles and debated whether this year's Australian Syrah would outsell last year's. Then they would jump to some technical discussion about the price of pork bellies, and they didn't mean McDonald's ninety-nine-cent barbecue lunch special.

To Luke, they were like young gods and goddesses. Shit, they looked like they could fly to the executive floor. Watching them all day, he longed to fly with them. The Gresham team made their living with their minds, not their fists.

Instead, Luke trudged down the dark steps to his basement apartment on Jane Street. The streetlamp had blown out or had been broken by a vandal's flying rock six months earlier, but no one in the building knew who to call at City Hall. Besides, boxers weren't scared of the dark anyway, were they? He slipped the key into his paint-chipped door. The crusty lock usually required him to pull the knob toward him as he turned the key. Not this time. The door swung open with a creak that oil could not cure. Had the door been unlocked? Instinctively, he brushed his hand against his nose and tucked his chin, taking his old boxing stance. Suddenly, he felt a crack against the back of his neck and crumpled to the floor. He grabbed the side of the sofa and hauled himself up and turned toward the dark figure, ready to charge.

He screamed an intimidating, "FUCK OUT OF HERE!"

The dim bulb flashed on. Luke saw Buck Roberts wielding a cane like the last of the Three Musketeers, the one who lived long enough to collect Social Security. Luke rubbed the back of his neck where the cane had struck him.

"Buck, what the fuck are you doing here? And why're you trying to kill me?"

The old man was out of breath, but grinned broadly. "I'm here to drag you back to the gym. I didn't train you to be a wuss security guard," Buck said.

Even in the dim light of a dusty 40-watt bulb, Luke could see that Buck had lost weight. Six months ago he was eighty-five, but looked like a spry seventy-five. He was still eighty-five, but now looked ninety. Buck's ticker was ticking down.

"Besides," Buck added, "you can't be very good at your job if you let an old man beat you with a walking stick."

"Forget it, Buck. I'm done. No more corpses. The next one could be mine—"

"Kid, I believe in you."

"Yeah, well that makes one of us." Luke slipped off his blue blazer and slumped onto the sofa, massaging his neck. Buck leaned against the wall, wheezing.

"So that's how it ends, Luke? You just quit and watch elevators fly up and down an office building the rest of your life?"

"Yeah, Buck. It ain't the fights. But lemme tell you this. When a guy rides a corporate elevator up, it doesn't crush some guy waiting for his turn."

Luke thought about Buck all night. After he made his first few million, he'd donate a chunk to a home for old boxers. Buck deserved a rest.

CHAPTER 3

The 150-foot yacht with the 3,000 horsepower, triple-turbo engines bounced in the high waves a few miles off the southeast coast of Key West. The boat had massive power, but, weather permitting, Tremont preferred to sail under the wind power. The skies had darkened, and a storm was flying in from the Caymans. Paul Tremont clutched the mast and wondered whether he'd be able to drink his Glenfiddich before it spilled on him. He looked below deck at his guests, Senator Harold Leopard of Florida, the president of the Metropolitan Museum of Art, and the executive director of the Peace Corps. They looked like a rainbow coalition huddled together, not because of their ethnicities, but because sea-sickness turned them into shades of gray, green, and blue.

"Can I get anyone some aspirin or Dramamine?" Tremont offered. His guests shook their heads.

A motorboat appeared about a hundred yards off the port side. Tremont threw his Scotch overboard and picked up his binoculars. It was the Coast Guard. He looked at the motorboat's trajectory and saw a smaller, flat vessel. He twisted the lenses of the binoculars, squinted, and concluded that it was a raft. Now, why would the Coast Guard chase a raft? To help it? No. To commandeer it and arrest the raft people— Cubans, no doubt—to make sure they did not make it to the shores of America. To Tremont, the Coast Guard boat was like graffiti on the Statue of Liberty, an attack on America's principles.

"Patrick," he yelled at his skipper, "full speed ahead! Catch the Coast Guard."

The captain was cautious. "Mr. Tremont, that's dangerous. You wouldn't chase a highway patrol car on the Jersey Turnpike, would you?"

"Patrick, don't argue. I'll pay your bail if anything happens."

With the waves slapping against the hull, the yacht cut through the wave-tossed waters and finally caught up to the Coast Guard cutter. By then, two officers had hustled the boat people onto the government vessel. Through his binoculars, Tremont could see a man and woman, probably in their forties, hugging two little kids. They all wore ragged pants and T-shirts. Tremont suddenly smiled. He ran below deck to his guests.

"C'mon up here. Look at this. Senator, look at this!" he said excitedly. "Look at those shirts."

By the time Tremont's woozy guests got on deck, they were just a few feet from the raft and the Coast Guard. The parents and children wore T-shirts haphazardly hand-painted with stripes: red, white and blue. On the rickety raft, Tremont could see three small paint buckets.

"You see that, Harold?" Tremont said. "They didn't have the nerve to paint stripes until they'd escaped the Cuban Navy."

The Coast Guard officers angrily waved at Patrick to stand off. Patrick began to shift into reverse.

"Hold it, Patrick!" Tremont shouted. He picked up a megaphone.

"Officers, please let these people go. This is Paul Tremont. I will take them into my custody and sponsor them. You can check my credentials with Florida Senator Harold Leopard."

The officers smirked. One of them, a thin man in his sixties, cupped his hands and shouted, "I don't care if you're the pope, you're not messing with Coast Guard business! Now move off or we'll impound your vessel."

Senator Leopard turned from green to red and nearly jumped off the yacht. "Jesus Christ, Paul, don't get me in the middle of this! I'm not here." He ducked below.

Tremont furrowed his brow. He needed a new approach. He picked up the megaphone again and asked, "Permission to come aboard, sir?"

The officers conferred with each other and appeared to agree it would do no harm. After all, they knew who Paul Tremont was. Everyone did. He was very rich and very famous and very powerful.

"Granted," the skinny one answered, "if you can get here without killing yourself."

Patrick brought the bouncing yacht within seven feet of the Coast

Guard cutter. Tremont quickly grabbed a line and tied a knot around his mainmast. With a few steps as a headstart he swung out over his yacht and then shimmied down to land on the motorboat.

Tremont saw that the Cubans were shivering and that their faces were badly sunburned and covered with sores.

"What's this about?" the other officer, a young guy in his twenties, asked.

Tremont realized that the family needed more than a first aid kit. "We don't have time to bullshit, fellas. These people mean nothing to you, just another traffic stop. They mean a lot to me, though, because I'm a patriot. The storm's picking up. You could be helping other people if you didn't have to waste your time here, right?"

The officers just stared, hands on hips, seemingly unmoved.

"It's a lot of water, the Gulf of Mexico. You could go days without running into somebody, right? Let's say we never ran into each other." Tremont reached into his pocket.

The young officer flinched. "He's reaching for a gun!" The officer tried to withdraw his revolver from the holster, but before he could do so, Tremont pulled his wallet from his pocket.

"Here's $2,000." He counted out a stack of 100s. "Just a random event in the great big sea. Let me get these people some help."

"Hey," the young officer said, "we turn down bribes from drug dealers."

"I'm glad you do."

"Why should we take this? Just because you're Paul Tremont?"

"Because this one's going to make you feel more like an American and less like a bureaucrat or, even worse, a stooge of Castro."

The older officer looked down at the quaking family.

"Forget it, no deal," the young one said to Tremont. "Keep your cash."

But the older one put his hand on his partner's shoulder and whispered, "Put it in your pocket, son." The kid was young, inexperienced, but he knew enough to obey his superior, and that few people said "no" to Paul Tremont.

A few hours later, Tremont delivered the frightened family to a church relief mission near the docks of North Miami Beach.

The following morning, Tremont was sitting at his desk in Manhattan.

Paul Tremont could never be president of the United States. Only people born in the U.S. could be president. He missed by 600 miles, having been born to British parents in Bermuda. But that didn't stop the mogul from ruling over his own empire from an oval office, sitting in front of a white-fluted fireplace in a rocking chair that was a replica of Jack Kennedy's. Behind him, eighty stories above Manhattan, grew a rose garden.

The tall man wore thick pinstripes, which made him seem even taller and more massive than his six-foot-three frame. His hair stylist combed back his reddish-brown hair in a way that added an extra inch. Tremont rocked back and forth in the chair, gazing serenely down Broadway.

The hottest architects in the world had lobbied to design Tremont's headquarters on Broadway, the biggest project since the 9/11 memorial. He set up the most furious and frustrating competition ever designed, a humiliation to name-brand architects. For a fee of $25,000, the architects logged onto a closed-circuit presentation by Tremont, in which he presented his ideas for an office building. Then the entrants had five days to design a model that fulfilled his mission. That was not the humiliating part. They did not know that after submitting their models, Tremont would submit the bids to a nationwide American Idol-like poll—of eighth-grade schoolchildren. This ensured that the winner, as well as the losers, would feel stupid. It also put Tremont's smiling face on the coveted cover of *People* magazine under the headline, "Mogul for Children." The body of the story also touted his charitable gifts to UNICEF and the Peace Corps.

As for Tremont's headquarters building, the exterior looked like a teenage boy's dream: a sleek, edgy, steel skyscraper with corners sharper than Ginsu knives. But the staid Georgian interior offended everyone born after 1850. On the whole, Tremont had bred a cross between James Bond and James Madison. The critic for the *New Yorker* called it a "derivative nightmare." To which the financier famously responded, "And that's where the money came from, derivatives."

As Tremont rocked in his chair, two men entered his oval office. The first was Dr. Stuart Burns, a five-foot-five dandy who would've looked splendid on top of a wedding cake. He'd picked the perfect silver Gucci frames for his round, pink face. Every evening he wore a tuxedo, whether he was attending the symphony or just strolling down to check out the prostitutes on Ninth Avenue. But why did a super-financier like Tremont need a trained psychiatrist? The firm's secretaries figured that Burns's job was to ensure that Tremont didn't lose control of his vicious temper and throw someone off his rose garden terrace. In fact, Tremont relied on Burns to vet new personnel and make sure they fit in with the Tremont "ethos."

Burns strutted into the oval office with a clipped gait, pocketwatch dangling from his hip, like a noble aide to Kaiser Wilhelm. No one would have guessed his family was from the slums of Palermo, and Burns was a translation of the Italian *Bruciare*. He told people he was a Scot and each year he celebrated Robbie Burns's birthday with bagpipes and a haggis dinner. Tremont knew the truth, but played along. He liked employees with secrets. The threat of exposure kept them honest.

Burns entered one step ahead of Christian Playa, who wore short-sleeved shirts to show off his bulging forearms. He was about the same height as Burns, but if the shrink belonged on a wedding cake, Playa would be the Teamster delivering it from the bakery. His sixty-year-old tanned face was marked by creases so deep you could run a credit card down them. No one really knew the color of his eyes because no one wanted to stare into them long enough to see.

"What do you have for me, boys?" Tremont asked, knowing that Burns and Playa couldn't stand each other.

"I've got your man, Mr. Tremont," Playa said with a grin that exposed tall, narrow teeth like tombstones.

"He's nuts," Dr. Burns replied. On the street he might be afraid of Playa, but he felt that his close relationship with Tremont would keep Playa at bay.

Playa pushed a button on the wall, and an oil painting of George Washington transformed into a projection screen. A bird's-eye view of the Braden/Perez match filled the screen. The image then closed in on Luke Braden delivering the death blow to Perez's temple. Then the crumpled Perez writhing on the canvas, followed by a shot of Braden, torn between horror and triumph.

Tremont stared, recalling his $50,000 bet on Perez. "Life is cheap under Castro. At least I got to screw him out of an oil well."

Burns bit his lip to stay quiet.

"Is Braden our man?" Tremont asked.

"Yeah, DNA confirms it," Playa answered. "He's your secret weapon for the Cuba mission."

"Where is he now?"

"Gresham Bros. So we can hire him anytime."

Burns had to jump in.

"Are you guys crazy? Paul, this kid knows nothing about finance, and you're going to invite him into the inner sanctum?"

Tremont was always amused to hear his psychiatrist allow the pitch of his voice to rise from tenor to boy soprano.

Burns continued. "Why? If you're going to hire a tool to do your dirty work, at least find one with some brains and a working knowledge of Wall Street. NYU and Columbia spit them out by the hundreds. And they'd all die for the chance to work for Tremont Advisors."

"You're wrong this time, Stuart. I don't need another brain to churn out multiple regression equations; I need some muscle. This kid's got just enough IQ points to do the job. I believe in giving young people an opportunity. Plus he's got the right connections. And, God knows, he's not afraid of blood."

Burns tried to contain his frustration. Tremont usually deferred to him on hiring judgments. "So he's perfect, Paul?"

"No, not yet. He needs to be tested. We need to test his loyalty. Make him dependent on us. Then he's ours to do what we need. Anything. You'll see."

Tremont rocked in his chair, while his loyal aides jockeyed to see who could exit the room first.

In the hallway, Burns turned to Playa. "He never blinks, does he?"

"Blinking is weakness," Playa explained. "How many negotiations has Tremont won when the other guy blinked?"

CHAPTER 4

Why did all those guys look so good? Luke snuck into Gresham's executive gym and grabbed a bottle of L'Oreal moisturizer and Abercrombie aftershave. None of the guys at Delancy's spread exfoliants on their faces. It would have gotten clogged in the pockmarks, gifts from steroid use. But if the Gresham Bros. team exfoliated and used emollients, so would he. He had started reading GQ, and realized that the security guards were all wearing the wrong shirts. Slightly frayed button-down shirts from TJ Maxx didn't cut it on the thirtieth floor. He picked up some spread-collar shirts on sale at Bloomingdale's. Then he invested a day's pay in a haircut at Oscar Biondi's salon. Shorter on the sides, longer on top. On the way out he snagged some mink-oil hair gel. He couldn't afford to go back to Oscar, but now he knew what to tell the guy at Supercuts. From now on his $10 cut would look like it cost $150.

One morning after a vigorous loofah rub in the shower, after fifteen minutes of pore-cleansing, toning, and moisturizing, he looked in the mirror and saw a guy who might finally get out of the lobby and into the elevator on the way up. But what would he say? Now that he had upgraded his face and shirt, he needed to talk the talk.

Luke started taking notes on conversations. He noticed that none of the Olympians carried the *Daily News*. Always the *Wall Street Journal* and a pinkish-looking newspaper called the *Financial Times*.

"It's for wrapping fish," one of his coworkers said. "That's why it's the color of salmon."

Rather than mock the newspapers, Luke tried to read them. He couldn't get past the first page of the *Financial Times*, with its obscure discussions of euros and sovereign debt. The *Wall Street Journal* was a little better; it sometimes had a sports column toward the back. He needed a tutor and a lot of help. It was the only way to climb those thirty floors to Olympus.

He needed a coach. He called his father's cousin, Ted. Ted and his father had only one thing in common—they shared the same last name. If Francis Braden, with his collection of Shelley poems and Rothschild wines, was the blue blood in the family, Ted's blood ran with Pabst Blue Ribbon. Francis could tell you his golf handicap and Ted could handicap the Belmont Stakes. Besides beer and ponies, Ted also knew something about finance. He ran a small investment fund, TB Capital. It never made much money, but it kept Ted busy and in on the buzz of Wall Street. In addition to the racing form, Luke was pretty sure that Ted read the *Financial Times* and the *Wall Street Journal*.

Luke had always liked Ted, who had even attended some of his boxing matches. Luke picked up the phone to tell his cousin about his job at Gresham Bros.

"Great, kid," Ted said, "I hope they gave you stock options." He gave a gruff laugh.

"No, I'm just a street man now, but I swear I'm going to get a job upstairs as soon as I've learned a little more about the business."

"C'mon, you sound like you took too many punches. Gresham Bros. only hires Harvard and Princeton. I've been in the business thirty years and they wouldn't take me even now . . ."

Luke couldn't imagine his pot-bellied, polyester-clad cousin amid the Olympians.

"I know I can break through, Ted," Luke said.

Luke described his plan. He would call Ted every morning with questions about the *Times* and the *Journal*. Then he'd call at noon to get Ted's briefing on the markets. Then he'd call again at four P.M. to see how the trading day finished up.

"Are you serious? I don't talk to my wife that often. My ex-wife's lawyer, maybe. All right, I'll help you. But don't get all excited about Gresham. You can always aim a little lower. In fact, I could use a little help . . ."

After a few weeks, Luke no longer imagined wrapping fish with the

FT, as he learned to call the salmon-colored paper. After the German finance minister resigned, Luke noticed a "widening spread in the Treasury-German bond yields." Then he turned to the foreign exchange page and, sure enough, the euro/yen exchange rate had broken through its 200-day moving average. He was starting to sound like CNBC.

CHAPTER 5

Jon Hardiz, president of Gresham, was of Mexican descent although he didn't know a burro from a burrito. Or at least he wouldn't admit to knowing. Hardiz learned the Wall Street adage "Dress British, think Yiddish." Hardiz looked like a British auctioneer from Sotheby's in starched collars and gilded cufflinks, and you saw those cufflinks when he wrapped his chunky arms around his star traders and called them "bubbe" or "mensch." His opponents were either "schmucks" or "putzes." No one had ever heard the word "amigo" or "hermano" slide past his lips. And what were those blond highlights streaking through his dark hair?

Luke didn't exactly stalk Hardiz, but he did wrangle a deal so that he got to work the special executive elevator that only Hardiz and a few loyal lieutenants could use. At first Luke did nothing but hold the door and tip his head to Hardiz and the other bigwigs. One day, he got up the nerve to say, "Happy Tuesday, Mr. Hardiz," just as Hardiz was stepping off the elevator. Hardiz looked over his shoulder at Luke and winked. Luke grinned all day. That wink beat a winning knockout.

A week later, his confidence building, Luke called Ted moments before Hardiz stepped out of his limo.

"Why's the S&P jumping, Ted?"

"Hedgies are covering their shorts."

Luke clicked off the phone, opened the elevator for the CEO, and said, "Good Friday, Mr. Hardiz. Watch out for that short-covering." For four long seconds, Luke's heart thumped in his chest. With one foot in the elevator, Hardiz looked him over. Luke felt his face flush.

Hardiz stared at Luke's name tag. Was he squinting or sneering?

Hardiz spoke. "And who's behind it . . . uh . . . Luke?" he said, reading the name tag.

"Damn hedgies." But I need more, Luke thought. He reached into his memory bank for a likely suspect, a big, swinging-dick speculator. "I'd bet it's Les Burger."

Hardiz broke into a huge smile while stepping into the elevator. "Just had breakfast with Les."

The elevator closed.

Then it opened a crack.

"Nice job, Bubee."

CHAPTER 6

Luke waited impatiently in the 8th floor office of Gresham Bros.' human resources director. He snuck upstairs during his coffee break, not wanting to admit to his security guard brethren that he was applying for work as a trader. From her office window, the sixtyish Ms. Turp had a view of a cement wall. She glared at Luke.

"You must be joking, Mr. Braden," she said in a phlegmy, smoker's croak. "We're not hiring. We're firing. Profits are down. You see this pile of papers? I got MBAs from Stanford, PhDs from Harvard. I got tenured professors at Yale who would kill for a job here. As far as I can tell, your main qualification is some kind of informal training or yammering with your cousin. And you think the aura of smart people as they pass you in the lobby has clung to you."

Luke would never hit a man with glasses or even a woman who looked like a man with glasses. But he was tempted.

"But Ms. Turp, I have studied and read—"

"Where? Where? I need Ivy, I need resumes dripping with statistical formuli!" She coughed and pulled out a hard candy from her desk drawer.

Luke gambled. "Call Mr. Hardiz."

"You're crazy. Go back to work."

"Can I use your phone to call Mr. Hardiz?"

With her bird-like frame, she pushed herself back from her desk.

"Be my guest, but don't tell his secretary it was my idea."

Luke pushed the buttons and told Hardiz's secretary that Luke "from Les Burger's elevator service" was on the line. But Hardiz refused the call.

Luke made a degrading retreat out of Ms. Turp's office. He slumped back into his swivel chair in the lobby.

CHAPTER 7

"I can't explain why, Braden, but Mr. Hardiz wants to see you. Something about Les Burger," Ms. Turp told Luke on the telephone.

"Oh, you don't have to apologize," Luke replied.

"I won't. Just another nutty thing to talk about with my cats."

Luke zoomed up in the mirrored executive elevator, straightened his tie, ran his fingers through his newly stylish hair, and checked his fly. There was no carpeting on the CEO's floor of bird's-eye maple. Hardiz's office was lined with paintings of Thoroughbred horses. Tall, skinny-legged beasts with big snouts. Why were they always painted in profile? Hardiz wore a shirt with a red-striped pattern and a white collar. He was staring at a bank of about fifteen screens. He waved Luke in.

"Exchange rates, Mr. Hardiz?"

"No, Luke, come around and look."

To his surprise the CEO of one of the world's preeminent trading companies was staring at closed-circuit security cameras. They were the same bank of monitors Luke and the street boys watched at the lobby desk! Hardiz also had the standard Bloomberg and Reuters screens, but he seemed more interested in the revolving doors in the lobby.

Luke felt strange and almost giddy walking behind the CEO's desk. How many of the MBA hotshots, who aroused his envy, had been invited behind the power center of the firm, indeed, one of the great power centers of the world? All the terminals on Hardiz's semicircular desk presented Hardiz with maybe 500 buttons he could push, like a mini-version of NASA's Houston Control. Luke was so dazzled he forgot to listen as

Hardiz talked. They weren't just buttons, knobs, or touchpads. They were the loom that knit the world together. Only instead of yarn, they used dollars.

Hardiz loudly tapped a computer screen with his fingers, bringing Luke back to attention. He noticed red lights flashing on a clear glass pane suspended over Hardiz's desk. It looked like a politician's teleprompter.

"What's that?"

"Ah, STATE SECRET, my boy. Well, at least a Gresham secret. But you can't make much use of it, so I'll tell you. STATE SECRET is our security system to prevent insider trading. Seconds before any trades over $10 million get executed, a computer in Bermuda cross-references the stock with all the p.a.'s of the m.d.'s," he explained.

M.D.s? Doctors? Luke was confused.

"Managing directors, personal accounts," Hardiz explained. "The system will stomp on any trader who tries to buy a stock for somebody else when he has a conflict of interest. They don't even know it, but we are monitoring their personal wealth 24/7, and STATE SECRET keeps them honest. See, Luke, we're all about honesty."

Even if you have to spy on your own people, Luke thought.

He tried not to stare at Hardiz's blond highlights.

"You're leaving the firm, Luke," Hardiz said matter-of-factly. "Your life is going to change forever. Now I don't know if you ever had money or saw money or played with money before. Isn't your father a teacher? But you're going to be flying high and moving up."

Luke imagined his dream job, perched on the trading desk, dealing in bonds. A smile spread across his face.

But why was he leaving the firm?

"Pack up your things, and go up to the roof."

"The roof?"

"Yeah, the roof. With the helipad. Ever hear of Paul Tremont? His helicopter will be picking you up in four minutes and taking you to his jet at LaGuardia. I hear he's flying you to Vegas. Roll snake eyes for me, kid," Hardiz said. "You got less than four minutes."

CHAPTER 8

The windy roof had no railings. As Luke stood on the helipad—just a circle painted on the roof, he felt like the dot in the middle of a bull's-eye. A roar came from the east and a chopper suddenly appeared. Not one of those little round choppers resembling VW bugs that the traffic reporters fly. *This was a freakin' Black Hawk.* It had missiles and guns and more firepower than the entire NYPD. Hardiz said he was going to LaGuardia, but the chopper could have been headed to Baghdad.

Could this gunship fit on the roof's bull's-eye? Luke would not find out. The raging bird didn't even attempt to land. Instead a rope ladder dropped down about forty feet. The wind from the chopper blew with such power that bits of grimy dust flew into his eyes. He wanted to cover his ears, especially the left one, where that damaged eardrum sent painful impulses into his spine. He was ensnarled in a tornado fifty-three stories above the ground, with no railings to keep him in.

He turned around and took a few steps back toward the stairwell door. He watched the rope ladder dangling and the chopper hovering. What was going on? Luke knew that Paul Tremont had a reputation for drama. He'd backed some Hollywood producers and thrown outrageous opening-night parties, including one where he turned the Paramount studio backlot into a white-water rafting route. What did Hardiz say? *"Your life is going to change forever. Now I don't know if you ever had money or saw money or played with money before."* What was holding him back? Luke asked himself whether he was too scared—but scared of what? Scared of holding onto a rope? If a seventeen-year-old ROTC cadet could do it, he surely could. Or was he scared of changing his life and finally succeeding at something? Then the Black Hawk circled around again. Luke saw the TA logo, Tremont Advisors. It seemed that the forty-foot rope ladder waving and swinging in gale-force winds was all that separated him from wealth and self-esteem. In his mind, he heard again the sounds of the Perez fight, the teasing chicken clucks and cackles. At that moment, he decided he simply would not walk down that stairwell and descend back to the lobby. He would grab Tremont's ladder. He jumped a few times and after several attempts finally wrapped his hands on the second rung and started climbing. When he was just five rungs up the ladder, the Black Hawk jerked higher while hovering above the Gresham building.

He tried to climb higher as the rope twisted, thrashing his body against the wind. He looked at his forearms, which had never failed him in the boxing ring. Blood ran down from his left hand, which had been gashed by the rope. Were they trying to kill him? The rope started tugging at his hands with more force. Within seconds he felt himself coming closer to the whirlwind of the chopper's blades. Then a hand—a strong hand—pulled on his right wrist and, aided by the momentum of the recoiling ladder, flung him inside the narrow, vibrating deck of the Black Hawk. Two beefy guys in goggles and sound-deadening headphones pushed his butt onto a hard bench and said nothing as the bird whirred toward La Guardia.

CHAPTER 9

"See the Gulfstream over there," one of the guys shouted as the helicopter touched down. He shoved Luke off the Black Hawk. "There's your ride. Run for it!"

Dizzy and sweaty, his forearms covered with dried blood, Luke trotted across the tarmac at La Guardia to the gleaming jet. One side of the jet's tail was painted with the face of a lion, the other with the calm profile of a lamb, the dueling symbols of Paul Tremont's investment funds. Yin and yang. Lion and lamb. Ali and Liston.

He dashed up the steps that descended from the lamb side of the plane. The plane was empty, unless you counted eight plush, calfskin lounge chairs, eight flat-screen TVs, and a green felt blackjack table right in the middle of the aisle. The table could have been ripped right off the floor of the Bellagio Hotel in Vegas. It had the odds and house rules sewn right into the fabric. "The house wins on a draw—"

Who was the house? The Federal Aviation Administration? Hanging along the side of the interior were bottles of cognac, Scotch, and Courvoisier, along with Baccarat crystal glasses. Lobster tails stuck out from a large bowl of ice, and a crystal vase was brimming with caviar. Luke didn't know whether the pink eggs or the black eggs were more valuable, but it didn't matter. There was plenty of both, but he was too shaken to eat a Ritz cracker.

The engines hummed while he leaned on the blackjack table.

"Hello?" he called. "I'm Luke Braden. Am I supposed to see Mr. Tremont here?"

No answer. He picked up a shoe of cards from the table and nervously shuffled until he heard a loud clank and the cockpit door slid open.

Luke raised his hands to his chest, the Pavlovian reflex of a fighter. A tall, gaunt, fiftyish man leaned forward to avoid bumping his head on the ceiling. Luke quickly figured he was no threat. Probably the pilot, but why was he wearing an outrageously colored scarlet uniform, like Superman?

"I'm Captain Lucern," the man said, reaching not for Luke's outstretched hand, but for a bottle of Coke, which he poured into a glass. "It'll take four hours to get to Vegas, so sit down and relax. If you get bored of solitaire, you've got online gambling on that screen, plus the latest Disney flicks, plus some porn. It's just me and you on this flight tonight. We'll be on automatic pilot for most of the way, but I don't want company in the cockpit. And here's a note from Mr. Tremont."

Luke opened the letter, handwritten on thick, almost tufted stationery.

"Luke, I've been a fan of your previous career. More to come. As they say in the fights, 'let's get ready to rumble.'" It was initialed "PT."

The pilot slurped from the Baccarat glass, slipped back behind the cockpit door, and slid it tightly shut. Luke heard the bolt engage.

CHAPTER 10

THE LAS VEGAS STRIP

In the old days, the Mob did a fine job of vacuuming. Sure, they cleaned up thousands of paper cups littered around the slot machines, but they also cleaned up people who were enemies of the "organization." Where once stood a genius card-counter, there was now an empty space. Bones ground to dust scattered across the scalding deserts of Nevada. Bugsy Siegel had been lucky. At least his widow knew where he got knocked off. But for the thousand other mugs? Maybe Vegas needs a "Tomb of the Unknown Gambler," protected by a pacing honor guard made up of tough guys named Augie without necks. Sure, today's magicians like Lance Burton and David Copperfield strut on stage conjuring up spirits to awe the Vegas tourists, but real ghosts from those rip-roaring, Rat Pack days of the 1950s still haunt the place.

Outside Paul Tremont's favorite hotel, the Four Seasons, romped a leggy, freckled redhead who could've been high-stepping with a *Riverdance* troupe. Instead of dancing, she was stomping and waving a huge banner. In her left hand she held a megaphone from which came words she must've unearthed at an archaeological dig at a Vietnam protest site. "Tremont kills!" "Stop the senseless slaughter!" "Hell no, I won't mow!" She was supported by a barking crowd of Labrador retrievers that she had tied to a fire hydrant. In the old days, she'd have been whisked away and her dogs would have been served as sausage at a hotel's hot buffet.

A Channel 5 truck turned up within minutes, launching its satellite dish up its three-story pole. A grizzled reporter named Hank Strom rolled out of the truck, a press release rolled up in his hand, his camera guy unpacking the equipment.

"What's this about? What do you have against Paul Tremont? Didn't he just give $100 million to the Red Cross?" Strom asked the leggy redhead.

The dogs started sniffing his trousers and he brushed them from his crotch.

"Tremont's a saint. I'd sleep with him—"

Strom pointed to his ponytailed cameraman. This could be a fun segment. "Roll camera!"

"Repeat that into the mike, please," Strom requested of the woman.

"That was to get your attention," she replied. "Tremont's businesses in Central America mow down rain forests, slaughter native birds, and force the peasants to grow coca."

"All right, lady. Who are you anyway?"

"Not only that, he's spent $200,000 lobbying Congress to stop building the new Moynihan National Park near the Hoover Dam. That's just an hour's drive from here, so citizens of Las Vegas should—"

"What's your name?"

"Cori Leopard." She rushed ahead, "And the Moynihan National Park would provide a sanctuary for—"

Strom started losing his cool. "Chrissakes, that a stage name or a streetwalking name?"

He turned to his cameraman. "Cut. We're done. Just another nut."

Cori mumbled to herself. Just another nut with a degree from Harvard Law, a black belt in yoga, and a very powerful father.

Paul Tremont was getting ready to enter the elevator from his rooftop suite and stroll down the Strip to the Luxor, the Egyptian pyramid of Vegas, when his advance team noticed the commotion. Ordinarily, they would ignore the lone cry of a protester. But the megaphone and the half-dozen barking Labs pushed the limits of the Tremont handbook. Meanwhile, Tremont had a show to attend. His henchman rushed into action.

CHAPTER 11

The hum of the jet's engines lulled Luke to sleep in one of the leather lounge chairs. He woke up to see the Statue of Liberty through the plane's window. Had they been circling Manhattan? Then he figured things out. Why, there was St. Mark's Square in Venice, or more accurately the Venetian Hotel on the Vegas Strip. Neon and halogen lights shone like sunbursts in the desert. He looked down at his hands, which had turned scabby and crusty from blood. Last time he was in Vegas he arrived and departed unscathed—that was for a boxing match at the MGM Grand.

Almost as soon as the aircraft thumped onto the Las Vegas airfield, two goons in sunglasses jumped onto the plane and hustled Luke into a waiting stretch limo that looked like three Cadillac Escalades bolted together.

A bald guy, about three hundred pounds, with wraparound shades sat across from Luke.

"You don't smell so good," the guy grunted.

"Screw you. I've been airlifted across the New York skyline by a Black Hawk, thrown into a jet with a weird pilot, and I'm still wearing yesterday's clothes. You'd be sweating too, Jumbo," Luke replied.

"I mean you smell like some high-priced perfumed bond trader."

"Yeah, that's me. I'm Luke Milken." Luke said.

"Here," the big man tossed Luke a black suit. "Put this on. Mr. Tremont don't go for the gray pants-blue jacket security guard look. Especially when you have a show to attend."

A show? At first Luke felt shy about changing in front of these thugs, but then he felt the soft, wool material, saw the Armani label, and figured, what the fuck, I made my career beating up guys in front of ten thousand people while wearing boxer shorts.

"What else can you tell me about Mr. Tremont, besides his taste in men's clothes?"

"You got nothin' to worry about. It's the chicks who disappear fast." He looked out the window.

Luke slipped on the Armani. Jumbo winked at him. Luke looked out the window. The last thing he needed was to hear a three-hundred-pound bouncer tell him that he looked cute.

The stretched Escalade pulled up to the Mandalay Bay driveway but wove past the lobby entrance, and swerved its way behind the huge concrete complex. Where was the Bay? Luke wondered. This was the desert.

Jumbo and his partner, a black man with skin so dark he looked like he was wearing a mask, escorted Luke through the doors of the convention center, where a few tourists followed signs for a dolphin show. They walked across a golden carpet that seemed to go on for miles. Luke was confused and tired. Hardiz said that this adventure would change his life. So far, the Gresham president was right. Never before had Luke been dragged across skyscrapers and handed a $3,000 suit by a fat man who winked at him in a limo. He finally saw the end of the hallway and a series of doors. Which door would Jumbo choose for him?

Then he heard a roaring crowd. At first, he thought his bum left eardrum might be playing a trick on him. But it wasn't just a crowd. He heard blaring horns, screams, the distorted voice of a disembodied announcer. Luke's nostrils instinctively started to flare, he felt his heart beat faster. His nervous system knew those sounds. He was being led into a fight. Shit! They've stolen me from New York to push me into a ring? The giant center doors sprung open automatically as Luke, Jumbo, and his partner stepped within ten feet of the threshhold. Then he saw the oddest scene he'd ever witnessed.

CHAPTER 12

Cori Leopard felt a wave of failure sweep across her. Despite the dogs, despite the megaphone, despite the placards, she wasn't getting much attention. Hell, in Vegas a girl needs a pair of at least double DD silicons to get noticed. Here she was a twenty-six-year-old depressed pixie, trying to control a herd of Labradors without knocking over her own protest signs. She had borrowed them from a trainer who supplied animals for Vegas circus acts. They were due back in an hour.

Her cell phone, tucked under her stocking in the vibrate mode, buzzed. She read the I.D. with dread. And anger. For decades she'd tried to break through to this man, knock some sense into him, and try to stop him from using his power to pollute the earth.

"Hello, Dad, Senator Dad," she said. "Please tell me you're calling because you hit your head, passed out, and woke up a liberal Democrat and now you're supporting Moynihan Park."

"My head feels just fine, Cori."

"Darn. That means more dead caribou in Alaska. Ding, ding. Machiavelli wins another round."

Senator Harold Leopard of Florida chaired the Foreign Relations Committee. In his sixty-nine years on earth, Cori could bet he'd never read Machiavelli. He had never bothered to read anything to her. Not even *Goodnight Moon*. He ruled the committee and U.S. foreign policy with a titanium fist. Literally. The former NCAA wrestling champion had been mugged near the Senate parking lot ten years earlier and had thrown a fierce left hook that flattened the twenty-year-old attacker. The senator's chiseled gold ring (a relief of an oil well) tore the man's cornea and ripped the cartilage across his nose. The senator hurt only his fist, and the surgeons inserted a titanium metacarpal in his hand.

"Why do you libs have such a love affair with caribou? I wish you'd find a man instead. Then maybe you'd cut out this resentment of my politics."

Cut it out? Cut what out? Twenty-six years of neglect? Twenty-six years of shame? Her father played the Miami social scene like some lothario in a Desi Arnaz tune. For all his right-wing moralizing on C-SPAN, he had ignored his wife and daughter except to pose for an occasional election campaign picture. While he lived the wild life in his South Beach condo, Cori and her mom made do in Celebration, Florida, the Disney development where every porched house looked picket-fence perfect. Sometimes Harold Leopard would send money home. Not much, but just enough to allow her mother, a nurse, to pay the mortgage. To make matters worse, he used his political power for evil. Offshore drilling? Great! Recycling? Stupid! Hispanic migrant laborers? Don't let them unionize! Pretty Hispanic girls? Screw them. Literally. Cori figured that the only thing he'd ever done to protect the environment was wear a condom. Of course, he probably tossed it out a car window and added to the litter problem.

She was about to bite back with more sarcasm when he interrupted. "I need your help, not as a protester, but as a daughter."

She felt her eyes well up. A tear began to slide down her cheek, connecting the dots among her freckles. She wasn't sure why she was crying. Was it the stressful, frustrating life of a failed professional protestor? Or a little girl longing for her lost daddy?

"I'm in danger. Or you're in danger," he said.

CHAPTER 13

As he stepped through the giant doors, Luke heard cheers and beer bottles clinking. But he saw no people. About ten thousand empty seats surrounded a boxing ring. The soundtrack of a frenzied crowd bounced off all the seats, creating an ear-splitting racket. In an empty room, sounds reverberate like the inside of a turbine jet engine.

Luke looked at Jumbo. "What the hell?"

Jumbo and his partner turned and left. Luke raised his eyes to the upper deck, where he saw faded bunting and peeling posters. He couldn't quite make out the words, but the style looked dated, like the old felt Knickerbocker banners hanging at Madison Square Garden or like a rebroadcast on ESPN Classic Sports channel. The place smelled like cigar smoke and the air seemed hazy.

Luke just stood squinting at the banners, trying to make some sense of the soundtrack. The crowd roared and then got quieter. A few random shouts. A thud, followed by some ripping noises. Suddenly, the crash of a thousand shifting chairs and bleachers, as if everyone jumped up to yell and cheer and boo. Definitely a boxing match. What was that snapping sound? Every second a click-click.

Luke tried to digest the surreal scene. An empty boxing hall in Vegas? Was he losing his mind? Didn't Hardiz promise him a new career in finance? After killing Perez, Luke had been trying to run away from the boxing ring. All those tutorial calls to his cousin. In just hours, he'd soared from the ground floor of Gresham Bros. to standing behind the CEO's desk. Surely, Paul Tremont didn't arrange a Gulfstream jet so that he could hang out in a barren, but deafening arena. And why the hell was he wearing a new Armani suit?

A voice cut through the noise of the screaming crowd and the constant click-click. Tense, hyper, fast-paced. Excited, as if the treble was turned up too high. Nasal and staccato. He remembered this voice from old fight tapes. Howard Cosell, the Brooklyn Bombast, a machine-gun-voiced, hard-drinking lawyer who had more vocabulary than Roget's *Thesaurus*.

Everyone enjoyed hating Cosell, with one exception. Professor Francis Braden. Luke recalled that his father didn't care much about sports, but loved Cosell, incessantly reminding his son that the annoying broadcaster had graduated Phi Beta Kappa from NYU before "entering sports." Didn't his father understand that talking into a microphone was not the equivalent of getting into the ring? All Cosell had to worry about was his famous toupee and his Nielsen ratings. Real athletes get their skulls cracked. But even a dropout like Luke could understand the subtext of his father's advice. First graduate Phi Beta Kappa. Then consider hitting people.

But what was Cosell's New Yawk voice doing now in Vegas, a decade after his death? He listened to the galloping rhythm of the voice, like the *William Tell Overture*:

> *Clay, still dancing around the Bear. Round three. Clay, a left to the cheek. Now a quick right to the Bear's left eye. The champ is hurt! The champ is hurt! I see blood! I see blood! Rock, that twisting punch by Clay has cleaved his face, the blood suddenly dripping down the jowls of the beleaguered champion. The winded gladiator wipes his cheek and sees the blood on his glove. Look at the expression on his face, Rock. For the first time in his brutal career, the scariest man in boxing looks scared—*
> "Jesus Christ, Howie, Liston's become an old man," *Rock said.*

Rock? Clay? Of course. Luke was a lousy student of his father's twentieth-century literature, but he knew boxing history. This was the first Clay-Liston bout. Miami Beach. February 1964. Just three months after the Kennedy assassination. Rock was former heavyweight champ

Rocky Marciano sitting in the broadcast booth with Cosell. In front of another microphone was Joe Louis, who thought Liston would squash Clay like a Miami mosquito. But Clay had foiled the 8:1 odds and demolished Sonny Liston, aka "the Bear," in six rounds. After the fight, Clay exploded like a supernova onto television screens and radio waves: "I shook up the world! I am the greatest thing that ever lived! I upset Sonny Liston and I just turned twenty-two-years old. I talk to God every day! I'm king of the world!"

Luke quickly figured out where the click-clicks came from. The old film cameras from the mid-twentieth century, each picture snapping like an old-fashioned revolver. But why was he listening to this replay in a empty hall in the desert?

The soundtrack stopped, though Cosell's voice echoed for a few more moments. From the opposite corner of the arena slowly emerged a tall, ghostly figure, wrapped in a long white robe, his head hooded. Luke could not make out the face. In the middle of the ring appeared a stool, just like the wooden corner stools Luke had sat on, slumped on, and spat on during his boxing career. The figure slowly ambled to the stool and then turned its back to Luke and sat down. Luke rubbed his eyes when his brain processed the black letters on the white robe.

CASSIUS MARCELLUS CLAY

CHAPTER 14

A spotlight beamed on the figure of the boxer Ali? Could it be his hero, Ali? The man who floated like butterfly, stung like a bee, and lit up television screens with more personal wattage than ABC could come up with? The sparkling champ who had faded into near silence, the victim of Parkinson's? Now in his sixties, Ali's gait had become a shuffle. Luke replayed in his mind the slow walk of the figure who sat in the middle of the ring. The figure looked very tall, matching Ali's six-foot-three inch frame. The white lace-up high-top shoes looked right, too. He had never met his hero, though Luke once received a cartoon sketch in the mail from the Greatest, congratulating Luke on a fight. Ali had drawn a boxing glove and scribbled, "You win."

With his back to Luke, the spectre waved his arm stiffly, commanding Luke to come forward. Luke hesitated but then stepped toward the ring. He gradually got to the outside of the ring and grabbed the corner post, where he saw the stains of blood, snot, and sweat that others had left behind as their only lasting impression of the sport called "The Sweet Science."

Suddenly a clanging, the ringing of a boxing bell.

A hoarse voice yelled over the loudspeakers, "One, Two, Three—"

The sound of a referee counting out a fighter who'd been knocked down.

Instinctively, Luke jumped fully into the ring and rushed to the figure on the stool.

"Champ?" he called. "Ali?"

The figure rose off the stool, his limbs extending until he stood tall. Facing Luke, he looked down from a three-inch advantage.

CHAPTER 15

"Danger? What do you mean?" Cori asked her father. Though she stood on the Vegas Strip, her mind ignored the taxis and limos darting through traffic. Instead she pictured her father's deeply lined, deeply tanned face. Sunken eyes that sparkled in photographs, but in person looked dull like shark eyes. He was big, but Cori sometimes wondered whether he wore lifts in his shoes to get an additional inch or two over the competition. She had never seen him barefoot.

Her mind raced back to her mother's brutal death, just two years before. A sniper had fired two shots into her neck as her mother accompanied a patient in an ambulance racing to the hospital. The gunman had not been a very good sniper. He was aiming at the patient, a Colombian drug dealer poisoned while treating his family to Disney World. Instead, a solid citizen like Ruth Leopard got the bullet. The president went to the funeral. So did twenty prime ministers out of respect for the chairman of the Foreign Affairs Committee. Everybody who was anybody was there. But the only one who mattered to Cori lay in the casket.

"Danger like your mother faced," he replied.

"But that was an accident, the FBI showed us all the records. And besides they extradited Nunez."

"That's a load of crap. And since when do you believe in authority?" he added gruffly.

"Since when do you *doubt* authority? You're the *go-to* guy, Dad. Why don't you hold a hearing or something? You're a power broker. You're not some poor, helpless widower!" She felt her anger starting to build. "You'd have a lot more credibility if you had visited mom and me without a camera crew from time to time. Kids used to ask me who my father was. I would tell them that I don't have a father. I have a photo-op."

Senator Leopard slumped on his leather and palm wood sofa in his "personal office," a vast, tropical-looking hideaway tucked just eighty-four seconds from the Senate floor. He had timed the walk, so he'd know how much time to allot when he had to cast a vote. Leopard inherited the office from a dying senior senator four years earlier. These mysterious minivillas are so supersecret that CIA spooks wouldn't know where to look for a missing senator. You think when you write to your senator's office that he's sitting in a chair behind a desk reading important memoranda from the Congressional Research Service? Forget it. In these covert condos, the important senators can relax, slouch and watch soap operas, and make deals. This is where a senator can let his hair down or his pants for that matter. Senator Leopard's personal office looked like the parlor of a Caribbean plantation owner. Pricey wallpaper embedded with straw, lamps embossed with tropical pineapples, and to top it off, a few indoor tangerine and tobacco plants.

Leopard took a puff of his cigar; here he could smoke and damn the EPA! He felt like spitting, but he had removed the spittoon a few weeks earlier.

"Listen, Cori. I know you think I wronged your mom. I don't care about your rebellious feelings right now. But I do care whether you get hurt. And, I might add, I'm somewhat concerned about getting hurt myself."

"You could carry mace."

"Cori, I don't know where you are—"

In fact he knew damn well. The FBI had told him.

"—But you need to find a computer," he continued. "I can't be too specific while talking on an unsecured phone line. Do some research on the legislation that funded Moynihan Park. I played a key role apparently. I'm sure you'll agree with me that it's a mighty frightening bill." He hung up.

A key role in a park? That was like Benedict Arnold playing a key role in the American Revolution. Cori looked down at her tangled pooches and decided to log on. She furiously began punching buttons on her telephone's Web browser, looking for information on a park that somehow frightened her unmovable father.

✻   ✻   ✻

Luke stepped back while the figure turned to him. The tall man slowly lifted his hand over his head and pulled back the white hood, revealing reddish hair flecked with silver. It was not Ali or Clay or anyone else Howard Cosell raved about. Luke felt as if he were watching a super-slow-motion replay when Paul Tremont turned and revealed his face. Then the billionaire methodically removed the vintage robe and folded it as carefully as a U.S. marine honor guard folds an American flag and hands it to a widow.

Luke watched silently, almost reverently, staring at the robe. Was it the original? That could be worth a million.

Tremont appeared to enjoy his performance. His blue eyes seemed to twinkle with delight, like Santa choosing the right toy to put under the Christmas tree. But unlike Santa's soft, rosy cheeks, Tremont's cheeks looked high and hard like the headlamps on an aggressive '56 Chevy. Underneath the robe, Tremont wore a chalk-stripe silk suit that must've taken a whole farm of Chinese silk worms to cough up. He ordered his suits a little on the tight side. Though he was just over seventy, he looked like a recently retired athlete, a star pitcher or quarterback. The tight suits made the chalk stripes ripple at his pecs and lats. Luke could tell Tremont's body was cut and ripped. He had heard, though, if Tremont disliked you, *your* body would be cut and ripped. "Yes, Luke, it's the real deal," Tremont said with a lilting Boston Brahmin accent. "Take a look at the note in the pocket." Tremont pointed with his long index finger, the finger of a pianist, not a boxer. His prominent nose helped point the way, like de Gaulle's or Lincoln's.

Luke, as if under a spell, patted the robe, heard a crumpling sound, and pulled out a yellowed handwritten note. He instantly recognized the handwriting.

"Read it," Tremont gently prodded him.

"*Round 8 to prove I'm great!*" Luke read calmly. "It's Ali, I mean Clay, that's what he shouted to Liston at the weigh-in."

"You know much about the fight, Luke?" Tremont asked

Tremont knew damn well that Luke knew about the fight.

Luke tried to control his excitement. "Yes, Mr. Tremont. Liston said his only concern was how to get his fist OUT of Clay's big mouth once the fight started. That was a long time ago. But I don't understand what you're up to today, Mr. Tremont. Flying me off the roof in a chopper, dressing up like Ali?"

Tremont snickered. "I guess there's a little drama queen in me. Here's my philosophy: if you want to win, you have to control not just the money, not just the people, but the atmospherics, everything from the room temperature to the signs on the exit doors. The Kennedys knew that. Whenever Jack planned a rally, old Joe Kennedy would book a room 50 percent too small for the crowd. That way the news footage would show a crowd going nuts, climbing over each other, in a frenzy over the young candidate. Here in Vegas, the comedians like to keep the showrooms at sixty-four degrees. No one can fall asleep when he's shivering. Laughing feels good. So, Luke, forgive me, if I went a little over the top today."

Tremont brushed back his hair and went on.

"It's yours, Luke," Tremont calmly said.

"I got a job?"

"No, not just a job. The robe, the note. They're yours. I just better not see them on eBay. You want to sell them, you need some money, you see me. We'll auction it right at Sotheby's in Mayfair. Should fetch a million or two."

Luke gave Tremont a questioning look. "But what's my job? I can't accept gifts like this."

"Why not? You a senator or something? You afraid of internal affairs? What are you, a cop?" Tremont teased him and bared his long, gleaming teeth. "You know something about Tremont Advisors, don't you? You know I run fights, but you also know I run a hedge fund. We buy and sell currencies, commodities, and international stocks. You're probably the only person in the world who understands both sides of my business. You think those pencil-necked MBAs at Gresham have a clue about negotiating with Don King? And you think those knuckleheads in the gym even know that the rest of the world trades in euros, yen, and yuan, instead of dollars? You're my bridge man. You're my link to sports and money. I've had my eye on you for awhile. I need muscle and money. M&M. That's you. M&M." Tremont looked up at the lights in a reverie "M&M. Paul Tremont's Candy Man," he slowly pronounced.

Luke fumbled for a response. It was like the pope offering you a bishop's seat even though you weren't sure you believed in Christ. Then he said something stupid.

"Do I get a contract?"

Tremont roared. "Don't ever mention *contract* in Vegas, or you'll end up in Hoover Dam." Still chuckling and shaking his head, Tremont asked, "How much did Clay get for the first Liston fight?"

"Six hundred thirty thousand dollars," Luke shot back.

"Right. Well, that should do it for you, then."

Luke gathered his nerve. After all, he'd been literally dragged from his prior job at Gresham. "But Liston got $1.3 million."

Tremont laughed again. "Hey, he got paid for breaking heads for the Mob. And where'd he end up?"

Luke knew. In his bedroom. Naked. Murdered by a hot shot of heroin torpedoed into his veins.

"You don't really want that, do you, Luke? You're on the fast track now, M&M. Take my advice, don't fall off."

Luke felt his knees almost buckle, though nobody had touched him.

Tremont continued. "You're used to a boxing ring. That's just five feet off the floor. When you fly with me, you got a lot more altitude. Meet me in the Four Seasons's sauna tomorrow at seven A.M. You'll never be the same."

Meanwhile across the Strip, Cori Leopard was nervously punching numbers into her telephone. Paul Tremont's security detail, composed of Jumbo, his dark partner, and a skinny young lawyer with acne who had just passed the Nevada bar approached her unnoticed. Jumbo grabbed her dog leashes and the dark man tore up the sign that said TREMONT KILLS! The acne-faced lawyer tried to swipe her telephone, but Cori quickly slapped him on the cheek with it.

"Hey, get lost, you freak-show contestant," she yelled.

"Just a minute, Miss Leopard," said Jumbo. "You're creating trouble for Mr. Tremont here."

The wimpy lawyer held one hand to his bruised cheek and used the other to hand her a piece of paper. "This is a summons—"

Cori ignored him and stared into Jumbo's round eyes. Was this the danger her father warned her about? On a public street, traversed by a hundred thousand people by day and five hundred streetwalkers by night? She wasn't going to be intimidated. Hell, she'd protested for women's rights in front of an Iranian mullah at his mosque. She had parachuted into a civil war in Liberia to protest strip mining.

"Lemme speak to him, then," she insisted.

"What?" said Jumbo. *The nerve of this chick.*

"You afraid?" she asked. "I'm not even sure you work for him." Yeah, question their authority, their manhood.

Just then Jumbo's phone rang. It was Tremont.

"Yes sir, yes sir," Jumbo said. "Should I dump her at the airport? One-way on Southwest?"

"No," said Tremont in a soft voice.

"Then what?" Jumbo put his lips directly on the phone and whispered with a confused expression on his face. "What? *Hurt* her?"

"No, no, no. *Hire* her. Put Ms. Leopard on the phone." Jumbo rolled his round eyes and handed the phone to Cori. He looked at his partner and the lawyer and turned his palms upward, shrugging in exasperation. This had happened before. He held onto the leashes as the dogs sniffed his shoes.

Cori didn't believe it was Paul Tremont on the phone until he reminded her that they met once when she was a freshman at Georgetown, and he gave a lecture at the Foreign Service School. Well, it wasn't so much a lecture as a name-dropping performance. He'd say "Henry," and the students would wonder, " Henry Kissinger? Henry the VIII?"

"I need a girl like you."

"First of all, I'm not a girl," she growled. "Second, I hate half your life. Yeah, you give money to the Red Cross and the Peace Corps to build bridges. But then your companies strip mine African towns, making it necessary to build those Peace Corps bridges."

"Good lord, Cori. You sound like you're reading from a "Wanted" poster. That's exactly why I need someone like you to make sure my managers don't run amok and undermine all our good charitable work. Look, do you want to work on the *outside?* Do you want a chance to really make a difference on the *inside?*"

"I've seen what the inside does. You must know who my father is. The inside ate up his insides and left him empty."

Tremont paused, dramatically. "I don't want to be a father figure. That's someone else's job. But if you truly want to repair the ravages you rage about, don't miss the chance I'm giving you. I could easily hire an aggressive, amoral, gold-plated, asphalt-hearted urban Wharton MBA for the job. He'd be happy to rip up some more earth. Do you prefer that?"

Is he threatening me? If I don't take the job, he'll do more damage? Cori's mind raced to consider her options. *What's the worst that could happen? I could quit an hour after accepting the job. I won't be a prisoner.*

I could take notes on his company's devious deeds and take them to the EPA or the Department of Justice.

"All right. I'll hear you out," she said, brushing back her hair.

"Fine. Come to the Four Seasons tomorrow morning at seven thirty."

CHAPTER 16

Clutching the dog leashes, Cori started jogging back to the pet trainer's office. She patted the dogs good-bye and then walked quickly to her motel, a few blocks from the Strip, which is like saying a few feet down from Niagara Falls. In Vegas, hotel driveways seemed miles long. Her seedy joint was a two-story walk-up. When she had checked in, she saw a recycling bin in the dimly lit lobby, which was really just an alcove with mildewed indoor/outdoor carpeting. In her mind a recycling bin was as good as a three-star rating from the *Michelin Guide*.

When Cori got to her room, she immediately started typing on her laptop, searching for Moynihan Park, obviously named after the brilliant and distinguished New York senator, who grew up in Hell's Kitchen but somehow spoke like a particularly posh leprechaun. Other than President Reagan, he was about the only man in Washington who imagined that the Soviet Union could collapse. Gossipers said that Moynihan's afternoon cocktails started arriving at ten A.M., but even sloshed, he could outwit his most sober Senate colleagues. If Moynihan were still alive, he'd insist that the national park named after him have an open bar.

Cori went to the Web site for the Congressional Research Service. Moynihan Park popped up, alongside Hoover Dam, followed by all sorts of specs: one hundred coyotes, an estimated thirty black bears, a pack of twenty wolves. It sounded like a shopping list for a zoo. Then the list of synthetic features: three hundred parking places, forty-two low-flush toilets, and so on. No big deal. What was her father worried about?

Cori typed in "Harold Leopard" and read the description of a twelve-foot by twelve-foot concrete fountain named for him. Her father annoyed her even more. At the last minute—after fighting against the park for a year—he must have thrown his support behind the bill in exchange for some lasting glory. A *concrete* fountain display! In a nature preserve! The water for the fountain would've been better used on a prickly cactus or diverted to help the Maopa Band of Paiute Indians, who struggled nearby.

Then Cori read the next line, cocked her head, and froze: *"The Harold and Cori Memorial Fountain, in memory of the late senator and his daughter."*

Luke had been to saunas before, but not Four Seasons-style. He'd been down at the Russian Baths on 10th Street, where naked, flabby old men encouraged deaf attendants to beat them with platza brooms made from bunches of oak leaves and softened in tubs of hot soapy water. Why were the attendants deaf? So that they couldn't hear Mob secrets. The sauna had three tiers of concrete benches. On the bottom tier, the temperature was so hot the hair on your chest could singe. That was nothing. Each tier brought more pain, or pleasure, depending on your point of view. The second tier brought 150-degree air flaming through your nostrils. And the third row? Nobody had survived the third row in a decade, not since before the Soviet Union fell.

But this sauna was different. Instead of peeling linoleum, Luke stepped onto Carrera marble and walked through reed curtains. On the Lower East Side, his masseur was named Bruno. At the Four Seasons, lovely Asian beauties sat behind a bamboo desk and offered him a menu featuring peppermint body scrubs, floral shea butter wraps, and cocoa vanilla massages using "Thai and lomi lomi techniques." What would his old schvitz buddies think?

He felt out of place in his Armani suit and alligator shoes. He had had trouble sleeping last night, wondering what to wear. Though Luke felt more at home in locker rooms and steam rooms than in fancy restaurants or oak-paneled clubs, he thought it would be bizarre to get naked with his new boss in the steam room the first day on the job. Also, he wasn't sure he was even being invited to partake in the spa. Would it be presumptuous to assume that Tremont was giving him a spa treatment? Luke had played back in his mind the conversation: "Meet me in the

TODD BUCHHOLZ

Four Seasons sauna tomorrow at seven A.M. You'll never be the same." Hedging his bets, Luke had stopped at the sporting goods store in the lobby and bought a swimsuit to wear underneath the Armani. With a salary of $630,000, he'd be buying more designer suits. Then he thought about his friends at Delancy's gym, especially old Buck Roberts, who couldn't make rent payments as expensive as the Armani. He'd take care of Buck with his first paycheck.

Tremont was delighted to keep Luke off-guard. His cardinal rule was that only he should feel entirely comfortable. The other guy should be tapping his feet, rubbing his hands, or twitching. Tremont had learned this from watching an intimidating character—Lyndon B. Johnson. At six-foot three-and-a-half inches, Johnson loved to peer down on shrunken old politicians, twisting their arms literally and figuratively into humiliating positions. He loved to pull rank, forcing aides and even congressmen to accompany him to the bathroom. Forcing a young hire to wear Armani to a sauna would've been pretty tame stuff for LBJ.

A beautiful Asian girl in a Hawaiian sarong took Luke's hand in her small, soft hand and led him to the steam room. He kept his suit on as the thin girl opened the door and gestured for him to enter. Heat assaulted him, blinding him for a moment. He backed into a wall, where he felt the droplets seep into his suit. Wiping his eyes, he saw Paul Tremont, shirtless, sitting on a towel.

"Did you bring a pad, M&M?" Tremont asked.

"Lot of good that would do, Mr. Tremont. It's a rainforest in here."

"I suppose you're right. Take off your jacket and trousers and hang them outside the door."

Good idea, since they're disintegrating, Luke thought. He wanted to strip off his shirt, too, but Tremont specified only the jacket. As his eyes adjusted to the wafting clouds of steam, he noticed something odd on Tremont's left leg, like a big tube sock extending from his ankle to his upper thigh, next to which rested the crown jewels of the Tremont empire.

Tremont noticed his stare. "That's a thrombosis sock. I'm trying to keep my leg. Take my advice; don't become diabetic."

"So's my father. Watches his diet closely, I'm told," Luke responded.

"Tell me about your father. I like to know my employees. A teacher, right?"

"Professor. An endowed chair. Columbia." Luke rolled his eyes.

"Colombia, the country? Or the university?"

"Upper West Side of Manhattan. Please, my father knows English literature. Guys like Milton, Pope, and Wordsworth. Like he learned it direct from God. He wouldn't speak Spanish if he was stranded in a Puerto Rican jail."

"Was your grandfather a snob too?"

"No idea. Died before I was born."

"How about your mother?"

"Car crash. I was a kid in the back seat. Mr. Tremont, I thought we were here to talk about me. I stand on my own. I fall on my own."

"Sorry if I offended you, Luke, but the DNA code in your blood-stream helps determine whether you're a genius or a dolt, an honest man or a crook. I'm going to give you an amazing role at Tremont. I can't afford to cast the wrong man. Let's make this quick. Sonny, the girl who let you in, has a check for you—$100,000. I want you to deposit it in your checking account and then write a check in your name to the Robin Hood Foundation. It's a charity that raises money from hedge fund managers. They do good stuff. Mostly for poor kids."

"That'll feed a lot of kids," Luke said, brushing the sweat off his eyebrows.

"They deserve it. We don't all get lucky breaks. Give some back. Give lots back." The sizzling steam made Tremont speak in short bursts. "I don't know what you've heard or read about me. But I send out a lot of checks with other people's names on them."

Tremont continued in a quickened pace: "Take the Gulfstream back to New York, go to Barneys, and buy some more suits. Go see Dr. Burns at our office, and he'll set you up with a new apartment. Your choice, West Side or East Side."

East Side, Luke immediately thought. West Side was too close to Francis Braden, Mars Company Professor of Literature at Columbia.

"Your first assignment, M&M, is to talk with Bloomberg News about Boeing. It looks good to us."

Luke didn't follow Boeing very closely, but he knew that Airbus was trouncing it every day by signing up jet deals with nearly every country on the globe. Boeing executives sat in Seattle as their market share plummeted from 80 percent to 40 percent. But Tremont must know something he didn't, so Luke just nodded.

"Any questions?"

"Just one. Who's Dr. Burns?"

Tremont chuckled. "That's our firm psychiatrist. You'll like him. Keeps us steady. Crazy world out there." He waved Luke away.

"One last thing," Tremont said. "Send Sonny in here after you get the check."

Luke walked out soaked and excited. New job, new clothes, new apartment. And a psychiatrist. Sonny walked up to him and handed Luke the check. Luke read the sum: "$110,000."

"Mr. Tremont is a big tipper," she said, as she sashayed into the steam room.

Luke patted down his suit, walked over to the spa bar, poured himself an iced lemonade, and slouched against the wall. Suddenly, he heard a woman screaming from the steam room. He bolted upright and wondered what to do. At that moment Jumbo appeared and signaled for him to leave.

CHAPTER 17

Cori stared at the screen. Memorial fountain. The late senator and his daughter. Was this a prank? A mistake? She did a wider search. Did they make other mistakes? She searched for Senator Billings, chairman of the Authorization Committee. Surely, he'd have a monument in his honor. Within seconds her screen displayed a diagram of the Billings Living Desert Museum, "dedicated to preserving the plant and animal life of the desert." The legislation also authorized $150,000 for a dedication ceremony chaired by the senator himself. No "memorial" there. A Living Desert Museum for a living senator.

Cori tried to call her father at home, but he wasn't there. Story of her life. Next she tried his office. Only an answering machine with "God Bless America" humming in the background. Typical. She hung up and prayed for the evening to go by quickly.

The next morning she hobbled over to the Four Seasons in uncomfortable shoes she had picked up at TJ Maxx a few days before. If she had known that she was going to such a plush refuge for rich people, she would've left the price tags on the shoes, just to bring some proletarian spirit to the elegant hotel. What in the world was she going to talk to Paul Tremont about? It was hard to focus on a job offer when you have just read your own bizarre obituary in federal legislation.

On her way into the sauna, she passed a doe-eyed young man in a soggy suit who had an athlete's build. She never read the sports pages, so the quick-walking Luke Braden meant nothing to her.

Cori found Paul Tremont relaxing on a chaise longue, an unlit cigar between his lips. Cori vowed that she would run out if he asked for a match. She spent her senior year of high school gathering signatures to ban smoking in private clubs in Washington, D.C. She had firmly believed that the underpaid waitresses, busboys, and masseurs of the Metropolitan Club and the Cosmos Club should not be forced to inhale nicotine.

Tremont waved her in with a smile.

"Cuban?" she asked, pointing to the stogie, and he nodded in agreement.

"Of course. Only the best."

"I wish those dolts in Washington would lift the Cuban embargo," she said, figuring he'd agree.

He didn't. His face began to turn red, and he almost bit off the tip of the cigar.

"Young lady, the animal dictator who rules Cuba deserves a cage. Good thing your father has been right about that."

"Well, that's Dad. Mr. Courage. Nodding his head along with those million Miami-Cuban votes. Do you think he gives a damn about Castro?"

Tremont decided to drop the subject. Why get annoyed right after a "spa" treatment from Sonny? He pointed to the chaise longue next to him, and Cori haltingly took a seat. She didn't like being so close to a Mr. Big, especially one reclining in a silk bathrobe.

"Here's the deal. I'll make it quick. You are my new vice president for global landscaping."

Landscaping? she thought. *What am I, a Mexican gardener?*

"Cori, you'll have a great deal of power. I've got projects from Tierra del Fuego to Toronto. Hotels, bridges, parks—"

"Coal mines," she inserted forcefully.

"Yes, mines, too. Some of them a bloody disgrace."

"Yes, I've seen them."

"Then, goddammit, clean them up! You report to me. Anyone stands in your way, you tell me. Stop bitching and take the reins. My dear, you've spent your whole life complaining, just playing the part of a protester. As if wearing a pair of Birkenstocks and using Tom's of Maine organic toothpaste would make a dime's difference. My researchers have told me about you. And I can't figure out whether you're trying to make a difference or just trying to *be* different. You can just as well save the world holding a Hermès handbag."

"How can I trust you? Maybe you're just using me. I'm no token, Mr. Tremont."

Tremont smiled. Nobody's a token these days. The only difference between a token and a full partner is a pension and membership at a fitness club, he thought.

"I'll trust *you* first," Tremont replied. "My assistant Sonny will be giving you wiring instructions to deposit $10 million into an account in your name. You will have sole authority over that money. Save the children, save the animals, or place it all on the red space at the roulette table."

"Ten million? And I choose the charities? You're joking."

"The money gets deposited at midnight tonight."

Stunned, Cori felt the color drain from her face. But she would not let this opportunity slip. "You're on."

He told her to rush to the airport and catch a ride on his Gulfstream heading to New York.

"There's an interesting young man for you to meet," Tremont said. "You have so little in common, I'm sure there'll be turbulence and possibly a food fight by the time the plane flies over Denver."

Tremont gave a little salute and Cori stood up to leave. But then he added something so chilling that it almost made her leap out of her TJ Maxx sandals.

"Frankly, Cori, I don't understand why Fidel didn't have your dad killed years ago."

CHAPTER 18

Paul Tremont sat at the Mandalay Bay baccarat table in his double-breasted blue jacket and splashy pink Zegna necktie, looking audaciously nautical for the desert. But when you own yachts and planes, no one questions whether you just stepped off your schooner. His scurrying staffers jostled with the Mandalay Bay waitresses, each eager to pour his drink, repour his drink, and line his shoulders with beautiful girls, half of whom somehow, accidentally, brushed their hands across his lap. A brush stroke was the only way to communicate with the master, to apply for work in his harem. Tremont loved sex but he had important work to do. These fools think that rich guys can afford to just lounge around and screw around. He noticed that none of the truly rich men he met had the simple capacity to relax and turn off their 500-horsepower brains or egos. Almost all CEOs suffered from attention deficit disorder. If you dispensed Ritalin in the corner offices, the Dow Jones average would crash 5,000 points.

What concerns were ricocheting inside Tremont's brain? He took inventory as another hand grazed his upper thigh. His bankers in London were bidding for Harrods, a consortium in Shanghai was after him to urge the Chinese premier to approve yet another skyscraper, last night his bond traders in New York bet five billion dollars that the European Central Bank would cut interest rates the following month, a gossip columnist in Florida was threatening to print a story about him and Paris Hilton's alleged abortion, the Guggenheim was hitting him up for another anonymous gift to bail out its sinking museum in Venice, and

UNICEF wanted him to sponsor a global conference on child pornography. He hated the pressure; and loved it too. Tallying up the calls to make and to receive, Tremont cast his eyes at the mirrored, spy-cammed ceiling of the casino. Meanwhile the tintinabulations of the slot machines in the low-rent district of the casino echoed. Why couldn't they banish to the basement those pitiful dollar machines played by porky shaped Americans clutching plastic cups?

One more concern struck Tremont: Luke Braden, another pet to add to his collection. Some of his human pets became close advisers, like Christian Playa, the murderous Cuban-American and Stuart Burns, the dandified shrink. Tremont had been keeping his eye on young Luke for a long time. A hungry fellow longing for respect, money, and the approval of a father figure. Luke would be shocked at the price he'd pay to satisfy his longing, especially the latter one. But before Luke would be ripe, he would first would have to pass some tests.

Tremont gently sloughed off the clinging arms of his sycophants and slipped away from the Baccarat table and the disappointed bevy of Vegas talent.

"Get me Dr. Burns," he whispered into his cufflink, embedded into which was a cell phone.

In Manhattan, the diminutive Burns picked up the phone with the same expression of awe and fear as Moses addressing the burning bush.

"Stuart, my dear shrunken shrink, it's time to start testing Luke Braden. Tell him about our training program. I've set out three tests for him: media, corporate finance, and diplomacy. He should make us some money while proving himself," Tremont said in the calm and instructive tone of a high school guidance counselor.

"But, Paul, do you think he'll ever be ready for the endgame?" Burns asked, almost pleading. "You could cut glass with his rough edges."

Burns stared into the phone. Was it a secure line? Was any line secure from the FBI or CIA or Mossad?

"Oh, that. Why, of course he can destroy Castro."

CHAPTER 19

Two men were telling nasty jokes about her in the lunchroom. So Sara Hartman leaned back against the flimsy partition that separated the Formica tables. She recognized their voices. They belonged to two lugs who worked in the Bureau of Western Hemispheric Affairs. They had publicly denounced the paper she published in a right-wing journal, calling for a blockade against Cuba. She argued that the forty-year-old embargo against Cuba was not enough; the U.S. Navy should encircle the island and choke it off. Bureaucrats had no imagination, Sara thought. These two had probably eaten at the same table since joining the State Department in the Carter days.

In a few hours the U.S. Senate would confirm her appointment as assistant secretary for international enforcement. Then she would eat in the executive dining room and leave those goons and their jokes behind. No more tuna or egg salad sandwiches. She knew that the secretary of state had worked out a deal with the chancellor of the exchequer to fly in fresh Dover sole on the first British Air flight from Heathrow Monday, Wednesday, and Friday. A later flight left Dulles with live Maryland blue crabs, their claws nipping all the way across the Atlantic. Sara had also heard that Secretary Hubert tried to negotiate a similar deal for pastries from the French, but their minister for cultural affairs found out and argued that Paris did not need any genetically modified foods from the U.S.

In just two hours Sara would face a real test, her confirmation hearing. The State Department's Legislative Liaison had warned her that the

Senate Foreign Affairs Committee would pierce and grill her like a shish kebob.

Senator Harold Leopard chaired the committee. Sara had spent weeks cramming her head with all sorts of important and trivial information so that Leopard couldn't stump her. For the past week, she'd had nightmares about Leopard. Yet soon she'd be squaring off against the committee and against all the senate aides who, no doubt, scripted trick questions to trip her up.

Back at the office, one last cram session. She picked up the flash-cards that she kept in her desk, next to her eyebrow pencil and her calculator. She'd been carrying around these smudged cards for a month and couldn't wait to get rid of them.

"What's the capital of Zimbabwe?" Sara read from the card.

"Harare," she shot back at herself, flinging the flashcard into the trash.

"Who won a Nobel prize in economics for his work on currency zones?"

"Robert Mundell," she replied correctly.

"What's the name of the Vietnamese currency?"

She hesitated. Something off-color, she remembered. The Wang? No.

She turned over the card. "The Dong." She wasn't too worried about missing that question. They'd never ask about the dong, not after the senators forced Judge Clarence Thomas to discuss "Long Dong Silver" in his X-rated confirmation hearings.

The phone rang.

"You ready, my princess?" her mother asked in a honey-coated voice. *She* would be ready, if *she* were the nominee. She knew all these answers. Hell, she invented some of these answers during her days as the first woman vice chairman of Merrill Lynch. Couldn't she send Sara the answers through a special infrared earphone?

"I hope so, Mom."

"Are you biting your nails?"

"No," Sara assured her, while silently pulling two fingers from between her teeth. "Thanks for calling. I love you."

"Dad would've been proud," her mother added before hanging up.

The phone buzzed again, and the Virginia drawl of her assistant filled the office.

"CNN and C-SPAN, Ms. Hartman."

What! Sara didn't even want a live audience for the hearing. What if she embarrassed herself? CNN Headline News would replay it again and again, every half hour, like the sports blooper of the week.

"Get me Legislative Affairs," she yelled, as her assistant placed the call.

"I don't get it," she said to the Legislative liaison What's all the attention for? CNN *and* C-SPAN?"

"I just got off the phone with Leopard's staff. Seems like he's got something up his sleeve about corruption that he's going to unveil in front of the cameras," the young man said, trying to hide his alarm.

"At my hearing?"

"Your turn at bat, Sara. Sorry. I'll let you know if I hear more."

Sara wanted to call her mother back, but instead decided to study her flashcards one more time.

Sara strode into Room 419 of the Senate Dirksen Office Building with the steely determination she usually displayed in public. But when the camera crew turned on the searing television lights, she could feel her makeup melting and tiny beads of perspiration forming on her upper lip.

The senators took their seats. Sara felt lucky that only five committee members showed up. But where was Leopard? Then the big oak door opened and the fiery Floridian sauntered to his center seat.

"Ladies and gentlemen," he began. "We're here to meet with the State Department's nominee for assistant secretary for international enforcement. Miss Hartman, we will treat you with respect and, I hope, fairness. My staff has prepared a few basic questions for you."

Sara gripped her notebooks and gave quick, not always eloquent, answers to his questions about World Bank funding in Sierra Leone and dam projects in China.

During a reply a pimply faced aide slipped a piece of paper to Leopard, who scrunched up his bushy eyebrows.

"How many guards does the United States have along the Mexico border?"

"About 9,000." Whew. Easy.

As Sara drew her finger across her eyebrow, Christian Playa squeezed his brawny buttocks into a pew in the back row. He peered toward the front of the room, studying Sara. Then he examined Senator Leopard. He hadn't seen the man in person in about forty years, but only the hairline looked different, slowly receding.

As Leopard continued with his questions, Sara noted that he was not really paying attention to her answers.

The fierce tiger was playing the role of pussy. He asked whether any of his distinguished colleagues had questions for the nominee. They had the blank stares of lobotomy patients.

The pimply aide returned with another missive for the senator.

"Do you agree with the president of Harvard that we should loosen the embargo on Cuba?" Leopard stretched "Harvard" out for an extra few syllables and added a sneer that made the university sound more like "aardvark."

"Not at all, senator. As you know, I have strongly argued that we should tighten the embargo on Castro. A naval blockade would be even better. Let the island screech to a stop. Then the Cuban expats in Florida and New Jersey can return and reclaim their stolen land. They'll be greeted with flowers and rum," she stated.

In the back row, Mr. Playa shifted his weight and looked nauseated. He pulled out of his pocket a small card, on which was written: *Cuba para los Cubanos.*

Finally, Leopard stood, and he pointed at Sara with his gold oil well ring, gesturing for her to stand too.

"You're a smart girl, I mean, woman, Sara Hartman. But too clever, if you thought you could fool this committee. Sure, you had slick, carefully rehearsed answers to my questions—"

Sara felt her face turning red and watched the television cameras swivel in her direction, their laser-like eyes drilling in on her.

"Tell us about the finance minister of Sri Lanka!" he thundered.

She searched her brain for the man's name. "That would be Mr. Hulati, senator."

"Not anymore, Miss Hartman. He's dead. Stabbed to death last night, throwing the Asian financial markets into a frenzy. Americans with stock in India, China, and Malaysia have just watched their savings evaporate. You may be in contempt of Congress for keeping this crisis from this committee!"

She had no idea. When was he stabbed? Why didn't someone slip her a note about the Asian stock markets? Leopard turned his back on her and aimed his ample body toward the oak door.

"Senator Leopard, I assure you that if I had any idea, I would have given advice—" Sara felt she was going to vomit.

Leopard twisted his shoulders back toward her and pointed. "Here's my advice, Miss Hartman. Get a lawyer."

The oak door slammed behind the senator, and Sara was left naked on center stage.

She didn't know that Mr. Playa was ready to pounce.

CHAPTER 20

Luke hopped onto the new Gulfstream 450 like a twelve-year-old into the stands of his first Yankees game. He had left New York literally kicking and screaming. Now he was flying back in style, with a big paycheck and fancy wardrobe. He thought about how he'd spend his $630,000 salary. When he landed, he'd call Buck and give the old man more than spare change. Despite a bum heart and arthritis, Buck lived on the fifth floor of a six-story walk-up. After easing Buck's pain, he might even place a phone call to the disdainful, distinguished professor at Columbia. Not to boast to his father, but just to keep him apprised. Your son, the yahoo, just shook off the dunce cap.

Luke had spent the past ten years trying to become self-sufficient, getting by with his street smarts and his fists, but those alone never paid the bills. Hanging sides of beef at Smith & Wollensky's or patrolling the lobby for Gresham Bros. kept him from eating dog food. But now things were different. Thanks to Paul Tremont, he could walk through the front door of Smith & Wollensky's rather than slip through the blood- and saw-dust-covered rear entrance.

Luke had no idea he'd be sharing the ride to New York. Not until Cori Leopard slowly climbed up the fold-away stairs, each step accentuating her long, sleek legs and the emerald green skirt that cut away just above the knees. She was a few pounds too skinny, he thought, but the cascading curls of her long, reddish hair framed an angular face with bones that God must have chiseled with Michelangelo's tools. She looked like Mary in the Pieta, except for two differences. First, she wasn't cradling a slumping Jesus. Second, she didn't quite look like a virgin. It had been months since Luke had been with a woman. And Las Vegas was like an aphrodisiac: breasts, arms, and legs waving at you all day and night on the billboards and in the flesh. Cori turned to him and her icy blue eyes pierced him like darts.

As she met Luke's eyes, she brushed back her hair and stared just a second too long at Luke's face. Then she looked him up and down frowning as she pointed to his feet. Politics got in the way of her instincts.

He was wearing Goddamn alligator shoes.

"You hunt them yourself?"

"I don't hunt." It was true. He had killed a man in the ring, but he'd never picked up a shotgun. He pointed to the shoes. "They are a bit pricey for my taste," he added.

"The belt too, oh my god," she moaned.

"Hey, I was about to tell you I liked *your* shoes," Luke said. He had read in *GQ* that women really like it when you compliment them on their shoes. It's less threatening than commenting on their shirts or skirts. "Besides, I didn't even buy the shoes and belt."

"Sorry," she said. He looked young. Did his mother still shop for him?

Luke thought he was doing okay. "Actually, Mr. Tremont bought them for me. Before I met him at the sauna." He just smiled, figuring she'd struggle to make sense of that.

He was right. She struggled. Was he a kept man? Was Tremont gay? Figures. Just when she gets locked aboard a plane with a cute guy, he turns out to be playing for the other team.

She plopped into one of reclining chairs and looked out the window. She had more important worries than this guy's shoes. Who in the world would want to scare her family with a "memorial" fountain? She had heard about mistakes in the *Congressional Record*. An aide's telephone number once showed up in a law because on the way to the printer it was scribbled in the margin. But everyone knew Senator Harold Leopard. No one could have accidentally thought he was dead.

Luke, for his part, wanted to learn more about Cori. "Should we start this conversation again? Would you like a drink?" He pointed to the well-stocked rolling bar with the Grey Goose bottles in four flavors and the plump olives in a frosted glass.

"Here's the scoop. My name's Luke, and I just got hired by Tremont. I'd never met him, but I accepted the job to help him with his hedge fund accounts and some sports marketing." He thought about full disclosure, but most women were totally turned off by boxers, which conjured up blood, sweat, and idiocy. He twisted the truth just a little. "I used to do some sportscasting back in college." He finished with a warm smile.

Cori turned in his direction, this time ignoring his politically incorrect clothing. "All right, I'll call a truce. Here's my story. I just got hired too. I think Tremont's creepy, but I'll give him a chance."

"Excuse me," Luke said while shaking the vodka, "you don't seem like the Tremont corporate type."

She laughed nervously. "Hardly. I haven't figured it out completely. Yesterday I led a protest denouncing him. Today I'm on his plane. Frankly I think he's using me just to repair his reputation as a strip-mining capitalist. But he's making a big mistake if he's underestimating me." Cori did not mention anything about her father.

Yes, Luke realized, Cori was a force. Opinionated. Arrogant. Maybe a pain in the ass. Luke couldn't keep his eyes off her.

CHAPTER 21

As Christian Playa trotted down the spiraling interior steps of the opulent Dirksen Building, the rain begin to fall outside. He passed by the elevator marked MEMBERS ONLY and swiped an umbrella from the gilded stand. *Fuck the members. They're public servants, and I need them to serve me an umbrella.*

He dashed out onto Constitution Avenue and leaned against a sturdy marble wall a few blocks from Union Station. Playa knew the escape routes and had even memorized the Amtrak train schedule. It was three thirty P.M., and there was a four thirty P.M. to New York, just as the December skies would darken. His phone buzzed.

"Do you hold the ace of hearts?" asked the calm voice.

"No. A little more time," Playa replied. "Ace of hearts" was the code for Sara Hartman's life.

After Senator Leopard had adjourned the hearing, Sara turned to her legislative aide with a combination of humiliation and anger. She ordered the twenty-four-year-old man to stay in the Dirksen Building. "We weren't prepared. We were punk'd." She started to use the language she'd picked up during her year as a Mob prosecutor in the New York district attorney's office. "I want you to infiltrate the Foreign Affairs Committee. Work them like a whore on a high-paying John. I don't care if you have to go down on your knees and crawl from one member's member to another, but you make friends with them! I don't want to be surprised by anything anymore, not even a stray fart!"

A moment later the ace of hearts vaulted down the grand steps onto Constitution Avenue. There was no limo waiting for her. Earlier that morning, Sara had calculated that with rush hour traffic, the Metro would be a much faster route across town back to the state department. The trip from Union Station to Foggy Bottom would take only fifteen minutes, including a quick switch at Metro Center.

Christian Playa followed her. His compact five-foot-six-inch body almost created a wake as he plowed along Second Street.

Sara started jogging, loping to the intersection of D Street and Second Street. The rain began to pound hard, and her shoes were soaking from the puddles, which were turning to slush as the temperature dropped. Her mind raced even faster than her legs. She started composing a to-do list, and would stay all night at Foggy Bottom till it was done. First, she'd call in the desk officer for Cuba and Sri Lanka. Demand a full report. Second, after reviewing the report, she would send it by messenger to Senator Leopard and his colleagues on the Foreign Affairs Committee. Maybe she'd hand deliver it herself. No shame in kowtowing a little. Third, she'd call the CIA chief at Guantanamo.

At Union Station, Sara kept moving and darted to the escalator to go underground to the Metro. She tried to take two steps at a time, but she was not alone. A boisterous group of Boy Scouts laughed and joked on all sides of her, flinging their soaking hats at each other like wet towels in a locker room.

Mr. Playa hung back, assessing the crowd.

Sara stepped onto the Red Line train just as her phone rang. Squeezed in between the Boy Scouts at the front of the car, she struggled to withdraw her phone.

"Department of State security, Ms. Hartman. Be very careful. We have a report of a man—" Then a crackling noise.

The line went dead as the train accelerated out of Union Station and out of range.

She looked down at the phone screen. "Text Message" flashed. "Suspect at hearing. Return home base. Call security."

She shuddered, not from the messages, but from the chill on the subway train. She rolled her eyes at the telephone. Ever since 9/11, the FBI and Secret Service were constantly running photos of Capitol Hill visitors through their computers, looking for matches. Bogus warnings flashed almost daily.

Playa leapt onto the crowded car behind Sara. He felt in the lining of his pocket for the strip of plastic explosive and its fuse, a long cord packed with black powder. He felt along his inseam for his alternative weapon, a Plexiglas knife that could easily pass through a metal detector and even more easily slice through a carotid artery. Which would he choose? It all depended on how close Playa could get, and what kind of cleanup task he wanted to create. A knife wound could be addressed by a cardiac surgeon. The plastic explosive would require three fire engines, four paramedic trucks, and a lot of sponges, squeegees, and brooms.

The train would stop twice before reaching Sara's switching point at Metro Center. Her phone started vibrating as the train screeched into Judiciary Square.

Sara looked down at her vibrating phone again. This time a fuzzy image was displayed. A man. Dark hair. A deep five o'clock shadow. She stared at the picture as the train approached Gallery Place/Chinatown. And then she looked at the baby-faced and peach-fuzzed Boy Scouts.

Playa walked through the passageway between cars and entered the back of Sara's car. He started moving between the passengers and the poles, like an Olympic slalom skier, picking up speed with each pass. He kept his left hand on the leather handle of the Plexiglas knife.

Sara's eyes shifted among the Boy Scouts. They looked so innocent, which seemed sexy to a hardened civil servant. Then she spotted an older face coming at her quickly, staring almost through her. She glanced at her phone. The Face. The image transmitted by State security was bearing down on her, just as the train slid into Metro Center station. Suddenly the brakes whined and locked, and the jumbled Boy Scouts tumbled against her, pinning her to the door.

The doors opened and Sara burst out. She tore up the steps, desperately searching for a guard to grab, or a guard station to run to. She ripped her pants and sliced her calf on a trash can, but kept running. Playa hustled to his feet and shoved Boy Scouts aside like an NFL linebacker in a Pop Warner football game.

Sara saw the guard room about two hundred feet away and looked back to see the face gaining on her. She tried to scream, but nothing came out, as she focused all her energy on keeping her distance. At nearly six feet, she was not used to losing foot races, but the face moved swiftly. Then suddenly, a new alternative. To her right, the orange line train to Foggy Bottom beckoned, its doors open just twenty yards away.

She heard the bell, warning that the doors would close in three seconds and the train would pull away. A better choice than the guard station, if she could make the twenty yards. She calculated instantaneously. She could run one hundred yards in fifteen seconds. In three seconds, she could do one-fifth of that, twenty yards. But the face was just four steps behind.

She bolted right and leapt onto the train, praying for the doors to shut. They began to close. The face had no time to squeeze through the doors. She hustled back away from the glass doors and retreated to the far end of the car, pushing her telephone buttons in a panic.

But Christian Playa didn't have to squeeze through the doors. Before they closed, he tore the plastic strip from his pocket with his left hand, yanking hard on an attached ring with his right. He hurled it into the car and then slapped a green sticker on the outside panel of the train. The plain sticker displayed two initials. C.L. Then Playa, the Face, ran as fast as he could toward the safety of the guard station.

CHAPTER 22

Luke arrived for his first day on the job at Tremont Advisors an hour ahead of schedule. He woke up early, checked Bloomberg television for the overnight market news, and hopped onto the B train near his apartment. He left plenty of time for blackouts, brownouts, and burnouts on the New York subway, and felt sharp and confident, bounding up two steps at a time to the lobby of the glistening glass building on Columbus Circle that was Tremont headquarters.

He stopped at the black onyx guard's table to announce himself. The guard, a white guy about Luke's age who still had acne on his thin face and a nametag that said "Justin" was dressed in a starched blue uniform. He punched Luke's name into the computer.

"How'd you get here, sir?" he asked in an unmistakable 718 accent—the area code for working-class Queens.

"A train," Luke replied flatly, which launched the guard into a guffaw.

"You're joking, right, Mr. Braden?"

"Not really."

"You've got an A-pass. That means there was a black car waiting in front of your apartment to chauffeur you up here. We don't see many A-pass guys on the B train."

"What does 'A' stand for?" Luke inquired.

The guard hesitated. "Sir, may I have permission to be direct?"

"Sure."

"Officially, it stands for 'All-access.' But down here in the lobby, among the help, we think it means 'Asshole.'" The young man smiled apologetically.

"Thanks for your candor, er . . . Justin. I'll try not to live up to my new rank."

Justin looked down again. "There's a message for you. Dr. Burns will see you at nine eighteen this morning. That's four minutes. Elevators to the left."

"I'm off," Luke said as he stepped toward the elevators. He looked over his shoulder. "Hey, Justin, what's Burns's rank?"

"A-pass. First class," the young guard answered.

Luke still was puzzled that he was seeing a psychiatrist. He'd never doubted his sanity. He had learned in his boxing career that half the guys were total nutcases. Unstable, untrustworthy, drugged up. But the other half were exceedingly sane. Fighting requires constant self-analysis: Can I take another punch? How can I psych-out my opponent? How can I stop my manager from cheating me?

That's how Cassius Clay took out Liston, by fooling the dumb old champ into thinking that his "sting like a bee" opponent was certifiably crazy. At the weigh-in, Clay ranted into such a sweaty rave that the boxing commission doctor reported his pulse at one hundred twenty and his blood pressure at two hundred over one hundred. The doctor officially opined that "This fighter is scared to death." Liston grew overconfident, just as Clay wanted it.

Luke knew enough about his own sanity to know that he needed a shrink as much as he needed an English lit scholar as a father. But if Tremont insisted, he'd go along. This was his big break, and some guy with a goatee dangling a pocketwatch in front of his eyes would not stop him from collecting his paycheck and moving uptown. He assumed that Dr. Burns would ask him to discuss his childhood. Probably sit there nodding and popping questions like "How did that make you feel?" Introspection was not Luke's strong point. Too much bullshit. He quit school because he felt as if he was strapped to a chair for six hours a day. Nothing deeper than that. He had no personal despair or feelings of guilt over his mother's accidental death. He didn't screw a chick because of an evolutionary desire to spread his seed. He screwed because his orgasms felt good.

Dr. Stuart Burns paced his office in his short, clipped steps, looking down at his shiny Prada slip-ons. When his heels hit the hardwood floors, they clicked like a hailstorm. While most of the other offices were carpeted, Burns had insisted on imported cherrywood from Bali. For some reason the sound of his steps ricocheted even louder outside his office than inside, inspiring the secretaries in the hallway to secretly refer to him as Dr. Bojangles. Burns thought Tremont was making a big mistake, trusting a young kid and grooming him for the biggest gamble of Tremont's career. But Burns couldn't challenge the boss; the boss made him the best-paid analyst in the history of medicine. Not even the Park Avenue Jungians pulled in $2,000,000 a year. And now he knew too much to leave the firm. He got the big bucks to keep his mouth shut about Tremont's unorthodox and aggressive trading methods.

Burns had no intention of psychoanalyzing Luke. He knew about Luke's childhood. His assistant had tricked the New York Public School system into turning over the boy's records. Burns perched on his taupe suede sofa, flipped through the records, and stroked his chin. The records showed some harmless pranks done with other boys, like signing up his newlywed ninth grade teacher for Internet dating sites.

The surprise came on his IQ tests, where Luke consistently scored higher than the average boxer or the average dropout or the average teacher or even the average psychiatrist. He had tested between 142 and 149. The boy was a borderline genius. Not Mozart. But he probably showed up in the same range as Paul Tremont. Burns quickly tossed aside the folder. He knew his own IQ. He'd taken dozens of tests over the years, including monthly exams emailed to him by Mensa. He'd never cracked 130 and it ate at him like termites in a rickety tree house.

Burns's square-shaped office reminded Luke of a boxing ring, and for a moment he had an urge to walk to the center and touch gloves with the shrink. Dr. Burns gave him a smile that displayed the large porcelain teeth of an orthodontist's advertisement in the back of New York magazine.

"Dr. Burns, I'm Luke Braden. Mr. Tremont asked me to see you." Luke said politely, even with some deference. "I don't have much experience with mental health professionals."

"Let's hope not," Burns said. "Luke you have a big fan in Paul Tremont. He wants to turn you into a power player at Tremont Advisors. I'm not sure I understand it myself. I guess you must have really wowed Mr. Hardiz at Gresham."

Luke, too, did not fully understand the sudden change in his life.

He thought he had potential, but a power player? Seemed premature to him. But he was willing to ride the wave.

"Dr. Burns—"

"Let me interrupt you there. I'm not here as your doctor. Paul Tremont wants me to be your coach. You're an athlete. Call me 'Coach,' if you want," Burns said. "By the time you get to be sixty-five, you play a lot of roles. I was just a few months shy of my PhD in English literature at Yale when I decided to veer off course toward the psychiatry building. I never thought I'd end up dealing with hedge funds."

Luke thought he'd left English lit behind with his father.

"Here's the deal," Burns explained. Tremont Advisors has two basic components: a hedge fund business and a sporting events business. You're familiar with both. We use Gresham as our prime broker for our hedge fund, doing much of our trading through their systems. And of course, you've been in the ring. I saw you knock out Perez."

Luke winced. He'd just recently gotten beyond the nightmare of the bloodied Perez crumbling to the canvas.

"We also do some IPOs, like Yahoo. Mr. Tremont is the genius, though. I told him Yahoo would fall flat because they concocted such a nonsense name, a random bunch of letters, for their company," Burns admitted.

"Come with me." Burns opened his cherry wood door onto the terrace. A burst of wind blew into Luke's face. In front of him, eighty stories above Manhattan, bonsai trees and feng shui fountains flourished. A Japanese tea garden. But the calm of the garden was punctuated by the whishing sounds of traffic choppers overhead and the distant wail of ambulance sirens below. He followed Burns around the corner, as Burns's shoes made a tip-tap sound on the cobblestones. Luke noticed roses growing along a colonnade. It looked familiar. Where had he seen this? Wait, he remembered a photo of President Kennedy walking with Bobby down a similar path shadowed by the columns.

"Dr. Burns—"

"'Coach,' please," Burns interrupted.

"Okay," Luke continued without uttering the word, which would be an insult to Buck Roberts, "This looks like the back lawn of the White House."

"Good eye, Luke. In fact, Paul Tremont asked Jackie Kennedy to design it for him. You'll find that Mr. Tremont is fascinated with the

Kennedy era, Camelot and all that. Optimism, America's promise. That's why he gives so much money to UNICEF and the Peace Corps. He's kind of a Robin Hood character. He outsmarts superrich money managers and then writes checks for kids."

Burns kept quiet about the darker side of Paul Tremont's soul that emulated the worst of the Kennedy's: the throwaway women, the phone-tapping, and the hobnobbing with the Mob.

He led Luke to a white bench and small table, on which sat a silver tea service gleaming in the bright sunshine. Luke felt dazed. In a matter of months he had gone from bludgeoning a poor Hispanic guy to having tea in a fake Japanese garden, next to a fake White House Rose Garden, hosted by a pompous shrink. The image of Cori Leopard suddenly flashed across his mind. What would she make of this grandeur, she who hated his alligator shoes?

"Luke, you're probably wondering what the deal is. Here's the way Mr. Tremont works. The setting may be complicated but the system is very simple. You get assignments. You pass or fail. You pass, you rise higher, you make more money, and you get more challenging assignments." Burns was telling the truth.

"What happens to those who fail?"

"You fail, you say good-bye, no harm done. We wish you luck and happily provide references." This time, Burns was lying.

"Tell me about the tests," Luke said. "Is this one of them, drinking tea on a rooftop?"

"Hardly," Burns chuckled. "You need to display three basic skills to be a complete player here. First, deal with the media. I believe Mr. Tremont has already roped you into a Boeing matter. Second, corporate deal-making, maybe a takeover. We have the world's best investment bankers. In comparison, Citigroup's look like a bunch of tellers dispensing lollipops. Third, diplomacy. Mr. Tremont is negotiating with a small country and its leader. Luke, if you can prove yourself on all these fronts, there's a corner office with a plaque waiting for you. We want to see how far you can go. We're all in your corner." Burns grinned at the clever boxing metaphor.

Luke peered down the eighty stories to a gridlocked Broadway. It was a long way down should he turn out to be a bad student.

"What do you say, Luke? You in or out?"

CHAPTER 23

The doors to the D.C. Metro were slicing closed with a "whoosh" as Sara Hartman tore into the car. She didn't dare look back at Christian Playa, the Face. As the train began to crawl away from the station, Hartman lowered her hands to see another troop of fresh-faced Boy Scouts talking, teasing, and baiting each other. She dodged past the kids, past the aluminum poles and the orange plastic chairs until she leaned against the door that connected her car to the one in front. Wiping sweat from her forehead, she scanned the car for the Face. She had escaped. She patted her jacket for her telephone, but must have dropped it during her frantic run.

On the floor, kicked under the seats, sat a small ribbon of material named after the Czech town, Semtin. It could have been a stick of gum. A blend of cyclonite and pentaerythritol tetranitrate, it could rip apart the doors of a tank. Just two hundred fifty grams of Semtex could tear apart an airplane, sending shrapnel all over the sky. The Libyans used a little extra, three hundred twelve grams, to explode Pan Am 103.

Christian Playa, the Face, briskly hustled up the escalator to grab the red line to Wheaton, Maryland. He did not bother to look back. He whistled softly. He would know without doubt whether he succeeded. Khaddafi did not need to hang around Lockerbie, Scotland to see the flotsam of Pan Am 103 raining down to earth.

✳   ✳   ✳

Connected to the stick of Semtex, a small wire glowed a faint shade of pinkish orange about six inches from the stick. Next to that wire lay Sara Hartman's telephone, lost, abandoned on the floor. The phone began to ring a no-nonsense ring. By the fourth ring, a Boy Scout spied the phone under the seat, bent down, said "excuse me," thrust his arm between the legs of the mailman, and pulled up the phone. He did not notice the stick about a foot away. The Nokia rang again in his hand. The screen said "FBI," so the kid pushed "Talk," and held it to his ear.

"Sara Hartman?" a deep voice asked.

"Uh, no. Who's this?"

Under the mailman's seat, the pinkish orange wire glowed within two inches of the stick, crawling toward its goal.

"It's very important that I speak to Sara Hartman!" the voice demanded.

"Okay, okay. I'll look." The boy covered the receiver and called out, "Is Sara Hartman here?"

The pinkish orange wire had crept to within an inch of the stick.

When Sara Hartman heard her name, she felt a pulse throb in her neck. She took a deep breath and dashed toward the boy.

The boy held out the phone toward the tall woman in the trench coat who was approaching quickly, her hand outstretched. He heard the deep voice shout: "Now! I need her now!"

Sara grabbed for the phone, just as the pinkish wire touched the stick. A tidal wave of sound and fury shook the car, briefcases shattering windows with the force of bullets. The walls of the car exploded, then imploded with steel, aluminum, and glass cross-cutting through the Metro tunnel, trading places like electrons vibrating from one orbital state to another. Human flesh had no hope in this concussive display of deadly chemistry and physics.

The *Washington Post* headline reported: "A Dozen Boy Scouts Die in Mysterious Metro Explosion." The President said a prayer at the National Cathedral for the Scouts. The FBI director wept over the young men, but ordered his staff to instead focus on Sara Hartman. Under the dust of bones and plastic resin, the FBI had found a clue.

CHAPTER 24

The lights burned the back of his neck, and his turquoise tie felt way too tight. Despite the heat, Luke was shaking. His first test in the Tremont triathlon. He stared ahead, looking for the red light that was aimed at him from atop the camera at Bloomberg News headquarters on Park Avenue. Before he became mayor of New York and a billionaire, Michael Bloomberg believed in "open architecture." No one has a private office at Bloomberg News. Radio, television, and print reporters literally trip over each other trying to get scoops and file reports. As a boxer, Luke Braden preferred just two guys in the ring and a ref. Standing in the middle of the Bloomberg studio felt like a free-for-all.

He gripped his script so tightly his sweat smudged the ink into a blur of fingerprints. Paul Tremont had emailed it a few hours earlier, and Luke had spent the morning memorizing the script, which spelled out the virtues of Boeing stock. Ever since Tremont mentioned Boeing to Luke in Vegas, Luke had been studying 10ks, 10Qs, annual reports, and every news story he could find by Googling the company. He phoned his cousin Ted, who called Boeing an "old dog that won't hunt, and certainly won't fly." Not the answer Luke wanted to hear. Now, Tremont was sending him to Bloomberg to talk up the stock. Tremont owned shares worth about $90 million, but Wall Street analysts were beginning to sour on the company. No doubt the Bloomberg reporter would press Luke on his optimism.

A big-nosed, big-hipped woman of fifty with bright red eyeglasses,

Jane Cowell looked better suited to report on a tractor pull at the county fair than a sophisticated Wall Street maneuver. But when she spoke, Luke realized that her sweet voice did not match her face or body. She actually sounded sultry, like one of those 1-900 sex-talk kittens Luke had once phoned up during his lonely, post-Perez slump.

Burns had coached Luke: "Stay on message." No matter what they ask you, stick to the script.

"What happens if they ask me something about Xerox or GM or OPEC, instead of Boeing?" Luke asked.

"Duck the question; take them right back to Boeing."

Luke wondered if he could pull this off. "What if they ask me something obscure about Boeing?"

"Ah, here's an old trick: cough."

"Huh?"

"Cough. Give some benign answer but cough through it. They won't use the tape. It's an old politician's trick. I'm sure Bloomberg himself coughed his way through some debates."

Jane Cowell brushed her bangs away from her eyeglasses and brought the microphone to her lips. The floor manager, a twenty-something guy with a ponytail, pointed to roll the cameras. Luke glanced at the television monitor, and noticed the symbol BA 80k@52.45–.75 scroll across the screen. Boeing was down seventy-five cents for the day. Eighty thousand shares had just been traded. No big deal.

Luke's phone rang. Cowell dropped the microphone, and the floor manager yelled "Wait!"

Luke was turning off the phone when he noticed the incoming telephone number.

"Yes, Mr. Tremont."

"News on Boeing. The Chinese deputy premier, Wang, just called me. South China Airlines is going to pick Airbus. No more 747s. Bad for us," Tremont said, though he did not sound upset.

"What should I tell Bloomberg? We're about to start the interview."

"Stick to the script. You'll be rewarded for it."

Tremont buzzed his deputy trader. "Glenn, call around town. Citi, Goldman, the usual suspects. Check prices on Boeing. Toss them all a little buy order, maybe a million. Let 'em spread the word for us."

Luke turned off his phone and tossed it onto a nearby desk. He looked gray. *How can I keep saying great things about Boeing when the Chinese will dump it? Is this insider trading? But, wait, I'm not trading, I'm talking about a stock we currently own.*

"Are you okay, Mr. Braden?" Jane asked.

"Uh, yeah, just a moment." He grabbed the phone again and tried to redial Tremont's line, but it was answered by the general voicemail in-box.

Should I go ahead with this? Why would Tremont want me to push the stock higher? He considered walking out, postponing, or just coughing through the interview.

"Mr. Braden," Jane said in her sultry voice, "studio time costs us money. We can do it tomorrow if you prefer. But we can't just hang out here. What do you want to do?"

Luke weighed his choices. "I'm ready," he said in a steady voice.

"Mr. Braden, your firm owns a lot of Boeing stock, aren't you worried about simple things like airplane sales? Airbus is stealing market share every year."

"Well, Jane, it's not just about market share. Profits count, too. If Airbus wants to throw away money on cut-throat pricing, that's okay with Boeing investors. We get paid dividends because the company actually earns some money on the planes."

He looked past the camera at the trading screen. *BA400k@ 54.5 + 1.3.* Boeing shares had jumped $1.30.

Across the studio, a young reporter jumped out of his cubicle and whispered to his colleague. "Tremont's loading up on Boeing! Just heard it from Lehman Brothers—wait—got it from Bear Stearns, too."

Jane lobbed another one at Luke. "Isn't the 747 looking obsolete?"

"Hardly." Luke continued, "Airbus is not proving as fuel efficient as promised. And I hear that orders for Boeing's 7E7 Dreamliner are going to be pouring in."

BA 700k@ 55.2 +2.0 zipped across the screen. Then *BA 800k@ 56.3 + 3.1.*

"And don't forget the Pentagon's orders for satellites, which we expect—"

BA 900k@ 57.1 + 3.9.

The streaming caption under Luke's picture now read, *"Tremont Advisors purportedly buying up Boeing shares."*

Paul Tremont picked up the phone and called Stuart Burns.

"Home run," he said.

"Yes, sir. You wrote a great script."

Tremont buzzed one of his secretaries, a former Ford model. "Get me Senator Leopard."

Then Tremont buzzed his head trader again.

"Glenn, now I've got a huge order for tonight. Heads will roll."

CHAPTER 25

Jane Cowell winked at Luke through her big eyeglasses, dropped the microphone like a Vegas crooner, and said, "That's it, thanks Mr. Braden."

"How'd I do?"

"Great. I'm sold," she said, dreamily focused on his eyes instead of his answers. "I'll call you again."

Luke still wasn't sure how well he performed until he took a final glance at the trading screen behind the camera. Boeing had jumped $4.10. That was more than 7 percent! He quickly calculated that Tremont made over $6 million during that interview.

After the brief feeling of elation, his mind wandered back to the nagging question: Hadn't the Chinese leader told us bad news?

On his way to the elevator, he stepped past the famous Bloomberg food court. To keep morale high—and to keep employees from leaving the building—Michael Bloomberg gave away—free food! Carrot sticks, sandwiches, Fruit Loops, and doughnuts enticed workers to regularly pop up from their cubicles to go grazing and networking. Luke grabbed a protein bar and kept walking.

When the elevator door opened, he was surprised to see Cori Leopard stepping out. He hadn't seen her since the flight back from Vegas. She wore a black silk suit and black pumps, instead of the organic, granola outfit he'd last seen her in.

"Hey, Cori Leopard. You look like New York, I mean, New York becomes you." She grabbed his arm and pulled him back into to the elevator.

"Come with me, Luke. We've got work to do."

On the Tremont trading floor, Glenn, a pixie-like trader who had been the coxswain on the Cambridge team that beat Oxford in 1993, was sweating.

"An about-face, sir?"

"Yes," Tremont said. "Dump it all, and sell short $90 million. And Glenn, take off those headphones. The crash could be dangerously loud for your ears."

CHAPTER 26

Within minutes of the explosion on the Washington Metro, grisly photographs popped up on computer, television, and cellphone screens. Whether on fifty-inch plasma sets or tiny palm-sized phones, the color of blood covered the screens.

Nick Larsen tucked some choice photos into his pocket as he waddled out of the J. Edgar Hoover Building with his partner, James Carmody. Larsen had the face of a sour pickle that had spent too much time at the bottom of the barrel. He was in his early sixties but looked ready to collect Social Security. When he walked, he carried his 230 pounds like a couple of bulky bags of fertilizer. Along with a sleek shooting range, the Hoover Building has a magnificent gymnasium in the basement offering the latest in recumbent bikes, rowing machines, and Pilates classes. Larsen had been there just once, when the malfunctioning elevators during a terrorism drill brought everyone to the cellar.

In contrast, Carmody looked like he spent his life in the gym. Twenty-five years old, his smooth, bronze skin contrasted with his partner's pocked puss. While Larsen's eyebrows seemed to crawl around his forehead like hairy caterpillars, Carmody's looked like an advertisement for plucking and waxing. Carmody looked like the one black guy featured in the Abercrombie & Fitch's *A&F Quarterly*. He subscribed, of course.

They were hunting big game. The two walked to the Capitol looking for Senator Leopard. They showed their badges at his main office in the Russell Building, but were told to make an appointment. They weren't constituents.

Leopard's admin officer would give a backrub and deep massage to any Florida orange juice grower who stumbled through the door, but the back of his hand to a couple of FBI agents.

"Where's his hideaway—the office the constituents don't know about?" Larsen barked at a young black intern.

"I'm not allowed to say. But we can leave a message for him," she replied.

"Who do you think you're dealing with here, Miss?"

Carmody wasn't going to waste his time with old-school badgering. He whipped out his BlackBerry, tapped a few keys, and zapped a message to his tennis partner, Hank Franklin, who worked in the catering office of the Senate cafeteria. Hank was good and fast. He could throw together a clambake on the Potomac in forty-five minutes, complete with Maine lobster tails and checkered blankets. He knew every senator's favorite snack, bottle of wine, and where to send it. Hank played squash with a guy in the Senate post office who knew which senators got deliveries of Botox and which got Viagra. Carmody trusted Hank.

Hank tapped back a few letters. Carmody flashed the BlackBerry screen in front of Larsen's squinty eyes, and the two men hurried through the labyrinth of hallways under the Capitol. They passed a stream of delivery men pushing carts, interns carrying stacks of paper, and a few women who looked like they billed by the hour. Larsen hoped they were undercover cops spying on terrorists, but even undercover types don't wear stilettos in the winter.

"Turn here," Carmody said, as he ducked behind a huge pillar roughly the width of the front line of the Redskins. "What's that smell? Smoke?"

Larsen knew right away and smiled to himself. Carmody was too young to know the scent.

Carmody pushed on the gilded handle of the oak door. Feet up, reclining on a leather sofa, Leopard appeared to Carmody as a big man. Old-fashioned mustache crawling across his upper lip, white sleeves rolled up showing solid forearms. He looked as if he made the leather sofa by ripping the hide off the bull himself.

Carmody turned back and whispered to Larsen, "Cigar." Ah, yes, the source of the smoke. Carmody couldn't identify the scent because they had banned indoor smoking while he was still in high school.

"It's about time, fellas! Now, who are you?" Leopard grumbled.

"J. Edgar Hoover sent us," Larsen responded.

"Then you should be wearing dresses."

Carmody blushed.

Leopard reached for a glass of Scotch that rested on a wicker table.

"I need your help. That's why I called." Leopard said.

"You called *us*? Senator, what are you talking about? We're here to question *you*. Did someone tip you off that we were coming?" Carmody interrupted.

Leopard unfolded himself from the sofa, tossed his wire-rim glasses on the coffee table and flicked his cigar ashes into an ashtray carved from a coconut. He looked much taller than six feet. A huge head topped with graying hair and a scar on his forehead. His barrel chest seemed to extend up to his head, like a wrestler without much of a neck. He's not a leopard, he's a bear, Carmody thought.

"Let's get this straight," Leopard said. "I called the deputy director because of this strange—and frankly unsettling—legislation establishing the Harold Leopard *Memorial* Fountain."

Larsen and Carmody traded confused looks.

"Senator, we're here to talk about the Metro crash, not a fountain. We don't know anything about a fountain, memorial or not," Larsen explained.

Leopard backed up a step, furious. The FBI had sent a team to interrogate him about a terrorist act? Without warning? Was the deputy director ignoring his own request? How dare they! He'd call a committee meeting and grill the director himself.

"You know who Sara Hartman is, right?" Larsen asked.

"No." He turned back to his Scotch.

"No? Didn't she come before your committee? Didn't you threaten her?"

Leopard took a sip. "Oh, yes, of course, Hartman the nominee from State. Threaten her? I think I scolded her for being ignorant. Who cares? She wasn't involved in the Metro attack, was she?"

"Yes, she was." Carmody interjected.

Leopard eyebrows jumped.

"Not as a terrorist but as a victim. She's dead," Carmody quickly added.

"Why didn't I see that in the papers?" Leopard asked. "The *Post* and *Times* devoted a whole Sunday supplement to the attack. Every frame of every closed-circuit camera. Every name."

"Not every name. Too much information can spoil the investigation and tip off the bad guys."

"Well, I'm not your bad guy."

"Still, we'd like to understand—"

"Understand this—the next time you come here, you better wear Kevlar underwear. 'Cause I'll squeeze your balls in a vise. Now get the hell out of my office!"

Larsen and Carmody shrugged and backed out, leaving Leopard to his Scotch and cigar. They knew he was at least guilty of smoking in a public building. But what else?

Leopard picked up his phone and called Paul Tremont.

CHAPTER 27

Shares of Boeing began plunging as soon as Glenn pulled the trigger on the sales. Not only did Tremont dump his $90 million stake in the company, he was selling shares short, betting that Boeing would fall even further.

For amusement, Tremont turned on CNBC.

"What's going on with Boeing today, Frank?" asked the host.

"Stocks are a bit like airplanes. Just as a plane needs forward momentum to stay aloft, stocks need buyers to stay up. We hear that a major hedge fund is selling, but nobody is willing to step in. It's a vacuum," responded some badly dressed guy on the floor of the New York Stock Exchange.

"Whoosh," Tremont said to himself.

CNBC then called up the president of Boeing, asking whether they had any comment. An official press release was faxed around Wall Street. "Boeing has no comment. Stocks go up and down. We stick to our fundamentals."

Tremont pulled a pencil from his drawer. Boeing shares were now selling at $41.25. Nice work. He made about $6 million when Luke Braden's interview sent Boeing flying, and another $26 million when shares fell into a tailspin. He called up the director of endowment for the Kennedy Center for the Performing Arts.

"Hi Trish, I just wanted to get back to you on the fund-raising appeal for the children's music center."

"Yes, Mr. Tremont. We're a little short on the campaign, what with the stock market being down this quarter, the heavy hitters are swinging with light bats."

"What are you calling the center?"

"Right now, it's the Kennedy Center's Center for Children, KCCC."

"Sounds like a kennel. You can put me down for $4 million. Just change the plaque to the Kennedy-Tremont Center. I am, after all, a philanthropist."

Luke stepped into the crowded elevator at the Bloomberg Building, his shoulder rubbing against Cori Leopard's chic, black suit. He glanced to his left to see her reflection in the mirror, her reddish hair cascading down her neck. He wondered whether she saw the interview or whether she cared.

He turned his head and whispered, "What do you mean, we have work to do?"

"Shhhh. Never speak in an elevator. Not even about the weather. Especially at a news channel."

Ever since the flight back on the Gulfstream, he'd dreamed about her. But that didn't mean that he had figured her out. Their conversational sparring on the plane showed that she had a few chips piled on her shoulders, perhaps put there by a manipulative parent or maybe some bad boyfriends. The whole left-wing, environmental, save-the-rain-forest-at-all-costs attitude mystified him. But what explained her sudden switch from Birkenstocks to Bruno Magli?

As the elevator doors opened in the lobby, Cori led him to a limo.

"You must have done a great job," Cori said, stepping into the vehicle.

"How do you know?" She seemed the type that watched the National Geographic Channel, not Bloomberg Television.

"Tremont called and told me to buy you a thick steak after our meeting."

It better be an expensive steak, Luke thought, since I just made him $6 million.

"*Our* meeting?"

"Yeah, we're going downtown to the Boys' Club of New York."

"Why?"

Cori explained to Luke that Tremont had given her a $10 million account with which to write checks to charitable groups.

So maybe that explains her attire, he thought. She's willing to wear a suit if it means she can give away his money.

"Why do you want me to come along?"

"Isn't it obvious?" she replied with a sly grin. "They try to help poor kids by getting them involved in healthy athletic activities. You're an athlete. You can help me figure out if they'll spend the money wisely. You and the Boys' Club; it's a natural fit. Besides—" her voice dropped off.

"Besides what?"

"You're Paul Tremont's newest boy."

The driver was about to pull away, when suddenly the door was yanked open with great force. An angry face glared into Luke's eyes. "You set me up! You used me! I've never been so humiliated!" screamed Jane Cowell in his face. "I know what you did! You tricked me into running a puff piece on Boeing, and then after you drove up the price, you bailed out. You think the SEC is going to let this go?" Her lips were flapping so fast and the words came tumbling out with such fury, Luke had trouble following her.

Cori looked back and forth between Jane and Luke. She felt as uncomfortable as a mistress caught by a husband's wife.

"Jane, Jane—" Luke tried to interrupt.

"Just who do you think you are? You think it's some kind of game or sport to dupe reporters? We're just trying to help the everyday guy keep up with the market. Do you care what this means for my career?" She was working up a sweat, and her red eyeglasses were sliding down her big nose.

"But Jane, give me a chance." What was she so upset about? Everybody knew that Tremont owned a lot of Boeing stock. Didn't he actually say that during the interview? Of course, Tremont would benefit if people believed his positive forecast. That was fair, wasn't it? Could they have heard about the Chinese guy, Wang? Unlikely, not in the past five minutes. It was four P.M. in New York, and four A.M. in Beijing.

"Short sellers destroy the market. Rob people of their confidence—"

He held firm. "Who sold Boeing short? Just tell me, and stop screaming."

She blinked a few times. Confused. Exhausted.

"You don't know?" she asked.

He shook his head. "Tell me, tell us," he nodded toward Cori.

"You did. I mean, Tremont did," she answered. "Maybe I'm not the one who was punk'd here."

Jane slammed the door and ran off.

Luke seethed. Cori looked sympathetic. She didn't give a damn about the stock market, but she was starting to like this guy, Luke Braden.

CHAPTER 28

During the long ride downtown, Luke's mind turned over his Bloomberg/Boeing predicament like a Rubik's cube. He considered asking the quirky Dr. Burns to explain Tremont's maneuvers, but quickly abandoned that idea. Burns seemed even less straightforward than his employer. As troubled as he was by Jane Cowell's pronouncements, he was also happily distracted by Cori's presence.

Was his life going in a better or worse direction than a month ago? A month ago he was a dead-end security guard checking packages and dreaming of taking an elevator up from the lobby. Now he was floating in a limo with a gorgeous redhead who was carrying a checkbook with $10 million to give to poor kids. Despite the Boeing frustration, he was on a good ride.

When the limo pulled up to the Boys' Club on 10th Street, Luke slid out first and ran to open Cori's door before the driver could beat him to it. An old guy in a Boys' Club T-shirt stood waiting, his substantial belly hovering over the curb.

"How long have you been waiting, Mr. Napoli?" Cori asked.

"Since 1937," he said, his eyes crinkled. "They called it the Tenth Street Club when I joined. Now I volunteer here. It's a good place. C'mon in."

"When I came here they didn't have televisions, of course," Napoli said in his raspy voice, "but they showed first-run movies. And then they'd open the swimming pool for us on Saturday mornings. You know, that was before air-conditioning. In my neighborhood—in Little Italy—

the streets would melt in the summertime because of the heat and humidity. Gelato and the pool. That's all that we had. But we loved it."

"Did you have to pay for any of that?" Cori asked, as they slowly strolled through the game room.

"Pay? Hah! For summer camp, I think it cost a quarter a week. I could swipe that from the church collection plate pretty easily." He chuckled and led them down the basement steps, where the atmosphere quickly became more humid with the dank, acrid scent of chlorine and sweat. In the pool, six black and Hispanic boys, about thirteen-years-old, were splashing around a water polo net.

"Water polo? In Greenwich Village?" Cori blurted out.

Napoli turned serious. "We do send some kids to college, Ms. Leopard. Do you have any idea how valuable a black inner-city water polo player would be to, say, Harvard? These kids can't afford tuition; but they can compete for scholarships, even if they compete underwater."

Napoli turned to Luke. "You were a boxer, right? Bet you trained pretty hard."

"I used to bleed every day and eat steaks just to avoid losing weight."

Napoli continued, "Take a look at these guys in the pool. A water polo player swims a mile and half a game. Meanwhile other players are climbing all over his head and shoulders, slamming him under the water and shouting nasty things about his mama when he comes up to sneak a breath of air. Do you think you could eggbeat your legs for thirty-two minutes? They've got spin moves that would make LeBron James jealous."

"I couldn't do it. I'd rather take a left hook to the face."

"Oh, they got that too. It's a hardball flying fifty miles an hour into your face while your lungs are full of water."

"He's right," Cori added.

"How do you know?" Luke asked.

"Four years of breathing chlorine for the Bethesda–Chevy Chase High School water polo team." She smiled, proud to have surprised Luke. "See this red hair?" she stroked her curls. "In the 1990s it was fluorescent green."

Luke imagined her in a swimsuit diving for a ball and scoring. Wasn't water polo awfully preppie for a left-wing, enviro-nut?

Napoli took them upstairs to a basketball court and then to a roomful of computers and student desks.

Cori sidled up to Luke, "I'm sure impressed."

"You ready to write a check?"

Napoli paused at a faded picture of an old man, balding and mustachioed. "Here's our founder, Edward Harriman—"

"Oh, yeah, a robber baron," Cori interjected.

Luke whispered into Cori's ear, "Can you keep the politics in the closet?"

"We prefer 'railroad magnate,' Miss Leopard," he responded. "Back in the 1870s he was touring a girls school when a rock came hurtling through a window. 'What's that?' Mr. Harriman asked. 'That's just a bunch of boys raising Cain; this happens all the time,' the principal explained. 'That's terrible!' he said. So he set up the Boys' Club. We've gone from rock throwing to water polo. It just took a few generations."

When they finished the tour, Cori gave Napoli the good news. A check for $400,000 would arrive by messenger the next day.

Luke turned to Cori. "I'm thinking Paul Tremont is a bit like Mr. Harriman."

"How?"

"Bags of money, and he's unloading it for good causes."

"Maybe." Cori had only $9,600,000 left of Tremont's money to give away. She would be shocked to find out where the next $9 million would go.

CHAPTER 29

She knew where the bodies were buried. Hell, she had bought the shovel. But who would know that to look at her now, strolling along El Paseo, the chic gallery district of Palm Desert, a few miles from Palm Springs? Though she had to be pushing seventy, she moved with the sexy, fluid gait of a panther. She wore only black, which was stifling in the desert. But she could pull it off, with her chauffeur-driven Bentley always stocked with an iced Coca-Cola splashed with rum and a twist of lime. She didn't rush after this year's fads, those fizzy Cosmopolitans and fruit-flavored Martinis. She was convinced that the Grey Goose mania that gripped Palm Springs today was no different from the tacky Bartles & Jaymes wine cooler mania of the 1980s. She had no nicknames. Oriana was her first name, and she insisted on it. Her hair as dark as her dress, her eyes as searing as the desert sun, she looked like Elizabeth Taylor, if Liz still looked like Liz, that is. She'd met the actress a few times. You can't avoid it when you live in a stone mansion near the corner of Bob Hope and Dinah Shore Drives. She was sure that Liz looked at her with envy. Of course, now Oriana had wrinkles, who doesn't? She didn't Botox or chemical peel or heat or freeze them away. She had a simpler trick. Create a decoy. The wrinkles faded from view when you were drawn to her lush eyelashes and eyes the color of the Caribbean. Did contact lenses intensify the color? After forty years she had convinced herself that Caribbean blue was her true color. Anybody who doubted Oriana was simply guessing. Screw them.

Strong words, yes. But under the sexy dress and beguiling eyes beat the heart of a female panther. Oriana could be ferocious, especially when injured. And she had been holding a grudge for forty years, unable to pounce and seek revenge. Until now. She was hunting the most dangerous prey in the world: Paul Tremont.

She walked down El Paseo, past the Coda art gallery, where she admired a pop-art painting of a Pez dispenser that looked like Michelangelo's David. She ducked into a store called Legends. She dropped down on a black leather sofa and surveyed the room festooned with autographed photos of movie stars and athletes. There's Bob Hope with Bing Crosby, Sinatra and Ava Gardner, Jerry just before breaking up with Dean. She closed her eyes and heard music. Was it coming from a stereo or was it in her mind? A swinging Nelson Riddle arrangement. Rodgers and Hart? Harold Arlen? A small smile emerged. So many years ago, but she could dive back into the memories as she could dip into her Palm Springs pool. She closed her eyes, and when she opened them noticed a new display. A framed receipt. From eight feet away, she recognized the curves in the handwriting. She stood up and as she marched toward the display, her smile changed into a sneer. She was disgusted. She read the text. A receipt from FAO Schwarz listing a selection of toys. Legends was selling the framed, signed receipt for $300. Oriana plucked the frame off the wall, threw it to the floor and drove her black heel into the shattered glass. *That whore!* she said to herself. She opened her purse, withdrew a stack of 100s and plopped three of them on the desk like a high roller at a blackjack table. "This should take care of that," she seethed.

The young man at the desk watched Oriana go and then craned his neck to read the damaged receipt. There it was—the signature of Mrs. John F. Kennedy.

CHAPTER 30

When Luke arrived back at his dumpy basement apartment, his answering machine blinked twice. The first message was from Tremont's secretary: "Luke, Mr. Tremont asked me to arrange your move to the Trump International Towers across the street from our offices. Unless you call me by seven P.M. tonight, the movers will be there tomorrow morning at ten. They'll do all the packing—"

What? Luke looked at his clock. Shit. Ten thirty P.M. Dinner with Cori lasted longer than he thought, but he had enjoyed lingering with her. Neither Tremont nor Burns had ever discussed having Luke move to the Trump building. Of course, he planned on getting out of his crappy place. Each morning the Tremont limo driver shook his head as Luke walked up the cement steps from the basement of the brownstone. But Luke wasn't sure he'd leave Greenwich Village. He could just move from the basement to the top floor and get a view of the Chrysler Building. He felt more free in the Village than in Midtown, where even the midnight shift workers wore neckties.

He looked at his shaky aluminum floor lamp, with its dim forty-watt bulb, and the dangling red boxing gloves. Then the peeling, yellowed linoleum floor in the four by six foot corner the landlord called a kitchen. He pictured the Trump building with its lavish restaurants, swimming pool, and lobby filled with beautiful women, rather than the triple-tatooed, quintuple pierced chicks who meandered through the West Village. If he didn't like the Trump, he wouldn't have to stay. With his salary, he could easily reclaim the basement dwelling. He could have it both ways, he realized. Money does that.

" . . . I'll have your keys for you when you get in tomorrow."

Luke scribbled a note to the movers and pasted it to the lamp. "Take the lamp; carefully pack the gloves." The irony! Treat gingerly the gloves made for bashing brains and crushing cartilage.

The next message was from his Cousin Ted. "Hey, Luke, what the hell are you trying to do to me? You told me you were going on Bloomberg to talk Boeing. I know Tremont's long, so I buy. You deliver the goods. Then the stock nosedives. You trying to kill me or something? Are they trying to humiliate you? Call me when you want to grab a coffee and cruller sometime. None of this latte, biscotti crap."

Luke brushed his teeth, staring at himself in the mirror with the rusty edges. He was annoyed with Tremont for being so presumptuous. Moving from the Village, manipulating his Bloomberg interview. Maybe he should fight the move, turn down the high living at Trump Towers. Should he demand a chance to go back on Bloomberg Television and try to explain the Boeing shenanigans? In the ring, he knew when to jab, when to unleash a left hook, and when to hang onto the ropes. But now he was playing in a ring much bigger than 20 feet by 20 feet.

He walked back to the lamp and tore up the note. He grabbed the red boxing gloves, ripped the Muhammad Ali/Sonny Liston photograph off the wall and tossed them into his duffle bag. Then he grabbed another piece of scrap paper and scribbled on it: "Hey Movers! Leave everything. Move nothing." He taped a $50 bill to the note.

In the morning he'd confront Paul Tremont.

"I have to see him," Luke demanded of one of Tremont's secretaries, all of whom had been plucked from the Ford Model Agency catalogue. He leaned forward on her wooden desk, which everyone called "Rosemary." It was the actual desk that Nixon's secretary, Rosemary Woods, used when she "accidentally" produced an eighteen-and-a-half minute gap in the Watergate tapes. Tremont had outbid the Nixon Library and the Smithsonian for this modest piece of the historical puzzle.

Tremont's secretary giggled. "Mr. Braden, I know you're an important new hire here, but who should I put on hold—Senator Leopard, the secretary general of the UN, or the chairman of the New York Olympic Committee? You're at the end of a pretty distinguished line, I'm afraid."

TODD BUCHHOLZ

"Tell him I'll be waiting for his call." Luke pushed back from Rosemary and sauntered back to his office like a minor leaguer in Columbus who'd been called up to Yankee Stadium only to find that he was pinch-hitting in an exhibition game against the hot dog vendors.

Luke raked his hands through his thick brown hair, two shades lighter than his long eyelashes. This was still Round One. Yeah, he'd taken a blow with the Bloomberg fiasco, but he suddenly had money, a view of Central Park, and a white-collar job, instead of a job that required him to run around a ring practically naked. Plus he was more than intrigued by his fellow Tremont employee, Cori Leopard. Luke swore he'd get to the bottom of the Boeing embarrassment before the end of the day.

He plopped down in his Herman Miller chair, although he would've preferred to sit on the old-fashioned hide of a steer.

As a little boy Luke had once spied Willie Mays's car in the parking lot of Shea Stadium: a bright pink Chrysler Imperial with fluffy white leather cushions that looked like marshmallows. The license plate said, "Say, Hey!" His father had taken him to the old-timers game. Though never a sports fan, Francis Braden allowed that baseball had some literary potential. The first time Luke heard his father declare that "Redford ruined Malamud," he thought it must have been about a boxing match, not a mismatch between literary and film lions in *The Natural.*

Luke swiveled in his chair and tried to look uptown toward Columbia University, but his view was to the east, over Central Park. Up above the park somewhere, his father was strutting in front of his students, parsing paragraphs of Roth, Bellow, or Hemingway, declaiming his insights into the twentieth-century soul. Professor Braden enthralled his students with the complaint of Portnoy, but Luke's tortured teenage nights hadn't ever grabbed his attention.

"How come you're willing to spend a week on the latest Roth book, but won't take me out of the city for a day?" Luke demanded sometime around his fifteenth birthday.

"Dear boy, don't tell me that you're jealous of fictional characters!" Francis tossed off with a nervous grin.

"Since Mom died, I've never seen my cousins on her side. I've never even met relatives on your side, other than Cousin Ted. Are you ashamed of me or something, 'cause I'm not in the freakin' National Honor Society?"

"Ashamed of you? Don't be silly. I'm up for a new professorship that would give us some security in this tempest-toss'd city. And if that means I have to spend more time between the covers of books, that's the price we have to pay. It's as simple as that. Some day you'll understand." He tugged on his Vandyke beard.

"*Some day?* Is that what you promised Mom when you guys got married? Some day you'll have time for her? When that car hit her, did that speed up or slow down your precious schedule?" Luke screamed.

Francis threw down the book and bolted upright. Luke was sure that his father was going to hit him. Instead, to Luke's disgust, his father quoted Tennessee Williams: ". . . the future becomes the present, the present becomes the past and the past becomes something you regret all your life unless you plan for it."

Francis grabbed Luke by the shoulders and stared into his eyes: "I don't give a damn about the past, about long-lost cousins. I'm trying to give you a future. And if you're too young to appreciate it, that's between you and a slowly flipping calendar."

"Damn you, Dad! You're *only* about the past. You're a dust mite on a yellow, dog-eared page!" Luke stormed into his bedroom and sobbed teenage tears, dousing his pillow with rage, confusion, and longing.

CHAPTER 31

Luke grew tired of his memories and of waiting for Tremont to return his message. On his office desk was an envelope he hadn't seen before, white with a dark blue stripe. He slipped his index finger under the flap and opened the envelope. Money came tumbling out. Not cash, of course, but modern-day money, a slim slip of paper with bar codes and strings of meaningless numbers. Except for one set of numbers, which bumped up against a dollar sign. *$20,200.* A paycheck, a relief, a validation.

Giddy with delight, Luke dashed across the street to inspect the new apartment. He zoomed up to the forty-fourth floor and stood in the empty space. He could not stop smiling; he felt energized in a way that had eluded him for years. Was it the sunlight pouring in through the floor-to-ceiling windows? The imagined aroma of the pine trees in Central Park? The ceilings were twelve fuckin' feet tall. He jumped to try to touch them with his fingertips. And how big is my living room, he wondered? He counted twenty paces across and then started dancing, shadowboxing with verve and glee, firing his fists toward Central Park, the East Side mansions, the horse drawn carriages trotting along 59th Street. It didn't matter that he was wearing Fendi shoes, not Converse trainers. It felt good. Alone in his skybox suite, for the first time in his life, Luke had no one to fight.

He kicked off the Fendi shoes and started sliding on the sleek bamboo floors. With a running start, he could swoosh in his socks from the foyer through the master bedroom, maybe forty feet. A *master* bedroom? As he slid across the foyer, he heard the door open. Paul Tremont stepped over the threshold, watching Luke slide by. Luke froze and skidded to a stop. Tremont had brought with him a familiar and puzzling companion.

Her rage must have receded because Jane Cowell had traded in her fierce glower for a cordial smile. Luke wondered what Tremont and Cowell were doing together. The slick billionaire and the no-nonsense reporter for Bloomberg News who had pumped Luke for his expertise on Boeing's stock price? Luke was embarrassed, of course, for sliding across floors like an eight year old, and for his empty apartment. But he was far more annoyed at Tremont for the role that Tremont had him play on television—the stooge, the dupe.

He refused to show his embarrassment at being caught in his shoeless performance. Instead Luke used an old boxing trick that Buck Roberts had taught him. "Don't let him know he's hurt you!" Buck would shout when a sparring partner rocked Luke with a particularly powerful blow. "Slap your abs, slap your abs!" According to Buck, slapping your gut with your own gloves distracts the other guy from looking at your dazed eyes, and it shows him that your core muscles are going strong. At first, Luke thought it looked foolish, but as with most of Buck's tricks, it worked.

And it worked on Tremont and Jane Cowell. Luke wasn't wearing boxing gloves, but his big hands slapping his abs drew attention away from his blushing face. He quickly shuffled over to his loafers and slid them on.

"Quite a welcoming committee," Luke said, nodding at his unannounced guests. He was determined not to let Tremont off the hook.

"Ms. Cowell was very impressed with your Boeing interview, Luke," Tremont reported, sounding like a friendly high school principal.

Huh? Cowell nearly threw a rock at the taxi window when Cori and I left Bloomberg. What the hell is going on?

"We'd like to talk to you about a follow-up interview," Jane interjected, showing no sign of her rage.

Luke had a choice. He could go along with this farce or not. As long as Cowell had calmed down, forgiven him, what was the point of disagreeing with Tremont's détente? But there was more to the Bloomberg encounter than Cowell throwing a fit. What about cousin Ted? What if Mr. Hardiz at Gresham or Lenny or even his father saw the interview and the subsequent bizarre trading in Boeing? He hadn't left boxing for Wall Street in order to throw a fight.

"Mr. Tremont, can I speak to you privately?" He glanced around his apartment. "In my kitchen." Tremont's blue eyes turned icy.

Through gritted teeth, the big man spat out, "Of course, Luke." He followed Luke to the empty kitchen, and they both leaned against a Viking refrigerator so tall Ted Williams could fit in it.

Luke didn't wait for Tremont to speak first.

"Sir, why did you set me up? I look either like the biggest fool ever to talk into a microphone or the most dishonest."

"You weren't set up. And even if you were, I'd remind you that you're no longer sleeping in a dump downtown, no longer begging for tips from butchers at steakhouses. You weren't even renting a walk-*up* in the Village. You had a walk-*down*," Tremont sneered. "More important, you should ask me where the profits went. I'll tell you. Thousands of poor children will be banging drums and blowing trumpets at the Kennedy-Tremont Music Center."

Luke wanted to believe that he hadn't been set up. He wanted to keep his new life on the forty-fourth floor. But did he want to swim in the sewer to get it?

"I wasn't set up? C'mon. Talk to the reporter in the next room. She thought I set her up, talking up the stock and then ripping the floor out from under it. Can you explain to me why we shouldn't both feel ashamed? Boeing shoots a roundtrip from $52 to $57 to $41 per share, and you want me to believe it's all legit, no shame, no guilt?"

Tremont laughed. "For a guy who used to smash people in the teeth, you are one naïve newbie. First of all, anyone on Wall Street who has the capacity for shame should go to the Port Authority bus station on Forty-second Street, walk past the strippers and hookers, and buy a Greyhound ticket to Kalamazoo. Wall Street's not immoral, but it's not moral either. Wall Street is like the weather. A natural phenomena. A hurricane hits and two hundred Floridians in trailer parks watch their corrugated steel strip away and swirl high over the Everglades. Does the weatherman feel shame? When the Mexico City earthquake swallowed up five thousand children, did anybody feel shame? Sorrow, maybe. Sympathy. But guilt? Who the hell are you, God? Let him feel the shame." Tremont's eyes bore deeper into Luke.

Luke slumped. Was Tremont right about the market? Maybe. But that still didn't answer the question about his role.

"Mr. Tremont, I still feel as if you used me, selling when I was telling the folks on TV to buy."

"Don't flatter yourself. Of course, I used you, but not in the way you think, and not in an illegal way either. Listen closely, Luke. You were the thermostat. I sent you out there. Then I watched how Boeing's share price responded. If it had jumped 18 percent, I would have held on to it. But despite your brilliant, persuasive recommendation, it rose only 7 percent. Sure, I made a lot of money on that, but the price action told me that Boeing could not go much higher. I decided to sell based on *public* information — how Boeing's price reacted to your *public* statements. We all heard you speak into Ms. Cowell's microphone at the same time, and we all could see the ticker blip up. That's all legit. The only thing that is not legit is your accusatory, paranoid attitude. Maybe I need to rethink things about you."

Tremont grinned a sharklike grin that Luke found unsettling. Tremont had made his case. He stepped away from the stainless steel refrigerator. Luke decided to back down. What did he know about the rules of insider trading? Later he could get a tutorial on the Internet.

"All right, Mr. Tremont, I'll drop the guilt, and skip the bus station for now. You could've warned me though. One more question. Why did you burst into my apartment in the middle of the day unannounced? With a reporter?"

Tremont grinned again. "You have secrets to keep from me? I'm a neighbor. You know I've got the penthouse. After I tried to return your message, I was scheduled to meet Ms. Cowell at Jean-Georges. The bellman told me you were checking out your new place. So I decided to see whether it met your needs. Sound innocent enough?"

"I guess so."

"Good. Now, how about offering us a glass of champagne?"

Luke was puzzled. "The fridge's empty. I just moved in."

"Open it."

Luke pulled open the massive door. Inside was a magnum of Dom Perignon.

"You don't mind if Tremont security keeps a key to the apartment, do you?" Tremont asked. "You never know what kind of treats they could leave in the fridge."

"No, no problem," Luke answered. Did he really have a choice? "*Mi casa es su casa,* as they say in the Bronx."

CHAPTER 32

After their failed interview with Senator Harold Leopard, Nick Larsen and James Carmody received a call from FBI forensics to race back to headquarters. Larsen couldn't keep up with Carmody, who leapt two steps at a time, barely perspiring. Larsen seemed worn out just pushing the elevator button. If Carmody was the sleek, sexy jaguar, Larsen moved his heft more like a hippo. When Larsen finally arrived at the desk of Dr. Ronnie Funk, Carmody was already peppering the forensics specialist with questions.

"Do we have any proof that Sara Hartman was the target? Were any fingerprints left? Any motive?"

"Only circumstantial evidence regarding Hartman, the phone log of State Department security," answered Funk, brushing away the Rastafarian dreadlocks from his brow. Funk was the supersmart son of a Jamaican tour guide and a horny Boston Brahmin divorcée who was vacationing on a cruise ship that docked in Montego Bay.

"We did find one clue that looks intriguing. I've been running linguistic tests this morning," he announced. He spoke with an odd combination of Caribbean lilt and Back Bay lockjaw, as if Thurston Howell III was actually born on Gilligan's Island.

Larsen looked suspicious. "Linguistic tests? Doc, we got dead Boy Scouts. We need DNA and blood work, not words, don't we?" He plunged his rotund frame into an uncomfortably narrow chair next to Funk's desk.

"Nick, let the brother speak," Carmody insisted.

"Brother?" Larsen laughed. "Don't pull out that race card with me, James. You want to talk brother? Jim Brown was a brother. Even that cokehead Mayor Marion Barry was a brother. You guys are not brothers."

Funk didn't care for bickering among partners. "Try marriage counseling, fellas. In the meantime, I wanna talk linguistics. The investigators brought me a bunch of text, fragments of poster board and shit that survived the inferno. Come along here," he said leading them to a small, dimly lit laboratory room. The lab, lined with stainless steel drawers and cabinets, smelled of disinfectant and glue, which was a relief compared to the stench of the FBI morgue, which Larsen and Carmody had visited earlier in the day. Along one side was a sophisticated, hi-tech plasma wall, eight feet high by six feet wide, where billions of light impulses raced within the thin frame propelled by gases. Carmody and Larsen both squinted and tilted their heads when they saw that hanging in front of the plasma wall were scraps of disorganized, disjointed litter. Carmody recognized some of the snippets: torn shreds of a paper that said "FOG" and "CIA"; a top half of a black-and-white face that looked vaguely like an animal; the symbol of a wheelchair, identifying handicap seating. Although Carmody could piece together a few more letters here and there, the scraps looked like a three-year-old's nursery school project, a collage of junk.

"Hey, Nick, look at that." He pointed. "Do you see CIA up there? Sounds fishy," Carmody said.

"It's garbage, James," Larsen blurted. "Funk, I thought you were going to show us the latest advances in linguistic science, not a trash collection," he said.

"So it seems," said Funk. "But let me turn loose the gasses." He pushed a button on the wall, which ignited a hissing sound and then streams of purple, orange, and pink light began to steam within the plasma wall, a supernova exploding. Larsen thought the light beams resembled worms migrating in all directions around the trash collage, some parts of which were splattered with blood, Jackson Pollock style.

The plasma screen began to replicate the scraps of evidence in front of it, copying the mess of disjointed letters, words, logos, and symbols, including splashes of blood and burn marks.

"We call it the Lacunator," Funk announced.

Larsen was not impressed. "Okay, so now you've basically taken a photo of the evidence and flashed it on an expensive television. Big deal.

I could've done that with a disposable camera and a computer monitor left over from the Reagan administration."

Funk brushed away the comment. "A little patience, Larsen. That was just foreplay. You sure you're ready for the money shot?"

Larsen rolled his eyes again and waved his right hand in the universal symbol for masturbation.

Funk pushed a button on the remote. "Shoot, baby!"

The colorful gasses started merging, separating, reuniting, synthesizing with such fury and beauty that Carmody thought he was watching the creation of life from nothingness. But it wasn't just a laser light show. The plasma screen began to fill in the blanks, providing the missing letters, symbols and words that had been either burned beyond recognition or reduced to smoke in the inferno. The slice of Metro map started to grow outward, so that the "FOG" expanded into "FOGGY BOTTOM/ GEORGE WASHINGTON UNIVERSITY," and "CIA" grew into the third syllable of JUDICIARY SQUARE. In half a second, a complete Metro map evolved on the screen, displaying in vivid colors the Red Line to White Flint, the Green Line to Anacostia, the Blue Line to the National Cemetery. The portion of the animal face became a panda bear, part of an advertisement for the National Zoo. Five seconds later, the plasma screen had grown into a full-sized replica of all the hard evidence as well as the missing evidence that had been incinerated. Carmody and Larsen were staring at an electronic copy of the subway car before it was blown up.

"Shit! How'd it do that? How does it know?" Carmody asked.

Funk pushed another button and the 3-D image turned and flipped over, showing the subway car's interior from several angles. Funk stared at the crusty agent and asked, "Well?"

"Okay, that's a money shot, Funk. Now answer James's question."

Funk took in a deep breath and leaned against a stainless steel table. "You need Google, quantum computers, and probability theorems. We live in a probabilistic universe. Are we standing in this room today? We could be. We think we are. But we could be dreaming, or we could be existing in a parallel universe. Every time we make a decision— do I choose paper or plastic at the grocery store—two new paths, two new worlds are created."

"Funk, I'd like you to beam me up there, 'cause in this world I'm spending too much time locked in a Buick with James here."

"Well," Funk continued, "speaking of beaming, physicists have actually shown that molecules sometimes act like billiard balls following normal Newtonian logic, and sometimes act like lightwaves, zooming wherever they want to go. Sometimes they seem to be in the same place at one time—"

"So where does Google come in?" Carmody interjected. "I can handle the probability stuff and the physics. It's like a dozen sci-fi movies I've seen."

"Okay, let's cut right to it. Google has given us a database for just about every piece of text and image that exists on earth. The Lacunator—the name comes from the Greek word *lacuna*, which means gaps or spaces—scans the available evidence from the crime scene. In this case, a lot of burnt and bloody trash. It then deploys a probability algorithm on Google to gauge which image or text most likely fills in the gaps. When we saw the plasma gasses synthesizing, they were building out the missing evidence based on probabilities. It's like if I show you an hexagon with the letters 'S' and 'T', your brain will fill in the blank and tell you it's a stop sign. Are you 100 percent sure? No, it could be a drawing by an artist who has actually written "Stew," but that's highly unlikely."

"You mean that replica of the subway is not for certain?" Carmody asked.

"No, it's not. But there's a 95 percent probability that the Lacunator filled in the blanks correctly. I'd be damn sure that the panda bear is a sign for the zoo, for example. Same thing for the subway map, of course. In fact, just about everything the Lacunator came up with is based on standard D.C. signage."

"What if it's trying to fill in the blanks for a place that isn't so public?" Larsen asked.

"It would be tougher for the Lacunator to build a replica of, say, the inside of a North Korean bus that has never been seen by modern people."

"So if we're talking about the District, why did you say our odds are just 95 percent? Should be 99.99999, right?" asked Larsen.

Funk took off his small round glasses and rubbed them against his lab coat. "That's the wrinkle in your case, Agent Larsen. One of the shreds the FBI brought in has stumped the Lacunator. Never seen that before—"

"But how can it be stumped when millions of people ride that Metro and tourists file millions of photos on the Internet? Look, I've been working here since 1976, when they opened the Metro. There's nothing new down there," Larsen said.

Carmody thought that Funk seemed suddenly nervous or embarrassed. Although he had unveiled the Lacunator with bravado, he was coming up short.

Funk picked up an infrared device and pointed to a small blue oval, actually half an oval, hanging in the trash collage.

"See this letter in white? It looks like the beginning of a 'C' in a Franklin Gothic font. I thought it was a part of a 'G' or an 'O' but the computers think it's a 'C.' The Lacunator tells us there's room for one more letter. Sure enough, the trash collage gave us the horizontal line of an 'L.'"

Carmody and Larsen both saw where the Lacunator displayed a full oval with white letters CL. But the outline of the oval was flashing with a red light. Funk explained that the red light indicated a level of confidence less than 50 percent, unheard of in the testing of the machine.

"What's so tough about a blue sticker? CL? Could stand for anything. Columbia Lions. Car Loan. Cock licker." Larsen blurted out like a game-show contestant.

"Precisely. It could stand for anything. But according to the Lacunator, examining trillions of data sets, it stands for nothing. No one in the history of the world has ever put together that shape, that font, and those letters. And if they did, they never did so in a Metro car," Funk said.

Carmody couldn't stop himself from thinking of other CL combinations, Chicago Lamp, Complex Litigation, and more.

"But why do you think this is important to the case?"

"Gentlemen, it is the missing evidence. The unexplained. The improbability. It's like finding kryptonite. It doesn't usually show up on earth. If it does, Superman must be showing up too. You solve this mystery that stumped the Lacunator, and I think you'll figure out a lot more."

Larsen and Carmody realized they had nothing else to learn from Funk. As they waited for the elevators, Larsen's mind wandered back to Senator Leopard's office. Should they have left his office so quickly when he booted them out?

"Hey, James, I think we need to speak again to the senator. And his family. He's got a daughter, right? A radical? What's her name?"

"Cori. Cori Leopard."

At the same time, they both saw her initials in blue.

CHAPTER 33

Luke tried to focus on the bridge of Dr. Stuart Burns's beak. It was tough. The good doctor seemed to over-salivate when he spoke and foamy spittle kept gathering at the corners of his mouth. Luke would have loved to toss him a towel, or even better, administer a rabies shot. Burns might be Tremont's right-hand man, but that hand seemed miles away from the brain. Even though Tremont was unpredictable, Luke felt attracted to Tremont's swagger, his complexity, and his charm. Burns, however, seemed like a phony. A rich dandy buying Saville Row suits, Burns merely road the coattails of his benefactor. Though Luke refused to call Burns "Coach," he knew that he must pay attention to the supercilious shrink.

Luke sat with a yellow legal pad on his thighs, scribbling notes on his next task in the triathalon. He'd passed the media test by performing on Bloomberg, and now he moved on. Next test: Mergers and Acquisitions. Burns called in Arnie Letts, the head of Tremont M&A. Arnie was a quick-talking forty year old from New Orleans. With thinning blond hair and dull brown eyes, Letts looked like the son of a preacher: too innocent, too inhibited, and too confined. In fact, Letts's father and grandfather were auctioneers, which explained why his lips moved so fast. There was no time for a southern drawl.

"Here's the deal," Letts said. "Tremont is working with Zeton, the pharma company, and we're looking to acquire a new brand, looking at buying—" He interrupted himself and stared at Burns, waiting for assurance.

"It's okay, Arnie. He's on our team."

Letts continued. "We're looking at buying a new pharma company with some good R&D and a new product that surgeons are raving about. Medcentric makes—"

"Stents," Luke somehow inserted into Letts's runaway sentence. "And pacemakers and defibrillators."

"Yeah, that's right," Letts said with surprised expression. "How'd you know?"

"I'm not that new to the Street. Guidant, J&J, Medtronic. Stents have been a huge business. They're those little springs keeping arteries open." In fact, the only reason Luke knew about stents was because Buck Roberts had had one implanted into his neck.

Letts was impressed. "Ok, Luke, we're shooting to close this deal next week. That gives you three days to figure out how stable Medcentric's business is. How good is the new technology? I need primary and secondary proof—"

How the hell was he going to figure out that for Tremont? Luke looked over at Burns, whose eyes had glazed over. You'd think a doctor would've paid more attention. Luke kept looking, hoping for some advice. "Tremont's put a lot of pressure on me, Luke." Letts gave Luke an imploring look. "He wants to do the deal, but he wants me to sign off on it. I don't care if you have to kidnap Dr. Christian Barnard, you need to give me some hard evidence. Today is Wednesday, and I need it by Friday noon. It can't be later and there can't be any excuses," Letts said, rising from the chair and tossing into Luke's lap a manila folder filled with drawings and patent filings that Luke would not decipher in a thousand years.

Finally, Burns piped up. "As your coach, I'm here for you," he pronounced. "But if you're going to meet the deadline, you'd better get the hell out of my office and investigate some hospitals. Quickly."

Luke didn't sleep. Instead he sat in front of his laptop and poured coffee down his throat while trying to become an instant expert on cardiovascular medicine. It was impossible of course. But also necessary. He downloaded data on Medcentric from the Web site of the Food and Drug Administration. In a preliminary finding, the FDA had approved Medcentric's technology for patients with extremely rare aortal aneurysms. But Tremont needed to know whether the product technology could help Joe Six-pack after he keeled over. At three o'clock in the morning, when the only sounds from Broadway were ambulances, Luke came up with a plan. It required some deception, but nothing dangerous, he thought.

At seven A.M. he quickly walked four blocks from his apartment to Roosevelt Hospital on Ninth Avenue. He'd been to the old red brick building quite a few times, to be patched up after a fight, or to undergo brain scans to make sure he wasn't turning punchy. The New York Athletic Commission had once sent him there to pee in a cup to ensure he wasn't bulking up with steroids.

Luke ran up three flights to the urology lab, where he knew a nurse. He stopped at the glass doors and noticed a brass plaque to the left. THANK YOU TO OUR FOUNDATION PRESIDENT, PAUL TREMONT.

Luke pulled open the glass doors and saw Jamie sitting behind the counter. She recognized him immediately and gave a tepid half-smile. Their first and only date had been a disaster. Now, Luke turned on the charm and gave her the full two hundred watts. He motioned for her to step into the stairwell.

"I lost your number, Jamie." Lame.

"And you lost your ability to dial 411?"

"Seriously, Jamie, I'd love to see you. You name the restaurant. Or a concert. I don't care. Your choice. This Saturday night—if you can get me in today or tomorrow."

"*In?* What do you mean? Surgery? You got a prostate problem?"

"No, no. I want to watch a cardiac procedure," he said eagerly.

"Why the hell would you want that? Too much blood. If you're not used to it, you'll pass out, for sure."

Luke explained his predicament. In the process he leaned close to her, whispering, confiding. He wasn't trying to deceive her, exactly, but he needed her help deceiving the cardiology staff.

"There are just two ways to get in. You either have to be on staff or an immediate member of the family. And you're neither."

"Isn't there some other way? You know, a student or something?"

"Nah, they come in with doctor chaperones. I'm sorry, Luke. I hope this doesn't screw things up for you. I'd love to help, but—" her voice faded out. Then her eyes perked up. "Hold on, there is one other way."

"Educate me, Jamie.

"Salesmen. Salesmen representing the drug companies and medical instruments companies routinely go into the O.R. They even help with the surgeries sometimes," she added. "I couldn't believe it, but I saw a surgeon in the O.R. turn over his patient to a dude in a tie. When I did a cardio rotation, the doc asked the salesman to demonstrate a new saw to cut open the patient's chest. The man might not have graduated from high school, but now he was holding the saw, brushing away bone fragments and dust from the patient's heart. Amazing."

Luke saw his chance to get some real inside dope for Arnie Letts. But could he pull this off by noon tomorrow?

"Do these salesmen come around a lot?" he asked.

"Every few days. There's someone back in urology now. He's selling some kind of catheter. Let's go back to my desk and I can tell you where he's from." She leaned into him and whispered. "Then we can talk about Saturday night."

In the waiting room, an attendant carrying a clipboard called for Jamie. While she was gone, Luke looked down at her desk. There glistening in the harsh fluorescent lights was an ID badge: AL HUMPHRIES, VP SALES, MEDCENTRIC. Luke's face got flushed thinking about the temptation and the guilt. This was theft. Or was it? The badge cost about ten cents to replace. He wouldn't actually do anything in the O.R., just watch. Was it illegal to witness a common hospital procedure? Hell, the Science Channel on cable TV probably broadcasts operations every night. Luke debated with himself for another few seconds, until the interests of Tremont won the argument.

He scribbled a note to Jamie, stuffed the badge into his pocket, and tore out of the room so quickly he nearly yanked the doors off the hinges.

CHAPTER 34

Oriana's Learjet was not for sale or for rent. Many rich people who owned jets actually made money off them, renting them out when they weren't in use. But Oriana had insisted on an orange-colored décor that made her plane unrentable. Dark orange leather chairs, light orange carpeting on the walls. The Lear representative gently warned her that "distinctive tastes might not be commercial," but she tossed his comments aside.

"Sinatra tucked an orange hankerchief in his tux. Orange brought him gold and platinum albums. Would you have told Oleg Cassini to drop the hemline?" she sneered. Her reference to 1960's fashions baffled the 30-year-old sales rep.

Oriana's jet rolled to a stop at the private aviation runway at Reagan National Airport. She looked small sitting alone on the back sofa. But she had a mission. And a deadline. From her cushy lounge chair she looked to her left and saw the Capitol Building. She'd not visited the building in forty years, but she didn't have to. She wielded her influence by telephone, and occasionally from the runway at National.

"Welcome to Reagan National Airport," the pilot said.

"If you ever use that term again, you'll be flying back in a middle seat on Southwest," she barked. She refused to acknowledge Reagan's legacy or his existence. Her mantra was "fuck the Berlin Wall" and all that evil empire, super-Ronnie hero stuff that was just a collective wet dream for conservatives.

"Is he here yet?"

"Must be caught in traffic," reported Sam, her chirpy assistant, a forty-year-old bachelor who used to work for Dinah Shore in Palm Springs. He was rumored to have slept with either Dinah or Burt Reynolds or both. Oriana could have found out if she cared, but what in the world could she possibly buy or sell with that information?

Oriana was fuming. She'd flown four hours. Couldn't he make the ten-minute cab ride? She'd make him pay somehow. She lit a cigarette and blew unfiltered smoke in rings around the cabin. She thought about the mission and the memories.

A black car raced across the tarmac. A knock at the airplane door. Sam fiddled with the heavy door and unfurled the stairs down to the ground.

Up the stairs trudged Senator Harold Leopard.

When he ducked to enter the cabin, he drew in a breath of smoke. It lifted his spirits. All morning he'd been stuck in a subcommittee meeting on global warming, dominated by leftists who worried about everything from tailpipes to cooking spray. Hell, they even worried about flatulence. Apparently 20 percent of CO_2 gasses come from cows belching and farting in the meadows.

But what was this meeting about? How many pounds of flesh would Oriana demand this time?

The tall man lumbered past the orange chairs and took a seat across from Oriana. His usual seat. She didn't let people sit beside her. She felt her turquoise eyes could not weave their spell from the side. Leopard looked at her skin, which seemed to glow both from the décor and from her determination. Did she have a heart or a furnace tucked under her ribs?

"You owe me, Harold," she began with a hint of smile so fleeting you'd need a Zapruder film played over and over again to make sure you caught it.

"Oriana, my dear, as long as I don't have to reimburse you for your jet fuel, I'm sure we're okay." He gave a "senator's smile," one that lasts a second too long, because they're trained to hold it until the last camera flashes.

Oriana turned to serious stuff. "Shame about that Hartman girl. She seemed so smart. I think the Venezuelans did it. All her talk about strangling Cuba.

"I felt even worse about the Boy Scouts. One was from Florida. That was a tough funeral to attend," Leopard replied.

"How much are they offering you, Harold?"

"Who?" He knew who. It was always the same "who" whenever he met with Oriana, his campaign's favorite ATM machine.

"Miami. The Cubans."

Leopard was currently in the middle of a squeeze play. But it was good for him. He was being squeezed with money. The Cuban exiles in Miami ruled South Florida politics and had a huge influence over the whole state. Twice they delivered Florida to Bush. But Leopard figured that they only cared about one thing: punishing Castro and planning for the day when they would take back their homeland, while still collecting the cash they earned in Florida and in New Jersey on their bakeries, automobile dealerships, and real estate conglomerates. The Miami Cubans will carve up Cuba into mini-malls and McDonalds. They've already decided among themselves who gets the Starbucks franchise in every neighborhood of Havana. Of course, they won't have to consult with the poor schmucks who stayed on the island for the past forty-five years.

The Cubans loved Leopard, and he loved their money. They helped him keep his job as chairman of the Foreign Relations Committee, despite fund-raising scandals, reckless sex affairs, and arrests for drunk driving. As long as he didn't get caught smoking Cuban cigars. He regularly denounced Fidel and condemned boobs like Jimmy Carter who had toasted the dictator. In 2004, when Fidel fell off a stage and broke his leg, Leopard rushed to the microphone and sarcastically offered him asylum in Miami—in the very house from which young Elian Gonzalez was swiped in 2000.

Leopard looked into Oriana's eyes. She was the other side of the squeeze play. She'd been dumping money into his campaign to offset the Miami-Cuban dough. Even though the Cubans were generous with their pledges, Leopard got few votes north of Fort Lauderdale. Palm Beach socialites were embarrassed by the man they called "Senator Cringe." The last time Leopard tried to stroll down Worth Avenue, the Rodeo Drive of Florida, an elderly woman told him, "You should really be from Louisiana." The Tallahassee and Tampa crowds figured he was in the back pocket of Miami. They just didn't know he was also in Oriana's back pocket.

CHAPTER 35

Luke rushed down two flights of steps to the cardiac ward, clutching in his hand his new ID, or rather, Al Humphries's ID badge. Roosevelt Hospital's cardiac ward was a factory, repairing valves and replacing pumps every thirty minutes like a Jiffy Lube shop. The waiting room was pure white with just a few framed black-and-white Ansel Adams posters on the walls. Luke figured that the real Al Humphries would be looking for his badge pretty soon, so he did exactly what he'd seen in the movies. He put an arrogant expression on his face and bolted past the receptionist, flashing his ID as a formality. Luckily, she was just a candy striper.

"Excuse me sir, who are you?" she squeaked out.

"Al from Medcentric. Didn't you hear me paged?"

His heart was beating so fast, he felt like a patient suffering from arrhythmia. He worried that Jamie Hooton might have called security. What were the stakes here? Tremont, Letts, and Burns demanded a quick diagnosis of the Medcentric stent. After spending the night checking out medical Web sites, Luke realized he needed some firsthand field research. What better way than to watch a procedure? Hell, with Humphries's ID badge, he could straight out ask the surgeon what he thinks of the product, and whether he'd invest in Medcentric.

Luke glanced back at the freckle-faced candy striper. She had lifted a telephone off its hook on the wall. Was she reporting him? Luke darted around the corner. He looked to his right and saw an "Exit" sign. To the left he saw a whiteboard: "Wm. Turner, 46. Angio. Drs. Patric and Singh."

Luke took a deep breath and thrust open the door of the operating room. He grabbed a mask off the wall dispenser, along with rubber gloves.

Blinding white light assaulted his eyes. A bitter disinfectant smell rushed up his nostrils. He froze for a moment then stumbled forward. Despite the glare, he could make out the operating table and four bodies, presumably Dr. Patric, Dr. Singh, and two nurses. They hardly noticed him, their hands deep in the chest of patient Wm. Turner. Luke slid along the wall until he was behind them.

"Nurse, who is that?" he heard.

A large woman with bulbous, veined cheeks sidled next to him and in a clipped voice asked Luke what he was doing there.

Luke felt nauseated. He still had a chance to retreat. He thought about Turner, the lights, the blood, the risk of arrest. He thought about Buck Roberts, who probably had saved nothing for retirement. Luke calculated that if he could survive six months with Tremont, he'd save enough money to fund Buck's retirement.

"Al Humphries, Medcentric," he said. "Authorized to check out product performance. I'll just hang back here and ask questions later."

The nurse hobbled toward the doctors and whispered. *For too long,* Luke thought. Then he realized something worrisome. The doctors might know Humphries! Wouldn't a salesman have taken them to lunch or dropped off samples or done something to bribe them into using his stents? The nurse shuffled back, looking more determined, her face frozen.

"It's very unusual for you to walk in here right in the middle, but Dr. Singh says you should step to the table."

He'd tricked his way into the inner sanctum. Luke ambled to the operating table, feeling a little cockier now, though he was ready to squint his eyes to avoid looking at the gruesome open chest of Wm. Turner.

Luke looked Dr. Singh in the eyes because that was the only part of his face not covered by a mask and cap. Dr. Singh had sad, old eyes surrounded by the wizened, thick skin that you see around the eyes of an elephant.

"You've got great timing, just in time," Singh said with the lightest of Indian accents and an Oxford trill. "Look at this," he said gesturing to his bloody hands twirling about in Turner's chest.

Luke looked, sorry that the halogen lights illuminated so clearly the mess of muscle, tissue, and guts. But what in particular was Singh pointing at? To Luke it was like a butcher asking him to comment on a lump of ground chuck.

"Six. I should get a commission." Singh gave a little chuckle. "I've never done more than five before. But results with your stent are very impressive. I'm actually giving a talk on it this afternoon to the rest of the cardiology department. The drug release seems to work, and so far the antibacterial coating has diminished infection risk."

Luke felt a burst of energy and luck. He had his story. Then the tables turned.

An announcement reverberated through the public address system: "Mr. Al Humphries, please call security. Mr. Al Humphries, please call security."

Singh and the others looked at him. "Must've double-parked in a doctor's space," Luke joked. "I'll go now. Thanks."

"Wait," Singh said, "if it's so trivial, you can wait another minute. Why don't you earn your commission, Mr. Humphries," Singh said. "You insert number six, right there in the left main artery."

Oh, shit! Luke quickly started backpedaling away from the table, sliding off his gloves. "No, no. That would be against the rules."

Singh wouldn't let him off the hook. "But my colleague Dr. Bumpers said you did a great job in the O.R. last week. Just slide it in."

"Yeah, well, Bumpers seemed a little unsure last week. You're doing great."

Singh pressed on. "Do you want me to cancel my recommendation?"

Luke was cornered. The rotund nurse handed him a sticklike slinky. He figured he'd place it near Singh's hands at the artery and then fumble it. He could blame it on too much coffee. He wouldn't have to fake having shaky hands.

Luke fondled the stent for a second and began lowering it toward the artery.

Just then Singh interrupted. "Hold it. That doesn't look right—"

Luke tried to cover. "Oh yeah, I grabbed it wrong. Sorry."

"No, I mean the coating looks funny. Is that a chip? Right out of the box? Lemme see that." He took the stent from Luke's hand and rolled it around, bringing it close to his sad eyes, which seemed to darken. "Yes, that is a chip. My God, that'll erode the artery. You ever see this before Humphries?"

"Uh, once, maybe, but I'm not sure," he stuttered.

"That's unforgivable. Nurse, get me another lot. No, just give me the J&J."

She reached for a box with the familiar Johnson & Johnson logo.

Just then, as things were looking sour for Medcentric, a new face entered the room, more frightening than Wm. Turner's bloody chest. The real Al Humphries strode through the doors. Al Humphries was not wearing a surgical mask, though he might as well have been wearing a Halloween disguise of a growling ghoul. He was short, maybe five foot four, but he was well grounded, at least two hundred pounds of fury.

"Who the fuck are you?" he screamed at Luke. "You fuckin' stole my ID?" His slitty eyes resembled a snake, and he pronounced "stole" with a sibilant "s."

Luke's eyes darted between Humphries and the door.

Dr. Singh's eyes widened, enraged at the intruder. "Hey, who are you? Get out of my operating room! Nurse, call security!"

Humphries spied the wrapping from the Medcentric and J&J stents.

For the first time, Dr. Patric piped up. He was worried about something else. "Jagdish," he said to Singh, "the pulse is slowing. And oxygen is down to 84 percent. We got to wrap this up and squirt some more meds."

Singh looked at the monitors. "Goddammit, this is taking too long." To Luke and Humphries, he yelled, "Both of you, get out of my O.R. now. I'm not going to lose a patient because —"

"Not till I figure out who this crook is!" Humphries shouted.

Luke needed a decoy, a diversion to slip out the door. His eyes spun around the room. Then he saw it: the chipped Medcentric stent, the smoking gun. He picked it up and started waving it at Humphries.

"You see this shit? What the hell is wrong with you?" Luke yelled, taking the offensive. "You could've killed this patient with defective equipment! That thing will destroy the coronary artery."

Humphries looked puzzled.

"Yes, very bad," murmured Patric, while trying to pump some steroids into the faltering Turner.

Luke twirled the chipped stent in his hands. Humphries squinted, trying to see the defect. Then Luke tossed the stent into the air, between the operating table and Humphries. Humphries shuffled his short legs and stretched his hands out, like an infielder trying to catch a pop-up to save a perfect game. As he dove to catch the stent, Luke tore out the door and down the stairs outside the O.R. He took three steps at a time, leaving his mask on until he flung open the door onto Ninth Avenue. He crossed the street and ducked into the Hudson Hotel on Fifty-eighth Street, known for its dim lighting and fashionable, young wannabees.

Now he had his firsthand investigation and his recommendation on Medcentric. He couldn't wait to deliver the news to Tremont and conquer his second test. Unfortunately, he didn't hang around the hospital long enough to learn the real story.

CHAPTER 36

Why did Oriana pay Leopard? Sometimes she wondered. She usually had little time for hacks. She usually didn't let her heart get in the way of her head or her wallet. In truth, she paid Leopard to do nothing. Simply nothing. Easy money. Like those tobacco farmers paid to sit on their verandas and watch ballgames instead of tilling soil and raising crops. Oriana funneled millions of dollars into Leopard's secret bank accounts so that he would not comply with the wishes of the Miami Cubans, who pushed for tighter embargoes on Cuba, naval blockades, and new and improved versions of the Bay of Pigs invasion. Over the years, Leopard felt the heat from Miami. The lobbyists would barge into his office demanding that the Senate pass resolutions that would authorize the U.S. Navy to block all but humanitarian goods from entering Cuban ports. Or insisting that the U.S. and UN weapon's inspectors snoop around Fidel's houses, looking for weapons of mass destruction. What a joke! She knew Fidel. They might find a Swiss Army knife, but that was about it.

Leopard had always been the perfect tool, and he was always perceived as the perfect tool for Miami. After all, he'd been a Marine assigned to the CIA battalion that landed in the Bay of Pigs in April 1961, when JFK stumbled into a Cuban liberation mess. Leopard was captured but not tortured. Embarrassed but not injured. Just a young man at the time. Big, strong, but outmanned and outmaneuvered by those who pledged their lives to Fidel. After returning to the U.S., he testified before Congress and revealed the military bungling. His finest moment, the testimony that made his career. He appeared in uniform, a fresh-faced, well-spoken kid who got screwed by the pinheads at the Pentagon and CIA.

He was asked, "How were you welcomed when your little craft landed?"

"The Cubans cheered, and shouted 'Viva Kennedy!' 'Viva USA!'" Leopard had a flair for drama and reenacted the shouts by raising his fist and smiling broadly.

"Then what happened?" asked the senior senator from Oregon.

"They asked us, 'How many more boats and ships are landing in your liberation force?'" Leopard paused dramatically. "We told them we'd have a few dozen more operatives arriving."

"How did they react?"

"They suddenly looked angry. One of them poked a bayonet at my belly. 'If that's all you brought, we're arresting *you*. You idiots. We can't afford to lose! We can only betray Fidel if we're sure we'll win!' They brought us to Fidel."

The Senators hung their heads. What stupid planning and execution, they all thought. Then Leopard capped his performance with a memorable line.

"They wanted to greet us with the Marine chant 'Semper Fi,' which means Semper Fidelity, Always Faithful. But we forced them into 'Semper Fidel,' Always Fidel."

The hearings were top secret but, of course, word leaked out. Leopard became a hero to Miami Cubans. As more Cubans arrived in the '60s, they eventually carried him on their shoulders into the Senate. He'd been carried by them ever since. For his five minutes of courage before the Senate committee in 1961, they forgave him forty years of booze and broads. It was only his daughter who held a grudge.

His eyes darting around Oriana's Learjet cabin, Lepoard suddenly felt claustrophobic. He wanted to roll down a window but that was impossible. She leaned toward him. The way she stared reminded him of Luke Wallace. Was she smiling or seething? Was she ready to take out her checkbook or throw him out onto the tarmac?

In fact, Oriana was not really looking at the senator. She was staring through his eyes into the swimming pool of the Havana Hilton.

"Did you ever meet him, Harold?"

"Who's him?"

"Fidel. The only him."

The only him? Leopard only knew what J. Edgar Hoover told him. That Oriana had been with Lansky, Sinatra, JFK, and RFK, aka, "the Runt."

"Oriana, I didn't spend much time with him. He yo-yo'd me in and out of prison before I could shake his hand," Leopard replied.

"He was a god at the pool. Really. Jack, Bobbie, Frank, they were all skinny marinks. Fidel was a man. He burst forth like he'd ripped his way out of Hemingway's typewriter. He held me—"

Oriana closed her eyes, her long lashes sweeping down, as if she was falling into her own spell. In her mind she pictured old Havana: men strolling in white suits by day and tuxedos at sunset, rum pouring into Baccarat tumblers at chic nightclubs. Fidel. Fidel, not in Army camouflage, but in a linen suit, holding her, and gently swaying, as a conga drummer tapped a rhumba beat.

Harold Leopard had heard this reverie before, as if Oriana were rewinding highlights from film in the vaults at MGM. Leopard couldn't stand time-traveling and sentimentality. He interrupted, "He jailed me. I can't get too worked up about him, frankly."

"We turned him into a dictator. When I met him he was a guest on the Jack Paar show staying at the Hilton. Meanwhile, Lansky, the mob accountant, was running around collecting Fidel's straw hats and packing his bags like a two-bit hotel bellman. Look at this. I just got it from QVC."

She held out a DVD disc and gestured at something behind Leopard. A DVD player. Leopard took the disc is his fat fingers, slid it into the machine and pushed "play." A grainy black-and-white image appeared, the old nightly entertainer Jack Paar holding a microphone, sitting next to a young, sexy Fidel Castro.

JACK PARR: Very late in Havana, Cuba, and Fidel Castro has just come down from his suite in the Havana Hilton after days and days and days of little sleep. And I'm very happy that he came down from his suite right upstairs to talk to me tonight. Mr. Castro, I can say not as a politician—I have no right to talk of politics; I'm an entertainer—but as an old friend of Cuba, not a newcomer, five years I've been coming here and speaking of

Cuba—you are a good neighbor to me personally. You live right up there. And you're not noisy. And you have not come down to borrow any sugar. You have been a good neighbor.

FIDEL CASTRO: Okay.

JACK PARR: And I know how tired you are, and I know how many questions you have been asked.

FIDEL CASTRO: Ah—mind? You can ask all that you want for the public opinion of the United States.

Oriana leaned over Leopard's shoulder and stopped the disc. "You see, senator, I was with him in the suite just a few minutes before. He was telling me how he wanted to bring Jefferson's philosophy and Lincoln's ideas to Cuba, after all those years of dictatorship and Mafia bosses—"

"Jesus, you really fell for it, Oriana. He's a dictator. Have you picked up a newspaper in forty years?"

"What paper are you reading, senator? The *Miami Herald*, which is frightened of its own readers? Or the *New York Times* and *Washington Post*, which are still so drunk on the Kennedys you'd think Old Joe had shtupped Katherine Graham and Mama Sulzberger in the same day." She chuckled at her own line. "I wouldn't put it past him."

"We turned him into a dictator. The press turned him into a monster. I knew Jack when he was just a senator." She paused, glaring at Leopard. "Intimately. I'll tell you the truth. Jack was the real monster. And *his* father and Jackie's father, Black Jack. These arrogant bastards juggled the whole world in their palms, but they were pricks. Perverts who couldn't control their own cocks. I did my time in their service, on my back, on my knees. And look at me now. I have the Lear and the diamonds. But forty-five years ago I was the girlfriend they tossed away like a used condom. Fidel was the only one, the only one who acted like a man, a mensch. You wouldn't believe the telephone bill he ran up at the Hilton, calling me in Chicago—"

All of a sudden, Leopard figured out her angle. This wasn't about money, or Communism or revenge against the Miami restaurateurs. This was about pricks. Oriana was protecting Castro because he didn't just fuck her and then tell her to fuck off. It turned out that the fate of American politics was resting on a thin reed, the manhood of Fidel Castro.

Leopard was startled by his conclusion. All he could do was look at

Oriana, the silence between them shattered by a buzz. His watch was vibrating. He needed to get back to the Hill to resume his committee meeting. He needed to close the deal, to get another check. He also needed to ask a question.

"Oriana, the Miami Cubans are leaning on me. They're squeezing me to expand Gitmo operations beyond the perimeter—"

"Fidel can't accept that, Leopard. Tell them no," she shot back.

"They smell blood. He's seventy-nine years old. Saying no has a price. I'll probably face an opponent in the primary next year." He shook his head wearily.

Oriana nodded. She knew he was playing her. That was okay. She enjoyed watching him debase himself. He could be bought for a pittance, a few hundred thousand. Maybe a million. Just two week's interest on her money. Lansky's money. The lost money of Havana. Oriana had spent enough time with Meyer Lansky at the Havana Hilton to earn some of the mobster's fortune. She had used it well—for Fidel.

He pressed forward on another topic. "Do you know anyone who's trying to scare me, Oriana? Anyone on your side?" Briefly he explained the Leopard Memorial project in Nevada.

She didn't blink. "You know, Leopard, I never get involved in the nitty-gritty of legislation. But I know someone who might."

The meeting was over. As Oriana watched Leopard walk away, she picked up her phone and called Christian Playa.

"The Memorial fountain has him scared," she said. "It'll keep him from going wobbly on us. Nice work."

CHAPTER 37

Luke needed to go underground, so the Hudson Hotel was perfect. The lobby was stylish; there wasn't a light bulb over forty watts. Dim is the new black, don't you know? In the soft glow, young waif wannabe models looked mysterious, and old people looked embalmed. Luke ducked into a corner and called Arnie Letts, Tremont's M&A guru. He explained to Letts that he wanted to stay off the streets for a little while, just in case the hospital security force was trolling the neighborhood. Luke didn't know that Letts was in Tremont's office at the time.

Letts smiled and covered the phone with his hand: "Looks like our boy's gone underground."

Tremont was staring, not at Arnie, but at his Bloomberg terminal. It was a rough day in the trading pits, and he had to cover his shorts in palladium, that is, buy back commodity contracts that he had sold the night before. "Did he get the goods on Medcentric?" Tremont asked.

Letts passed on the question to Luke.

"I got it." Mission accomplished. "Don't do the deal!"

"What?" Letts asked, astonished. He thought maybe he'd misunderstood Luke. *"Don't?"*

"Do not, I repeat, do not. I'll be there within the hour to explain." Luke saw a security guard walking toward him. He hung up quickly.

"That's fucking ridiculous," Letts said to Tremont, his lower lip spotted with spittle. "You're not gonna let a rookie call off my deal," he said defiantly. "Are you?"

TODD BUCHHOLZ

Luke slipped behind a brick pillar into the men's room. He leaned against the sink for a few minutes and then looked up at the mirror. Stupid! The surgical mask was still dangling from his neck. He ripped it off, stuffed it in the trash bin and then furtively emerged from the lavatory, looking for a security guard.

He didn't find a guard in the lobby. But he did find a welcome sight. Walking into the bar area was Cori Leopard and her long legs. He jogged toward her. She was wearing a short black skirt and a tight white shirt. He grabbed her by the waist. She didn't expect it. She turned on her heels, her fists clenched, ready to head butt the stranger, if necessary.

"Whoa, Cori," Luke said, as he felt her body tense up. "It's me, your friend the capitalist pig."

She smiled and her clenched hands turned to outstretched arms. They hugged, not just around the shoulders, but their waists bumped together, too. From the moment they had first met on Tremont's plane, sexual vibes seemed to orbit about them. It was just a matter of time.

"What are you doing here?" he asked. The Hudson was not exactly the place for left-wing, environmentally minded philanthropists.

She mumbled something about the hotel being historic and part of the city's landmark and monuments commission. Luke wasn't listening. In less than an hour he had to be in Tremont's office to explain why he would quash the Medcentric deal. He knew what to do in the meantime.

"I'll be right back," he said to Cori.

He walked to the reception desk, tossed out a credit card, and came back with a room key. He placed it in the palm of his hand and shook hands with Cori, who felt the plastic slip into hers.

"What's this, your credit card?" she asked with a giggle. She looked at his warm, confident smile and felt the urge to giggle, realizing she was about to indulge in something more than tea in the afternoon. Who could doubt her or stop her? He gave off sparks and had a spontaneity she had seldom felt from all the tree huggers she'd dated. Plus, he was surely easy on the eyes.

Luke took her hands in his and whispered, "Let's get to know each other's monuments a little better. You know, research for the city commission. It's a philanthropic gesture."

She laughed, brushed her red hair from her eyes, and moved close to him as they walked to the elevator. When they got to the tiny hotel room, they fell into bed and peeled back their clothing, along with months of frustration and loneliness. They began tenderly, nibbling, kissing, and stroking. But after a few moments, the bars of the cage broke free. They were sure their thrusting and the shudder of their climaxes shook the foundations of the landmark building.

CHAPTER 38

Arnie Letts couldn't wait to confront Luke. He had been working for weeks on Medcentric. How many dinners had he missed with his wife and kids, not to mention with his girlfriend? He hated traveling, and yet he was forced to commute back and forth between LaGuardia and Medcentric's headquarters in frozen Omaha. How dare Luke threaten to screw up the deal. Letts was fuming outside Tremont's office, ready to pounce. He was combing his fingers through his thinning blond hair quickly and repeatedly; fine strands drifted down to the shoulders of his brown suit.

Feeling energized by his rendezvous with Cori, Luke galloped toward the Tremont building ready to divulge his findings, the debacle of the Medcentric stents. Tremont would appreciate his originality, his daring. He'd pass the second test and move up the Tremont ladder, closer to financial security for himself, and for Buck.

When he arrived at Tremont's reception area, Luke saw Letts standing in front of the portrait of Washington crossing the Delaware. Letts was grimacing. The expression reminded Luke of a prefight weigh-in, where surly boxers try to scare their opponents. Letts's expression puzzled Luke. He should be happy that Luke had dug up some dirt. Who else on Wall Street knew that the Medcentric stents were plagued with chips and that the head of cardiology at Roosevelt was about to ban the product from the operating room?

The fast-talking Letts let loose a barrage of stinging questions: "What the hell are you doing, superboy?" he said in a hoarse voice.

"Screwing *my* deal? What'd you learn? What'd surfing the Internet teach you about cardiology?"

Luke thought Letts's left eye was beginning to twitch. His voice became louder and even more sarcastic. "I can see it now," Letts continued, "you're sitting there in your fancy, paid-for apartment, you boot up your laptop, you surf along some medical Web sites—probably stopping to jerk off to porn—and then you place an urgent call telling me you want to cancel Medcentric?"

Luke hadn't heard trash talk like that since he hung up his gloves and jockstrap. Letts took a few steps closer. Luke was nervous; he wasn't worried about a fistfight, but he was unskilled in office politics. What did he do wrong? Wasn't he supposed to discover the truth about Medcentric?

"Arnie, you've lost me. I followed your instructions. You came up with the assignment. You haven't even let me explain what I found out, and you're jumping all over me like I just killed your dog," Luke said.

Paul Tremont's first-year associate got up from her knees and was pouring tea for Tremont when Luke and Letts marched in, one behind the other. In the split-second that Luke stepped over the threshold, he had to decide how to act, how to respond. Should he just quit on the spot and move back to his Village apartment? Should he match fury with fury, pounding back at Letts? The electrical field in Luke's brain sparked. A lot was at stake: If he didn't win this round, he'd be back on the streets, or at best working as a "street man" at Gresham Bros. He now realized that Letts never intended for him to do a thorough job investigating Medcentric. Tremont and Burns had probably forced Letts to take on a rookie. Now Letts wanted to destroy him. Luke wondered, What would Buck do?

Letts began spitting out his verbal attack, skipping all opportunities to take a breath or let Luke slide in a rebuttal.

"Mr. Tremont, this is bullshit," Letts said. "I've been up to my earlobes in Medcentric for the past month, living, eating, breathing stents. Now this hick who crawled in from the outerboroughs through a tunnel comes in at the last moment to tell us to scuttle the deal—"

Hick? Hey, I was born in Manhattan; you're the jerk from Louisiana!

"Forget it. Forget him. How the hell would he know anything? I don't even know if the kid's got a high school diploma. What are you gonna rely on here, my Wharton MBA or his membership card to Gold's gym? I agreed to take on this ignoramus, but I never imagined he'd have the balls to try to block my deal!"

Luke was turning shades of scarlet that clashed with Tremont's Picasso from the Blue Period. He wanted to lunge at Letts, and shove his MBA degree down his pencil-necked throat. What would Buck do? The answer came to him: Rope-a-dope. A glittering page out of Ali's book, his rumble in the jungle against George Foreman in 1974. The experts were certain that the beastly, menacing Foreman would tear off Ali's head. So Ali leaned against the ropes and let Foreman fire all his bombs, until the muscles on Foreman's arms ached and sagged, exhausted, the last neuron refusing to fire, refusing to instruct the fast-twitch muscles, refusing to talk to the slow-twitch muscles. The beast turned into two hundred fifty pounds of heaving, helpless blubber. Luke looked at Letts, foaming, fuming, stinking up the room with his vitriol and flop sweat.

"And then he thinks he's some kind of expert? Christ, might as well appoint an ape as surgeon general—"

Buck would let old Letts punch himself out, and then push him over with a few precision blows. Luke looked over at Tremont, eyebrows arched, nodding his head. Hadn't said a word. Tremont stared at Letts. Luke didn't have a clue how to read Tremont. And then Luke noticed Letts shifting gears. He started running out of words, but started waving his arms, pounding an imaginary table. Chopping, cutting, slicing, like a two-bit hawker at the county fair demonstrating the new Ronco vegetable dicer. Suddenly, Letts had shed the patina of his Wharton MBA and was now starting to resemble his father, a hillbilly auctioneer.

He was sputtering, tossing off a string of unconnected words: "Internet junk and rumors and bullshit and porno and crap research—"

Luke remembered something. The plaque in the Roosevelt urology lab thanked Paul Tremont for his generous contributions. He had his opening. Luke raised a finger. Letts swiped at it, though he was at least three feet away. "I'm not done, and another thing—"

Tremont brought his cup of tea to his lips. Caesar watching the gladiators. Then he finally uttered a word, "Speak." He looked at Luke. Luke calmly asked a simple question. "Mr. Tremont, what do you think of Roosevelt Hospital?"

"Fine place, I've raised a lot of money for them. They performed New York's first open-heart surgery in the 1950s—"

Good. Perfect answer.

But Tremont wasn't finished, "So what? Mr. Letts here thinks you're a buffoon who will destroy Tremont Advisors. What say you, Luke?"

"What if I told you that Roosevelt's cardiology department was banning Medcentric's stent?"

Tremont's eyebrows began climbing toward his hairline, but Letts interrupted, "I'd say you were reading too much Internet crap. The shorts on Wall Street are always sneaking negative rumors onto the Net. Oldest trick in the book—"

Tremont waded in, "How do you know, Luke?"

"He doesn't know anything, Mr. Tremont. It's innuendo bullshit, like UFOs and Roswell area 51—" Letts blurted out.

"I was there," Luke declared.

"Where?" Tremont asked.

"In the operating room. With the head of cardiac surgery."

"Jagdish—" Tremont began.

"Singh. Yes, Jagdish Singh. He's banning the Medcentric stent today."

Letts started coughing. His cheeks turned ashen, and he backed up to the wall, at first leaning awkwardly against the precious Picasso. By the time he slid down to Tremont's white sofa, Luke had explained his discovery—the story of the chipped Medcentric stent. Letts appeared disoriented, groping for a pitcher of water, while Luke beamed, knowing he had conquered his second test. Buck would be proud.

CHAPTER 39

James Carmody broke into a sweat, his paisley Ferragamo tie flapping behind him like the tail of a kid's kite. Back in Asbury Park he had set high school records for the 100-meter dash, but this competitor was more formidable. Carmody was racing to catch up to the Amtrak Metroliner, which was pulling away from Union Station with a zillion horsepower. But Carmody was not unarmed. He boasted a fat ratio of just .12 and a Porsche's coefficient of drag, aided by his gelled-up fade haircut. He pumped his arms and nearly kicked his own butt.

In the second car sat Nick Larsen, munching on a Krispy Kreme, a dab of glaze now smeared across his upper lip. Where the hell was Carmody? If Larsen could haul his fat ass to the train all the way from Fredericksburg, Virginia, why couldn't his Dupont Circle partner make it? A few years earlier, Larsen might've chalked up Carmody's absence to the color of his skin. Larsen wasn't afraid of stereotypes. Chocolate City, he called D.C. But Carmody wasn't a black-power guy. Larsen once snuck over to his partner's desk and picked up Carmody's iPod. He expected to find who knows what—James Brown, Snoop Dog, or some filthy rapper he'd never heard of. After all, Carmody often spoke of his "street cred." Larsen quickly scrolled through the songs. Most of them were by Johnny Mathis! "Misty," "Wonderful! Wonderful!"

But where was his Muzak-loving partner?

Pump, whoosh, pump, whoosh. Carmody was keeping pace with the train. But he looked ahead and realized that he was running out of concrete. His leather satchel banged against his lower back with each stride.

What would Larsen think? That he slept in? Stayed out too late? Misread the Amtrak schedule? In fact, Carmody had been up at five A.M. and had already hit the gym, burning his abs with three hundred sit-ups and creaming his glutes by loading massive iron plates. He wouldn't have bothered if he knew he'd be chasing a train forty minutes later. But he couldn't ignore the phone call that had interrupted his daily ritual and made him late for the train. Who tipped her off? He had to tell Larsen, had to catch the roaring locomotive.

Pump, whoosh, pump, whoosh. Carmody calculated he had about forty more feet before he'd be jumping onto the rails, which would get him nothing except the sounds of his own ankles snapping. He considered giving up and catching another train in an hour. But there was his pride. No way was James Carmody—a black kid from Asbury Park who fought his way off Springdale Avenue and busted his ass to get through Rutgers and Quantico—going to give his overweight white partner the satisfaction of looking at his wristwatch, shaking his head.

Carmody spied a metal handle on the side of the last car. It was a tall three steps up, four feet from the concrete and looking more like a blur. He'd have to jump up and forward at the same time. As he stepped forward he drew back his arms and then whipped them forward, stretching out toward the train. He heaved and thrust his hips forward. But the handle started to move away from him. His leap was just a few inches shy. He would bounce off the side of the train and roll along the concrete. As he started falling toward the concrete, a meaty arm thrust itself outward. Nick Larsen caught Carmody's hand and pulled him onto the train's landing.

Larsen gave the slightest smile. "Now can you tell me what that goddamned phone call was about?"

"She called me. Told me she might be able to help."

"How did she know? How did she know to call you?" Larsen asked.

"The senator told her." Carmody shrugged.

"I hope you've prepared some tough questions."

"Oh, I think she'll squirm. And she'll speak."

Carmody felt along his left arm and realized that his satchel was missing. He began sweating, a funky sweat of worry, not the perspiration of an athlete. He tried to think: What FBI secrets had tumbled along the railroad tracks of Union Station when he jumped to catch the train?

CHAPTER 40

Larsen and Carmody came up from the lower levels of Penn Station in New York like rats escaping a maze. Though the station had banned cigarettes years before, somehow a haze of smoke and body odor floated through it. Larsen insisted they stop at a Nathan's hot dog stand. Carmody's stomach growled, but he couldn't imagine stuffing a fattening, chemical laden weenie into his lean body.

"But it's 100 percent meat," Larsen assured him as he chomped on a mustard-coated tube of flesh.

"Squirrels are made of meat," Carmody replied. "You're probably eating squirrel testicles right now. I'll wait for a bran muffin."

Larsen chewed as they walked onto Seventh Avenue. They had come to New York to solve the mystery of the "CL" sticker that had stumped the Lacunator. Their mission: to surprise Cori Leopard and interrogate her about the D.C. subway explosion. Could CL stand for Cori Leopard?

"According to our files, Miss Leopard has led protests in almost every major city. She's a known agitator, and she doesn't care if she embarrasses her father," Larsen said as they hailed a cab.

"But she's not a violent terrorist, Nick. Yeah, she's been caught carrying a handgun, but a subway attack is way beyond her."

"Well, we'll talk to the agitator and find out, won't we? I can't believe she had the balls to phone you this morning. Maybe it was part of a plan. Keep you yapping on the phone so that you miss your train. You think?"

Carmody wasn't sure what Cori's motive had been, but he was shocked that she'd been tipped off. FBI agents don't like to give suspects a lot of warning.

Instead of surprising Cori at work, Carmody suggested they meet in the lobby of the Palace, an ornate hotel near St. Patrick's Cathedral. In *Vanity Fair*, he had seen photos of billionaire investors and Bulgari patrons crisscrossing the lobby. A grand double staircase carpeted in red added drama and mystery to the scene, like a plunging neckline. Larsen had suggested the hotel with a spark of irony: It had been owned by Leona Helmsley, who went to jail for tax evasion. The place had the ghost of felons about it.

Just like the senator, Cori had a different agenda from the two agents. They were trying to solve a vicious terrorist attack, while she and her father wanted the FBI to figure out who put the word "Memorial" in front of their names in the Congressional record.

Indeed, Cori clashed with the room when she arrived. Her red hair was too auburn for the red carpet, and her own plunging neckline stole attention from the staircase. Larsen was surprised. Every FBI photo showed her looking more like a tree hugger than a reader of *Vanity Fair*. Carmody noticed the black leather handbag with the white stitching from Tod's. The Manolo Blahnik shoes matched smartly.

As Cori crossed the lobby like a runway model, her mind was still focused on her tango with Luke at the Hudson Hotel the prior day. He was bursting with strength and confidence. When he took her to the room, she felt as if she were being kidnapped by a wave of testosterone. But what would come next? Was she just a roll on the mattress? When she saw him next, at Tremont headquarters, how would he behave? Like a man falling in love or like a frat boy who'd added a notch to the bedpost?

Larsen took the first step. "Have you gone straight, Ms. Leopard? You look like a million bucks. Where are the Birkenstocks and ripped woolen sweaters?"

Cori didn't understand why he sounded so antagonistic. Weren't they here to help her solve the mystery of the Leopard Memorial fountain?

"It's none of your business what I slip on at the office or at home. This morning on the phone I told agent Carmody that I was working on the inside now, for Paul Tremont. I'm not stupid enough to walk into his offices looking like Davy Crockett's cook. If wearing Prada lets me write bigger checks on Paul Tremont's account, I'll suffer with it. Enough about the dress code; I'd like to talk about the subject at hand."

"Yes, what *do* you know about the subway explosion, Ms. Leopard?" Larsen interjected.

Huh? She knew only what she'd seen on CNN. "You're joking, right?"

"We don't joke much," Larsen remarked. "Not with dozens of dead people, including Boy Scouts."

"But why would I have anything to do with that? My mother was murdered by terrorists. That should be in your files, right?"

Carmody's antennae told him that she was being honest, that she was shocked at Larsen's question. Nonetheless, he pushed another angle. "Your father just chaired a hearing with the nominee for assistant secretary of state. We think she, Sara Hartman, was a target of the terrorist strike. Have you had any past connections with foreign cells? You've been involved with all sorts of protest groups, fighting smokestacks, gas emissions, and even French fries. Did any of the money ever come in euros, yen, yuan, or rubles, I mean, from abroad?" Carmody leaned closer to her. "Even if you didn't know about the attack, might you have unknowingly funneled money or passed information on to someone who might have been working for, say, Al Queda, Bader Meinhof, or even a renegade group of the Mafia? Our agents in Vegas tell us that you were leading a protest there a few weeks ago. Who put you up to it?"

Cori began to pale. "This is ridiculous," she shot back. "I'm not in anyone's hip pocket. I deal my own deck; I don't take orders. I was in Vegas protesting Paul Tremont's mining techniques in Latin America. That's got nothing to do with the Mafia or Al Queda or anything else. Where do I get the money? From a small trust fund courtesy of a life insurance policy on my mother."

Just then a waiter came by. He was an ancient Hispanic man with his hair dyed macadam black, but behind his neck furry white tufts sprouted. "What'll it be?" he rasped, resting his order pad on the table next to Carmody.

"Dewar's on the rocks," said Larsen.

"Manhattan," said Carmody.

"I don't have much time for a wild goose chase," Cori said. "One drink and I'm out of here, unless you've got something better to talk about. Or a warrant." She turned to the old waiter. "Rum and coke. Twist of lime," she said.

The waiter jotted it down on a pad. "Back in the old days, we called that a Cuba Libre," he said wistfully.

Carmody looked down at the old waiter's pad, as he jotted the initials "CL."

"That's it!" Carmody shouted.

CHAPTER 41

When Luke foiled the Medcentric deal, Arnie Letts felt like hitting the rookie. But instead Letts hit the road, joining a private equity firm based in Greenwich, Connecticut, one of those boutiques where hotshot MBAs put bandaids on dying firms, hoping they'll stop bleeding just long enough to resell them. After Arnie left Tremont Advisors, Tremont called a special staff meeting in the so-called Roosevelt Room. Like so many other touches in the Tremont office, this room was an homage to the West Wing of the White House. Following the original 1902 architecture, Tremont's Roosevelt Room had no windows, just a skylight, similar to the one FDR had installed in 1934. Luke worried that Tremont would blame him for losing a key player like Letts. No one really knew whether Letts quit or was fired. What secrets might he have packed in his bags when he bolted for Greenwich?

Luke gingerly entered the Roosevelt room. He was immediately struck by the huge sailfish hanging on a wall, like the kind that could grace a strip mall's seafood restaurant in landlocked Nebraska. He sidled closer and saw a small plaque that said, "Caught by J. F. Kennedy, Acapulco, 1960." Luke looked back at the table and saw name cards written in calligraphy leaning on sterling silver stands. He started to circle the table squinting at the elaborately scripted writing. He had moved about halfway round when his stomach started rumbling, butterflies he hadn't felt since grade school. Where's my chair? He could not find it.

At that moment Paul Tremont strode through the entranceway, followed by a beautiful receptionist holding a pot of coffee and a small white bag. Dr. Burns tapped loudly at his end of the table. He gestured for Luke to take the empty seat next to him. Luke dashed over and sat down seconds before Tremont lowered himself into his leather chair, raised slightly higher than the others. The receptionist placed the white bag in front of him.

Tremont did not look happy, his blue eyes did not twinkle; they stared. This was the Tremont of the stressful trading room, the Tremont with steel balls, not the charming Tremont who hosted charity balls. He looked coldly at Burns and simply nodded his head. Burns seemed unnerved, but he cleared his throat and began. "We don't usually meet in the Roosevelt, but as some of you know, this room is *unwired* for sound, that is, it is more secure because BlackBerrys, cellphones, and other electronic devices are blocked by lead, new ceramics, and other absorbent materials, similar to what the Air Force has developed for Air Force One. We're off to a rough month according to Ryan, with the collapse of the Swedish krona really hurting—."

Ryan probably made $5 million last year, but he had a lousy job. The PhD from Yale was responsible for understanding the billions of digits of data spit out by the risk-management software. He walked into Tremont's office every day at 4:01 P.M. and broke the good news or bad news, the daily P&L. At just thirty, his wispy reddish hair had already retreated halfway down the back of his head. You could tell by his posture how the trading day went. His height seemed to fluctuate between five seven and five ten, depending on the action on the floor of the NYSE and the Chicago Merc.

But a simple plus or minus sign next to the daily P&L would not tell the whole story. Ryan was responsible for RiskMatters, the in-house risk-management software for Tremont. RiskMatters calculated how much risk the fund was taking in its portfolio, how much it was borrowing in order to place big bets, and how historically risky the investment vehicles were. A fund could be up 30 percent, but the managers may just be rolling the dice and come up lucky. A day later, they could hit snake eyes and drop 50 percent. Tremont hired Ryan in 1998, the day that Nobel Laureate geniuses nearly blew up the world, when the hedge fund called Long Term Capital Management exploded. Grizzled Wall Streeters scoffed that only a bunch of professors could have screwed things up so badly. They didn't return their Nobel Prizes.

Ryan had tweaked RiskMatters so it could assess almost any scenario.

How much would today's investors lose if the markets collapsed in the same magnitudes as after 9/11? Or the Kennedy assasination? How would another December 7, 1941 impact the stocks, bonds, and currencies in the portfolio? Ryan could answer those questions. It was like compressing all of modern history into a little disk. He handled the software disks as if they were vials of nitroglycerin. Tremont called them the "playbooks of prosperity." Each evening Ryan locked the disks and a printout in a small vault behind Tremont's office.

Burns turned the floor over to Ryan, who nervously described the overall portfolio. Luke didn't understand everything such as options on palladium and copper that were hedged but somehow not hedged enough. Ryan threw around so many Greek letters like gamma, theta, and delta, that Luke began to feel as if he were touring fraternity row. Ryan also explained that even though the portfolio was down 8 percent, the stock investments were virtually market-neutral: "We have about $30 billion longs and nearly $29 billion shorts, so it shouldn't matter to us whether the S&P goes up or down—"

Tremont finally spoke. "That's right." Everyone immediately looked at him, their knees resisting the urge to genuflect under the conference room table. It's hard to resist the instinct when you're sitting with someone who can drop a $10 million bonus in your pocket come Christmas.

Tremont paused and luxuriated in the rapt attention. "But I'm looking to buy, load up on the longs. Big time. Seismic shift. Tectonic plates and tsunamis. We're talking forty-year floods. Floods of prosperity for Tremont Advisors." His lips seemed to be resisting a smile. "So, as Ryan has just described, we're doing badly right now, boys, but the year's not over." This was not a dry market forecast from *Barron's*. This sounded more like the chanting of a Puritan prophet.

Everyone at the table had the same two questions: Why does Tremont think that stocks will be exploding higher? And when? Unfortunately, no one had the nerve to ask. To them, Tremont was like a ripped and jacked Buddha who could not be questioned directly but should be studied for signs. Luke didn't understand god worship, so he leaned forward.

"Mr. Tremont, the portfolio has been roughed up badly, even though we're market neutral. I guess the stock picking is in a slump. Could you give us a clue to the change ahead?"

Tremont stared at Luke and let the seconds beat. The others wondered if the rookie had stepped over the line. Tremont didn't blink. Luke felt as if Tremont were conducting a full body scan, like an MRI. Finally, Tremont answered.

"Luke, you will be among the first to know. You're part of the plan. But it's too early to tell."

Luke's whole body tingled. He didn't get an answer, but he got something better, further assurance that he was a player.

Burns jumped in. "Mr. Tremont, there's one other matter you might want to discuss. Arnie Letts is gone of course."

"Yes," Tremont said calmly, "Arnie Letts has gone to Greenwich. We wish him good luck." He took a deep breath and then took on a sterner tone. "But no one, I repeat, no one, should have any contact with him whatsoever. If he calls, hang up. If he emails, delete it. Any security breaches can be—well, fatal."

He turned back to Luke. "Though we've suffered portfolio losses and the departure of Letts, we do have a bright spot here. Let me tell you about Luke's performance on Medcentric. We were this close," he held his thumb and forefinger an inch apart, "to buying a loser."

He described Luke's investigation and then lifted a glass of water toward him.

"Here's to playing defense. We need to find good deals to make and good stocks to buy. But we also need to know when to shoot down a deal and when to go short on a stock. Luke stopped us right before we signed on the dotted line for a merger that would have hurt us badly. He did it through good old fundamental research." *Pause.* "And a little playacting at Roosevelt Hospital." He laughed, and forty partners and associates joined in. They had heard about Luke's performance as Al Humphries. "So Luke, you're our defensive player of the week. Congratulations."

The team applauded, and then Tremont opened up the bag he had placed on the table. He held up a New York Yankee's jersey. The pin-striped shirt was stitched with Luke's name. Luke tried to contain his smile. He had passed the test, climbed to the next level, and done so without compromising his integrity very much, although Al Humphries might disagree.

Back in his office, Luke looked out over Central Park and realized that he had started to feel at home in the Tremont world. Those days in the Village, those stinking memories of Delancy's, and bloody nights in Smith & Wollensky's butcher room belonged to another person, some-one who had been literally and figuratively airlifted to a new life. In the middle of his reveries, the door burst open, banging against the wall. Paul Tremont's smiling face leaned into the office.

"Put on your shirt, young man," Tremont said.

"What shirt?"

"The Yankee's jersey. We're going to Steinbrenner's box tonight."

Luke knew that this was an order, not an invitation. No one turned down Tremont, and no one would turn down the chance to sit in Steinbrenner's skybox.

An hour later, Luke was at Yankee Stadium. When he looked down on the field, he felt like a kid who'd just opened his first box of Crayolas. My God! The green grass was so intense! The smell of the turf! The buzz of the crowd as the players warmed up. He could hear a vendor's Bronx accent scream: "Get your hot dawgs! Get your hot dawgs! Get your goddamn hot dawgs!" Naturally, the hot dogs didn't make it up to the Steinbrenner suite, where waiters carried trays of New Zealand lamb chops.

"Your career path has just begun, Luke," Tremont said. Tremont wore a gray cashmere so soft and luxurious it had an added dimension of depth.

Luke wasn't sure how to respond to Tremont's observation, so he kept quiet, not wanting to spoil his ascent.

"There are no limits to what one can do. Do you understand?"

Luke gave a tentative nod.

"I'm talking about markets. Markets. There are markets everywhere."

"Of course, Mr. Tremont, equities, bonds, currencies, real estate—" He was trying to think of others.

"No, No!" Tremont was getting excited, or maybe frustrated. He put his arm around Luke's shoulder. Had Luke ever been embraced by a billionaire?

"Look down at that field. What do you see?" Tremont asked.

"Yankees? Grass? Babe Ruth's monument?"

"I see the kinetic energy of the markets, coiled ready to send prices spiraling up or downward. I see goods and services begging—searching—for a new market price. You see grass, but I see grass seed and fertilizer. What can I do to drive up the price? How can I invest in it? You see vendors hawking hot dogs. I see pork belly futures. You see a raving crowd in the bleachers, but look down there." He pointed to a guy in a good suit and an ostentatious green scarf. "I see a hotshot banker trying to impress his girlfriend by buying last-minute seats from a scalper at three times the cost. What if it rained today? Would cabbies charge more to drive the fans home? Everything has its price—all I want to do is change the dynamic forces that create that price." Tremont removed his arm from Luke's shoulder.

"How do you change the price of grass?" Luke asked.

"Oh, I don't know yet." A beat. "Try this: What if everybody read in tomorrow's paper that grass and fertilizer caused cancer, whether you were the shortstop, or the guy in the mezzanine deck inhaling the aroma? Secondhand cancer from watching baseball played on natural turf. Imagine that. You bet your ass that ESPN and the *Wall Street Journal* would cover that story. Suddenly, fertilizer prices collapse and the company that makes artificial turf flies through the roof."

Tremont pointed up to the sky. "God is a mover and shaker, right? But he's omniscient too. Can you imagine his P&L if he were speculating in the commodity markets? He knows when the hurricane is going to wipe out the orange crop because he creates the furious winds that rip the buds off the trees." He paused and put his arm around Luke again. "That's how we need to think, Luke. Not just as investors. We need to be movers and shakers. I don't mean the chickenshit kind, those who make money flipping apartment buildings and then brag about it at the New York Athletic Club. I mean we have to move and shake the markets because we control the kinetic energy. Like Zeus firing thunderbolts. Like Zeus firing thunderbolts." His voice dropped off, as he repeated his refrain. "Like Zeus firing thunderbolts."

Luke had never thought of the markets that way. To him, investing was simply a matter of judging which way a stock would go. He only knew how to ride a stock. He never dreamed that Paul Tremont could be the prime mover. Or that he, a washed-up boxer, a high school dropout, could rise to Olympus.

CHAPTER 42

Dr. Francis Braden paced his musty classroom like a matador teasing a bull. He didn't wave a red cape to incite his opponents; he didn't have to. The literature majors at Columbia came ready to fight. Three hundred of them, with standees in the aisle. Though Braden was around fifty, he belonged to another era, when men wore fedoras, not backward baseball caps. The word "dude" wouldn't emerge from his mouth unless he was watching someone rustle a horse on a range in Oklahoma. And Francis Braden hated to go any farther west than Princeton, New Jersey, so you could just forget about it. He once responded to a thug on the subway by stating that "the mills of the gods grind exceedingly small." Mills? Gods? In New York? Unlike so many of his colleagues in the English department, Braden did not have the sickly pallor of a vegetarian who lacked animal protein.

"Professor, your theory goes against everything I ever learned about Hemingway!" shouted a frustrated senior in the third row, who pointed to a stack of dissertations. "Cohn is a loser." She formed the letter "L" with her left hand.

Braden raised his thick eyebrows. "Is that a gang symbol, Ms. Rushton?" Patty Rushton was a convenient foil, someone who seemed to have ingested every conventional concept ever covered in CliffNotes.

"No, it means loser."

"Well, let's remove ourselves from the shopping mall, or the hip-hop video for a moment, shall we?" He smiled, tugged his Vandyke and then suddenly thrust the spine of *The Sun Also Rises* toward the girl. "Explain why you think Cohn is a loser?"

"He loses his wife, his girlfriend, then he complains and beats up Romero—"

"All true, Ms. Rushton, but it's 1926. Now scroll forward. Hitler stalks Germany and then stampedes to power. What does France do?"

"Nothing," the girl answers.

He takes a step forward. "The Great Depression throws half the world into the poorhouse, the rich would eat dog food, but there's not even dog food to be found. What, Ms. Rushton, do the world's leaders do?"

"Nothing." Another step forward, going in for the kill.

"Now, Ms. Rushton, in the face of this emerging world of terror, of desperate famine, of meandering soldiers and demagogic madmen, what would the conventional hero, the hero of all your high school teachers, do? What would Jake Barnes do?"

She blanched and murmured, "Nothing"

"Excuse me, Ms. Rushton? What was that answer? A little louder, please."

"Nothing, Professor."

"So would you consider that Hemingway perhaps does not despise Robert Cohn, the outsider, the wandering Jew, the only character who even bothers to express his humanity? Yes, Cohn talks too much, exposes too much, fights too much. But at least he's got guts. At least he's in the ring." Braden slammed the book on a desk.

The students started scribbling and nodding. Ms. Rushton looked at her shoes. Silence. The silence that comes when precious paradigms begin to crumble.

A voice piped up from the very back.

"But why would he make Cohn a boxer?"

Braden shook his head and muttered, "God knows." He squinted toward the questioner. He should've brought his opera glasses. "Interesting question, Mr . . . uh?"

"The name's Braden." Luke Braden swallowed hard as three hundred students stared at him. He had stepped into his father's ring.

Luke sat across from his father at the Columbia faculty club. The décor and the menu were frozen in the Edwardian era. Salisbury steak went nicely with crushed velour in purple. Carrots and peas from a can made sense when you were staring at dusty tapestries. Luke had suddenly decided to reconnect with his father, show some common ground. He also wanted to explain his burgeoning career at Tremont, his ongoing relationship with Cori. Though he and Cori hadn't spent a huge amount of time together, he knew there was something solid and true between them; this was the real deal. He'd never felt this way before, and never before had the slightest urge to share his personal life with his father.

Luke no longer earned his income by hitting people. He now wore a white collar and was pulling in over half a million a year. While Luke felt a wave of pride, he also felt an undefeatable urge to rebel against the stuffiness of the place, as if he were fourteen again. His father ordered iced tea, but Luke asked the addled waitress whether she could bring him an Iron City beer. The woman didn't know what he was talking about.

When Luke first started acting up in junior high school, Dr. Francis Braden did what any Upper West Side academic would do: he took a class in child psychology. But all those hours couldn't bridge the gap between his son and him. That was before the Internet, of course, so he actually had to sit in a library, which meant he spent fewer hours with Luke. Now, years later, he sat staring at a son who seemed more confident. And more prosperous. Why was he wearing a trendy suit to a faculty club more accustomed to elbow patches?

Luke decided to start the conversation with the most innocuous inquiry: "How's your blood pressure and blood sugar, Dad? Still skipping dessert?"

"I'm fine. A dish of crème brulee never hurt anyone. And you? What's with the suit? You look like you just stepped off a runway in Milan."

Luke explained his whirlwind trip from being a street man at Gresham to a rising exec at Tremont. He waited for a response.

Instead, his father muttered a series of "ums," and "uh-huhs," and "I see's."

Luke then went to a leading question. "Dad, what would you say to a student of yours who got a job at Tremont?"

"*Pacta sunt servanda.*"

Christ, couldn't he just speak English! "Dad, I thought you were an English teacher? What's with the Spanish?"

"Latin. It basically means, Keep your promises," his father said.

Luke felt his temperature begin to rise. He tried to smile, but he was sure he was scowling. It was hard to have a father-to-son talk when your father talked like a page from the *Encyclopedia Britannica*. "All right, Professor, what are you trying to say?"

The professor stroked his Vandyke and took a deep breath. "I've had graduates work for Tremont. Some got filthy rich. Those who did got filthy in other respects too. Kids who would marvel at the Metropolitan Museum of Art and sit with sketchpads in front of the Seagram's Building on Park Avenue lost their ability to contemplate or to appreciate aesthetics. It was all about real estate, setbacks, double-dip leveraged tax leases, and a bunch of accounting mumbo jumbo. Who was Mies van der Rohe? A great modernist architect? Nah, just some guy who generated a double-digit EBITA for Seagram's. Who is Philip Roth? A guy who rewrote the twentieth-century novel, twisting the Jewish experience into a modernist torture chamber? Nah, just some guy whose pages might get you a two-picture deal with Miramax."

"So what's the problem? Your former students figured out how to make a living? They didn't have to starve in graduate student hell?"

"There's nothing wrong with earning money. But before these kids signed up with Tremont, they'd promise me that they'd never lose their sense of wonder, their appreciation for art, for music, for creativity. But they broke those promises. More important, they broke themselves. *Pact sunt servanda*, my son."

Luke stifled a groan. He was never going to be a literary scholar or an architect or an aesthete. Surely, Tremont Advisors was a step up from the grime, graft, and blood of the ring. Luke looked at his father and slowly shook his head, frustrated that they could not even speak the same language.

Just then a familiar figure appeared. Paul Tremont glided into the faculty lounge. as if surrounded by an aura, an aura that seemed to fray the tweed on Professor Braden's well-worn jacket.

CHAPTER 43

Luke couldn't believe that his father and Tremont could be in the same place at the same time. Call the Hayden Planetarium! Matter and anti-matter were about to share the same space. Luke wasn't sure whether to spring up from his seat to greet his boss or to duck down and hide. He looked at his father, who would not have looked more uncomfortable had Jake Barnes shown up in the flesh.

The professor cocked his head as if his son had orchestrated this meeting with his new boss. And Luke didn't have a chance to hide, for Tremont was walking straight toward them.

"I heard you were here, Luke." He cheerfully looked over at Luke's father. "Is this your tutor?"

Luke stood up to grab Tremont's hand. "Mr. Tremont, meet my father, Professor Francis Braden."

Luke was relieved that his father was sufficiently well mannered to hide his grimace. Nonetheless, Francis Braden shook Tremont's hand as if he was half expecting a concealed buzzer in it.

"Would you like to join us for lunch?" Luke asked, quickly slurring the words together. *Please don't! Go back to the Roosevelt Room or to your oval office!*

"No, thank you—" said Tremont.

Tremont looked down at the table, at the Professor's spinach frittata and Luke's hamburger. "But I'll have a glass of wine with you."

Silence. Luke wasn't sure how to begin. Did Mao ever play chess with Chiang-kai-shek? How could he relate his father's ivory tower to

Tremont's business world? Capitalism didn't often cross paths with English Lit, except when Saul Bellow cashed his advances. Then Luke had an idea, an entrée to a conversation.

"Mr. Tremont, you know my father has an endowed chair here in the English department, endowed by the Mars candy company."

Professor Braden added, "The students like to joke about taking courses from the Mars Professor of English. Term papers show up with Milky Ways taped to them."

It was a lighthearted topic. Father and son waited for a response from Tremont.

"I'm long cocoa futures. And short the Sri Lankan market," Tremont replied with not a tinge of humor.

A dead end.

"Actually," Tremont added, "I don't eat much chocolate, too many near misses with diabetes in my family."

"Me too," Luke's father said. "A supreme irony for me. Like a breadmaker who's allergic to yeast."

Luke exhaled. At last some connection, even if they had to dive to the cellular level to find common ground. They were not from the same generation. Luke's father was near fifty, while Tremont was around seventy. Nonetheless, Luke always considered his father excessively mature. He could have qualified for an AARP card at thirty. And Tremont seemed younger than his true age.

Tremont slid his chair closer to the professor. "The dean told me that you teach Hemingway."

"You know the dean?" Francis asked.

"Sure, Columbia hits me up for fund-raising, and we recruit from the B School. When I heard about your teaching, I wondered, have you ever been to Cuba?"

"No." Francis sounded dismissive or defensive. "Would I have to live in Elizabethan London to teach Shakespeare?"

"You never wanted to go to Sloppy Joe's or any of his other haunts, Professor?" Tremont started to sound like a slightly aggressive tour guide.

Francis waved his hand. "Mr. Tremont, for almost all my life, Cuba has been off-limits to Americans. I don't break the law. Besides, there's plenty of Hemingway memorabilia in Key West, including a Sloppy Joe's bar—."

"You know the real Papa loved Havana, not Florida!" Tremont

sounded annoyed, as the waiter poured a glass of red. "Key West is a fraud. Just a big Tommy Bahama store overrun with gays and frothy drinks. I'm not sure Hemingway could get a man's drink there anymore."

Francis pressed on. "As for Cuba, the law is the law."

"Well, you should try it. I've been there quite a few times. Since I've got a British passport, I don't have to kowtow to silly congressmen. By the way," he leaned closer to the professor and spoke through his excessively white teeth, "the Cuban ladies are unbelievable. And available. All of them. Just like the old days, when the Mob had a piece of the action. Remember that?"

Luke watched his father wince as Tremont spoke. Was it embarrassment? Disgust? Political correctness?

"No, Mr. Tremont, I must have missed out," the Professor replied with a slight tremor.

"Pity. Pity," Tremont said while slowly sniffing his glass of wine. "You sure you haven't been? Something reminds me—" his voice trailed off.

Luke couldn't wait to change the topic.

His father glanced at his watch and announced that his class on World War I literature would begin in ten minutes.

He stood up and put his hand on Luke's shoulder. "Call me soon, Lucas."

He nodded at Tremont and said "I hope you're giving this school a lot of money."

Tremont tipped his glass in a halfhearted toast.

CHAPTER 44

"Are you sure it's him?" the voice whispered.

"Of course, I'm the one who brought him here," said Christian Playa in disgust. He was repulsed at both his guest and at himself. "He's in the back, in the bathtub, as usual. And he's not alone. That pig."

The former Havana Hilton droops over the Havana skyline like an addled dowager who's misplaced her bra. Where once strolled men in tuxedoes and ladies in ermine, now skulk pimps and prostitutes and petty gamblers. In 1959 Castro chose the Hilton as his headquarters, a twenty-seven-story slab casting a shadow over La Rampa, the sloping action-packed boulevard of the 1940s and 1950s. Only the cars look the same now, the 1950's Chevys and Cadillacs spewing soot through tailpipes constructed from tin and any other metal that can be bent into a tubular shape in someone's alley.

Christian Playa had escorted Paul Tremont from the airstrip to the former Hilton, now the Havana Libre. Playa hated this work. Even more than blowing up a subway car in D.C. or murdering a finance minister in Sri Lanka, Playa hated escorting Paul Tremont through the alleys and, ultimately, the genital canals of Havana women.

His brother, a simple milkman, once asked him, "Why do you do it? The money must be good, no?"

But Playa didn't pimp for Tremont simply for the money. This crease-faced assassin also had a heart, a heart that still beat for the old Cuba. He and Tremont had but one thing in common. They both hated Fidel Castro. Playa calculated that Paul Tremont could do what no U.S.

president had succeeded in doing: depose Fidel. That was the greater good. When Fidel fell, the people of Cuba would take over the island, Playa believed. No more Fidel, no more godless, penniless Communism, no more Batistas, no more fascist mobsters.

The voice spoke into Playa's ear: "Can you get photos of this?"

"Yes, of course. His favorite sport, a bathtub strangle."

"He got that from Jack Kennedy, of course. The chair, the décor, even his sex life. He's obsessed. Did you ever read that book I sent you, the biography by Thomas Reeves?"

"Yes, Oriana," Playa answered.

A few feet away, Paul Tremont lay smiling in a huge gilded bathtub. His eyes wide like a madman, he was looking down at the face of a Cuban woman, maybe nineteen years old. She was lying on her back, her face submerged. She had not drowned. She was alive, but trying to hold her breath as Paul Tremont—benefactor of the Red Cross, Doctors without Borders, and UNICEF—stroked his member in and out of her mouth. Her eyes began to bulge in a desperate plea, but Tremont placed his hand on her forehead to hold her down beneath the rippling surface. Air bubbles had escaped the narrow space between his cock and her lips. She was out of breath, writhing, trying to lift her neck to get one more breath. The money was on a table next to the tub, enough money to feed her parents and brothers for six months. Hard currency. Tremont looked down and pushed her forehead once more, like a crazed preacher trying to exorcise the devil. She looked as if she were weakening. Tremont figured she had half a minute left. Then twenty seconds. Ten seconds. He suddenly grabbed her hair and then shot his semen into her mouth. Then he yanked her head up and watched her cough and suck in air. She survived, of course. They almost always did. With big heaving breaths, she climbed out of the tub, wrapped herself in a towel stitched with a faded HH insignia, and grabbed her bounty.

Playa wanted to puke as he saw the girl run to the stairs. The image brought back flashbacks of Castro's soldiers raping his sister. Tremont would pay for this, more than the couple hundred dollars. Soon.

Back in New York, Luke Braden was about to receive disastrous news.

CHAPTER 45

Once again, Luke was watching the Yankees from Steinbrenner's skybox, sharing popcorn with Cori Leopard, feeling like a titan. He and Cori had just met with lawyers for the Tremont Foundation. The Foundation would support his idea for an old-age home for New York–area athletes like Buck Roberts, those who never got a big payday.

Luke's phone rang. It was Dr. Burns.

"Hey, Luke, you're in deep shit—" Burns never spoke like that. Perhaps he misheard Burns because of the din of the crowd.

"Arnie Letts has completed the Medcentric deal—"

Luke knew this. *So what? It was a doggy company. Bad product.*

"Letts is making a fortune for his fund. It should've been our deal. Your research was bogus. The stents work just fine. No chips, no leakage. You better get here fast. Tremont is on his way back from the Caribbean— furious. Wear a Kevlar vest, if you can." Burns hung up.

What happened to Burns, the "coach"? Now he was just a messenger of bad news. *How could my research be bogus?* Luke wondered. He had been an eyewitness to an operating-room disaster. The doctors at Roosevelt Hospital would back him up, except that he entered the O.R. under a fake identity. He tried to look calm, but Cori could tell that they would be leaving the game long before the seventh-inning stretch.

There was a traffic jam on the Westside Highway, and it took Luke fifty-five minutes to get to the Tremont offices. He dashed past the receptionist into his office to grab his notes on Medcentric. He knew he had precise quotes from Dr. Singh at Roosevelt. It was an airtight case.

TODD BUCHHOLZ

Dr. Burns and Tremont were sitting on his desk waiting for him to burst through the door. Frowning. This could mean just one thing: money was at stake.

"Sit down, Luke," Burns said.

A more timid man might have slumped in a chair, but Luke knew his facts. Surely, Burns and Tremont must have erred. Tremont stood up, arms folded. He spoke crisply with a superior tone that reminded Luke of his father.

"Luke, Arnie Letts is a very rich man today. The Medcentric deal went through and now he's flipping his shares. He's going to pull in $15 million just for himself. That should've been Tremont money. But you bollixed things up. I sided with you, but Arnie was right."

Luke was puzzled. "Arnie made money because they haven't figured out yet that the stent will end up killing people. It's just a matter of time. I don't think I made a mistake." He was puzzled by another thing, too. Tremont didn't usually worry that other people were getting rich. Why would Tremont be jealous of a dweeb like Letts? Even with the Medcentric payout, Letts was still a billion dollars short of Tremont's net wealth. Then Luke was struck with the obvious answer.

"Oh my God," he said to Tremont and Burns, "you didn't just pull out of the deal; you sold Medcentric short, didn't you?" Medcentric had jumped 40 percent.

"Luke, you should have known that," Burns said. It was listed on Ryan's dailies." Burns pulled a sheet of paper from his suit jacket and practically threw it at Luke. All senior analysts were required to read those sheets each day. Luke looked down the list of shorts.

A million and a half shares! The shares leaped $25 per share. Luke quickly realized that Tremont had lost $37.5 million. Luke was paralyzed. Burns and Tremont just stared. What could he do? Write a check to make up for the loss?

"Despite the near-term losses, those stents are damaged goods, time bombs for cardiac patients," Luke blurted out.

"That's where your research was bogus," Burns said. "The stents you saw in the operating room turned out to be fakes made in, I don't know, India or some other place. They looked like Medcentric stents but were cheap knockoffs. Can you blame Tiffany's if there's a scratch in the cubic zirconia on someone's costume jewelry? This happens a lot in hospitals, with patients getting killed by germs from unsterile instruments. Places like India and China don't give a damn about protecting patents, so any guy named Chin or Chopra can go into the medical business."

Luke felt dizzy. His daring, original research had been foiled by frauds. He stood there, trying to stay upright, straining for a ray of hope, a new argument to save his ass. It seemed like ten minutes of silence passed, as Tremont and Burns awaited his reply. But he had no brilliant insights. Then he recalled that he once heard Tremont say, "When in doubt, blame the lawyers." With this adage in mind, Luke answered their stares: "But if patients end up dying, class action lawyers will sue Medcentric anyway, right? They still have an urgent liability problem if doctors can't tell the difference between their stuff and unsterile knockoffs. Medcentric will be paying out a billion dollars in class action lawsuits."

"*Ultimately*," Tremont repeated in a mocking tone, "but how is anyone going to know about it?"

Tremont marched out of the office shaking his head.

Burns and Luke watched Tremont's broad back disappear around the corner.

"This could be a career-ending blunder, Luke," Burns said. "You don't drop $40 million and keep your job in this industry."

Luke thought of Cori, Buck, and his father. How could he be chewed up and spat out so quickly?

"But," Burns said, "I have an idea. Someone you can call."

CHAPTER 46

MIAMI CRUISE SHIP TERMINAL

James Carmody looked like a million bucks. His casual baseball jersey, boldly striped in pumpkin and gray, cost about $300 in the Anthony + Mo catalogue, a lot for an FBI agent to spend. His brown skin glistened in the sun as he walked up the ramp of the *Carnival Ecstasy* in Miami. He had enough hair gel in his curls to outdo any oil slick on the high seas.

Nick Larsen followed him wearing an old turquoise-colored Hawaiian shirt, a shirt not old enough to be a classic, and not new enough to be fashionable. He stroked Carmody's sleeve, "Hey, is that cashmere? Who the hell ever heard of a cashmere baseball shirt?"

After the meeting with Cori Leopard at the Palace in New York, Carmody was positive that CL, the initials that stumped the Lacunator computer at FBI headquarters, stood for *Cuba Libre*, Free Cuba. Forty-eight hours later Carmody and Larsen had flown down to Miami to meet the leader of the Cuba Libre Agency, Tito Marti. The Cuba Libre Agency was a citizen's group aimed at bringing the downfall of Castro through nonviolent means. Because fighting for the collapse of an entrenched dictatorship in Cuba doesn't pay very well, Marti had another business to pay his bills. He owned a company that supplied slot machines, baccarat dice, and casino chips to cruise ships sailing in the Caribbean. And so the two agents boarded the *Carnival Ecstasy* to interview Marti.

Marti looked to be in his late thirties with slicked-back hair and wraparound sunglasses. He was so slim that the cigar dangling from his mouth looked as wide as his neck. Moving through the casino like a pinball bouncing off the posts, Marti quickly yanked slot machine handles, brushed his hands across the felt craps tables, and spun the roulette wheels.

"Hey, bro," Carmody called to him, "why are you running so fast?"

"Ya gotta be kidding," Marti replied. "Look out the window. There are fifteen ships in today. They all leave between four thirty and six P.M. That gives me less than a half hour to check things out, replace parts, and all that shit. You wanna know why I smoke such a big friggin' cigar?" he asked while dashing over to the baccarat table, "it's 'cause they last longer. I don't have time to keep lighting up those skinny-ass stogies."

"Yeah, well, at least they let you smoke here," Larsen said with some sympathy. "You try lighting up in the Hoover Building. They'll bust you faster than Capone."

Marti had little time for the agents. "What do you guys want? I'm clean, my business is clean. All I need is for Fidel to fall and I can do business in Havana too. My parents taught me to spit whenever I faced south toward Cuba. But they made it clear I was spitting on Castro, not on the soil of Cuba," Marti explained. He took the cigar out of his mouth. "You cannot believe the rage my people feel." His face started to turn darker, his eyes narrowing. He stepped within a few inches of Carmody's face. "How would you feel if next year white people in Nantucket took black slaves and made them work on plantations? Well, now you know how we Miami Cubans feel about Castro defiling our people. So we lobby senators, raise money, and write books and articles demanding that Castro go." Marti paused, biting his lip as if to hold back tears and then pronounced, "But we have never, never, never picked up a gun or a knife to make that happen. No violence. None."

Larsen and Carmody spent the next couple of hours chasing Marti from cruise ship to cruise ship. They believed his story. The Cuba Libre clue looked like a dead end, until Carmody's phone rang.

CHAPTER 47

"What's your idea?" Luke asked Burns, who wore a sly smile on his thin lips.

Luke didn't trust the man. He was a fop and a phony. But the bigger question was whether Burns was on his side. Luke hated to admit it, but the doctor had helped catapult Luke up the corporate ladder. He'd even made room for him in the Roosevelt Room when Luke couldn't find a chair. Now Burns said he had an idea to save Luke's career. Perhaps Burns, the psychiatrist, was just a harmless head case himself, someone whose ego was both too big and too small for his body. Besides, it must be pretty tough playing second fiddle to a maestro like Paul Tremont. Forget second fiddle. Compared to Tremont, everyone else blew into a kazoo.

"Here's how it goes. We know that sooner or later a fake Medcentric stent is going to be placed inside somebody's chest or neck. And the patient will bleed to death. Sooner or later, the sharks in the tort bar start circling Medcentric. Just a matter of time, right?" Burns asked rhetorically.

Luke had a queasy feeling about the direction of Burns's idea.

Burns steepled his hands under his chin. "Now, we could simply move that schedule along—"

"Good lord, Dr. Burns, you're not suggesting we help murder someone by pushing knockoffs into the O.R.? I'm not looking for jail time, are you?"

Burns put on the appearance of surprise. "Of course not. I'm a doctor, not a ghoul. Luke, I'm trying to save your career, not destroy my own. Now, I've been checking up on meetings with the Tremont Foundation and your, uh, contacts with Ms. Cori Leopard." He sounded more avuncular now. "I think your idea for a retirement home for old athletes is quite noble. And her pledge to the Boys' Club downtown makes a lot of sense, too. I don't know too many hotshots in our business who give a damn about charity until they've socked away $10 million for themselves. I'm impressed, and so is Mr. Tremont."

"I appreciate the pat on the back. But what's your idea that will save my career but won't land us in jail?"

"Call her," Burns said tersely.

"Who?"

"That woman. The one with the microphone."

"At Bloomberg? Jane Cowell?"

"Tell her."

"Tell her about the stents? But she hates me. She distrusts me. She thinks I screwed her over Boeing."

"Doesn't matter. She's a journalist. She lives and dies on tips. Some pan out and some don't."

"You want me to tell her that Medcentric stents will kill people?"

"Luke, you keep thinking that I'm a monster! No, I want you to tell her the truth. Cheap, chipped knockoff stents are being substituted for Medcentric stents. That's it. Let her run with it. Then the lawyers will run after the corpses."

What was wrong with telling the truth?

"Giving her a true story, a real scoop will make you golden again at Bloomberg News, and also around here. It's your only way out. The truth will set you free. And make us some of our money back. Will you do it?"

Burns strutted down the hall to Tremont's office, leaving Luke slumped in his chair wondering whether he should tell Jane Cowell the truth. Luke hated the idea that he was being pressured to call Cowell—pressured by Burns—and by his hopes to salvage his own career. His conscience was itching, not just itching but scraping at his brain cells. There must be a way out.

He was tapping his finger on his desk when an ambulance siren penetrated the double-paned glass. He suddenly sat upright. That's it! he thought. Wouldn't he be *saving* lives by blowing the whistle on Medcentric? Once Bloomberg broke the story, surgeons would carefully inspect any stents, and Medcentric would take immediate action to encode the authentic products so they could be distinguished from the counterfeits.

"Will he do it?" Tremont asked Burns.

"I leaned hard. Told him it was a make-or-break career decision," said Burns.

"Stuart, he better go along with this," Tremont said. "The stakes are high. If he says no, then he torpedoes his career here. If we have to fire him, we're the big losers. He's our wedge to Havana. He needs to stay with us."

Burns looked edgy. He took his glasses off and rubbed them on his paisley necktie. "But what about the $37.5 million he cost us?"

"Screw the $37.5 million! You think that's worth more than the chance to get back at Castro? Is it worth more than the billions we'll make in Cuba? Where are your priorities? I can make back $37.5 million in a few days. Hell, I could fire you and have a good down payment on that loss, Stuart."

Burns looked at Tremont's color-coded bank of telephone lines through which he could tap into any call made to or from the Tremont offices. "Braden's line just lit up. Who's he calling?"

The computer display registered the phone number.

Burns shouted: "That's Bloomberg. He's gonna do it. Let's listen."

Tremont nodded, happy to have scared the hell out of Burns if even for a moment.

They listened as Luke explained to Jane Cowell that Medcentric was the victim of a counterfeit ring. She was excited and appreciative.

"Do you realize," Tremont began, "that this was a twofer? Not only do we get Medcentric back in the plus column, but we also have more leverage on young Mr. Braden."

"How so?" Burns asked.

"I'd say that the attorney general would be very interested in a young hotshot who leaked damaging information about a publicly traded company, a company about which he had inside information," Tremont said calmly.

"You wouldn't call the AG, would you?"

"Of course not. But Luke doesn't know that. And we can always use it as a threat to keep him in line should he resist his next test, his next assignment."

Jane Cowell was a solid reporter. She contacted Dr. Singh at Roosevelt Hospital; he backed up Luke's story. Then she called the FDA in Washington, as well as the office of Senator Tom Rathbone, who chaired a senate investigation on hospital negligence and wrongful deaths. Coincidentally, when Cowell called, the Senator was in the middle of an interview with CBS's *60 Minutes*. It took less than sixty minutes for word to hit Wall Street. Medcentric shares gapped down 20 percent and were halted from trading.

Luke hadn't been watching the trading screen and didn't see the collapse of Medcentric reported by CNBC. His eyes were glued to a local news channel, which was reporting on the suicide of Arnie Letts.

CHAPTER 48

Paul Tremont always did the right thing at big events. Brides received Tiffany gifts, Bar Mitzvah boys got savings bonds for college, couples celebrating anniversaries were given expensive spa treatments. And so it wasn't much of a surprise when eight elaborate food baskets from Dean & Deluca arrived at the residence of Arnie Letts's widow. He also made a pledge of $5,000 in Arnie's name to the Mental Health Association of New York.

Tremont huddled with Burns to plot Luke's next career move. The next test would involve a corporate takeover.

"I think we need to test his loyalty some more," Burns announced.

"Yes, I *unexpectedly* dropped in on lunch between Luke and his father, the esteemed Professor Braden. An odd couple. Those two couldn't agree on the time of day," Tremont said.

"I've looked over all of Luke's school records. There's a lot of tension between them. But Luke still seems to be looking for his approval. Though I'm sure it's useless. How many English professors give their blessings to boxers?"

"Or investment bankers! I'm not sure which is worse!" Tremont laughed.

"But between the two, the father is the liar, right?"

"Of course. He's never told Luke where they came from. Some people are ashamed of their past, Dr. Burns."

Tremont smiled again. He knew that Burns had been hiding his own Sicilian heritage, instead masquerading as a descendant of Robert Burns, the great Scots poet.

"We all have our skeletons. Some just jangle louder when someone else peeks into the closet," Tremont added. "Call Luke in here," Tremont said. "Let's push him a little now, so that later we can push him a lot."

Luke hadn't spoken to Tremont since Arnie Letts's funeral, but Tremont sent a letter out to each member of the Tremont organization expressing his sorrow and urging them to make charitable donations in Arnie's memory. According to the letter, Arnie had frequently displayed "erratic behavior." To Luke, the most interesting passage in the letter admitted that the Wall Street world was like "working in a convection oven—it's too damn hot and wild winds sometimes blow us to places where we don't really want to go. That's one reason we are fortunate to have a certified mental professional on our board. If any of you for any reason feel you need to speak to someone on a totally confidential basis, please get in touch with Dr. Burns."

In the week since Letts's suicide, Luke had trouble sleeping. Had his call to Jane Cowell at Bloomberg added to Letts's mental trauma? You pack a million Type A's between Wall Street and Rockefeller Center, dangle millions of dollars in front of their wide eyes, and demand that they each negotiate a better deal with all the others, and you're sure to get some guys flipping out. Hadn't some famous French chef recently killed himself because he was going to lose a Michelin star? He died a three-star chef instead of living with just two. Arnie died for the sake of a Med-centric stent.

Luke walked into Tremont's oval office as the afternoon sun started to descend over Jersey. Tremont and Burns sat waiting to push him around. With his call to Bloomberg, Tremont Advisors must have made up some of its $37.5 million in losses. By following Burns's instructions, Medcentric was no longer a black mark on his record. Or at least, so he thought.

But Tremont still seemed annoyed.

"Didn't we make back the losses after the stock sank again?"

"That's naïve, Luke. We were losing so much when the stock soared that we had to cover our losses." Tremont explained that as the stock jumped by $25 a share, he had instructed the traders to take off the bet, to buy back shares at the higher price. "We couldn't take the chance that Medcentric could soar 50 percent or 100 percent. When you sell a stock short, you have *unlimited* risk, because the share price could go parabolic, theoretically to infinity. When you buy a stock, when you are long, what's the worst that could happen?"

"It could just go to zero."

"Right," Tremont said, enjoying the Socratic dialogue. "That's why you've got to watch those shorts more than anything else. Unlimited risk."

Luke knew this in theory, but it seemed like the theorem for a book, not for a real discussion.

"Where were you when Medcentric took off and we started bleeding?" Tremont asked.

"Yankee Stadium."

"Where in Yankee Stadium?"

"The Boss's box."

"Steinbrenner?"

"Yes."

Tremont stood up and gazed out the window, pointing his finger uptown toward the Bronx. He raised the pitch of his voice slightly. "So let me get the picture here. There you were, hobnobbing in Steinbrenner's skybox, sharing caviar with Senator Leopard's daughter, no doubt, cheering as grown men hit a ball around the grass. Very nice. And you have access to this luxury because of whom?"

"You."

Luke wanted to back out of the room and start over. He should've learned from his father never to get caught in a match of Socratic inquiries. He still didn't feel that he'd made a mistake on Medcentric. And, he'd followed Burns's advice in trying to repair the damage. Burns sat quietly, his stubby legs crossed, taking notes on a yellow pad.

Tremont continued. "And while you're dining at the Ritz, I'm left here with my palms sweaty, my mouth dry, and my heart alternating between beating too fast and beating too slow." His voice got louder. "Why? I'll tell you why!" Now he was shouting. "Because my hotshot new vice president claims he's got proprietary research on Medcentric. Research he got through false pretenses, and research that turns out to be bogus anyway!"

For a moment Luke wanted to trade places with anyone, Lenny from Gresham or even Arnie Letts. His father used to yell at him like this, but this was much worse. His father would scream because of things Luke chose not to do. Not to take math courses, not to accept tutoring in French, not to learn to play the piano. Here Luke was clearly failing at his chosen work.

Tremont sat down behind his desk, picked up a piece of paper and let the moment sink in. After a few moments, Luke gathered the nerve to restart a conversation. He reached for a piece of advice he had once read in GQ.

"I can't change the mistakes, Mr. Tremont. But I'd like to know what we can work on together going forward. I'd like to take up a new project."

Tremont didn't bother looking up. "I'm sure you would."

Silence. Neither Tremont nor Burns seemed interested in making eye contact. Luke tried to compose his next sentence. *Should I ask whether I should leave? Leave the office or leave the building? Should I go through the Medcentric analysis again? Or recount my conversation with Bloomberg?*

Tremont lifted his head. "I have an idea. Maybe you can save your skin, after all." He sounded somewhat more friendly. "I prize men who are quick thinking, guys with ideas overflowing. Surely you must have some idea up your sleeve, Luke. An investment, a scheme, an opportunity. Now you've been here long enough to know we sometimes test the limits of the SEC. So I'm not expecting some plain vanilla recommendation, like 'buy shares of GE.' Tell us where you really think there's money to be made. Just tell us."

"Could I get back to you later today? I want to do some preliminary analysis first," Luke replied, pleased with his quick thinking.

Tremont did not respond well. "Don't give me the hyperrationalistic bullshit, Luke. All those annoying fucking clichés. You're going to 'run the numbers' or 'create some spreadsheets.' Let me tell you, there's nothing creative about a spreadsheet. It may be called 'Excel,' but only mediocrity ever came out of it. If Edison had a spreadsheet, we'd all be sitting in the dark today because nothing would get fucking done. They'd just sit around with their hands on their mice."

Luke knew that Tremont was calling his bluff. His previous encounters with his boss had proved that the man had an internal pendulum that violently swung without notice from rational to irrational. If Luke didn't come up with something in the next minute, he knew he would be packing up his belongings and going—where? Back to his hovel in the Village? To his father's arch stares? To Delancy's gym?

Suddenly, Luke had an idea that could save him from ever going back to his former life and the basement apartment.

As Luke began to unveil his idea, Stuart Burns and Paul Tremont stared at him, mouths agape, stunned by the opportunity.

"You're joking! How can you know this?" Dr. Burns said, his eyes bugging out so far Luke thought they might be dangling by the optic nerve. Tremont was only slightly more composed.

"What do they call it?"

Luke said slowly, "They call it STATE SECRET."

Tremont and Burns nodded. "Nice touch," Tremont murmured.

"Here's what Hardiz told me," Luke said softly, with a little shame in his voice. He would simply describe the system, then leave it up to Tremont to follow up. "STATE SECRET is their security system to prevent insider trading. Apparently before anyone can execute any trade over five million dollars, a Gresham computer in Bermuda cross-references the stock with all the personal accounts of the managing directors. The system will quash any trader who tries to buy a stock for somebody when he has a conflict of interest. They don't even know it, but Gresham monitors their personal wealth 24/7. STATE SECRET keeps them honest."

"Brilliant," Tremont responded. "But what are you suggesting?" Tremont knew damn well what he would do with the information. Order Christian Playa and his secret operations boys to tap into the Bermuda line, which would give them a quick heads up on any major trades. Since Gresham handled twenty percent of the action on the New York Stock Exchange, this would be like having God hand you racing tips five minutes before the windows closed at Belmont or Saratoga.

Luke leaned back in the armchair. He felt dirty, sharing Hardiz's platform. But surely Hardiz must have all sorts of security protection built around the STATE SECRET platform. And besides, Luke had not taken any confidentiality oath. It was foolish of Hardiz to blab about his security systems. Nonetheless, Luke refused to point Tremont any farther. He would not state the obvious: hack into the computers. Instead he offered a more benign suggestion.

"Mr. Tremont, I think STATE SECRET is the kind of system that Tremont Advisors should adopt. It would reduce internal conflicts of interest and help the efficacy of our SEC compliance operations."

"You're a real Boy Scout, Luke." Tremont said. But he was salivating. Luke had just dropped a windfall in his lap, and had saved his job after all.

As Luke was about to leave, Ryan the head trader poked his nose into the office. Ryan was always permitted to interrupt. He looked taller than usual. Must've been a good day in the pits. His green eyes flashed.

Tremont didn't have to verbalize the question. He just turned up his large palms, shrugged a shoulder, gestures that immediately translated into "How's the baby?"

"Up 6.1 percent. Good looking baby." Each afternoon like a ritual, Ryan came by to deliver the news. Each day was a new day. A year or so earlier, Tremont started using the metaphor of a newborn baby to describe the daily results of trading. Sometimes the P&L looked like a "handsome young slugger." Or a "bouncing bambino." On a bad day, though, the portfolio could look like a "hairy, infant weasel" or a "skinny baboon."

"Best day in a long time," Tremont remarked. "Go out tonight and toast with the boys," he said to Ryan. He knew Ryan was gay, but Tremont didn't care. Referring to the "boys" was his way of telling Ryan that he knew.

Ryan continued the ritual by placing the daily results and the updated "playbook of prosperity" in the vault right outside Tremont's office. Tremont interrupted. "Hold it, Ryan." Tremont walked over, licked an envelope, sealed it, and tossed it into the safe.

Luke wondered what else went into the safe, but averted his eyes and started to make his way out of the office.

"Just a moment, Luke," Tremont said. "Sit back down. Now I have a new project for you. It's a takeover operation. Another test."

Tremont explained that he was looking to acquire a food company that was privately held. "Time to get it into shape and take it public."

"Sounds reasonable," Luke said, thinking of Safeway and some other companies that had gone through leveraged buyouts, only to be spun out again as publicly traded companies. What's the name of the company?"

"I'm sure you know it. Very *familiar* in fact. You might even say it's a member of your family already."

Luke titled his head like the old RCA dog.

"It's the Mars Company."

"But that's my father!"

"Precisely," Tremont answered.

CHAPTER 49

Nick Larsen was tired of the yo-yo he thought that he and Carmody were riding. First, the fouled-up interview with Senator Leopard, second, his daughter in New York, and then this cruise ship tour with Tito Marti. He was slumping against the gold-plated elevators on the *Carnival Valor* when he saw Carmody talking on his phone, waving his hands toward his partner.

"This could be it," Carmody said.

"I'm tired of this chase. It's a dead end. A waste," he mumbled. He looked over at some swaying palm trees. "It's Margaritaville."

"Not anymore." Carmody pulled Larsen by the arm out to the promenade deck and passed him the telephone. "Tell him, Ronnie."

Ronnie Funk, the brilliant Rasta guy at the FBI, explained: "We've been trying to analyze the remains of any electronic devices found at the explosion site. Just this morning, a security guard at the D.C. Metro found a chip. Believe it or not, he was chasing a rat near the tracks when he saw a glint. The chip contains a video clip from inside the subway car. We think we might be able to trace it to Sara Hartman's cellphone camera." Funk's nerdy, analytical style made his findings sound downright dull.

"And what does it show?" Larsen asked.

"I don't know yet. We just got it an hour ago. Most of the pixels seem to be damaged, so we're seeing just a smattering of dots," Funk said.

"Oh, just swell," Larsen moaned. "Get me out of this high-tech FBI. It's a crock. We used to chase bad guys. Now I'm supposed to chase pixies."

"Pixels," Carmody corrected him.

Larsen placed his hand over the phone and turned to Carmody. "Face it, James. We don't have shit. Let's catch a cab back to the airport."

Carmody was disappointed, too, hoping that Funk would have something juicier than a badly damaged computer chip. With a sigh, he looked at a stream of passengers boarding the Carnival ship and wished he could join them for their Caribbean vacation.

They heard the whiny squawk of Funk's voice through the phone. Larsen removed his hand from the speaker. "We're running it through the Lacunator right now. I think the Lacunator might be able to fill in some blanks. Just give me ten minutes."

Larsen had had enough. But Carmody was more patient. "Nick, go explore the ship. Come back in ten. Give Ronnie a little time, will ya?"

Larsen trundled off, looking for the lunch buffet. He'd have no trouble blending in with the passengers, many of whom were overweight retirees, also wearing cheap Hawaiian shirts.

Carmody waited for the electronic breakthrough. He strolled toward the back of the ship and squinted at South Beach. That's where he belonged, instead of on a Carnival "Fun Ship." Carmody wanted to cruise the late-night scene in SoBe, which made D.C.'s DuPont Circle look like a rock exhibit at the Smithsonian. He would love to show off his eight-pack abs on Collins Avenue.

Ronnie Funk called again. "We have a home run, dudes. Or at least a double."

"Hold it, Ronnie. Lemme grab Larsen," Carmody said. He waved to his partner. They both listened to the speakerphone.

"The Lacunator came through! It couldn't fill in all the pixels, but enough of them. We have an image. A face."

"What's it look like?" Larsen asked.

"I'll send it to your phone right now," Funk said.

Twenty seconds later, a photo showed up on Carmody's phone. A person entering a car on the D.C. Metro holding something. Another image followed, displaying an explosion of twisted plastic and fire. Carmody and Larsen recognized the suspect. The Lacunator had produced a remarkably clear photo of a woman. Cori Leopard.

CHAPTER 50

In the oval office, Luke fell back into the armchair. Why the hell would Tremont be interested in Mars? After chasing high-tech and medical stocks, why would an old candy company have any appeal? It seemed beneath Paul Tremont's stature to be discussing Skittles.

But Tremont was a masterful storyteller and soon had Luke intrigued. "Mars is based in McLean, Virginia. So is the CIA. But guess which one is more secretive? You guessed it, Mars. Old Forrest Mars, the son of the founder, and the one who invented M&Ms, died in 1999, but his handprints are still there. He was a shark. He went to England and worked for Nestlé and Tobler. Know what he came back with?" "Secrets! Recipes! Know-how! Intellectual capital! You ever read *Charlie and the Chocolate Factory?*"

"Like the Willy Wonka movie?" Luke asked.

"And do you know why Wonka fires all the human factory workers? Because machines don't steal ideas. Only humans do!" Tremont announced triumphantly. "And Forrest ran the place like Mussolini, the conveyor belts always ran on time. He was ruthless about quality, too. He'd throw out millions of M&Ms if the writing looked faded or smudged. After he bought a pet food company, he forced his staff to taste the kibble!"

Luke gulped, and Tremont relaxed for a moment. "Don't worry, Luke. I'm not interested in buying Alpo."

"Very interesting, Mr. Tremont, but what makes the company valuable as a financial proposition?"

Tremont was waiting for this question. "Forrest Mars demanded efficiency. When he took full control of the company in 1964, shortly after the Kennedy assassination, he dropped to his knees and prayed. He also fired his French chef, sold the fancy art collection, and forced all his employees to punch the clock. Every dime was accounted for. No one flew first class. Heavy-handed? Yes. But it turned the Mars Company into a global giant."

Tremont moved behind his desk and pulled out a file marked "SECRET." He tossed a binder to Luke. Luke flipped through pages of financial statements. Bold red and blue charts seemed to show profit margins shrinking and revenues flattening.

"That's because old Forrest Mars died, and his sons aren't made of the same steel. Sometimes sons can't follow in their father's footsteps, I guess."

Luke nodded, his face flushing a little.

"So," Tremont continued, "we need to get in there, take over the company, and restore the principles of Forrest Mars. That'll get those margins back and add value. We might have to fire some people, but that's a story as old as Willy Wonka. I need your help."

Tremont went on to assign Luke the initial task—he was to research the unprofitable divisions and products such as the soft drinks that didn't sell well or the international divisions that didn't turn a profit. "Does Mars have to be in one hundred countries?" Tremont asked. "Is it the fucking UN? Are they in Albania because of pride or because of profit? Hubris kills profits, remember that." Tremont also asked Luke to inspect the nonprofit activities engaged in by the Mars Company. Luke scribbled notes and wondered how he would get information on such a secretive organization.

"You understand the assignment?" Tremont asked.

"Yes." But he was confused by one thing that Tremont mentioned in the history lesson. "What did Forrest Mars pray for in 1964? Lyndon Johnson?"

Tremont laughed. "Johnson? Hopeless. According to eyewitnesses, Forrest Mars fell to his knees and literally prayed for the success of Snickers and Milky Ways."

Luke glided out of Tremont's office with the SECRET charts and his notes. It was what every young executive craves, a new adventure. A chance to redeem himself.

In the office, Burns observed, "Very elaborate. Very persuasive. I didn't know you were so interested in candy."

"I'm not. I'm going to tear up the relationship between Luke and his father, the Mars Professor of English Literature at Columbia. By siccing Luke on the Mars Company, I can isolate the boy."

"The boy's got a tough outer shell," Burns replied.

"But I need to break it down to get him ready for the final test."

"Castro?"

"Yes, the Fidel test. After Mars, our young man is going to destroy Fidel Castro."

CHAPTER 51

Three thirty in the morning. That's when Luke's phone rang. Someone must be dead, he thought, as he reached across Cori, who was wrapped in his 500-count cotton sheets, and grabbed the phone. It was a nurse at NYU Medical Center. Buck Roberts was in the cardiac center, recovering from an emergency bypass. He had no insurance and no next of kin. They had found in his pocket a birthday card from Luke.

Luke and Cori rushed down to the hospital. A fair-haired young resident with bags under his eyes met them in the waiting room. He was blunt. "Your friend's probably on his deathbed. The surgeons did a bypass, but open-heart surgery causes a lot of stress to the rest of the body. For a sixty-two-year-old man he looks like he's got a lotta miles on him. Tough life."

"Why didn't they just do an angio or insert some stents?" Luke asked, his floppy hair tousled and matted from what had been a good night's sleep. He'd learned a lot in his research for Medcentric.

The young resident was caught off guard. "Are you a doctor?"

"I know just a little bit, that's all." He didn't want to get into a discussion. He just wanted to see his old friend.

Cori whispered to Luke, "I thought you said Buck was in his eighties?"

Luke pushed past the resident. A skinny black kid turned the corner, his eyes lighting up when he saw Luke. Henry Beetle, Luke's occasional cornerman. They hugged and Luke introduced Henry to Cori.

"Buck's not doing well," Beetle reported. "he's talking weird shit. Maybe it's the drugs."

Luke was surprised to find Buck looking, well, pretty good for Buck. His eyes were closed, there was a tube in his nose, and all sorts of machines beeped around him. He looked like he was connected to the control room at LaGuardia. Luke tapped his wrist. No response.

"Hey, Buck," he whispered, then repeated it louder. He looked up at Cori, who was mesmerized by the EKG lines and oxygen readings, as he placed his hand on Buck's deeply lined forehead.

Suddenly, Buck's left hand rose. He murmured, "Counterpunch, champ. Counterpunch." Then his eyes opened, and Luke saw his baby blues twinkling. Buck was going to be all right. Luke introduced Buck to Cori, and Buck winked at Luke to signal, "nice catch."

"Hey, Buck, why did the doctor think you were sixty-two? You're at least eighty-five, no?"

Buck grinned mischievously and begin to speak in a raspy voice. "You think they'd perform surgery on an eighty-five-year-old man without insurance? I know those doctors and HMOs. They'd figure he's lived long enough, let him die. But if they think I'm sixty-two, they don't want to do nothing and get sued."

Street smart.

Then Buck became quiet. He grimaced, but denied that he felt much pain. The morphine drip was steady.

"What's wrong, Buck? Do you want me to get the nurse?" Luke asked.

"No. But I want you out of there."

Out of *there?* "You mean you want us to leave?"

"I want you to get the hell out of Tremont," his scratchy voice said. "You're too young and naïve for that guy. You know him through Wall Street, but I've seen this guy promotin' fights and hangin' with gangsters, and it's a throwback to the old days. The days when fighters lost limbs for not throwin' fights. Ever hear of Tony DiSeppio?"

Luke shook his head.

"Let your old coach tell you about Tremont and DiSeppio.

"He was my fighter. Good kid. Shoplifted some from Woolworth's, but a good kid. Back in the late '60s, Tremont wants to break into the fight racket, he signs Tony D. for a big fight at the Garden—"

Buck was starting to work himself up, and Luke was getting worried whether the old man's body could take it.

"Tony's mother dies all of a sudden. Heart attack, I think. Tony naturally wants to go to the funeral, but Tremont says he's got too much money on the fight to let Tony out of the contract. The kid tells him to shove it. Goes to his mama's funeral. Two months later, they find Tony D. in the Passaic River in Jersey. Tremont wasn't too upset when they dragged Tony's body up the riverbank. I don't believe any of that shit about Red Cross Man of the Year." Buck took a deep, labored breath.

Luke was stunned. He knew Tremont played hardball with his portfolio, maybe even stretched the SEC rules, but Buck's story was ridiculous. He looked over at Cori. "Must be the morphine speaking," he whispered.

After a minute or two, Buck resumed his story. "After Tony died, I asked some of the boys I knew in Vegas to check out your Paul Tremont. They told me that Tremont was deep into Cuba in the late '50s. He actually ran arms to Castro, arranged financing for Castro. Why? Because he thought he'd get the concessions in Havana: the boxing, the casinos. He was going to take over when Castro ran Lansky off the island."

As Buck told his tale, he started to resemble a Rip van Winkle character, waking up from a long sleep with only memories of the past. "Luke, don't you remember anything I told you about the great Cuban fighters? Kid Gavilan in the '50s was a national hero in Cuba. Invented the bolo punch, a looping uppercut that confused the hell out of Robinson and inspired Ali."

"I remember, Buck, but what's that got to do with Tremont?"

"So Castro pushes out Batista in '59. I was there! I WAS THERE! Goddammit, I was there. I used to go to Cuba twice a month, recruiting, training. Three days after the revolution, there's a pro boxing match scheduled. What does Castro do? The Communist? He says the show must go on. He invites his brother Raul and Che Guevara ringside! The girls are parading nearly nude, the revolutionary soldiers are carrying guns, the palm trees swaying, the congas drumming. Rum overflowing. Some soldier fires his rifle into the air with joy, and everyone ducks. Then everyone laughs. Greatest night of my goddamn life. But do you know who else is there?"

"Tell me, Buck."

"Your friend Paul Tremont. White suit, fat cigar, trilling his "r"s like he's the ambassador from the Queen of England. He sees all of this and thinks: "It's mine. Cuban boxing and the casinos are mine. Fidel's going to throw out Lanksy and the wops, and put me in charge. That's my payback."

Suddenly, Buck arched his back, his face twisted. "I don't have to tell you what happens next, right? Castro slams the door on professional boxing, gambling, professional anything. He announces Cuban National Decree 82a: 'Professional sports enriches the few at the expense of the many.'"

Wow, that was strange, Luke thought. Buck actually quoting a statute? "So what happened to Paul Tremont when Castro signed the decree?"

"He loses his first fortune. I don't know what he had. Maybe twenty million. He was no Lansky, but he had a lot. So he gets angry. Real angry. Starts backing JFK and begging JFK to do something. Becomes a JFK wannabe, part of the entourage, like Peter Lawford and Sinatra. Even starts acting like JFK, the haircut, the gestures, everything. Joins up with the Miami Cubans to lobby the State Department and Senate. When the Bay of Pigs comes, he's sure he's gonna get his money back, but that turns into a fuckup." Luke noticed that Cori was nowhere to be seen.

"But here's what you gotta remember, Luke. Your friend Tremont helped Castro and then tried to nail him for one reason: to make money for himself and to control all the money in Havana. He didn't give a damn about the Cuban people. To him, they were a bunch of Tony DiSeppio's, just something to dredge up from the river."

Buck's voice started to drift off. Luke looked down at his old trainer, his coach, and whispered, "I'll come back this afternoon. Promise."

Maybe Buck's memory of Tremont was right, but that was over forty years ago. What in the world did these old stories have to do with a hedge fund king who was on the shortlist for a Nobel Peace Prize?

CHAPTER 52

"Cori Leopard?" Larsen was angry. After twenty-five years on the force, he hated to be snowed. Even more galling was that it was a young woman who fooled him.

"My gut told me she was telling the truth," he said.

"I'm usually pretty impressed with your gut," Carmody replied, looking down at the paunch that bulged from his partner's shirt.

They both realized that they were about to plunge headfirst into the crucible, a crucible filled with heat, bile, and the black ink from journalists who would be jumping all over this story: "Senator's Daughter Arrested in Terrorist Attack." Their lives were about to change. They would be applauded and denounced by every media outlet from ABC to Al Jazeera to the *Weekly Reader*.

Larsen felt like puking. He was planning on retiring with his pension. He had already hung enough scalps on his wall, enough bad guys caught and prosecuted. He didn't need the high-profile stuff anymore. Twenty-five years ago he thought he'd turn into a hero. Now he just wanted to crawl back to the lunch buffet with the retirees. But he had no choice. Carmody and Larsen dashed to Miami International and flew to New York, handcuffs at the ready.

Leaving Buck dozing in his hospital bed, Cori and Luke went back to his apartment. The sun was starting to climb over Queens and peek through the apartment buildings on the East Side, shining shards of early morning light across Central Park. A few weeks before, Luke had bought a telescope for gazing across the park and across the sky. From his window, he could see landmarks like the Central Park Zoo, FAO Schwarz, and even the co-op where Jackie Onassis last lived.

Since leaving Buck's room, Luke and Cori had not spoken. Luke was mulling over Buck's history of Paul Tremont. If it was true, did it make any difference to him? Why should ancient history matter? And besides, all those machines plugged into Buck—beeping, zapping, encoding—were they making Buck loopy?

Luke looked over at Cori, her hair sweeping across her shoulders as she slid back into the king-size bed. "What do you think, Cori? What if Buck's right?"

Cori brushed her hand through her hair. "Luke, I come to this from a different place than you. First of all, because of my father, I don't doubt that *important* people involved in politics do illegal things. I believe accusations even if they're in the *National Enquirer*. Don't you remember when we met? I'm the one who was denouncing Tremont on the Vegas strip for strip-mining and cutting down rain forests. But I've decided to use his money and power to improve things. I've got ten million dollars of his money in my checkbook. I don't care whether he's shaking down cops or shagging prostitutes. All I know is when I'm done, I'll have spent at least $10 million of his money helping needy people or cleaning up toxic dumps in Mexico or other stuff that's important to me."

"You don't feel like a hypocrite?"

"Are you kidding? Just because I'm carrying a Chanel purse instead of a canvas backpack with "Sierra Club" stitched on it?"

"So, you're using him? Is that it?"

"Exactly," she said with a wide smile. She leaned across the bed and pulled Luke toward her by his belt. "Now, I'd like to use you, if that's okay."

Luke started to feel warm all over, especially around his belt. He leaned one knee on the bed and bent down to kiss her shoulder. She slipped his belt off with her teeth and took a moment to admire the Tiffany buckle.

Crunch! A noise so jarring it sounded like a shark chomping on a rowboat filled the apartment. Followed by thuds. Cori dropped her grip on Luke's belt, and he instinctively straightened his back and looked out the window curtains for a clue. But the horrifying noises were not coming from outside. Before either Luke or Cori could identify it, two strangers burst into the bedroom, guns drawn, shouting:

"FBI! GET DOWN! FACE DOWN ON THE BED!" shouted a black man.

Cori, inclined to oppose orders, cast her palms outward and yelled: "What the hell are you doing?"

A heavy, white man charged toward her, ready to knock her to the ground like a linebacker. Luke's reflexes flew into action. He stepped in front of the man and threw a right cross that landed on his temple. The man crumpled and Luke stood peering down, trembling. It was the same punch he had thrown at Perez. The black man fired a shot at the window, which shattered and sent a thousand chips raining down on Columbus Circle. Five other guys in FBI flak jackets rushed into the bedroom.

Luke threw up his hands. "Okay. Okay. What the fuck is going on here?"

James Carmody helped lift Nick Larsen to his feet and fetched some ice for his head. Larsen staggered to a chair, while the other FBI agents handcuffed Cori and Luke. Carmody pointed to Cori, who was shaking in her slinky negligee. "She is charged with conspiracy to commit terrorism. And not just conspiracy. Murder One."

Carmody continued, "You!" pointing to Luke. "Resisting arrest."

The agents shoved Cori and Luke into an unmarked car and raced them to the FBI headquarters in lower Manhattan. On arrival, a gruff, young agent threw an old black phone at Cori and Luke. "Go ahead. Call for help. You'll need it."

Cori knew the call she had to make. She dialed her father's home office. Then Senator Leopard's Washington office. Finally some eager beaver answered at the constituent's office in Palm Beach. The Senator was off fishing in the Everglades and had left his cellphone behind.

The holding pens were dank and smelled of a combination of sweat and putrid incense trees that cabbies love to dangle from their mirrors.

CHAPTER 53

"Did they get her?"

"Yes, of course. Although we didn't count on her father being AWOL," said Christian Playa. He was speaking from the Staten Island Ferry, just a few ripples away from the Statue of Liberty. It was hard for the FBI to track a cellphone call to the ferry.

"Yes, I'm losing patience with him. I may need to buy myself a new senator. Are you ready for the next step?"

"I need a little more time. To set things up. And I have to lay low. I can't raise my profile just because the FBI's locked up Cori. One of these days they could track down my face on a computer chip too."

"I've been waiting long enough, Christian. Forty-seven years."

"Yes, Oriana. I know how you feel. But we'll get Paul Tremont out of the way soon enough," assured Playa, who was remarkably calm for a double agent straddling two vicious and rich people.

"Sooner than soon enough. As long as he's around, Fidel is not safe,"

Luke placed his first call to Buck. "Buck, are you okay? No setbacks, right?"

"No, champ," he whispered. "But I'm worried about you." Buck had the television on and was flipping through the channels at a furious pace. The story of Luke and Cori's arrest was inescapable. Even the Weather Channel ran a scroll about them. "Senator's daughter and boyfriend accused of terrorism."

Luke urged Buck to turn it off. "It's bullshit. I don't know who they really meant to arrest, but it can't be Cori and me."

"I'm sure you're right about you, Luke," whispered Buck. "But how can you be so sure about the girl? Maybe you were sucker punched."

Luke said good bye and then felt nauseated, not by the smells of sweat and fear, but by a sickening realization that Buck could be right. He looked through a soundproof window at Cori, her jaw fixed, her eyes refusing to give up a single tear. Luke tried to remember every data point on her. His brain assembled a montage. Meeting on the airplane from Vegas, and being both puzzled and enthralled by her radical fight-the-man attitude. Holding hands with her while she assessed the Boys' Club and eagerly took out her checkbook. The rollicking romp at the Hudson Hotel when he was elated about cracking the Medcentric code. But, in fact, he knew so little about her. Why hadn't he asked more about the father she hated? The mother who was murdered? The years spent in Latin America, supposedly fighting rural poverty and toxic runoff?

Carmody and Larsen tried to delay a bail hearing, but a press-friendly federal judge happily opened his hearing room. Every reporter and every editor in the country wanted a piece of this event. Even the obituary editor for the *Times* wanted a pass, claiming that it would provide better insight into those who died in the D.C. Metro explosion. It had all the elements of a boffo hit. A senator's daughter, an athlete, terrorism, Boy Scouts. By the time of the hearing, Senator Harold Leopard had put down his fishing rod and flown to the hearing along with his longstanding lawyer, a dry, Waspy lobbyist who was more used to getting drunken senators out of the D.C. holding pens. Carmody and Larsen sat behind the assistant attorney general in one of New York's grandest courtrooms, Carmody perfectly erect, Larsen slouching, still half-dazed from Luke's blow to his temple. The painting of Lady Justice on the wall appeared so majestic it could have been painted by Raphael five hundred years ago at the Vatican.

The U.S. attorney, a tall, bald man in his fifties had a pronounced speech impediment. His "r's" came out like "w's."

When he began to speak and the defect became apparent, Carmody panicked and looked at Larsen. "What the hell is this? Are we gonna lose this on account of him?"

Larsen smiled painfully. "It helps us. When he says, "tewwow" and "muwdew," everybody listens very closely. It's—what do you call it—subliminal."

Sure enough, the prosecutor emphasized those words in every sentence. He pointed the judge to the available evidence against Cori, the computer images from Ronnie Funk's laboratory showing Cori entering the soon-to-be-obliterated Metro car, the CL sticker, and assorted photographs of her in different stages of social combat: fatigues in front of the U.N., a beret in front of the U.S. Embassy in El Salvador, photos of her protesting against Paul Tremont on the Vegas Strip. In the photos she looked humorless, but not menacing. The prosecutor asked for bail to be set at $2 million.

Senator Leopard sat behind Cori, alternating between a stoic defiance and resting his head in his hands. He was confused about everything. Cori had done some stupid things in her life and had an aversion to her father's politics that seemed downright Biblical in its sweep and fury. But murder? Before flying up to New York from D.C. he had consulted with his crack political adviser, David Toms, a guy whose cigarette-stained fingers had touched every voting machine from Tampa to Coconut Grove.

"David, what do I do? I'm stuck, right?"

"Yeah, you can't totally support your daughter without looking like you're trashing your law-and-order reputation. After all, this is the People v. Senator Harold Leopard's daughter. You're trapped on the scales of justice."

"You know, the nice thing about getting old is you can throw away your damn scale. I guess I'm going against the People and with Cori," Leopard decided.

Washington Post editorialists applauded his stance. But no one knew his real motivation. Was it simple boredom after forty years of politics that was inspiring a new attitude? "To hell with the People; I don't care if I get reelected." Or was it, as the cynics wrote, a careful calculation that he'd gain more votes by sticking with his kin than abandoning her for some abstract principle like "fighting crime and terror?"

The judge sided with the prosecution and banged his gavel like a Sotheby's auctioneer, to the tune of $2,000,000 in bail. Cori refused to show emotion, but her father appeared not to be so stony and heartless after all. He wiped away a tear, while the reporters punched their stories into their BlackBerries.

Luke watched all of this on a small television as he awaited his hearing before the same judge. His mind spun as Buck's question about Cori bounced around in his head. He thought about bail. Where would Cori come up with the money? A girl in her twenties, who spent most of her adult life holding placards, did not generally have a big stash of cash. Nor did her father. According to Cori, Senator Leopard had blown most of his savings on mistresses and sputtering tech start-ups. And so Luke was surprised when a new source emerged to rescue Cori from her prison cell.

A few hours later, Cori shocked the judge and the bailiffs by slapping a checkbook on the desk, right in front of the judge, and wrote a check for $2 million.

"Young lady, what is this?" the judge asked.

"I'm authorized to write at my discretion funds up to $10 million," she said. Though still defiant in tone, she looked tired.

The judge asked where the money came from. How could she cobble together $10 million? He looked at the prosecutor who signaled a vague gesture to Carmody and Larsen that surely meant, "look into this."

The prosecutor then walked over to them and whispered angrily, "Twace the account. Could be tewwowist money."

Cori spoke softly and pointed to the checkbook. "This comes from Paul Tremont. I am an employee, and I have authority to use the funds for this purpose."

In fact, she did not have permission. But Cori was willing to take a chance. "Call him," she said. "Here's his number."

The judge, the prosecutor, Carmody, Larsen, and the bailiffs crammed into the judge's chambers and shook their heads. "Weediculous," the prosecutor barked.

The judge just stared at Cori, trying to fathom this odd girl with the dodgy past. He decided to call her bluff.

He called and immediately reached Paul Tremont, who was rocking in his Kennedy chair. It was a brief and profane conversation.

"Yes, I give my goddamn permission. I'm a man of my word. I gave her discretion. I'll go along. Yeah, send a goddamn affidavit to my lawyer."

Tremont's phone rang again. The judge asked another question.

"Yes, goddamn it. She can fucking bail out Braden, too."

Paul Tremont was fuming. He was barking, almost howling at Burns: "How could this happen?"

Meanwhile, Cori and Luke fought their way past the media throng into a limousine and escaped to an old beach house on the Jersey Shore owned by Tremont Advisors. For an hour and a half, as the car sped down the Garden State Parkway, Luke held Cori's hand and tried to shake off one repellent question: What had Cori been doing near that Metro car?

CHAPTER 54

The wind was howling in Bay Head, New Jersey, spraying the tops of the small sand dunes against the windows of the weather-beaten, shingled estate. Tremont bought it in 1970 from an Italian guy who owned half the boardwalk concessions in Asbury Park. The 1969 race riots destroyed Asbury Park and tossed the owner into a financial vise. Tremont was happy to help out by buying the man's properties for a about a quarter of their pre-riot prices. The Bay Head beachfront estate gave Tremont a convenient and quiet hiding place halfway to Atlantic City's casinos.

Cori and Luke threw their duffel bags on the king-size bed in a large room facing the Atlantic, but they might as well have been facing different coasts. Cori could feel a freeze in their relationship. But Luke could not tell her that he was worried about her possible connection to the explosion. Instead he confessed to being nervous about the follow-up court date, and worried about how they could salvage their careers at Tremont. After pacing the living room for an hour, Cori grabbed a plaid blanket from the cedar closet and trudged out to a sand dune. Luke looked down at her from the bedroom and thought he saw her crying. He sat on the windowsill feeling torn between rushing down to embrace her or hopping the next train to someplace he'd never been. He took in the aroma of the Jersey Shore: the salt, the reeds, and the scent of bluefish and flounder. As a boy, his father would sometimes take him down to the shore for a weekend, to Point Pleasant or Avon-by-the-Sea. The only physical moments with his father came when they dove into the waves. But this time, the Shore made him feel lonely, sick, and confused.

He heard a rumble and saw Cori look upward. A sudden thunderstorm? The sand started sweeping up. Luke rushed down the steps and out the screen door toward Cori. Then he saw it. The Black Hawk that had taken him from the roof of the Gresham Building into Paul Tremont's world. As the aircraft descended, the wind fired granules of sand like pellets from a shotgun. Luke reached Cori just in time to shield her face with the blanket, and they huddled together as the Black Hawk touched down in front of them. Out of the chopper strode Paul Tremont, his jaw locked in place, his lips pressed together.

The roar of the chopper drowned out the surf. Tremont didn't bother trying to speak above the racket, he just jutted his arm forward, pointing to the house. Luke and Cori followed him into the living room, brushing sand from their eyelashes and eyebrows.

Tremont had fumed during the chopper ride from Manhattan, angry that someone had interfered with his game plan. He kept banging his fist against the thin wall of the aircraft, which made the pilot nervous. Despite his expensive and far-flung team of consultants and informants, he was as surprised as Luke by the arrests. He hated to admit surprise. He always wanted his staff and his competitors to think he was omniscient. He pondered his choices. He had just gotten off the phone with Burns. "Fire them," Burns had suggested. "Denounce them in public."

Typical Burns. Cover your ass, and don't worry if you lose track of your ultimate goals.

"Look, I certainly don't believe that Luke has done anything wrong. Not even the FBI thinks so. Do you?" Tremont asked.

"No."

"Luke is guilty of being in his bedroom at the wrong time, when the FBI barged in. Besides, he's our key to get Castro."

Without Luke, Tremont felt his plan to destroy Castro's regime and lead Havana to the glory of its past would unravel.

Cori was useful, of course. She improved his standing among left-wingers in Congress, the environmentalists and the psuedosocialist do-gooders, and she was a bridge to Senator Leopard. Tremont might need some help from the Foreign Relations Committee in order to consolidate his grasp on Havana. Cori and her father might not get along, but he would always take his daughter's calls. But how heavy was Cori's baggage? Allegations of murder. Terror. He was horrified that she could ruin his good name. Just before landing on the beach he had called Christian Playa.

"Who blew up the Metro?" Tremont demanded.

"I have no idea, but I doubt Cori Leopard blew it up."

In the house, Tremont put his finger an inch from Luke's chest. "How could you let this happen? I've spent a lifetime building myself into a brand, the Tremont brand. That stands for honesty, charity, and bravery. I've got a desk full of medals, honorary degrees, and thank-you notes to prove it. But in one day, you and your girlfriend grab that drawer and dump the honors, dump my reputation into the East River."

Luke was not going to interrupt or even defend himself until Tremont had finished. Ali's rope-a-dope strategy goes to the corner office. He would let Tremont wear himself out, and then try to devise a prudent response. Still, Luke felt pretty sure that he would be axed.

Tremont continued his rant: "You thought you cost me money on the Medcentric debacle? That was nothing! That was just money. A measly—what was it?—$30 million. That's squirrel nuts to me. But now you're costing me my *name*. When this is over, you may be cleared by the judge, and you can go back to your basement apartment. The nice thing about living in the basement is that you can always go home again. No one stops you from walking *down* those steps. But when this is over, where do I go to get my reputation back? That's walking *up* a hundred stories, putting back in place what it took forty years to build. You and Cori have been a demolition crew. A giant wrecking ball crashing into my castle." He raised his right arm, sweeping it across a stainless steel counter, knocking the teapot, creamer and the sugar bowl to the floor.

The crash told Luke that it was now his turn. But what could he say? Surely, Tremont didn't think that Luke had anything to do with the Metro explosion. Nor could he think that Luke deliberately orchestrated the arrests or the publicity.

"Mr. Tremont, I feel miserable about what's happened. But, sir, I really would like you to tell me what I did wrong?" Luke asked contritely.

Tremont's nostrils flared. He answered the question with a story. "You know how Bobby Kennedy made his name? By helping Joe McCarthy, the most hated man in America, run his witch hunt. But Bobby quickly realized he was in bad company, he could *smell* he was in bad company. He then switched sides, changed his target, and started going after the Teamsters. Luke, to be successful in business or politics, you don't need great eyesight, you don't need good hearing, you don't need a big dick. But what you do need is a fine sense of smell. You need to run away from the guys who will drag you down. I believe in guilt by association. If you're too stupid to get away from guilty people, you deserve to be found guilty yourself."

"But what does that have to do with me?"

"Ms. Leopard. I don't know if she's guilty of murder, or just guilty of jaywalking. But she's a risk I can't take, and neither can you. I've been in business a long time. She doesn't smell good to me."

Tremont wanted to deepen Luke's doubts about Cori. "I have contacts at the FBI telling me that they've got a strong case. A polygraph will lock it up."

None of this was true. Tremont's informants hadn't cracked into the files yet. So why was he dripping poison? It was part of the larger strategy, the same logic that earned Luke the Mars assignment.

"I'm not sure I understand," Luke said. "Are you firing us?"

"No. Just Ms. Leopard. You've got more work to do."

Luke saw his reflection in the stainless steel refrigerator. His shoulders looked slumped, and he seemed dwarfed by the taller Tremont. He felt paralyzed because he couldn't be sure that the FBI was wrong.

Then Tremont made an odd request: "Go out to the beach and get in the Black Hawk. It'll fly you back to New York."

"But what about Cori?"

"I'm going to meet with her next. You head out to the helicopter."

"Let me speak with her first," Luke insisted.

"You've had all day to talk to her."

"I know, Mr. Tremont, but I'm not going to just leave Cori. I owe her a good-bye. I'm sure you understand that."

He walked into the living room where Cori sat slumped on a striped sofa. Behind her, on the other side of the window, Luke could see the Black Hawk blades rotating slowly, even gently. Luke looked into her eyes. He told her that Tremont was going to let her go. She nodded her head gently, but then he saw her gulp hard.

"Luke, don't you see what's going on here? He's turned us into pawns. He's trying to separate us."

"Can you blame him? When he offered us jobs, he didn't bargain for an FBI arrest and a trial."

"I think he'd be splitting us up anyway, even without the FBI." She had tears in her eyes. "He's got big plans for you. I don't know what, but something bigger than candy bars. He wants to make you even more pliable. And he's doing it by stripping you of your lifelines. Right now, since you don't really talk to your father, and since Buck is in the ICU, I'm your only buddy."

Cori fought back the urge to cry, but a single tear escaped and rolled down her right cheek. Luke kissed the tear and licked his salty lips. Life was a game of odds, of probabilities. What were the odds that Cori was a killer? Tiny. Like a single grain of sand. He wished he could take that one single remaining granule and make it go away like the tear that he licked off his lips.

As Luke and Cori said good-bye in the living room in Bay Head, James Carmody stood on Christopher Street in Greenwich Village. He didn't hear his phone ringing. It was Ronnie Funk at the Hoover Building. Funk left an urgent voice mail. "James, call me right away. There's been a huge development in the Leopard case."

CHAPTER 55

Buck Roberts was recovering quickly for an eighty-five-year-old man. Of course, the doctors were not impressed because they were told he was in his early '60s.

"Are you sure you're just sixty-two, honey?" asked a heavy-set, black nurse who was scanning the chart dangling from his hospital bed.

Buck barked back: "Yeah. If you don't believe me, why don't you call back the surgeon, cut off my leg and count the rings like an old tree. I was born during WW II."

The nurse wasn't listening. She quickly assessed him. He looked pale, but his heart seemed to be beating fine. His oxygen level was a little low, but stable enough. Half the people walking around Manhattan seemed to be wheezing and coughing. She scribbled her initials on the chart and left the room.

A visitor waited near the elevator.

"Go in now," said the voice on his telephone. "You're covered."

Christian Playa was wearing a light brown leather jacket, roughly the same shade as his face. Cowboy boots and dark khakis would've made him at home anywhere from Greenwich Village to Austin, Texas. But he was a quick-change artist. Within a second's notice, he could toss aside the jacket and instead reveal a light blue button-down shirt that would totally change his look, from rodeo fan to the local manager of any retail store, from a Blockbuster to a Best Buy.

The nurse walked past him and snapped, "Turn off the phone. No cellphones here. Can't you read the sign?" She pointed vaguely, over there somewhere. "We got patients on lung and heart machines. You'll kill somebody with that damn thing." She sneered and quickened her pace down the hallway. Playa momentarily held the phone down next to his thigh before picking it up again.

"My guys have taken out the cameras in the front. So you're safe," said the voice in a reassuring tone.

Playa walked directly into Buck's room. Buck's eyes widened. He didn't know the man, but he didn't look like one of his doctors.

"Who the hell are you?" Buck asked. "I'm tryin' to sleep."

"I know, that's why I'm closing the blinds." Playa leaned over and pulled the Venetian blinds closed. "I'm the respiration therapist," Playa replied. He reached to the cabinet next to Buck and grabbed the plastic tube with the floating ball that Buck had used to exercise his lungs.

"Blow into this," Playa said gently.

Buck held the tube to his mouth and took a deep breath. His chest expanded and his cheeks puffed out. Playa swiped the tube away and picked up a small pillow. He jammed the pillow into Buck's face and held it there. Buck squirmed for a moment, as the oxygen monitor started to spiral downward. A man recovering from a heart attack can't hold his breath very long. Within a minute, Buck was down for the "big sleep," and Christian Playa was lumbering down Fourteenth Street, having changed to a button-down shirt, looking like just another blue-shirted manager at Blockbuster.

Playa felt momentarily sad. Buck Roberts seemed like a decent hard-working stiff. But Playa had little time for sentiment. He needed to get back into the good graces of Paul Tremont. Tremont had left a bitter message for him a few days before, furious that Playa hadn't warned him about Cori Leopard's arrest. "What the hell am I spending $10 million for if not to keep tabs on the FBI!" Tremont bellowed.

Playa found it tough and sometimes confusing to be a double agent, to serve two bosses: Oriana and Tremont. He wished he could explain it to his brother Paulo, a milkman who struggled to feed his children outside Havana. Paulo's seven-year-old daughter had died from anemia brought on by malnutrition. Christian sent money, but it was often intercepted.

"Christian, what do you get from this?" Paulo asked. "Who are you really working for?"

"Myself, Paulo. I've got my own plans." He couldn't use Castro's name in conversation with Paulo. If he did, Paulo could be tortured.

Playa shared Tremont's vision for the collapse of Castro. But his view of what Tremont called "manana" could not be more different. Whereas Tremont wanted to rule Havana and dominate the Miami Cubans, Playa wanted to keep Miami out and leave the survivors of Castro's bloody regime to control their own futures, without the Mob, the gambling, the whoring, and the deep bow to Uncle Sam.

Playa called up Dr. Stuart Burns. "The job is done." As he signed off, he could hear Burns spitting out the tip of a cigar and then lighting it up. He was probably on his way to report the news to Tremont. For the first time, Playa wondered why Buck Roberts had to die.

Back at his office after confronting Luke, Tremont growled to Burns, "One day closer to manana."

"Braden will be upset, but not surprised. He was an old man," Burns said.

"One by one, we topple Luke's pillars. First, get rid of Roberts. Then fire his father. Later he'll learn the truth about dear old dad."

Tremont stood up and paced the room. His pinstripes were rippling with each step, like a tiger about to leap. "He's frozen Cori out. So now he's like an alien. Alienated from his father, his mentor, and his girl-friend. And he's alienated from his natural habitat too. You think he's comfortable on a high floor of an office building on Columbus Circle? This is a guy who thrived in a square ring on the ground floor. We've plucked him from his natural habitat, thrown away the familiar trees. Soon he'll be completely on his own. I'll be the closest thing he has to a father, friend, and confidant. That's when he becomes mine."

"And Castro falls," Burns added.

"I told you to mark your calendar, Burns. Manana falls on December 31. That's when Castro comes to Vegas for the first time. That's when he meets Luke."

CHAPTER 56

James Carmody walked gingerly into a bar called The Shaft. He was in the closet at the Hoover Building, but he felt liberated when he came to New York City. Washington was close-knit and uptight, while Manhattan was tight-lipped. Yeah, they made dumb jokes about J. Edgar Hoover and dresses, but nobody inside the building believed the stories. As he entered the doorway, Carmody untightened his skinny leather tie and pushed it askew, better to show off his black, high-sheen suit. The suit looked fashionably wet as he ambled toward the bar. I'm off duty, right? Aren't federal agents allowed to relax, be themselves once in a while? Carmody had spent years studying harder than his white colleagues. But he didn't want to surrender all of himself to the force. To become an agent, he put his hand on the Bible, not his dick. Sometimes he wanted to be just another cool black dude who could set hearts a-racing. At least that's what he hoped for. Still, he was nervous and his hands were sweaty as he touched the diamond stud in his right ear.

The bar was packed, guys leaning against barstools and a few pool tables used as makeshift chairs, rather than for playing the game. A thumping beat signaled Pink Floyd's *Another Brick in the Wall*, as the twenty-something crowd celebrated the early 1980's, their birth years. Carmody caught the eye of a bartender, a blond kid with a mullet. The kid winked at him, and Carmody signaled to the beer tap. He assessed the crowd. He thought a place called The Shaft would attract a much earthier crowd; guys in uniform and leather. This place was misnamed. It looked more like a Twinkie bar, filled with preppie young white kids. The only sign of sex Carmody noticed was the sign to the men's room, a neon ejaculating penis. Carmody sipped his beer, waiting to be approached. Someone always did, usually some white guy looking for a black stud. A few minutes later, Carmody felt a hand on his shoulder. He swiveled around and saw a guy with bright green eyes staring into his. He had long, reddish hair that crept over the collar of his white shirt, on top of which he wore a tennis sweater with bold stripes around the V-neck.

"Hey, I'm Jim," said Carmody, sticking out his hand.

"Me too," said the young man. "Hey, I can't stand '80's music. Wanna get out of here and walk?"

Carmody thought this was going a little fast, but figured he could always peel off and come back. "Sure."

They strolled along Christopher Street, looking at galleries and shops and trading innocuous comments. They didn't touch, except when occasionally bumping shoulders to avoid brushing against another pedestrian. The redhead was shorter than Carmody, and clearly not athletic. They talked about the Knicks and rolled their eyes at a pair of Goth punks who had pierced their cheeks and eyebrows so many times their heads looked like they belonged atop a set of studded western armchairs. Carmody and his new friend could've been two straight guys passing time, waiting for their girlfriends to show up. Then the redhead's phone vibrated in his pocket.

He read a text message and shoved the phone back into his pocket. "I gotta go, Jim. Call me, please. I'd like to see you again," he said, with just the slightest hint of desperation. He went to a telephone pole and tore off an ad for moving services. He scribbled on the back, handed it to Carmody, and jogged toward the subway entrance.

Carmody looked down at the paper. "R.F." and a 212 phone number.

CHAPTER 57

Nick Larsen sat on his desk and opened up a slim envelope that had been X-rayed several times by the FBI mailroom. It was cleared for explosive residue, anthrax, and a hundred other biological risks. After 9/11, the FBI director boasted to the worried mailroom staff that their new scanning equipment could identify a sender who had halitosis when he licked the stamp. The envelope contained a DVD disk. The last unmarked DVD he had received was a bootleg sex tape of a Moral Majority preacher. Who could it be this time? He was hoping it would be Hillary Clinton with a man or woman or preferably both. Larsen leaned back in his Naugahyde chair, touched his bruised temple, and popped the disk into his computer. The figure was clothed and alone. A hippie-looking Cori Leopard with a placard around her neck. No big deal, Larsen thought. That's how she spent the first twenty-five years of her life, it seemed. She was wearing boots and appeared to be holding something in her hands. From the right side of the frame entered a microphone, which was shoved close to her face.

"Tremont's a saint. I'd sleep with him," she said in a seductive voice. Then she shifted gears. "That was to get your attention," she said.

The camera began pulling back to show several dogs on a leash.

Larsen was not impressed. It was nothing new. The picture froze. She was standing in front on the Mandalay Bay Hotel in Vegas. He left the frozen image on his screen and considered using it as a screen saver.

"Hey, that's Cori Leopard," a female intern said, nodding toward the screen "What are those? Labradors?"

Larsen turned his head back to the screen. And then it hit him. Hard and low like a punch to the lower gut. Cori Leopard was innocent.

TODD BUCHHOLZ

CHAPTER 58

Enraged, Larsen ran up to Ronnie Funk's office. Funk was a little frightened to see the agent huffing and puffing. Larsen jammed the DVD into Ronnie's laptop, which projected the Cori video on the Lacunator.

"What do you see, Funk!" Larsen demanded.

"Ms. Leopard and, I think, Labrador retrievers," Funk responded, confused.

"You're fuckin' blind. Not the girl. Put your bugaboo eyes behind the girl. Look at the sign!"

Funk's eyes focused in on the sign for the Mandalay Bay Hotel looming behind Cori. It was a huge, brightly lit marquee. A thousand little golden lights spelled out an advertisement: "*Bayman vs. Ruiz* July 12, nine P.M." A boxing match. No big deal, right? But July 12 was crossed out with a blinking red neon line. Next to that bright red line blinked the word that could get Cori Leopard released from her hell: "Tonight!"

If Cori was protesting in Vegas on July 12, she could not have blown up the Washington Metro that very same afternoon.

"It's a fake," Funk said matter-of-factly.

"Which?"

"The video," Funk said.

"Or maybe your photo from the Metro is a fake," Larsen sneered. "Let's solve this now. Low-tech style." Larsen picked up a phone and called the television station in Las Vegas whose logo graced the lower portion of the screen. The manager returned to the phone in about three minutes and confirmed that the station had a video of Cori Leopard taped on July 12. It was time-stamped eleven thirty-five A.M.

"Holy shit!" the manager shouted. "I've got a scoop! This is like the Zapruder film."

"Yeah, quite a scoop. Go ahead and sell it," Larsen suggested. He quickly downloaded his media e-mail list from the computer and sent a copy of the footage to the main server of the National Press Building on Fourteenth Street. Only about two hundred media outlets would get copies.

Then he turned his anger to Funk.

"How can you be so calm? We locked up a freakin' senator's daughter on this! Do you know what we look like?" He shoved his hands deep into his pockets to avoid strangling Funk. "I told you this high-tech shit is no good." He stared at Funk's dreadlocks. "I'd rather you do some medicine man thing and rely on your mojo or some other bullshit like that."

Funk stared at the Lacunator. "Isn't is possible she hopped a flight to D.C. after the taping?"

"Ever been to Vegas?"

Funk shook his head.

"I didn't think so. I busted my ass for five years in Reno. Guess what?" he asked rhetorically and sarcastically. "Vegas is three hours behind D.C. Even if she caught a flight an hour later, it would have taken off at three thirty D.C. time. Unless she was flying on the space shuttle, she couldn't get across the country in an hour, in time to blow up a Metro leaving Union Station at five o'clock, could she?"

Funk was demoralized and out of ammunition. He shrugged his shoulders, as if to suggest there was nothing for him to do now. On to the next assignment.

But Larsen saw things differently. His face was plastered all over the *Washington Post* and the *New York Times* after they arrested Cori. The White House chief of staff had demanded a briefing from the FBI director. Now, the FBI would have to backtrack, backpedal, and get plowed by the Senate Judiciary Committee.

"Do you realize that you've destroyed our careers!"

They had plugged Carmody into the conversation through the field office in lower Manhattan. He was sweating for the same reason that Larsen was. Only for Carmody it was even worse; he was the guy who had placed his confidence in Funk's science.

"Ronnie, how could we get fooled?" Carmody asked. "Are you sure?"

"It's possible that the video was rigged somehow. More likely, though, the Lacunator picked up an image of Cori that coincidentally was on someone's camera phone. We got, bufu'd by a coincidence."

"What are the chances that someone happened to have a photo of Cori Leopard on their camera?" Carmody asked.

"Not high," Funk replied. "But wasn't an editor of the *Post's* style section on that Metro car? She probably had a thousand images of politicians and their families. I just don't know."

One person did know, of course. The morning of the Metro tragedy, Christian Playa had e-mailed a photo of Cori to Sarah Hartman, just to spur this wild goose chase. It was Oriana's idea. At first Playa resisted the idea.

"Christian, if we frame Cori, then Senator Leopard will feel more vulnerable. I need that. What could be worse than for the chairman of the Senate Foreign Relations Committee to have a daughter suspected of terrorism?"

Oriana had done enough hobnobbing in Hollywood in the 1970s to know that Jane Fonda cost Henry Fonda some plum roles. Senator Leopard would need Oriana more than ever. Hopefully, she would get his assurance that he would squelch the Miami Cubans and prevent them from deposing her idol, the man who held her tenderly, who rescued her from the Lanskys and liberated her from the Kennedys—that old man who still ruled Cuba.

"Where'd you learn to play such deadly chess with your pawns, Oriana?"

"From the best. Joe Kennedy and the wise guys in Chicago. Joe and Jack used me, but I used them too. They were my tutors. I got to peek behind that Camelot curtain. The gambling, the sex, Jack's drugs. And that smiling fraud on Jack's arm."

"Jackie? Even the French loved her, and they hated everything American."

"No wonder. She played to them. If Chanel, Givenchy, and Dior made extra-large sizes, Jackie would've dressed her horses in them." Oriana slowly strolled around her Palm Springs estate, a scissors in one hand, a flower basket in the other. Jackie. How innocent she pretended to be with those big round eyes. But Jackie just sat and smiled when her own father, and her father-in-law, and Jack used every Mary and every Marilyn they could find.

Oriana was bitter and she was lonely. Where was her Hyannisport? Her family? Where was her son, who refused to acknowledge she even existed?

Bitter. Lonely. But not defeated. In her garden, Oriana noticed a tall, miraculously bright, orange bird-of-paradise. She stopped, opened her scissors around the thick stem, and snipped.

CHAPTER 59

Luke passed Paul Tremont in the hallway as he was heading toward his private gym and spa.

"How's my Mars report coming, Luke? You ready for the big presentation?"

Luke tried to smile but knew he had more numbers to crunch before he would have the nerve to confront Tremont.

He had just received an email from Cori, but hadn't had time to respond. After the FBI issued its official apology to Cori, Luke thought that Paul Tremont would take her back into the business. After all, she had been doing good work for the Tremont charitable endowment. The Boys' Club downtown invited her to join their board of directors. Nonetheless, Tremont turned down the idea of rehiring Cori.

"I'm sorry, Luke. I know you care for her, and I thought she could help us, but let's face it, she's damaged goods," Tremont explained. "I mean that the Tremont brand has a reputation and we have competitors and enemies who would be delighted to sully it. I wish Ms. Leopard well, and I might remind you that I put up the money to get you two out of jail. As far as I'm concerned, I have discharged any moral obligation to her."

Luke couldn't argue with that. Tremont had provided the checkbook for Cori. Moreover, he gave her a severance package worth a few hundred thousand. She used the money to move out of Luke's apartment and into a more modest place near Broadway.

Tremont kept walking, loosening his tie as he leaned on the door to the spa. "One more thing, Luke. You need to be careful about your relationship with her. The FBI cleared her of murder, thank God. But that doesn't mean she's pure as Snow White, does it?" Tremont winked.

Luke wondered what else Paul Tremont knew.

Even though Luke and Cori had separated, they still tried to grab dinner once a week. He had thrown himself back into his work and was researching the Mars Company at least sixteen hours each day. Tremont expected a report on Mars ASAP. After Buck's death, Luke's good humor disappeared. Exhausted by his research, he felt stuck like a hamster in a Habitrail set, scurrying in an ever-narrower tube. How much could he see of life when he was walking to work across Broadway before the sun began to rise? And as winter approached, the sun fled over the Hudson River to hide in Jersey at four thirty P.M.

CHAPTER 60

On the morning of December 12, Luke tried to sit up in bed. Today was his chance to pass his next test at Tremont. He'd tossed and turned so violently that his duvet looked like it had gotten snagged on a boat propeller. He slipped into a dark Etro suit with alternating thick and thin violet pinstripes. "Daring," the salesman had told him. Even more daring, Luke chose a striped shirt and striped tie to accompany the suit. He looked at himself in the mirror. He didn't feel daring. Tired. Cranky. Too much work and too little sex. It was as Yogi Berra put it, déjà vu all over again. Like being an underachieving adolescent in his father's household. But he had a job to do and a test to pass.

At least he thought he wanted to pass the test. Wasn't that what he was working for? To climb the Tremont ladder, to escape forever the ghetto of the basement and the lobby-level reception desks? Tremont had promised him a future of not just riches for himself, but participation in all the good works of the Tremont Foundation too. "When I'm too decrepit to be honored by UNICEF and the Red Cross—and that date is coming pretty soon—I want protégés like you to keep up the good work," Tremont whispered to him. Tremont probably cut corners, manipulated stock sales perhaps. But these were misdemeanors compared with the Tremont Malaria Project in Ghana or the Tremont Kitchen in Camden, New Jersey. Right?

Luke had prepared loose-leaf notebooks and a PowerPoint presentation on Mars. Tremont's instincts were right. Old Forrest Mars had run a ship as tight as Captain Bligh. But now the company was run more like a candy store. Spending was up, perks were up, and efficiency was down. Luke had analyzed expenditures into three categories: (1) vital, (2) near vital, (3) flotsam. Among the flotsam, he found corporate helicopters that should be grounded and sold, as well as satellite offices that seemed to serve no purpose than to allow mid-level, and some senior, executives to work close to their homes. Forrest Mars wouldn't have put up with that. One senior VP felt compelled to take his staff to the Ritz Carlton in Maui each year. Luke added up the flotsam, which totaled nearly a hundred million in annual costs. Big stuff, Luke thought. Tremont would be pleased. He highlighted the flotsam in a special section with bright red tabs. This would be the crown jewel of his report.

Scrunch, scrunch. The sound was coming from the front door. The last time Luke heard an odd noise from the door, FBI agents barged in and arrested them. He walked over suspiciously and peered through the peephole. Cori was balancing a tray of Starbucks coffee and grinning at him.

"I thought you could use some oomph before the big presentation," she said, handing him the tray. She looked at the colorful loose-leaf note-books. "These look great. But you don't look so good."

"I'll tell you what's making me sick." He flipped open a notebook to a subsection of the flotsam analysis.

She looked down at the pages. Nothing jumped out at her. "What?"

"See this innocuous line item called 'additional consideration'?" He'd buried it in the middle of the spreadsheet. "I'm hoping Tremont skips over it. It's just $1 million total, a tiny percentage of the whole flot-sam analysis."

"I don't get it. If it's so teeny-weeny, why do you need to bury and camouflage it with a boring title?"

"Cori, these are Mars's charitable and nonprofit disbursements. A gift to a local symphony, scholarships to junior colleges, and research in-stitutions, that kind of stuff."

"Big deal. Tremont's going to care?"

"There's more. The annual $100,000 endowment for the Mars Pro-fessor of Literature at Columbia University. My father is a subdivision of flotsam, a matter of 'additional consideration'."

"That's not flattering."

"I'm not trying to insult him. I'm trying to protect the old man and his job."

An hour later, the meeting began in the Roosevelt Room. Tremont began by swearing everyone to secrecy.

"There's nothing touchier and more dangerous than one company trying to acquire another. It forces you to defend your manhood. It's very—instinctual, almost Darwinian." Tremont made a fist and tapped his chest. "The CEO who can't defend his company against a takeover is like a village leader who has allowed his women to be dragged into brothels for conquering invaders. If we're going to do the pillaging, we have to be absolutely silent until we attack."

Luke found Tremont's warnings both repulsive and thrilling. He wanted to be part of the pack, part of the hunt. But as he opened up his loose-leaf notebook and saw all of the spreadsheets, thousands of little boxes filled with long strings of numbers, he realized that they weren't preparing for a barbaric gangbang, but a long, dull slog through the muck of the Generally Accepted Accounting Principles promulgated by the Financial Accounting Standards Board.

Finally, Luke asked the team to turn their page to the section marked flotsam. His heart started beating faster as their eyes locked onto "additional consideration." He placed his index finger over the line so that it wouldn't distract him further. Tremont was delighted to hear about the corporate helicopters. Then Luke flashed on a projection screen a photograph of the vice president who turned Maui retreats into his own personal brothel. One of the analysts, a former frat boy from USC, scrunched up a piece of scrap paper and hurled it at the screen. "Loser!" he shouted. Luke was hoping that this tale of Maui would close the discussion on flotsam. Then he could turn the meeting back to Tremont, who would outline the logical steps for a corporate takeover.

"Very nice, Luke," Tremont said smiling. "Great job. Gentlemen, Luke has put in—what—four weeks compiling this report? Well done. I'd give this more than a passing grade."

Luke exhaled. He'd passed the test. For the next minute, Luke couldn't hear what anyone was saying because his brain kept playing back the sentence: "I'd give this more than a passing grade." His imagination inserted the line from ABC's *Wide World of Sports*: "The thrill of victory." He wanted to call Cori. Maybe she'd forgive him for being so distant over the past month.

When he stopped replaying Tremont's statement in his head, he realized that his colleagues were staring at him. Tremont had been asking a question, and they all were waiting the answer.

"What in the world is 'additional consideration'?"

"Yeah, is that the cash the Hawaii vacation guy slips to the pimp?" chimed in the USC frat boy turned analyst.

Luke tried to smile, but that sick feeling came back. Should he stonewall or cover up the truth? What was his obligation? Through his mind flashed a collage of awful images right out of Salvador Dali: At first he saw the local symphony that Mars endowed, then, suddenly, the violins started to melt and the strings strangled the necks of the violinists. At research laboratories with Mars nameplates, beakers and test tubes started bending and breaking, sending shattered glass into the eyes of scientists. He saw his father, Dr. Francis Braden, strutting in front of his students. His face began to twist and his features turned into shapes and colors, a Cubist festival on acid. While entertaining these images, Luke seemed to lose control of his own facial expressions. He couldn't tell if he were frowning or smirking.

"Something wrong, Luke?" Tremont inquired.

"Nothing," Luke managed to utter unconvincingly. He forced himself to blink a few times rapidly to shake himself out of this miserable reverie.

"Uh, okay, the question is . . . um . . . yes," he stuttered, "additional consideration." As he spoke, he realized he had no choice but to plow forward and reveal Mars's charitable-spending initiatives. After all, he thought, Tremont might go along with them. He could cut out 99 percent of the flotsam and have a compelling case for taking over Mars. Should Luke expose his father's subsidy? He would have to make that decision within minutes.

TODD BUCHHOLZ

CHAPTER 61

"Do you really think you can keep me out of his life forever?" Oriana asked.

"So far, it's worked well enough," he answered.

"Well enough? What the hell are you talking about? That boy's had three lives so far. Reckless teenager. Brutal boxer. And now, who's he working for? I can hardly spit out the name, that greedy prick who wants the world to think he's a combination of George Soros and Albert Schweitzer." She would have shouted the words but she was lying face down on a massage table at La Quinta Resort near Palm Springs, surrounded by cactus and palms and the occasional howl of a coyote. It brought back memories of old Hollywood, where gods like Errol Flynn and Clark Gable would cavort. A young Mexican man of about nineteen, massaged Oriana's buttocks with coconut oil and marveled at how tight her muscles and skin felt.

The man on the other end of the phone took offense. "Luke's not a killer! You think he wanted that Cuban boy to die? He would've been happier killing himself. You know he quit the ring after that. As for Tremont, I'm just as disgusted as you, but for different reasons, of course," explained Francis Braden.

"I just don't trust Tremont. I don't know what plans he has for Luke. I won't have that man manipulating my only grandson," she said. "If he needs money, I can wire some money—"

"Keep your money, mother. We don't need contaminated money. I'd like you to just stay out of it. The last time we spoke must've been five years ago. Let's schedule another call for 2011, okay?"

Oriana cringed, the thin, almost translucent skin around her eyes crinkling. She felt a bolt of pain along her spine. It was the recurring memory of men—a son, a grandson, a lover—ripped from her arms, leaving her so alone.

What was wrong with her son? How could he have turned out so effete, so feckless, so comfortable in a professor's gown? She was tired of hiding behind a curtain, kept so far away from her grandson.

Oriana hung up on her son. She knew a man with his head in the clouds or in his precious books would be no use in trying to save Luke. Or Fidel Castro.

CHAPTER 62

Luke explained how Mars funded the music scholarships in Virginia, the local symphonies, and a token gift to Meals on Wheels. He also explained the research grants into the impact of antioxidants on heart attack victims. Tremont and the team took notes and nodded their heads.

"It's pretty shrewd, actually," Luke said.

"How?" Tremont asked quietly.

"Chocolate *is* an antioxidant. While I was researching Mars, I also learned that you're better off giving a coughing child a piece of chocolate than an over-the-counter children's cough medicine," Luke reported.

"Interesting. Okay, here's my plan. The symphony goes. Kill the program. The music scholarships too. And Meals on Wheels? Zippo for them. Mars is a candy company, not the Red Cross. The research funding is different, though it stays in on one condition: It must be aimed at discovering facts that help chocolate sales. Like this antioxidant/coughing research. Very good. Shrewd."

Luke didn't want to give up so quickly on the music and the Meals on Wheels. "Mr. Tremont, it's such a small amount, what's the point of appearing hard-hearted?"

Tremont pounced. "Hard-hearted? How can anyone call Paul Tremont hard-hearted? There are thousands of little black babies in East Ghana, who are dying of dehydration right now. In West Ghana they are growing up big and strong. Do you know the difference? In West Ghana, the babies live near the Tremont Treatment Center."

"But I still don't see why we should slice up Mars's charitable activities."

"Let me spell it out for you. When I give money to Ghana, or Mississippi, or the neighborhood Girl Scouts, it comes from my pocket. I take the loss. I don't force others to chip in. But when a corporation writes a check, it comes out of the pockets of shareholders. They have no right to do that. That's robbery. And I'm going to stop it." He knew he was on a roll. "And when we turn Mars around and make more money for its owners, they can write their own damn checks for the Meals on Wheels do-gooders in their hybrid cars delivering free-range chickens that died of old age."

Snickers filled the Roosevelt Room.

"And one more thing," Tremont said. "According to my notes, the 'additional consideration' adds up to $900,000. Where is the other $100,000?"

"Educational stuff," Luke replied quietly.

"Yes?" Tremont asked.

"Some of you might know that my father teaches at Columbia. Literature." Too high-falutin'? Luke tried a self-deprecating smile, "I can hardly read the phone book, but my father loves books. Money doesn't exactly pour into literature departments. So this endowment from Mars is important to my father."

"Luke, there's no room in this hypercompetitive business to support people staring out a window and imaging what F. Scott Fitzgerald would think of Long Island today," Tremont said. "I have nothing against academia. But I have nothing against the profit motive either. We've got to get the order right. Profits come first. Then we can distribute the profits to whomever we like best, whether they be violinists or basket weavers or, English professors. I'm afraid we have to take out our red pen on this too."

"You're firing my father?"

"No, you are. It's your analysis. I'm just following through on your report."

"But I never suggested firing him." Luke felt his voice rising

"You didn't have to. The report speaks for itself. Besides—and forgive me for getting a little personal here—your father hasn't exactly been a big supporter of your career, either as a boxer or an investment banker, has he?"

Luke balled his fists in his lap and his foot began tapping rapidly.

"My father may not have been a big fan but he never tried to undermine me. He thought he was trying to straighten me out, that's all."

His colleagues started shifting their weight in their chairs, coughing, and clearing their throats.

The rest of the meeting was a blur. Luke couldn't bear to see Paul Tremont take a red pen and slice it through the line item, through the heart of his father. But what could he do? He couldn't argue anymore with Tremont. What standing did he have? There was a clear conflict of interest for him. This was a business meeting, not a family counseling session. What was Tremont trying to prove?

On the way out of the meeting, Tremont patted Luke on the shoulder and whispered. "I know how tough this can be. But you passed the test."

He had passed the test, but failed his father.

CHAPTER 63

Professor Francis Braden was worried. How long could he keep Luke in the dark? Would Oriana burst in on him unannounced? Francis felt like an alienated child—Camus goes to Columbia. So what was so wrong with a little white lie, telling Luke that his father was an orphan, abandoned at birth?

Francis sat alone in his classroom, slumped in a leather chair. This was the chair out of which wisdom was supposed to pour. Luke had called him and asked for a "meeting." How many sons request a meeting with their father? Each September, Francis would watch parents deliver freshmen boys and girls to Columbia. He'd watch them unpack computers and beanbag chairs. Then came the hugs, some accompanied by Niagara tears. When was the last time he'd hugged Luke? Fourth grade, maybe? The last time Luke lost a fistfight and came home crying?

Should he tell Luke at the meeting that he had a colorful grandmother named Oriana? Colorful? Was Capone colorful? Would it help Luke to know that his grandmother had been around the block a few times? And what blocks they were! Busted in the saloons of Chicago, the illicit clubs of Miami and Havana, usually on the arm of some Italian or Jewish mobster who touted a gun or an adding machine.

Francis had been a precocious teenager, who quickly figured out that he should be ashamed of his mother. "This is your Uncle fill-in-the-blank," his mother would say as another overnight guest tossed his jacket on the sofa. Sometimes Frank would sneak into their jackets and flip open their wallets. Sometimes their last names sounded Italian or Jewish or Spanish or Waspy. Some family. Was he the son of the United Nations? And, then there were the guests who left before dawn.

Over the years, the shame deepened. He ran away. In his mind, he convinced himself that some antibody in his anatomy had rejected her bloodline and his father's bloodline.

He used to call her once a month. Now, he screened his calls and would only pick up her phone calls at Christmastime. But he would never let her speak to Luke.

What good would it do? She had wealth; Lansky's mob money saw to that. But Luke didn't need money now, especially dirty money. Besides, Francis couldn't bear admitting he had lied all those years, covering up his and his son's past.

Luke's limousine pulled up in front of the Columbia campus. The sun was trying to slip from behind a low wintry cloud. He still was not sure how to break the news. What else did his father have in his life besides his chair at Columbia and his stack of books? Francis never seemed fragile to Luke, but doesn't every son wonder at some point whether their strong father is just a great actor, and is really quaking in his boots? Luke did, as he pictured his father's controlled, almost robotic stroking of his Vandyke while he mused about Philip Roth and somebody named Philip Rahv. He entered the classroom from the back door, paused before Francis saw him, and looked at the neutron in his nuclear family. The neutron stays in place while the electron swirls about. Francis had been at Columbia for almost twenty years. How many shots to the head had Luke absorbed since that time? He looked a little like his father. His father was darker, more heavily bearded. But Luke shared the squarish jaw and the full head of hair. Funny enough, Luke's face looked smoother, despite the cuts and scars from the ring.

"Dad," Luke said approaching. "Thanks for meeting me here."

"My home turf," Francis said pleasantly.

Luke wasn't going to toy with his father about the Tremont/Mars plan. He had explained his predicament to Cori. She said to just blurt it out. "Tell him that Paul Tremont plans on cutting out the Mars literature subsidy. He'll understand."

"I've got bad news, Dad," Luke said. "We've hardly spoken recently, and now I'm intruding in your life—"

Francis's face started to redden. Did he know about Oriana? Had she called him?

"Tremont Advisors is taking over Mars. There won't be any more grants to Columbia." Luke took a breath and bit his lip.

Francis felt relief. No mention of Oriana. But this! This! Tremont was going to destroy his life? He squinted at Luke just to allow a second for him to admit it was just a joke. But there was no relief, just an expression of shame on his son's face.

"But he was here last month! He sat at my table! Just what was he doing—scanning the faculty lounge to see which furniture he could sell off? Which books he could tear off the shelf, throw in a heap, and burn to generate heat for a chemical factory? And my own son is a part of this?"

Luke had no words. Words were never his strong point, certainly not in competition with his father. His stomach clenched in disgust with himself.

"Are you a henchman, Lucas? A bagman? What's your role in this? When you quit school and started boxing, did you know I cried? My son, my only family, beating people's brains in for a living. But this is worse. This is ducking through the ropes, climbing down from the ring, and diving into the nearest sewer vent. Tell me, what kind of air do they breathe at the top of the Tremont Building?"

Francis stood up from his chair and walked to the chalkboard. He scrawled in large letters: *PACTA SUNT SERVANDA*. "What does this mean to you Luke? *Keep your promises*. Not just to other people, but to yourself. Haven't you ever made a promise to yourself about how deep you would dive?" Francis hurled the chalk to the ground.

Luke wiped his brow and fought the urge to run over like a dutiful son and pick up the rolling chalk. "Dad, I'm sure there are other companies that would be willing to pick up the tab. I've built some good relationships with some firms—" *Which firms? Bloomberg, which I've lied to? Boeing, which I've lied about? Medcentric, whose salesman I impersonated?*

Francis Braden fought the urge to spit. This was his classroom, his church. He wouldn't defile it. "You don't understand this at all, do you?" he said. "I'm not nauseated because I'm losing my endowed chair, my $100,000 bonus. I don't need the money. I spend most of it buying books to donate to the library anyway. But look at yourself. You look great on the outside. The women must drool when they see you strut by. I look at your face. Your green eyes are as clear and penetrating as ever. That's what the world sees. But I'm your father. I care more about what's *inside* the suit. And now I'm afraid my son is turning into Dorian Gray—"

Luke couldn't even remember who Dorian Gray was. Some LBO sleazebag from the '80s, like Ivan Boesky?

"Take a look at that picture of yourself, Lucas—."

Now Luke remembered the story. The portrait of Dorian Gray in the attic ages and corrupts while the man stays young. He let Francis blow off more steam and hurl about more literary allusions.

A girl with a backpack stumbled into the classroom. Luke saw how the girl looked up to his father and smiled as she said, "Good afternoon, Dr. Braden."

As his father ignored the student and rushed from the classroom, Luke knew the time had come to confront Paul Tremont.

CHAPTER 64

The headlines hit with a force that reminded Wall Street vets of Daimler-Benz buying Chrysler: "Tremont Advisors Sets Sights on Mars"; "Candy-Coated Capitalists"; and "M&M's Melt in Tremont's Mouth." All the consumer-goods stocks started skyrocketing, from Krispy Kreme to Heinz. Immediately, all brand name foods were in play. The buzz wasn't limited to the trading floors or the chat rooms. Cocoa and coffee markets from Kuala Lumpur to Lima, Peru shuddered. That evening even Jay Leno led with: "Today, Paul Tremont said he's buying Mars. Guess his ego didn't fit on earth anymore." The worried heirs of Mars started huddling with their lawyers. Tremont could not have been happier with the exposure. Nothing like shaking up the world to give yourself a boost.

Luke stopped by the "21" Club and gulped down a Scotch on his way to face Tremont. He and Cori, now his unofficial strategist, had mapped out his approach. He would continue to work for Tremont—even work on the Mars deal—if Tremont would keep the charitable spending in the budget.

Paul Tremont was getting ready to leave his office for a rubdown at the spa on the floor below. He'd already changed into his silk, monogrammed bathrobe. Luke barged in without knocking and launched right into the debate.

"Take it out of my pay. You're paying me over $600,000 a year. I can't cover the whole mil, but you can knock me down to $100,000. The five hundred you save on me you can let Mars throw at the symphony and the schools."

"And Columbia, right?"

"Yes, my father's chair. I'll cover that too, as long as you don't tell him." Luke could still taste the Scotch, and he felt the heat of the alcohol circulating through his chest. Tremont didn't look disturbed. Obviously, yesterday had been a big day for him. Phone calls from titans. Jokes from late-night comedians. He was in a cheery mood. But good cheer alone wouldn't seal the deal for Luke. "Didn't you call me 'hard-hearted' yesterday?" Tremont asked.

"I didn't mean it personally, Mr. Tremont. I was just appealing to the great example you've set with the Tremont Charitable Foundation."

"In my book, 'hard-hearted' beats the crap out of 'soft-headed,' Luke."

"I suppose so."

"I'll be honest with you. I'm not enthusiastic about your proposal. But your plan does have one virtue. You've learned a lesson. And the charity comes from your pocket, not the shareholders. That's admirable," he stated, his noble nose tilting a little higher in the air.

Luke started to feel encouraged. "I'd still like to work on the Mars deal," he said, trying to turn the conversation back to the business of Mars nuts and nougat.

"That's impossible for two reasons. I'll give you the first. It would be terribly, terribly destabilizing to have you on the Mars team. Let's face it, you're a weak link."

A weak link? After I made a blockbuster presentation?

"If we scramble to make this deal happen, the negotiations will be brutal. The public exposure is not something I like and all that publicity makes the other side dig in their heels."

"What does any of that have to do with me? It would be brutal no matter who you put on the deal," Luke retorted.

"When word leaks out—and it will—that we went soft because we were protecting an English professor from a salary cut—the guys on the other side of the table will think I've lost my touch, my scent for the kill. That's important in this arena. We can't go soft and quit. It's the same thing in boxing, right? Look at your last fight against Perez. What if you had gone soft then? If you had let your hands down and allowed him to recover and then pummel you? Someone would have died in that ring anyway. But it would have been you instead of the other guy."

You've got no right to bring up the Perez fight! My nightmares are mine alone! Luke wanted to shout and protect his privacy. And yet he realized that the boxing arena was a public arena. How could you demand privacy when pay-per-view watchers are sustaining the sport? They turn everything into a goddamn peep show. They come up with the money, so they insist that they witness everything from a super-slo-mo replay of your nose getting busted to the prefight locker room scene when you're slipping the athletic cup over your nuts.

Luke bit his lip and spoke slowly. "I've never said this to anyone, Mr. Tremont. But there are many nights when I wish I had done just that, that I had dropped my hands against Perez. Let someone else wake up with bloody hands."

Tremont realized he'd stepped over the line. But that was part of the test. He was systematically separating Luke from the few slim pillars that supported him, while at the same time drilling into his psyche.

"Sorry, Luke, but Wall Street needs the killer instinct—or at least you need the other guy to believe that you would strangle him."

Luke had enough. He'd quit boxing. He could quit this too. If Tremont wouldn't accept him on his own terms, then he could take the elevator down to the lobby and walk out the door. He turned toward the door.

Tremont got ready to offer one more avenue of escape for Luke.

"Screw the Mars deal, Luke. Maybe I've got something else for you."

"Even if I don't have the killer instinct?" Luke replied with some sarcasm.

"Yes. I call it the Fidel test. Here's how it goes—" Tremont's eyes widened and his face grew more animated. He explained that Castro would be attending a boxing exhibition in Las Vegas in a few weeks. Tremont had been negotiating with Castro's energy minister over some oil properties. He wanted Luke to go to Vegas and meet Castro.

"Castro! Me? What's my role?" Luke felt he'd been flung into an extraterrestrial orbit. "Castro must travel with an entourage like the Giants' defensive line. How would we ever get to him?" This was like someone tapping you on the shoulder and saying, "Hey, wanna share a cigar with Churchill?"

"I'm afraid I can't meet him myself," Tremont said.

"You have a more important appointment? How often does Fidel Castro come north?

"Castro is still an outlaw in the eyes of many. He can speak at the UN and travel discreetly to the States, but if I were to shake hands with him, our Florida businesses would be picketed, and the FBI would start investigating everything from my bank accounts to the thread count of this robe. The politicians in Washington would have my ass."

"Why not Dr. Burns? Or Ryan or somebody else? Five minutes ago, you looked like you were kicking me out. Now, I'm going to Vegas to meet Fidel frickin' Castro?"

Tremont laughed. "You have something against him?"

Luke wasn't a politician or philosopher. He didn't hate Castro like many conservatives, but he couldn't understand the glassy-eyed look that so many of his father's fellow professors got when they mentioned his name. Luke figured they were just jealous of rich capitalists like Paul Tremont, and Castro represented the radical Marxist antidote: "Look at Fidel"—the radical professors say—"we Lefties can be powerful too, if we bothered to work at it like you Republicans!" To Luke, though, Castro wasn't politics, he was a mega-icon or mythical rock star. Like the pope or the Beatles. It didn't matter whether he was good or evil. Would he have rejected the chance to meet Napoleon or Stalin or Elvis?

Ryan stuck his head into the office, the afternoon ritual, bounding toward the vault outside the receptionist station.

Tremont smiled. "How's the baby?" The daily returns.

"Might as well be twins! Handsome boys!" Ryan reported.

"Outstanding. The BP dividend come in?"

"You bet." Ryan continued toward the vault.

Tremont explained to Luke that the fund had recently bought $50 million shares of British Petroleum. "We had some intelligence telling us that they would be raising dividends. Sure 'nough." He just shook his head.

Out of the corner of his eye, Luke noticed Ryan raising his hand and giving his cheek a little slap. Ryan had apparently forgotten something. He dashed back to the trading floor. The vault door was left open, but Ryan had the "playbook of prosperity" in his hands, the secret report that told the Tremont head trader where to invest the money in case of unforeseen events, whether calamitous or positive, whether a Toyko earthquake or the sudden collapse of the Communist party in Beijing.

Luke shook his head. "No way."

Back to Castro. Tremont laughed at Luke's awe. "Luke, Castro knows you! Don't you remember?"

"No way," Luke repeated.

"Did that Buck Roberts character keep you in the dark about everything? Castro was watching the fight. And who do you think paid for Perez? You think those poor bastard peasants have trust accounts? Or deals with Nike?" He took a deep breath and so did Luke. "Castro's an egotistical animal who destroyed a culture. His army stomped on commerce and freedom of speech. They've jailed or killed anyone with the *cajones* to speak out. You know Castro's nickname as a schoolkid? 'El Loco.'"

Tremont paused. "But there's one thing positive about him. He loves sports, especially boxing and baseball. His baseball teams won the World Series in 1992 and 1996. They say he was a damn good pitcher himself. There's been a rumor he tried out for the Washington Senators. If only they had signed him, we'd have peace in our hemisphere."

"But how does he know me?"

"He was watching the Perez fight! Don't you think the dictator of Cuba can get HBO or steal satellite signals? Remember when you had Perez in trouble, just minutes before, well—"

"Yes," Luke interjected. He didn't need to hear Tremont describe the punch that released the hemorrhage in Perez's brain.

"Perez stumbled and looked like he wanted to quit, but they got the signal from the corner, from his father to keep him up, keep him standing like a punching bag." Tremont stood up in his enthusiasm. "Who do you think made that decision? A peasant cornerman? Of course not. Fidel made that call! It was because of Fidel Castro that you killed Perez!"

Luke was both angry and pleased that Buck had kept him in the dark. How nervous he would've been if he knew that Castro was playing cornerman to Perez. Still, he couldn't shift the blame for the boxer's death to the dictator. He'd thrown the punch. He'd felt the juices of revenge aroused by the crowd's cries of *"pollo!"* and *"no cajones!"* On that night, even though he was watching by satellite, Castro was fifteen hundred miles away from Luke's uncontrollable anger and passion.

"Okay, but even if Castro pulled the strings on my fight, why would he meet me?"

"Because he respects you, and he respects my money and my business skills. We've dabbled in some oil fields projects together. I can't see him personally, and there's no way he would respect a weak little man like Dr. Burns or someone like Ryan." His voice dropped a few tones. "Luke, I hired you with this in mind—knowing that you could bridge the gap with Castro and help Tremont Advisors. It might sound incredible, but that's business today. Is it more incredible than Donald Trump? That stooge has gone bankrupt twice, and yet most Americans think he's a financial Einstein. Or Martha Stewart? Her stock price tripled after she started doing jail time in West Virginia. I hear that her staff petitioned the judge to give her a life sentence! Bill Clinton turned the Lincoln Bedroom into a Motel 6, leaving the light on for any contributor with a checkbook. Instead of shower caps, he probably left condoms. Is it so bizarre to think that the head of a small island country would want to create closer relationships with a powerful investment fund, and do it through an athlete/businessman whom I've mentored?"

As Luke tried to comprehend Tremont's words, his boss spoke into the intercom on his desk, called for Ryan and ordered the most startling trade that Luke had ever heard.

Ryan came running into Tremont's office, red-faced.

CHAPTER 65

Tremont looked perturbed, and asked Luke to leave his office for a moment, while Ryan stood there, biting his lower lip. Luke, his mind still fixated on an absurd image of Fidel Castro standing on a pitcher's mound, leaned against Tremont's receptionist desk, behind which a door to the little vault hung open. It was the size of small, old-style television set. He turned his eyes to the vault. It was empty. No wonder Ryan left it unsecured. Luke looked again, curious at the depth of the vault. He noted a manila folder lying flat on the bottom. He looked through the window into Tremont's office. Ryan was nodding away—the proper gesture for a loyal Tremont employee—but Luke could tell that Ryan was squirming. Luke leaned closer to hear the conversation.

Tremont lifted his fist and pounded it on his desk.

"Ryan, when I say *sell*, I mean *sell*. I don't mean that I want to have a conference and discuss it like a therapist."

"But, but . . ." Ryan's fair skin and freckles darkened with embarrassment, fear, and maybe some anger. "This is really unusual, even for us. As soon as we sent in that 13b filing, we have to assume that the SEC is bugging the trading lines." He was talking about the flimsy but fearsome 13b form, a paper that tells the SEC that you have already acquired 5 percent of a company and are probably aiming for more.

"Fuck the assholes at the SEC. We're not doing anything illegal," Tremont insisted.

Ryan wiped his forehead. "But you're ordering me to sell the million shares of Hershey Foods that we bought as soon as you decided to acquire Mars. When word got out that you were gunning for Mars, Hershey shares exploded. So we got a huge gain on Hershey—"

Tremont had no patience for this history lesson. "I'm telling you to sell Hershey. And then I want you to sell it short. Another trade in the books. We buy and we sell. That's why we exist, Ryan! Buy. Sell. Buy. Sell. It's binary. It's banal. And it made me a billionaire. Why am I justifying this to you, Ryan? Who built this business?"

Ryan pursed his lips. Tremont paid Ryan exceedingly well. He took home $5 million last year. Not bad for a guy whose demeanor made him look like he could be a manager at a local Wal-Mart. He had bickered with Tremont before, but the discussions never verged on insubordination. "That's fine, Mr. Tremont. But if you decide to call off the Mars bid, Hershey will tank and we'll make millions on the short, right?"

"You got it."

"All I'm saying is that the SEC lawyers could call this 'manipulating the market' or 'fraud on the market.' Do you know what happens to the head trader of a fund who performs the manipulation? Jail time."

"Are you afraid I won't protect you?" Tremont said smiling slightly.

"I don't want to do it. The trade or the jail time," Ryan declared.

"Then hand me the phone. I'll call JP Morgan. You can keep your nose clean." Tremont exhaled loudly. He punched some buttons, spoke to a shocked trader on the Morgan desk and hung up.

"There," he said to Ryan, "I've kept you safe. I guess boys like you don't do well in jail, do they?"

Ryan let the remark pass. "I'll fill out the paperwork and book the trade in the dailies," he said as he stormed out. He didn't notice Luke standing next to the vault, empty except for the manila folder.

Christian Playa knew the real reason Luke was being sent to meet Fidel Castro. Now he waited for Tremont outside the steam room of the spa. Sonny, the beautiful Thai girl that Luke had first met in Vegas at the Four Seasons, waited also. She was wrapped in a violet sarong, her hair piled high on her head, exposing smooth, creamy shoulders. She looked sexy and Playa did not with his seamed face and the scars that etched his veiny arms, some from knife fights, others from a heroin addiction he kicked in the early '80s. Tremont wagged his finger, dropped his robe, and ordered the killer for hire to accompany him into the steam room.

Amid clouds of swirling mist and the hiss of ten fans, Playa began to spell out his plan. Tremont nodded, trying not to speak. He was highly confident the spa could not be bugged, and even so, the roar of the steam fans would make it virtually impossible to decipher their words. But Playa didn't trust Tremont. So he had figured out how to tap into the steam room, in case Tremont wanted to use the conversations against him. Playa hated Tremont only slightly less than he hated Fidel Castro. Still, he was content to use Tremont to dethrone the bigger evil.

"Here's how Luke will get Fidel," began Playa. Playa was wrapped in a terry towel that covered his thighs, but exposed a tattoo along his left calf in the shape of the island of Cuba. "I've tapped into some interesting information about Fidel's health. He's been a horse, let's face it. Big and strong. But he's eighty now. When he fell off the stage and broke his arm and kneecap in October 2004, the doctors conducted a stress test. I've got some old buddies at the agency who were able to tap into the report when they transmitted it by wireless to his headquarters. For years, the CIA had been trying to get information, but they never knew when he was seeing doctors. They received medical data, but it could've been anyone's. This time, though, because he broke his arm in public, they knew that data transmitted on October 21 was highly likely to be about Fidel."

"I'm sorry he didn't fall down forty years ago," Tremont said. "So what did you learn?" The clouds of steam were swirling more furiously and felt hotter than usual. Playa's tattoos and scars made his skin look dirty. Tremont leaned back against the tile and made a mental note to ask the staff to clean the tiles more frequently.

"It's his heart. Significant arrhythmia. Borderline diabetes. And some intestinal complications."

"What can we do? I've got Luke ready to fly out to Vegas. He's so excited he could get there by flapping his arms."

Playa opened his hand and started to count on his meaty fingers various ways of *not* whacking Castro. "You're not gonna get Braden to knife him or shoot him, even if we jammed the metal detectors so he could pass through them. I saw the *Manchurian Candidate*. Hypnosis works great in the movies and at magic shows. But you're not going to turn Braden into a killer."

"So what's left?."

"You remember all the CIA plots against Fidel, right?"

"Sure, exploding cigars, mostly," Tremont recalled.

"Oh, Jesus, it got stranger than that." Playa shook his head, revealing a tattoo of barbed wire below his neck. "They also tried to lace his cigars with LSD, so that he'd trip out in public. And a scuba diving suit they infected with tuberculosis and some kind of terrible fungus. They tried to give it to him as a gift."

"So how do we succeed without looking like we're part of the CIA clown show?"

"We must go after Fidel's bodily weaknesses. In the '60s, the CIA and Bobby Kennedy were trying to waste a wily guerilla at the top of his game, a guy in his thirties who'd survived in the jungles of Sierra Maestra. Now, we're just trying to get an old man sick."

"Could Braden shake hands with Castro and 'accidentally' transmit an overdose of insulin or some supersugar agent that would spike his insulin levels? Braden wouldn't know about it. We'd slip it on his hands right before he went in to see Castro."

Playa explained that insulin molecules would not penetrate the skin effectively enough, except in extreme laboratory conditions.

"But I do have a better plan. I'm expecting a package from Shanghai tomorrow, enclosing a cellphone. An international cellphone. I found some engineers in Shanghai who have implanted Taser technology into a cell chip. You've got shares in Taser International, right?"

"We did," Tremont said. "Sold it when the revenue growth rate slid from 300 percent per year to just 100 percent per year. Made a killing, though."

Playa smiled. He loved knowing more about modern toys than other people. Here he was, a guy who grew up on a sugar plantation in Cuba, explaining hi-tech to a rich white guy. "It uses something they call EMD—Electro-Muscular Disruption. It temporarily overrides the central nervous system, taking over muscular control. Taser's salesmen say that EMD technology debilitates the toughest targets, without causing injury or lasting aftereffects. But that assumes that the target is a nineteen-year-old black kid looting a Korean grocery store. It works differently when 100,000 volts zap an eighty-year-old arrhythmia patient with a smoking habit. We'll ramp up the amps to an even more lethal dose."

"But how do we get Braden to pull the trigger?" Tremont asked.

"He doesn't have to shoot it. All he has to do is wear the phone."

"And you set off the ringer?"

"Yes. The ringer sends maybe 100,000 volts in all directions."

"Fidel collapses from the arrhythmia."

"And no one knows why," Playa added. "We can even set the ringer on silence. Not even Braden will know that he's killed Fidel."

"That is, until Luke collapses from the Taser."

"You forgot something, Mr. Tremont. Luke Braden is a young man. His body has been pounded by punches to the solar plexus. He's already been tested. His knees might weaken, but that boy won't fall down. Never got knocked down in the ring, did he? That's what makes him a perfect candidate."

"Brilliant."

"There's just one hitch, though. You've got to figure out how to get Braden within a few inches of Fidel, if we're really aiming for a lethal result. Shaking hands might be close enough, but a big bear hug would be better."

"No problemo," Tremont said. "We'll get a bear hug."

"How?"

"Oh, you don't know?" Tremont's smile grew broader. "That's the biggest secret of all." He looked around instinctively to make sure no one else could hear. "But if you let the word out, I swear Playa, you'll find the FBI arresting your ass, the attorney general personally plugging in the electric chair, and the president of the United States throwing the switch."

CHAPTER 66

Oriana was stewing. She hated stewing. She wanted action, but felt like she'd been in a slo-cooker for two generations, waiting for her day. She paced the living room of her Palm Springs ranch, up on the rocky hill. Her curvy swimming pool was embedded in that hill, tucked against a waterfall that cascaded sparkling water diverted from the mountain 9,000 feet above the arid desert. At night she looked out her windows, tall floor-to-ceiling panes that belonged in a church, not in the home of a single woman. But she wasn't so single. She had so many memories of so many men in so many wild places from Reno to Rio that the place felt crowded. She was a survivor. You could just take out a street map of Palm Springs and find the people she outlasted: Gene Autry Way, Frank Sinatra, Bob Hope, Fred Waring, and Dinah Shore Drives. Kirk Douglas still motored down Kirk Douglas Way, but when Oriana danced with him at his fiftieth wedding anniversary, the old fox couldn't trot anymore.

Ah, the memories, the glories, the jealousies, the monstrous indignities of strolling on Lansky and Lucchesi's arms. She opened her sliding glass door and dipped her long legs in the pool. She was proud of her legs, and her toenails looked magnificent! No sign of the yellow fungus splotches that plague the other queens of Palm Springs.

Oriana's memories returned her to the first time she sashayed to the pool at the Racquet Club. Marilyn Monroe had looked up and uttered in the world's loudest, breathy whisper, "Who's the moll?" Screw her! Oriana could see the dark roots crawling under the blond waves on top of Marilyn's head and even blacker hair peaking out from her upper thighs.

Oriana had had a Kennedy or two, long before Marilyn ever learned the words to "Happy Birthday, Mr. President." So what if Marilyn bragged about snagging a boring brainiac like Arthur Miller? *The Crucible?* Two hours of anti-McCarthy ranting, dressed up in black robes and pointy hats. The audience skulked out like seals trying to escape wielded clubs. *Death of a Salesman?* She saw it on Broadway with Lee J. Cobb. Slumped in the front row. That wasn't theater. It was like watching a coyote chewing off its leg to escape.

The only value Marilyn ever provided to the world was humiliating that high-falutin' bitch Jackie. So prim, so proper in her pillbox hats. What did she keep in those stupid hats? Pills. And why did people lap up her blue-blood fictitious biography, anyway? Old Black Jack Bouvier was a raving, womanizing drunk. What do you call the Kennedy/Bouvier men in a bathtub? A Bay of Pigs.

Oriana splashed her feet in her pool and spotted a coyote about a hundred yards beyond her waterfall. They were ubiquitous but harmless. Like wiseguys in the Mob. She thought about Luke Braden, the grandson who knew nothing about her. She had given up ever having a decent conversation or relationship with her son Frank, the bigshot literature professor. He probably worshipped Arthur Miller. With her grandson, Luke, she might have a chance. On her bedroom dresser, she had two framed photos of Luke, one in his blue boxing trunks, another in a tuxedo. She'd lifted these from the Internet, a trick she learned from her pool boy. She didn't really know Luke, but she adored the very idea of him. Though Luke didn't come along until the early 1980s, she had a hunch he'd prefer Joe DiMaggio to Arthur Miller.

Twenty years earlier, Oriana had reluctantly promised Frank that she would never show up in Luke's life. Why had she done that? Her son had persuaded her that her past—the Mob, the saloons, the midnight whoring of her youth—would crush a tender young boy. Bad enough that Luke's mother had died when he was so young, the poor boy would not be able to handle a grandmother with a past so shady, so *unsavory.* As if the scent of semen were on her breath. Frank had provided Oriana with reams of psychoanalytic testimony and research papers documenting the potential damage. Frank had sent her a clear message: Get back in your closet with your boas and your memories of Lansky, Castro, and Lucchesi. She had consulted her lawyers, who gently sided with Frank. And yet now an exception must be made. Luke was in danger. Anyone within ten feet of Paul Tremont would eventually suffer, either mentally, financially, or physically. The man's ambitions were limitless, and he did not hesitate to destroy employees to fulfill his quests. Playa had told her that Tremont had Castro in his sights. And somehow Luke was part of the plot. The two men she loved most were merging into the crosshairs. Fidel, her lover from another era, and Luke, the grandson she longed for but could not touch. She would not sit still. She must warn Luke.

Oriana settled on a sofa in front of her towering floor-to-ceiling windows. With a push of a remote control, the curtains closed, and one of the huge panes darkened and then transformed into a computer screen the size of a small theater screen. Oriana spent the next few minutes cutting and pasting photos of Paul Tremont that she had gleaned from the Internet, from her archives of the 1960s, and from a database selectively supplied to her by Castro's brother, Raul. She would send an anonymous warning to Luke, a warning that would wake him up from the slumber brought on by the smell of Tremont's cash.

CHAPTER 67

"I can't believe he's unwinding the whole deal!"

Cori was no longer surprised by anything Luke told her about Tremont. "He unwound *me* pretty quickly, even after the FBI dropped all the charges and apologized ten times over. What's so surprising about backing out of a chocolate deal?" She was sitting on the king-size bed, leafing through magazines.

"Listen to me, Cori," Luke said. "I've never seen Ryan shaking. Vibrating, really. He lives with pressure every minute. They wake him in the middle of the night if the Shanghai A shares start outperforming the Shanghai B shares. He's already worth millions and routinely lays on trades worth a billion dollars. But he looked like he was about to disassemble, like a jigsaw puzzle pushed off the table." Luke told Cori the story of Ryan's argument with Tremont, emphasizing Ryan's fears of SEC prosecution.

"At least you can go back to your father now that his professorship is safe."

"Hardly. My father accused me of trying to destroy his career. I'm an accomplice of a runaway capitalist. His career? He never let *me* have a career, with all the sneering. And those goddamn college applications he kept dropping on my desk. He never spoke with me directly. It was all innuendo. He would talk to himself, into the air. I'd be sitting on the chair trying to watch *Monday Night Football*, and he'd orate to the atmosphere: 'I can't believe how much college graduates make compared to high school dropouts. The *New York Times* just published a study,' he'd say to the crown molding in our apartment. It was like living with a carnival barker. 'See the amazing college graduate! Witness the miserable dropout!'" Luke announced loudly. "And my father wouldn't hand me the article. He'd neatly clip it with scissors and slide it in my in-box."

"You had an in-box?" Cori chuckled.

"Yeah, doesn't every kid? If I wanted a serious conversation with him, I had to schedule it during office hours, which he posted on the refrigerator." Now Luke chuckled at the absurdity and pretended to address his father. "Hey, Dad! Can I talk to you about my urge to screw Mrs. Halburt in apartment 4A? Oh? Sure. Well, can you pencil me in for Wednesday at noon 'cause my dick will explode if I don't deal with this by Friday!"

Luke wanted to change the subject to Fidel Castro, but wasn't sure how Cori would react. Her father was the Senate's fiercest Castro baiter and hater. And what about her? Was Castro good because he fought Yankee imperialists? Or was he bad because he trampled on free speech, anti-government protests, and gays? It was hard to know where Cori would stand. But he was too excited to wait any longer.

"Tremont has plans for me that are much bigger than Mars bars," Luke said, placing his large hands on her narrow shoulders. She was wearing an ivory-colored silk camisole that accentuated her long neck. He rested his lips at the base of her neck and nudged aside the camisole with his mouth.

"Oh?" She drew back. "Do tell? Being out of work I'm forced to live vicariously."

Luke stepped back and looked her straight in the eyes. "He's setting me up to meet Fidel Castro in Vegas." He shook his head as if trying to wake up.

"No way. Don't get me wrong, Luke, but you can't be important enough for that. Not even the UN secretary can arrange a meeting."

Luke recounted his conversation with Tremont, why Tremont couldn't meet Fidel, and why Fidel would be willing to meet an ex-athlete who had played the role of gladiator against a Cuban champion. It sounded almost plausible.

Just then, they heard a slight rustling sound from the living room. They jumped. The last time they heard a strange noise in the apartment, the FBI broke through and threw their lives into a Cuisinart. Under the door was a Chinese takeout menu, halfway exposed. Just another delivery man trying to drum up more business. Cori walked to the door and picked up the menu. When she did, something slipped out of the menu: a small computer disk.

"Cool," Cori said, "they must be putting the menu on disks. I guess you can just order online and watch a video of them carving Peking ducks."

Cori slid the disk out of the packaging. "Wait. This has your name on it. 'Urgent.'" She noticed that her name was on the disk too. And so was a photo of a landscape. It was a picture of the Leopard Memorial Fountain near Hoover Dam. Her heart started beating faster. She hadn't been able to solve that mystery and had let it slip from her list of worries. Now it crawled back from under the door.

"Boot up your laptop. We have to look at this," she said. Once the Dell flashed blue and welcomed them, she slipped the disk into the DVD drive.

A hazy video of Fidel Castro in fatigues filled the screen, a scene of him hiding in the Sierra Maestra with Che Guevara. There was no sound, and the film clip lasted about ten seconds. Then a video of a nightclub scene, the Tropicana. A middle-aged man with a five o'clock shadow sitting in the front row on a white chair. Someone had crudely inserted a caption with the date and his name: Fulgencio Batista. A young Caucasian man walked over to Batista, lit his cigar, and pulled an ashtray from his pocket. He was tall. The film was grainy. It could have been anyone. The camera panned the room: guys in white suits and hats; showgirls in feathery headdresses so tall they can hardly walk straight. A close-up and they saw the face of the tall man. Sort of familiar, but the hat blocked half the face. Then the man removed his hat, wiped his forehead.

"Holy Jesus, it's Tremont!" Luke cried. The frame froze. They waited for the next scene, but nothing happened.

"This is too spooky," Cori said. "Who would have sent this?"

"I know. It's got to be Buck. This fits right in with what he was telling us at the hospital. Tremont, Batista, the gambling world. We thought he was hallucinating but this is proof of his story, isn't it?"

"That's ridiculous. From the grave, the hand of Buck reaches out, passes through a Chinese restaurant, and slides a computer disk under your door?"

"How about your father? It's like he's putting something in your in-box without confronting you head-on."

"Too high-tech for him. The most I could expect from him would be, what do you call it?—that X-ray film stuff that libraries used to have?"

"Microfiche?"

"Yeah, something like that."

Cori could imagine her father ordering a Senate staffer to concoct a disk. But why would he bother? He had nothing against Tremont. Senator Leopard probably got campaign contributions from Tremont.

As they puzzled, a glimmer of light emerged from the laptop. Luke leaned over to see an icon for Audiomate, a Voice-Over-the-Internet company. An icon for a bullhorn popped up, and a woman's voice started speaking. He turned up the speakers, but could not get the sound much louder than a hoarse whisper. They both leaned in close and stared at the computer speakers.

> *Luke, we've never met, and probably never will. But I can't stay quiet while you put yourself in terrible danger. As you can see from this motion picture, Paul Tremont has a long history with fascists. He wants Havana back. His White House fantasy, his obsession with those Kennedy's, it is all an insane nightmare you should run away from. If you help him, you'll pay a dear price. He'll dispose of you or anybody else that gets in his way. And you are too dear to me for me to stay quiet, despite your foolish father. Ciao.*

The sound faded to just the faint hum of the disk drive. Cori looked at Luke. Surely, he must have an idea who this is. She waited for Luke to explain. But Luke's face was blank and ashen.

"This is getting crazy, Cori," he said. "You know what it's like, right?"

"What do you mean?"

"After you lost your mother, did you have any aunts or big sisters to step in and help you handle things?"

"Only for a few months. Then my father was back on the Senate floor and a bunch of nannies flew through the revolving door."

"For me it was similar, but no nannies and no national mourning ceremony. My father was just an assistant professor. His parents were dead. All I had was a slot at the daycare center at Columbia."

Cori looked at him. She didn't understand the connection.

"I've spent half my life daydreaming about my family, people I never knew. Like those stories of amputees who still feel pain in their legs. And some voice of a distant woman says I'm dear to her? It's the cruelest hoax. Like asking an amputee to kick a field goal. I don't know who sent this, but I'm ready to crack open a window and see whether I can send this disk flying across Central Park to the East Side. Maybe I'll get lucky and I can hit Jackie Kennedy's old apartment."

"Maybe you should show this to your father," Cori suggested. "He might have some guess about it. It's definitely the voice of an old lady."

"How do you know?"

"Have you ever heard anyone under seventy use the words "motion picture?" That's like discussing 'talkies.'"

"Oh, shit!"

"What?"

"I've gotta go back to the office for a minute. Now that Tremont's called off the Mars acquisition, he ordered us to shred our research before midnight."

"Is that legal?"

"Yeah. It's just our research for internal use. It's not like we're being audited."

Luke rushed down the hallway toward the elevator, hoping to bump into a Chinese delivery man along the way. He didn't. Instead he ran into a crime scene in the offices of Tremont Advisors.

CHAPTER 68

Luke jogged across the street, took the express elevator, and unlocked the door to the office. The lights were dim, though he could tell that a few associates were still working. He unlocked the drawer to his file cabinet. Inside were all the original, numbered copies of the briefing book he had prepared on Mars. He also had all the printouts he'd done of spreadsheets, balance sheets, and revenue forecasts. He started tapping keys on his computer and zapping files from his hard drive. Then he plugged in the shredder and started feeding the fruits of a month of nonstop labor into the hungry mouth of the machine. With a whirr, it would all be gone. But he had a new mission, the Fidel Test, as Tremont called it. He also had the unresolved missions swirling in his own mind: living with Perez's death, his relationship with his father, and with Cori, and the bizarre specter that slipped under his door wrapped in a Chinese menu.

It was ten thirty P.M. when the last page of the last document was spat out like paper spaghetti. With all the confused thoughts assaulting his mind, Luke decided to seek temporary refuge in the Tremont gym.

The spa at Tremont Advisors includes the latest weightlifting machines, stair-steppers, and about fifty spongy exercise balls. In addition to the exercise rooms, Tremont's architect had designed a steam room and hot tub, nicknamed the Grotto. The tub was the size of a suburban family's swimming pool and was constructed of purple and orange rocks brought in from Fiji. Fan palms and bamboo encircled the tub. "World music"—those airy sounds made by flutes and pipes from the Andes— filled the atmosphere. When you stepped into the spa area, you were transported far away from Sixtieth Street. Tremont wanted a place where he and his senior colleagues could trade in the violent waves of stock prices for the gentle eddies of the tropics. The Grotto was for men only. The few female executives at Tremont were compensated with an annual pass to the deluxe gym at the Mandarin Oriental Hotel nearby.

While Luke was feeding papers into his shredder, Paul Tremont was breaking his own rules about women in the spa. He'd called Sonny to join him. She was beautiful and discreet, two virtues Tremont prized above rubies. Her long black hair was streaked with strands of blond that rolled down in curls toward her round breasts. While other Asian girls might've looked silly or cheap with blond highlights, Sonny looked glamorous. She could afford glamour. Tremont paid her a $250,000 salary to file papers, fetch cigars, arrange jet travel, and keep him happy. Tonight he wanted to be happy in the spa, in the tub.

Tremont was still in his robe as he looked down at Sonny floating naked in the Grotto, her head resting on a step in the shallow end. He let the silk robe slide off his shoulders and fixed his gaze on her. She looked small, and he looked huge, his chest beginning to heave with anticipation. He didn't want to talk to her. Talk added stress. He wanted to relieve the tension. He stepped into the pool and leaned down brushing his lips over her eyes and down to her breasts. As he headed further downward, Sonny unleashed a fugue of ahs, oohs, uh-huhs, and yeses.

Tremont didn't pay much attention to her cooing, except when she said, "Oh, God." *Yes, I am your god, aren't I, he thought?* He looked up at her with a twisted smile. His acolyte. His peasant from the East. Where would she be without him? Clipping toenails at a nail salon? Was this how JFK felt when he commanded his rotating harem through the baths of Boston and Washington?

Her head bobbing gently on the step, Sonny looked straight up at the ceiling, where ceramic stalactites pointed downward. A wave sloshed over her face, over her eyes. The waves grew higher as Paul Tremont lifted his legs and marched three steps toward her head. Sonny took a deep breath through the sloshing water and then closed her lips.

"C'mon, Sonny, open up."

She could not refuse. That was her contract, her promise, his desire. He lifted a leg over her chest and straddled her. His hard penis jammed into the soft spot under her chin, which made her choke and open her mouth. She tilted her chin downward and allowed him to slide his hardness into her mouth. His large hands cradled her head and yanked her head to the side, off of the step. His thrusts, slow at first, became more severe, even angry, and those thrusts began to push her head under the surface of the Grotto. As he moved his hips, his member slipped out of her mouth, and she tried to sneak in an extra breath, but within a second another ram, bruised the back of her throat.

Then it happened. His drives turned deeper and pointed further downward, propelling her head not just an inch, but two or three or six inches under the water, now swirling with waves. He had turned the Grotto into a kind of whirlpool around her face, and she could not breathe. The slosh of the water, the sound of the music, and the grunts of this man were mixing together like a clashing symphony by Wagner. She began twisting her head but he held her in place with one hand and slapped her with the other. In that last twist, she tried to swallow air, but instead swallowed the chlorinated, rose-infused water of the Grotto. Instinctively, her brain told her mouth to open again and so she ingested mouthful after mouthful of water along with his semen. Before he had finished, her eyes rolled up.

Tremont looked down at the woman and realized something terrible had happened. Two thoughts collided in his brain. One expected; the other quite extraordinary: *What do I do?* And *How dare she!*

CHAPTER 69

Luke marched down the hallway to the Tremont spa and tried the door, but it was locked. Josh and Justin, the trainers, must have cut out early. He looked through the frosted glass door, hoping to find someone milling about inside. He thought he heard a loud groan, but there was no follow-through. No answer to his knock.

Inside the spa, only one person was alive and he was on the telephone.

"Burns, there's been a big accident here. I need you to clean up. Call Playa and tell him it's a red alert. When I say *clean up*, Stuart, you know what I mean, right?" Tremont spoke while grabbing his silk boxers. He rehearsed his story with Burns. "She should not have decided to take a swim here. The sign clearly says that women are not allowed in the Grotto. She had a terrible accident. We feel terrible about it. Tell our counsel's office to set up a trust fund for the family."

Tremont's face was covered with sweat. He looked down at Sonny. She didn't look injured or bruised. He wondered whether to drag her out of the Grotto or leave her floating. It was an accidental drowning of course. But he had an ounce of humanity. He reached down into the water and pulled her up on the step. He stumbled into the rest of his clothing and walked toward the exit leading to the main offices. His limo would be waiting downstairs, but as he swung open the frosted glass door, it struck Luke on the forehead. What the hell?

"Luke, you shouldn't be here." Tremont said sternly. "Go home,"

"But I was just finishing things up and felt like blowing off some steam."

"Do you have a key?" Tremont asked.

"No, that's why I've been knocking on the door," Luke answered.

Tremont locked the door behind him. He wished Luke a good night. Then he realized he'd been too abrupt. "Don't forget to learn some Spanish so you can greet Castro," he said while striding toward the elevator.

Luke said "Adios," but Tremont didn't hear. Walking back to his own office, Luke passed the vault outside Tremont's office. He glanced to his right and saw that Ryan was still sitting alone at the trading desk. He had not yet filed the final daily P&L nor the updated "playbook for prosperity." Ryan had sent his assistants home; the night trading desk crew would be reporting shortly. Luke decided to drop into the kitchen and scavenge for some snacks. The door swung shut behind him.

Then Luke heard Stuart Burns rush toward Ryan on the trading floor, his shoes clicking across the hardwood. "Ryan, anybody else here?" he asked urgently.

"No. Sent them home," Ryan replied, hardly looking up from his spreadsheet.

"Good," Burns said. "Look, Paul just called. There's been an accident, and paramedics will be here soon. We know we can count on you to keep it to yourself. If word gets out, it could damage our reputation. Paul Tremont has been good to you, Ryan. We've kept your secrets—"

"Of course, Dr. Burns." Ryan had no choice, really.

Luke wondered whether he should open the kitchen door and announce himself. But too much time had elapsed already. If he walked out now, Burns would think that he had been spying on them. Besides, Tremont had ordered him to go home. If Tremont found out that he was hanging around, it would look like insubordination. So Luke leaned his head toward the hinges of the kitchen door and listened.

"Go to your office, Ryan, and keep the door closed," Burns instructed him. "You can watch market movements on your desktop, right?"

Ryan walked to his office, grabbing his calculator and a stack of papers.

Luke leaned closer against the cabinets in the kitchen and waited.

A few minutes later, a short, dark-skinned man arrived, followed by two men who looked like New York City firemen. Then the sound of a gurney being wheeled toward the spa. Luke heard a crash, as the glass door of the spa was shattered. He held his breath. He squinted through the space between the door and the jamb. A woman lay on the gurney, head uncovered. She looked Asian and familiar. She was the girl he had met at Tremont's spa visit at Mandalay Bay in Vegas. His mind returned to that momentous day when Tremont anointed him a future power-broker at Tremont Advisors. Luke remembered the girl's scream from the steam room that day. Sweat started spreading out across Luke's skin as he watched the men rushing toward the exit.

"Take the freight elevator," someone ordered.

"Burns, get over here," barked the dark-skinned man. "It's worse than you said. I looked her over. Any detective could see it. Her mouth, her head. She was not alone."

Burns turned white. "I need a cold drink right now," he said staggering toward the kitchen

"Damn," Luke whispered to himself. Luke's eyes searched the kitchen for a closet or pantry. None. He looked down at the waist-high cherry wood cabinets and quickly calculated that he could not squeeze himself in. He thought about playing dumb. He could burst out of the kitchen, and preempt Burns by mumbling something about late-night phone calls to Tokyo. He heard Burns' footsteps coming closer, the tip-tap of the tall heels the small man preferred. Luke leaned back behind the door and held his breath; maybe there was enough room to tuck himself between the door and the cabinet behind it. Burns leaned his hand against the door and started to swing it open.

"Burns!" the dark-skinned man shouted. "You gotta follow her. Right now! Catch up to the boys in the elevator."

Burns was startled. "Why? She's dead, Playa. I can't do anything!"

"You're a doctor, right? You've gotta try first aid or something—or else it'll look like you came here without any purpose except to cover Tremont's tracks. Now, go!"

Burns immediately retreated toward the lobby. Luke waited for the men to dash out to the elevators.

Luke knew he was no Boy Scout. He had tricked Bloomberg re-porters, posed as a medical salesman, and looked the other way when Tremont's employees jogged through that shady neighborhood just on the border of insider trading. But he had not signed up for this. Luke had killed someone himself, under the blinding halogen bulbs of an Atlantic City boxing ring. He still faced flashbacks of Perez dropping to the floor, eyes rolled up in his head, lips hanging like loose blubber. But boxing was premeditated maiming; combatants were guilty of premeditated brutality. What had happened tonight was a nightmare, a twisted, ghoulish crime. Watching the dead girl roll through the Tremont offices like a sacrificial lamb to the great god Tremont nauseated him. What logic led to the snuffing of a girl? And the escape of a billionaire who boasted medals and awards bestowed by the Red Cross and UNICEF?

He had to call the police. Wasn't that obvious? He had seen a dead girl drowned in the spa, while Tremont was there. He could tell them that he saw Tremont exit the spa. He could report Burns's conversation. Burns was an accomplice. It was a slam dunk case. His hands shaking, he picked up the telephone and began to push the buttons 9-1-1 on his office phone. His fingers must have stumbled, though, because the familiar tones did not chime as he pressed down. He tried again. This time he hit 9-9-1 by mistake. A third try at 9-1-1. A voice answered. It was Paul Tremont.

"Luke, I thought you might still be there," Tremont began in that mid-Atlantic accent that sounded so calm you'd think he was going to invite his employee to a round of golf. Luke quickly realized that the outgoing lines had been shut down. "What have you been up to since I told you to go home?"

"I realized I had a few more Mars documents to file." He didn't want to use the word 'shred.' "I was actually about to lock my office door when you called."

"Good. Apparently there was a very bad accident here this evening. The paramedics were here but it's taken care of."

"How bad?" Luke opened his drawers and rifled through them, hoping to find a voice recorder or cellphone on which to record the conversation.

"I don't have all the details, but it could be serious. We'll take care of it."

Tremont must be suspicious. Had he known Luke was dialing 9-1-1?

"No matter what happens," Tremont said, "it's important to know that three former attorneys general serve on our board. Last year we donated $10 million to the New York City police department to buy Kevlar vests. We once had a disgruntled employee who tried to report us for a bunch of frivolous charges. Our lawyers buried him, drove him into bankruptcy. Then, of course, poor Arnie Letts didn't end up so well either. That was suicide."

"I'm not sure I follow you, Mr. Tremont."

"You know what Ben Franklin said, right?"

Tremont answered his question. "During the revolution against Britain, he said 'We must hang together, or we will hang separately.' Remember, Luke, Tremont Advisors is a revolutionary organization, and you are a patriot." He hung up the phone.

Luke understood the message. Arnie Letts was dead. If O.J. Simpson got off, wouldn't Paul Tremont be able to wiggle free? Who else could get blamed for the accidental death?

Then it hit Luke like a left hook to the chin: *He* could be tagged as the murderer. What alibi did he have? He was in the office where no one but Tremont had seen him. Luke's heart started beating with so much fury he thought his shirt buttons would fly off. He wondered if he could make it back to his apartment without passing out or vomiting or both. He had to run. He also knew he had to have some proof with him. But there was none, other than the voices he heard while ducking into the kitchen. He looked around his desk and saw shreds of paper. He knew he'd never come back to this office again. Tremont would figure some way to entrap him with his own fingerprints or some other clever ruse. Luke closed his door and made his way toward the elevators. Cori. Cori could help him figure this out. As he passed Tremont's empty office, he saw Ryan. Had the trader been there the whole time? Whose side was Ryan on anyway?

CHAPTER 70

Professor Francis Braden was teaching an evening seminar from seven to ten P.M. Just ten students and himself, sitting on sofas, tucked into a townhouse on 116th Street that an alumnus had donated to Columbia. The course covered ancient philosophies and twentieth-century myths. The students nicknamed it "Plato to Play-doh." Though Braden was riveting, the chenille-covered sofas and loveseats were so comfortable that he devoted his first lecture to Morpheus, the god of sleep. It didn't help that the students took turns bringing bottles of wine to the seminar.

This time, however, a lively discussion was underway when Braden's ecstasy turned to dread as Dean Chambers opened the door and called him off the couch. "A woman named Oriana is demanding to speak with you on the phone."

The students could see that the unflappable Professor Braden was looking flappable. He bolted from the room.

"Frank," Oriana began, "if you never listen to me again, listen to me now. I've just heard something. Luke is in danger and so are you. Be careful. I think you should get out of New York. Watch your back."

Braden was furious. "You interrupt me for this? For some cryptic warning? What are you, a Ouija board? I've got a class to teach. Please don't call again. If you were going to warn people about their backs, you missed your chance in November 1963." He slammed down the phone, but she had already hung up.

He returned to his classroom and forced the students to compare Greek tragic heroes with Willy Loman from *Death of a Salesman*. Could there be true Greek tragedy in the common man or did the gods reserve tragedy for only the noble and mighty? But after a few moments, Braden lost his train of thought. Distracted, he glanced out into the hallway and saw a man wearing a hat pacing and smoking a cigarette. Didn't he know that you can't light up inside in New York?

CHAPTER 71

Ryan was walking toward Tremont's vault with a small stack of papers and a computer disk as Luke approached. What had Ryan seen? Luke wasn't sure whether to confront Ryan. If Tremont would eventually try to frame him, it would be better to know what Ryan knew. Luke swallowed hard and started a conversation.

"Hey, Ryan, I just got a call from the old man. Do you know anything about an accident?"

"Nothing," Ryan said, too quickly. "Just been finishing up the sheets."

Luke looked into Ryan's eyes. He was trained to detect anxiety and fear. He found it in Ryan's enlarged pupils.

"You sure?"

"No worries," Ryan said. He *was* worried.

Luke did not let go easily. "Well, Tremont tells me that there's been a bad accident here, and somebody's going to get the blame. Could that be you, Ryan?"

"I don't know anything," Ryan repeated. This time his freckles seemed linked together by a reddening face.

As a trained fighter, Luke knew that he needed some leverage over an opponent. Paul Tremont lived in a world of information. Luke needed information for that leverage. He noticed Ryan's papers, a computer disk, and the folder inside the little vault. Could he steal them? He assessed Ryan. He outweighed the guy by twenty pounds. He gritted his teeth and began to draw back his arm to land an explosive blow.

Caution took over before he could pump his arm forward. If he leveled Ryan right now, surely the police and FBI would come after him with more force and more confidence. A *violent* offender, they would say. Prone to outbursts of uncontrollable anger and physical abuse. Certainly able to kill a woman. Luke relaxed his arm and watched as Ryan placed the materials in the safe. Then Luke noticed something odd. Ryan carefully placed the documents and the disk on the bottom of the safe. He gingerly closed the door. He then walked away and jogged toward the elevators. Luke was certain that Ryan did not spin the lock after closing the door!

He waited a few moments, watched the elevator enclose Ryan, and then he made his move, sneaking toward the vault. He was about to reach in when he was struck by a thought. What if this were a setup? What if Ryan was calling the police so that they could arrest Luke for theft, a nice foreword to locking him up for murdering the girl in the Grotto. In just a few moments, the night desk traders would be arriving. Luke had little time to weigh the probabilities, to gauge the outcomes, to perform a spreadsheet operation in his head. His body and brain were exhausted from the stopping and going. His shirt was drenched in sweat. He couldn't take any more indecision. He jammed his hand into the safe and pulled out the documents, tucking them between his jacket and his shirt. Luke stood up tall, and tried to compose himself before walking out the door of Tremont Advisors for the last time. He wouldn't be coming back. And if the Tremont machine had its way, he would not be going anywhere ever again.

He managed to race across the street and up to his apartment, planning to stay just long enough to tell Cori his story and make an escape. Tremont's crew would be close behind.

He resisted the temptation to open the documents until he arrived in his apartment and triple-locked the doors. He ran into his bedroom, reached under his bed, and pulled out a Louisville Slugger, thirty-six ounces of hard maple, signed by Steinbrenner and Reggie Jackson. Luke didn't own a gun, but he could swing a piece of lumber with a lot of torque. He heard the shower spray and figured Cori was in the bathroom. Luke dropped the papers on his bed and tried to put them in order. There were five documents: First, the daily P&L, showing which stocks made and lost money that day. Second, a spreadsheet of codes that he could not decipher, followed by dollar amounts. One line said SWB5B.

Another said BTP2.5B, and CNB7B, and NKR1B. He had no idea what these meant. But at the top of the page he had a clue. The heading said "P4P." His eyes locked on the third document like an infrared missile locking on an enemy jet fighter. The heading said it all: CIA. Another three-letter acronym appeared under the CIA logo: DNA. Luke opened the document and started scanning it. Then he flipped to the fourth document. His eyes were ablaze. He screamed to himself and to Cori and to the Western hemisphere: "Holy fucking Christ! Holy fucking Christ!"

CHAPTER 72

Cori rushed out of the bathroom before she could grab a towel. "What?"

Luke was quaking. He threw down the documents as if they were laced with anthrax and started coughing. Cori walked over to him, but he could only point to the papers. She picked up the CIA report with disdain. The agency had been useless when her mother was assassinated. She opened the report and began to read:

> The subject, Fidel Castro Ruz, was born 8/13/26 in Cuba. Samples of DNA have been extracted from a variety of sources over a number of years, including blood drawn at Manhattan Hospital during a honeymoon in 1949, saliva from discarded cigars, and hair samples taken from his personal barber in Havana. These samples have been tested and demonstrate a consistent array of gene chromosome locations. They corroborate widely held beliefs that Mr. Castro is highly likely to be of Spanish and particularly Galician descent. These DNA samples do not suggest any gene markers for commonly tested diseases such as Alzheimer's, cystic fibrosis, or sickle cell anemia.

Cori looked puzzled. "So what? All this says is that Castro is Castro. You didn't need the CIA to tell you he speaks Spanish, did you?"

Luke managed to blurt out: "Read the other one." He thrust out his finger and pointed to a single sheet, the heading of which said "Brooklyn Forensics — DNA Lab."

Dear Sir,

We have examined the DNA report submitted to us on a subject #106, also known as Mr. Ruz, birth date 8/13/26. We have compared the DNA to samples submitted for subject #402, taken from blood, saliva, hair, and semen samples.

Cori continued reading though she didn't understand the terminology.

Alleles are reported below as the number of tandem copies of the basic DNA repeating unit.*

She looked down at the bottom of the page, where a footnote explained that alleles were forms of a gene trait. The report then broke into columns a list of eleven gene chromosome locations, all in codes such as D9S302 and D22S683. She was a poli-sci major, and there was no science in poli-sci. After the series of columns and codes, her eyes fell to a final paragraph.

"Subject #402, a white male also identified as L. Braden exhibits some chromosomal coincidences with Mr. Ruz. However, it is unlikely that Mr. Ruz is the father of L. Braden, within a confidence level of 98 percent."

"They tested your sperm? Where did they get that? Our bedroom? Those goddam spooks!" Cori looked up at him. "Relax, Luke. The report concluded that you're *not* related. It was a wacky Halloween scare, right? So they're a bunch of conspiratorial quacks."

"Turn it over, Cori. Read the back of the page."

She flipped over the sheet and scanned the last sentence. "Oh, God."

Mr. Ruz cannot be excluded as being the grandparent of L. Braden. Based on these data, the probability of grandparentage is 99.999 percent compared with an untested, randomly chosen man from the Caucasian population on North America.

There was only one man who could explain this. Luke had to find his father, who was, most likely, the son of Fidel Castro.

CHAPTER 73

After the clock struck nine P.M., Professor Braden closed down the discussion on the Greeks and Willy Loman. He waited until his students left and then walked down the steps into the street. He turned right onto Broadway. The man he had seen from his window wearing the hat and smoking the cigarette was following him. Braden thought about turning and confronting his stalker, but this was New York, on the fringe of Harlem, and, in the tight logic of a tenured professor, any normal person would have made an appointment during office hours. Oriana's warning reverberated: "Get out of New York." Braden was in good shape, but he was wearing a long black coat that would make it difficult to run. He picked up his pace. He glanced to the right and saw that the man had no trouble keeping up. He scanned the street, looking for a busy store where he could get lost or a police station where he could slip in. He passed a half-dozen laundromats and pizza parlors, but their storefronts provided no escape and no privacy. The man seemed to be gaining on him. Braden looked to his left and saw refuge—the subway station at 116th Street.

He fumbled in his coat pocket. Did he have a Metro card? Would he have enough time to buy a card and run through the turnstile? Braden grabbed the banister and jumped two steps at a time down the cement passageway. He smelled urine, but he also smelled his own fear. He found a card in his pocket, but had trouble pulling it out. He heard the man shout "'Scuse me," and could tell he was jostling commuters who were blocking his entrance to the station. Braden landed on the bottom step and dashed to his left. Just ten feet in front of him was the turnstile, looking like a meat grinder. A train was waiting in the station. It could take him to Penn Station or the Port Authority, getaway points. Braden withdrew his fare card and slid it into the slot. A green light flashed and he pushed through the turnstile.

Braden heard a beep on the train and saw the doors on the train closing as he passed through the turnstile. He also heard a rip, his coat snagging on the prongs of the turnstile. He pulled and pulled, but the coat wouldn't tear cleanly enough to let him through. He tried slipping off the entire coat, but the turnstile was jammed with black wool. He had no choice but to face the man who had chased him down the avenue. Braden turned around. He didn't see the face because his eyes went directly to the gun in the man's hand.

CHAPTER 74

Luke called his father's home and his office, but heard only the answering machine message. He listened to his father's voice, so familiar.

Now, however, Luke listened with a different set of ears. Was his father a son of Fidel Castro? He listened to every inflection. Was there a faint, vestigial Cuban trill covered up in his father's pronunciation of the word "Terribly," as in "I'm terribly sorry I can't get to the phone right now—" He pictured his father's face. The nose, the eyes, the ears. As a little boy, maybe five, he noticed a slight nick in his father's left ear. That day Luke comforted himself by saying if his father were ever replaced by an android or an imposter, he could tell by the little nick in the left earlobe. Was this the kind of paranoia that all boys felt? Or was it just boys who lost a mother and didn't have many other relatives to hold them?

Then he tried to picture Fidel. He was no student of Cuban history. Everybody knew what Fidel looked like—the big beard and the commanding body draped in olive fatigues. Did his father resemble that picture? He tried but couldn't perform the simple mental exercise of lining up an image of his father with an image of Castro. Then it occurred to him.

He raced over to the mirror and started inspecting his own face. What would it mean to be Cuban? To have Castro's blood? To have his thirst for fame? His almost uncontrollable, epic hunger for power? Luke took his hand to his cheek. It was smooth in the morning, even babylike, but now his five o'clock shadow was spreading across his neck and jawline. He pulled at his hair. Luke had never fit in. Too rough for school. Too resentful for college. But ultimately too smart for the boxing ring.

Neither school guidance counselors nor his father's psych texts could help him. Was it because of Fidel's fire-red blood rushing through his veins? Finally, after years of rebellion he might have a clue what was wrong with him.

He felt Cori place her arm around his waist. "I don't believe that report. It's probably more lies from the CIA or Tremont."

Luke felt in his gut that she was wrong. "That disk from the old woman we received, she seemed to know something. Even if this is bullshit, I do know one thing: Tremont is going to kill me. I've got to get out of here. The guy owns a Blackhawk! And he sure as hell knows where I live."

"Let's go to D.C. If you have enough cash we can just hop a cab, give the driver a few hundred dollars to take us. I can get into my father's special hideaway office. Security is unbelievably tight. We'll hang out there." Cori was fired up.

Luke wondered how he could have doubted her during that nightmarish arrest and the FBI foul-up. "Cori, I can't let you dive into this whirlpool. I don't know how much danger I'm in. As far as Tremont knows, you've been cut off. He's not going to go after a senator's daughter. You're a lot safer away from me."

He kissed her forehead and then let his lips slide down to hers. "I want you to be safe—I don't even want to tell you where I'm going. If any of Tremont's goons ask you questions, you tell them the truth: you don't know."

"But my father—"

"I thought you'd renounced your father," Luke said.

"I hate to go to him for help, but this is no time for family squabbles."

Luke ran his hands through his hair again. He ran to his closet, grabbed a large duffel bag, and started to throw stuff in, including the CIA and DNA reports and the indecipherable "playbook." He tore around the corner to his bedroom and into the walk-in closet. After a moment he came out holding a picture frame. His old photo of Liston and Clay. He wasn't planning to come back soon. The rumbling in his stomach told him he would be leaving behind the patrician heights of Columbus Circle. He knew this sensation well, though he hadn't felt it since the opening bell clanged on his fight with Perez in Atlantic City. His instinct was telling him to prepare for a fight.

CHAPTER 75

"How dare you talk to me like that, you little weasel!" Tremont screamed at Dr. Stuart Burns. The December sun cast weird shadows on their faces as they stood facing each other in the Tremont rose garden, high above the city. Beyond them in Central Park a thin blanket of snow covered the grass.

Confrontation was unusual for Burns. He was used to playing the role of courtier, pimp, and fluffer to Tremont. Before the tall titan walked into his life, the diminutive Dr. Burns had a middling practice on Sixth Avenue.

Burns readily admitted that he had been riding the Tremont gravy train. He didn't want to get off. He wanted to keep the million-dollar retainer and the ski chalet in Beaver Creek, where the gorgeous girls at the Ritz Carlton bar would slide a mug of hot Bailey's to you as you stepped off the lift. Right now Burns wasn't worrying so much about falling off the gravy train. He was worried about Tremont becoming unhitched and the train itself derailing. That would take down Burns too. Over the years, Burns had tried not to leave his fingerprints on Tremont's shady deals. He didn't want to know exactly how Tremont exploited Braden's disclosure of STATE SECRET, the Gresham Bros. trading program. Burns knew that Tremont was planning to dispose or depose Castro, but that was Playa's mission. He made sure that he was on record as hating Christian Playa. Today he'd asked Tremont to see him outside, on the rooftop. Away from note-takers and hidden microphones.

"You need to call off the Castro thing, Paul."

"Are you joking? I'd sooner toss you off the roof, Burns," Tremont said. Burns instinctively counted the steps to the ledge. About ten.

Tremont continued. "How many more opportunities will I have? The last good one was '61, the Pigs. There's too much at stake this time to let it go." Burns watched a drop of spittle collect in the corner of Tremont's mouth. "I will destroy Castro. And by destroying him I will be collecting billions of dollars in the market. And inheriting the future of Havana. This is my symphony. My *Mona Lisa*. My hat trick. My perfect game. And I'm not going to let you talk me out of it."

Burns wasn't about to let go. "But what about Braden? You're not going to get him to do it. Not after what he's seen, I mean the girl thing — to say nothing of the Castro DNA test."

"Braden's precise quote was 'Holy fucking Christ! Holy fucking Christ!'" Tremont said.

"How do you know?" asked Burns.

"The wires are tapped; the ether is tapped. Every molecule of the air he breathes. We've heard him wake up at two A.M. screaming about killing Perez. By now he's probably figured out that we have the place wired. That's why he's packing his bags and skipping town. And he'll be packing a special gift with him."

"Special gift?"

"Playa was able to switch his phone to the rigged one with the taser. They look identical. It'll act like a regular phone. But when Luke meets Castro, Playa can call him and launch the taser ring."

"That's theoretically great. But you still haven't told me how you're going to get Luke back in your game. You just said he was skipping town."

Like a great oracle, Tremont proclaimed: "'The sins of the fathers.' — Euripides. I feel pretty confident that the Castro family tree will cast a shadow over Luke Braden that he cannot escape."

Tremont planned to grab Castro's son — Professor Francis Braden — giving him the leverage he'd need.

CHAPTER 76

Luke waited for the elevator in front of his apartment while his eyes
darted in all directions. He kept patting down his duffel bag, feeling for
the folders. He'd live and die by that duffel bag. He needed cash. His duffel bag might be worth millions, but all he had was five $20 bills. He
slipped his card into the slot of a Citibank ATM, and tried to guess his
balance. Probably $800. The machine rejected his log-in. He knew his
nervous fingers must have flubbed a digit, so he tried again. A mecha-
nized sound burped from the machine and he awaited his cash. Instead
he read a message: "INVALID. CARD RETRIEVED." The machine
had eaten his card! He picked up the phone attached to the ATM and
started clicking the receiver tab. But there was no dial tone. He had just
enough change to buy a subway card and within a minute found a seat
for himself and his duffel bag on the Number 9 train uptown. Luke realized he should leave the city right away, but he had to see someone first.
The Professor. Fidel's son. Luke didn't see the black man with glasses
trailing him.

When the train started pulling into 116th Street, Luke looked around.
The Columbia students with backpacks and iPods attached to their ears
and their belts crammed the car. A homeless man cupped his hands
together like a megaphone and announced: "Now arriving in Harlem.
Last stop for white people!" Nervous laughter spread through the car as
the white people lurched toward the opening doors. Luke climbed the
steps, looking in all directions for another ATM that would accept his
AMEX card. He spotted a scratched up ATM with the name "Apple

Bank." He pushed the buttons, slid his AMEX through, placed it back into his wallet and waited. A moment later, a message flashed in block letters so big and tall they looked like street signage: "INVALID. POSSIBLE FRAUD." He heard three computer tones from inside the ATM. A high note, followed by two identical lower notes. Was the ATM dialing a number? 4-1-1? Directory information? Wait a minute. It was 9-1-1! The damn machine was reporting him to the police! He looked up above the screen and saw the shadow of a tiny camera built into the ATM. Shit! Not only had Tremont pulled the plug on his cards, but he'd figured out how to get the NYPD chasing his tail.

Luke bounded up the subway steps, the duffel bag bouncing and chafing against his shoulder and hip. Within a few minutes he was at his father's apartment, faculty housing, first built in the 1920s and partially refurbished every ten years. It had fast Internet modems. Eugene O'Neill regularly got drunk in a flophouse that operated in the lobby in the 1940s.

Luke knocked at the door softly, then loudly. It was eleven P.M. No response. His mind shifted from "Don't wake the neighbors!" to "Wake the dead if necessary!" Then Luke decided to do the unthinkable. He reached into the duffel bag and pulled out a symbol of the long-lost relationship with his father. A key. Francis had mailed him the key five years earlier, "Just in case there's an accident and you happen to care," his father had said.

Luke inserted the key. It felt like a very rusty lock. He tried to turn to the left and then to the right. The tumbler would not budge. He pulled the handle toward him and tried turning. Then he pushed the door forward and sideways toward the jam. Nothing. He tried pulling the key out, and had the illogical urge to start all over again. He would walk up to the door as if he'd just arrived. A fresh start. But as he twisted the key, it got caught. He felt himself working up a sweat. He threw his jacket on the floor and laid the duffel bag on top. He felt his forearm muscles bulge as he yanked with all his might. Still nothing. He knocked one more time, shouted "Dad!" and then retreated back to the subway station. He didn't see the young black man who hid behind the pillars and pediments of Harlem's finest landmarks.

While jogging to the station, Luke took out his cellphone and called his father's apartment. Instead of his father's haughty message, he heard that annoying sterile female-like voice: "I'm sorry, your call did not go through. Please dial the operator." He tried again and a series of tones spelled out in his brain: 9-1-1. He tried to take stock of the situation. Down to his last $100. He couldn't find his father. Tremont had turned off his portals to money and to his father. Cori was off-limits. He loved her too much to endanger her. Don't panic. Think. He thought of Buck's raspy voice: "There's always a counterpunch! Always a counterpunch!"

CHAPTER 77

The man with the dangling cigarette yanked Professor Braden back from the turnstile and tried to hurl him against the wall. Braden thrust his elbow back and up, catching the man's jaw. The man's hat flew off, but he managed to hold on to Braden's neck.

"What the hell do you want from me?" Braden demanded before he could turn around to face the assailant. The ticket booth was empty. The distant voice of Oriana resonated in his head. "Luke is in danger and so are you." Braden reached for a billfold in his pocket containing a couple of twenties. When Braden went for the billfold, the assailant grabbed Braden's arms in a full nelson wrestling hold and threw him to the ground. They rolled across the floor of the empty station.

"Stop fighting!" the man said, somewhat winded. He sat on top of the professor and withdrew a badge from his inside pocket. "FBI!" he shouted, waving his ID in front of the professor's shocked face.

"Larsen. Agent Nick Larsen." Larsen helped Braden to his feet. Braden had trouble focusing for the next few minutes. Soon the professor found himself sitting across from Larsen in a Greek diner, each with a mug of bitter coffee. Larsen explained that he'd been involved in the false arrest of Cori Leopard and Luke.

"What is it about you Bradens? Your son cracked my jaw, too."

"So what do you want from me?"

"We haven't given up on the D.C. Metro case. Maybe your son is innocent. Maybe not. But we're continuing to get hot traffic."

"Traffic?"

"Intelligence cables from embassies and from the Agency."

"I thought the FBI didn't talk to the CIA."

Larsen tilted his head back. "I thought you lived on the Upper West Side of New York. I thought you read the *New York Times*. I thought you read the *New York Review of Books* and the *Village Voice*."

"I do," Braden replied, still mystified.

"Then you should know about the worst evil ever perpetrated on civil society," he said with sing-song sarcasm. "The, ooh, Patriot Act!" He waved his hands like Japanese actors running away from a Godzilla doll.

Braden had enough. "Please, Mr. Larsen, what the hell do you want?"

"I want to know what you know about a dame named Oriana."

Dame? What was this, a film noir festival? Larsen had dropped a bombshell.

"This Oriana woman. Today, she called you, your son, the FBI, and Tremont Advisors. I want to know why. Frankly, we haven't got wiretapping authority yet, but we'll be facing the judge first thing in the morning. When I mentioned her name to the Agency veterans, they reacted with silence. Silence so long and loud I thought their voice boxes had exploded in their throats."

Braden responded with silence. *How do I describe her? My mother? A mob moll? A Latin lover? A Palm Springs dowager?* He hadn't seen her in twenty years. He decided to let them wait until they got their fucking Patriot Act wiretap.

He took a sip of coffee and turned his palms upward. "I've taught about ten thousand kids at Columbia. I think I taught an Ariana once. But I don't remember an Oriana."

"Pity," Larsen said. "I thought I'd hear some truth, some wisdom from a professor." He shook his head.

"That's your first mistake, Mr. Larsen. Truth has little to do with wisdom. Good night." Braden stood up and slowly walked out the door.

As soon as he left the diner, he picked up his pace. He had to get to Luke.

CHAPTER 78

Luke was rushing back to the subway station when he noticed the skinny, black guy following him. He darted into an Adults Only video store, lined with X-rated DVD's, obscenely large dildos, and other plastic ware. He didn't make eye contact with the Arab guy behind the counter, but raced toward a staircase in the middle of the store, above which hung a sign: LIVE GIRLS! It was dark and smelled of incense.

A fat, dark-skinned guy with a pierced nose was perched on a rickety stool. He looked up as Luke came down the stairs. "Do you know what you want, dude?"

The fat guy pointed to a row of rooms, each glowing with a different shade of light: purple, blue, pink, mauve, chartreuse. In each of the cramped rooms with the spooky glows awaited a girl. One of them had a generous bosom but also a dick.

Luke knew what he was looking for. He rushed past the small rooms with their freak show peep shows. At last, he found it. A back door. He flung open the door and ascended the short flight of steps to the street level. The black guy was gone.

Luke raced over to Eighth Avenue. And then he found it. What he was really looking for. Not a young girl. Not an old lady. Not a she-male. But a middle-aged man in a torn, black coat that hung sloppily off his shoulders.

"Dad!" Luke cried as the man walked by.

Professor Braden turned around. "Lucas! What are you doing here?"

"Never mind, we've got to talk," the Professor said.

"You better believe it."

"I tried to get you at your apartment, but my key didn't work." Luke could barely resist putting his arms around his father.

"That's impossible. The lock worked fine when I left for class this afternoon," the Professor replied.

Luke showed his father the key. His father's handwriting was scratched into it. "FB." "Is it possible someone's screwing with your apartment?"

"Until an hour ago, I would've said 'no.'"

"An hour ago?" Luke asked.

His father explained his violent encounter with FBI agent Larsen. But Luke wasn't satisfied. They had more to discuss. More to disclose. "Let's go somewhere we can sit down," Luke said.

Francis had had his fill of diners. And now he couldn't trust his apartment. He guided Luke to the step of a brownstone. They both sat, brushing away a few crystals of ice. He didn't know how to begin. "Luke, have you heard from a woman named Oriana?"

"Maybe."

"Maybe?"

"I got a strange CD under my door. A woman—she sounded old-fashioned—you know, in the words she used—she started talking trash about Paul Tremont. Crazy Cuba stuff. And then she said something about you."

"Me?"

"Yeah, I think she called you 'foolish' and said you wanted to keep things quiet." Luke hesitated. Should he tell him about Tremont and the girl? The murder? The plan to meet Castro? The fact that he stole stuff from the file?

His father's shoulders slumped. Sitting next to Francis on the stoop, Luke could see only a profile. Yet, in a second, his father's muscle tone seemed to transform from a hale man of fifty to a guy over sixty-five worried about Social Security.

Luke asked, "Who is she?"

"Who is she?" his father responded through an exhale.

Luke was feeling the pressure, the frustration. His father was evading, not answering. He jumped to his feet and stepped right in front of his father, like a man at bat glaring down at the catcher.

"Answer my question! Wait, forget this Oriana person. Who in the fucking world are *you*? Who am *I*?"

"What are you talking about?"

Luke felt the urge to hit, to actually punch his father, but he held back. Instead he kicked a small rock resting on the step. "I can't believe you've been hiding this for—how long? My whole goddamn life! What kind of excuse do you have? What kind of opening did you need! What kind of segue were you waiting for? How many hours did I spend on the couches of guidance counselors and child therapists, where *I* was supposed to reveal *my* deepest thoughts? Well, well, well, it turned out that you—the perfect professor—you were the one hiding, weren't you!"

Francis seemed to age as Luke's ranting continued. "I almost told you a hundred times."

"Fuck *almost*."

"Even recently, when Tremont came to the faculty club."

Luke remembered Tremont badgering his father about Cuba and Castro. "Tremont told you, didn't he? God knows where he dug it up."

"No, he didn't tell me."

"Then someone else must know,"

"I stole the information from Tremont. He didn't want me to know." Luke explained the past six hours, the nightmare of the Grotto death, the theft of the documents.

"It doesn't matter," Francis said.

"*It* doesn't matter? What doesn't matter, Dad? You can't even say *it* out loud, can you? Can you?" He looked down with disgust and then grabbed his father's collar. He looked into his father's brown eyes, or were they olive like Fidel's fatigues? "Tell me!" he screamed. "Tell me!"

Francis summoned a bitter breath and pronounced the sentence that had haunted him throughout forty years. "I am Castro's son." One more breath, choked through Luke's shaking hands. "And you are his grandson."

Luke heaved his father back onto the step. Luke was overcome with shame, anger, frustration, a lifetime of failure. "And that doesn't *matter?*"

"No," Francis whispered. "You're a self-made man, Luke. You are not just some ectoplasm that oozes through from generation to generation. DNA is not destiny." He spoke slowly from exhaustion and passion. "I could not let you or myself be controlled by some cell, some wiggling sperm that my father once released with a grunt. That was not me. What am I? I am the books that I've read, the museum's I've seen, the works of art I've absorbed, the life that I have led. I am Hemingway, Fitzgerald,

O'Neill, Modigliani, Picasso and all the others that I've devoted my life to."

Luke had little choice but to let his father explain.

"Look Luke, bigots, church elders, and Hindi caste-determiners are always condemning innocent people because of some wart, blemish, or chemical imbalance in their fathers. If I had told you the truth, the truth would have crashed down on you like an iron cage. So I wanted you to cultivate your mind because I was afraid you could turn out like my father and my mother."

"Instead, I became, what? A brute? A capitalist pig? And now you're telling me—and you're right—that I need to run away. So, guess what, Dad? I'm a prisoner anyway. What did all the hiding, all your philosophy accomplish?"

Francis shook his head.

"I think you called it wrong, Dad. You left someone out, didn't you?"

"Mom. Half my life comes from her, even though she died when I was little. If you define me simply as the books and museums I've seen, then Mom contributed nothing. She couldn't lend me those Irish drunks like O'Neill or Fitzgerald, or even a copy of *Sports Illustrated* because she was dead before I could even read. Under your Ivy League logic, Mom was a complete zero. Well, I refuse to believe that. My bloodstream carries more than you imagine. Thank God, it carries more than a nightmare in Havana."

"Then she's right," Francis said. He stared into the distance.

"Who?"

"Oriana. She said we'd both be in danger. Luke, Tremont could squash you like a gnat. He *must* kill you. You know too much. You saw too much. You've got to get out. Not just off this island. Off the planet, I don't know." Francis shut his eyes.

The sight of his beaten father made Luke's adrenaline race. Then Luke figured it out. Buck's advice. The counterpunch. He had a counterpunch. Setting it up meant fleeing town, if he could manage it without being caught. He had to catch a train to McLean, Virginia.

He stood up and started walking away, feeling slightly groggy.

"Wait, Luke. There's something else. November 1963," he said weakly.

"I've heard enough for a night. We can talk about the '60s tomorrow. I gotta get out." Luke started jogging, his duffel bag bouncing against him.

All Francis could muster was, "Be careful, Luke."

Neither of them noticed that the thin, black man had tracked down Luke again.

CHAPTER 79

The thin, black man watched Luke fumble through his wallet at the Amtrak window at Penn Station. He made a phone call and then sat in a plastic chair watching Luke.

Luke carefully counted $76 and gave it to the man at the ticket booth. He was down to just over $20. How could he accomplish his plan in D.C. on $20? He needed hundreds of millions. Maybe billions. When the sign posted his train, he trudged toward an Amtrak car with a bunch of government bureaucrats and mediocre lobbyists. The better lobbyists would all be on the sleek Acela train, where tickets cost half again as much. An old security guard, who looked Indian, asked for his driver's license and any electronic devices. Luke took out his BlackBerry. And the telephone with the rigged taser. He had no idea. Then the guard pointed to the duffel bag. Luke's stomach tightened.

"Why?" Luke asked.

"Security, why else?" the old guard said.

Luke noticed a gun in a holster. He unzipped the top of the bag, knowing that Tremont's goods were in a side pocket. "Just dirty gym clothes, mostly."

The guard took a sniff and waved his hand.

No one sat next to Luke. He opened the duffel bag and withdrew Ryan's handiwork. The codes looked like a Scrabble game dropped from a rooftop onto the pavement. Luke started feeding guesses into his Black-Berry. BTP? British Thermal? No good. CL1B? Clorox? No. He thumbed down the list. M00.5? What could "Moo" be? He had to crack this code. It was his only chance at a counterpunch.

After a few more minutes of frustration he decided he needed more help. A newspaper, maybe the *Wall Street Journal*. He gathered his belongings, and four rows ahead, he found a man whose head was bobbing forward. On his lap lay the *Financial Times*. That would do. Luke scanned left and right again. Commuters were either dozing or nose deep in their papers. Luke dipped his left shoulder, pretended he was saying something to his fellow passenger and brushed his hand over the sleeping man's lap. Then the train bounced and lurched to the right. The man woke up with a jolt. "Hey! Whaddaya doing?" he shouted.

"Sorry," Luke quickly answered. "Is this seat taken? I slipped trying to slide in here."

The man was not convinced. "It's taken. Find another seat."

Luke caromed into the next car. He found the first empty seat he could and plopped down, shaking from his encounter. He took out his BlackBerry again and started banging away, hunting for clues to the code. A hand touched his shoulder.

"Cori! What are you doing here? This is a mistake. You shouldn't be here with me." He was angry and worried. He also felt a return of that gnawing doubt about Cori. How did she know? Could she somehow be part of Tremont's grand scheme?

She kissed his cheek and slid down next to him. "I'm a stowaway."

"This is crazy. Tremont is a killer. Do you think he'd hesitate about getting rid of us?"

"Yeah, but I'm not letting you go down without me or without a fight. Remember, we've got the goods on him."

"He's got better lawyers. For all we know the FBI works for him," Luke said. He was losing hope for cracking the code or cracking Tremont. Right now the counterpunch was just a theory, a prayer. "Who told you I was on this train?"

"Henry."

"Beetle? My cornerman from the Perez fight?"

"I asked him to keep an eye on you. He loves you, Luke. He told me he'd always be in your corner."

"Let's just hope he doesn't have to mop me up when this is over."

Cori watched Luke rapidly punching numbers and letters in the BlackBerry. "Why is this so important?"

"This is P4P, what Tremont calls the 'playbook for prosperity.' If we can crack this, we'll know where Tremont is going to place his market bets. He thinks he's going to kill Fidel Castro. If we can figure out what bets he's placing based on Castro's death, we can get a leg up."

"What can *we* do?"

"If we can lay a big bet in the opposite direction of Tremont, and Tremont gets it wrong, we can wipe him out," Luke explained.

Cori was not convinced. "But what if Tremont gets it right?"

"We're screwed."

"And where will we get the money to bet against him? How much do you have in your account?"

"They've destroyed my accounts. I've got a total of $24. That's why we're going to McLean."

Cori immediately knew that Luke's remark could mean one thing. The CIA. Maybe they could save her and Luke. But since when could she trust those spooks?

A former spook was peering at them from the next car. Christian Playa.

CHAPTER 80

"You learned nothing from him? That's pathetic," said Carmody as he and Larsen huddled next to a plastic angel adorning an evergreen tree in Rockefeller Plaza. "And you call yourself the bad cop! You couldn't shake down an English teacher?"

"No. For a professor he didn't talk much," Larsen reported. "But that's okay, the judge will approve the wiretaps. I planted a bug on the professor's coat."

Carmody leaned against the fence overlooking the skating rink. "There's only one guy that Tremont trusts with his money. It's not our boy, Braden. It's the guy who handles the trades. Name is Ryan Fleet. Supersmart. Apparently, he's been downloading algorithms from NASA Web sites and somehow incorporating them into Tremont's software system.

"Al what?"

"Algorithms." Carmody watched his partner's eyes glaze over.

"What's this guy look like?" Larsen sounded skeptical

"I Googled him, but couldn't get an image. Apparently he missed 'picture day' for his Princeton yearbook."

An hour later, Carmody announced himself at Tremont headquarters, posing as a salesman for a new kind of accounting software that would help Ryan reconcile stock trades and IRS reports. It wasn't easy for the elegant Carmody to look the part of a salesman. He had shed his tight-fitting black suit and found a boxier glen plaid, along with glasses that had gone out of style.

Ryan Fleet told the receptionist to brush off the salesman even though he had an appointment. But Carmody stood his ground, insisting that he had traveled on the train from Passaic to get to the meeting. Ryan had other things on his mind. He hadn't slept all night. He kept seeing images. Sonny. Tremont in his bathrobe. And he kept playing over in his mind the confrontation with Luke Braden. How could he turn in Tremont? What would he be without Tremont? Ryan looked down at his shirt. It was brown and wet. He'd spilled coffee on his shirt and it now dribbled on his pants. He hadn't slept since he refused to execute the Mars/Hershey trade. But this was something else. Ratting on Tremont was more dangerous than sitting out a trade. He looked around the trading floor at his junior staff. Was he going crazy or did they all have suspicious looks on their faces? He looked over toward Braden's office. Had Tremont sent Braden on some new assignment—or dropped him in Long Island Sound? Is Braden talking to the police? Would Braden point the finger at him, too?

Ryan threw down his pen and marched to the receptionist area, his clothes still damp, his body foul with perspiration and coffee. When he turned the corner and saw Carmody, his face twisted with shock and repulsion. Ryan gritted his teeth.

Carmody stuck out his hand but his face shattered at the recognition. Ryan Fleet was the guy from the Village bar that wanted Carmody to call him. Ryan returned Carmody's handshake and pulled him toward a chic conference room a few steps away. Carmody was muscular, but went limp as Ryan shoved him onto a leather chair. "You show up at my work! Are you an idiot? You concoct a sales story just to see me again!"

Carmody tried to remain cool. He sure as hell wouldn't be scouting out guys on FBI time. "Hey, dude, I'm sorry." He took off the nerdy glasses he wore to impersonate a salesman. "Look, I'm on the *down low*," code for hiding in the closet. "You think I wanted this?"

"So you're telling me you're really here to sell me software and you took the train from Passaic, where you kissed your 1.5 kids good-bye. Bullshit."

Carmody had to lay his cards on the table. He took out his FBI ID out and slapped it on the table. "Ryan, I'm not here to sell you software. I'm here because the Bureau thinks that Paul Tremont is planning something big. An international strike, maybe. Maybe you guys are trading Airbus stocks and looking for a killing. But the intelligence chatter is frying the wires from McLean to the Hoover Building."

"I don't know anything. Nothing."

Ryan would not give up any information, even though he admired Carmody's flawless skin and bright teeth. "We report big trades to the SEC. We're in full compliance. That's it. Your fishing expedition is over."

"What do you know about someone named Oriana?"

"Never heard of her."

"Luke Braden."

"Young guy. Washed-up boxer. I don't know why Tremont's so hot for him. He's just getting his feet wet here."

"Do you care about him?"

"You mean, do I *like* him? Or am I attracted to him? Not my type."

"We think that Luke might be targeted for a hit. Not just a punch. You know what I mean?"

Ryan nodded. It was plausible. Did Luke already spill his guts to the FBI? Now they were looking to entrap him!

"What's a playbook?"

"You tell me," Ryan responded.

"Stock trades, right?"

"Maybe."

"Would it worry you if Braden were running around with the trading playbook?"

"No. It's coded. He's a boxer, not the Enigma machine."

"'Scuse me?"

"Try Googling the name Alan Turing."

"Does he work here?"

"No. Turing killed himself in '54. My point is, a theoretical playbook is useless in the hands of a boxer."

Carmody took notes. "Ryan, can you help us decode the playbook?"

"Fuck you. No way. You think I want to end up like the others?"

Ryan cupped his hands around Carmody's face, a move that embarrassed the agent. He whispered, afraid that a hidden microphone could pick up his words. "The playbook could be worse than useless. The playbook could get Luke killed."

CHAPTER 81

Luke and Cori agreed to split up at Union Station. With the playbook in his grasp, he had the ultimate leverage. He could give it to the SEC or to Tremont's hedge fund competitors or even auction it on eBay. How much would rogue traders or gamblers in Shanghai pay for the secrets of the $90 billion Tremont portfolio?

Christian Playa watched Cori and Luke separate. She headed to the left, no doubt to the Capitol. He was cutting right. To where? Playa wasn't worried. He knew the terrain well. The last time he was in D.C. was for the Sarah Hartman mission. Playa followed a few steps behind Luke. Tremont had given him a simple mission: get the duffel bag. "Should I bag Braden?" Playa had asked.

"No," Tremont ordered. He was convinced that Luke would turn himself in later. The "Euripides strategy," Tremont called it. "We'll have blood leverage."

Luke walked through the food court, stopping to buy a spinach bagel. He had forgotten to ask Cori for money, so grudgingly he parted with a dollar. He grabbed a few plastic half-and-half containers. They were free and would serve as his breakfast drink. Playa watched Luke and thought he was pathetic. The boy wanted to be a hedge fund titan and now he was sucking off plastic shot glasses of coffee creamer.

Luke wiped his chin and started jogging down the steps to the Metro. The Orange Line would deliver him close enough to McLean. The platform was crowded with commuters, those that got off Amtrak trains, and those simply changing Metro lines at the Union Station hub.

He'd been able to arrange a meeting at nine thirty A.M. using Tremont's name. If he showed up without Tremont, they'd give him hell. If he showed up late, his chances of success would drop to zero. If they didn't believe his story about the playbook, his chances of being arrested would jump to a hundred percent.

Playa kept Luke in his sights. Wearing a long, gray coat, from the back Luke looked like dozens of young men amid the D.C. maze, from college interns to youthful congressmen. Playa watched Luke wait at the edge of the track, standing right on one of the floorlights that would flash when a train approached. Playa's eyes focused on the duffel bag. How strong was the strap? How close to Luke's shoulder? Could he just yank it? Or would he need a knife? It was hot underground. Luke was taking off his coat. That would make Playa's theft more dangerous. Playa wondered if he could slice off the bag without also slicing Luke's arm? How would the ex-fighter respond? Playa wanted to time the theft perfectly. If the knife ripped his bicep, screw it. Playa felt no responsibility for the good health of Luke Braden. Sarah Hartman got a lot worse.

Luke looked at his watch. Nine A.M. He had just thirty minutes to get to the meeting. He'd need perfect connections. Where the hell was that train?

The light under Luke's right foot started blinking. Playa's heart started beating faster. This was petty theft, right? And yet Playa's body was geared up for a kill. Playa stood three steps above the landing, about fifteen feet from Luke. The car slowly came to a stop. *Whoosh.* The doors opened. Luke tried to enter, but a dozen annoyed commuters tumbled out, tripping on each other. Once Luke saw daylight, he lifted his right foot off the flashing light and took a first step into the car.

Playa's eyes locked on the duffel bag. He leaped down the three steps like a hawk swooping on a rabbit and within half a second flipped open his switchblade. His first cut slashed open Luke's shirt, ripping into his forearm. Somehow the duffel bag strap escaped the blow.

Luke wheeled on Playa. It was so fast and the knife so sharp, he didn't even realize that blood had sprayed. He yanked back the duffel bag with one hand and jammed his fist into Playa's face.

Playa fell backward toward the platform, while Luke grabbed onto a metal pole inside the Metro car. He needed to stay on this train. He needed to get to Virginia by nine thirty. As Playa fell backward, Luke saw the duffel bag flying toward his attacker. Playa waved his knife to sever the last bit of strap and rolled toward the step. Luke then noticed the gash and the blood spraying from his arm. The Metro chimes sounded and the doors started to close. Luke winced in agony as he watched Playa pick up the bag and tear up the steps.

Luke's agony stretched far beyond his arm. What could he bring to his meeting now? The playbook was gone. He had no money. His past was dirty. His future was treacherous.

After reaching safety at the top of the steps, Playa took a deep breath and watched the Orange Line car roll away toward Virginia. He was sure that Luke was headed to the George Bush Center for Intelligence, the headquarters of the CIA. Playa hoped that Tremont had the "Euripides strategy" lined up. He would find out soon.

CHAPTER 82

Professor Braden did not go back to his apartment after his confrontation with Luke. If they had broken his door lock, they could be waiting inside. He thought about calling Larsen, but he couldn't imagine confessing the Castro and Oriana story to the FBI agent. He walked back to the townhouse where he had given his seminar. The comfortable sofas that put graduate students to sleep would serve him well. In the morning, the winter sun sneaked through vertical blinds in microthin slices. Braden sat up and rubbed his eyes. Suddenly, the slices of light vanished. Braden felt his arms pulled behind him. He heard a metal clink and then realized his hands had been cuffed. He awkwardly turned his body around. Standing over him were two young Middle Eastern men with small backpacks. In another universe, they could have been foreign exchange students. One of them balled up his fist and slugged Braden on the side of the head. Braden rolled back on the sofa. Before the professor could muster a howl or a "Help!" the other lifted him up again while the first man unleashed another blow. One more crashing punch and the Professor was unconscious, bleeding from his left ear, and breathing with a horrific wheeze. The men gagged him with a coarse hand towel and watched his body writhe.

"We got 'im," the puncher said into his phone.

In D.C., Playa got the message in text form. He was pleased. He hopped onto the next Amtrak train and whistled his way through Penn Station. Euripides was working just fine.

*　　*　　*

Luke wrapped his coat around his arm and pressed hard.

His bleeding slowed to an ooze by the time the train crossed over the Potomac into Virginia. That was the only good news. He would go to his meeting empty-handed. He would have to fake his way through. Bluff about having the playbook. Then his phone rang. He jumped out of his seat and scraped the gash hard in doing so. He looked at the caller ID. "NO IDENTITY."

The Middle Eastern man who had punched Francis Braden spoke haltingly over the phone. "Here are your instructions. I will say them once. Twice means more blood. Your father, the son of Castro, is our hostage. He is safe. I hit him only three or four times."

Each sentence struck Luke like a round of buckshot. He wanted to interrupt but was too stunned and scared to try. He tried to block from his mind the news photos of beheadings in Baghdad.

"Proceed to Las Vegas as you were originally commanded. You are an emissary of Tremont. Don't forget that. You are to meet the leader of Cuba on the evening of December 31, just as originally planned. If you fail to show up and fail to follow your original commands, nothing will happen to you. But I'm afraid your father will suffer more. Much more."

Luke felt heat flush through his body and swallowed bile. "Who is this? I want to speak to Tremont. I've got something he wants."

The Middle Eastern man laughed. "I hear that you lost your leverage. In a fight. Some boxer." Luke heard a thump and a low-pitched moan. The man hung up.

Luke had never been knocked out in the boxing ring. He'd been stunned and had staggered a few times. "Rang his bell," the broadcasters said. But now he felt such a blow that it ricocheted his brain around inside his cranial cavity. At least when you're knocked out, you get a few minutes to peacefully rest. And a referee steps in to protect you from further harm. He pictured his father, like a prizefighter bludgeoned and beaten to the ground by low blows and kidney punches. As Luke stood in front of the imposing brick building in McLean, empty-handed, late for his appointment, he bit his chapped lower lip so hard it split and bled. The stakes were no longer an SEC charge of insider trading or even a dead prostitute in a spa. Other lives depended on this meeting and the aftermath. His father's, Cori's, and his own. Oh, yes, Castro's too. The oozing red dribbling down his sleeve was the only proof he had that his heart had not stopped beating.

CHAPTER 83

"What do you mean you can't find him!" Carmody shouted at Larsen. "You bought him coffee last night." They stood in front of the City Court-house, waiting nervously for a judge to act on their petition to wiretap Francis Braden, Luke Braden, and Ryan Fleet. "Unless Judge Henriks sides with us, we might as well join the pigeons out there." He glanced at the birds pecking among the snowflakes.

Larsen was embarrassed. He was old school, and the old school just suffered earthquake damage. Now it was his turn to look helpless in front of his junior partner. Larsen wondered why he didn't take early retire-ment. "Hey, Carmody, get off my back," he said waving his scarred, liver-spotted hand. "So the English professor's missing," he went on. "Maybe he's gone to a hippie commune in the Catskills for the week. Breathe some fresh air at Woodstock." He didn't believe it. Francis Braden was not a man of action. He was a man of habit and a man of books. He was pro-grammed to lecture for fifty minutes, read, think, and write. That was his life. Skipping town was not in his repertoire.

Carmody wanted to take action. But what? Where? Unless Judge Henriks granted them permission under the Wiretap Act, they were lost. Carmody and Larsen had worked with the legal staff at FBI headquar-ters, but the petition was no layup. Larsen reminded his younger partner that New York had a tradition of bucking the FBI.

"Their judges only care about airy-fairy civil liberties. If they see a body bleeding in front of them, they'll step right over it on their way to an ACLU meeting."

Just then the bailiff called them into his Honor's chambers. The judge, a man who looked like an old turkey, with a pointed beak and a wattle, began by scolding them.

"This petition stinks. You say you've exhausted all normal surveillance techniques, but all you've given me is a one-page summary. I don't know what you fellas think about privacy, but I can tell you most of the people in this district want to be left alone. They don't want some Washington, D.C. spy hiding under their bed or hiding in the potted plants."

Larsen tried to interrupt, "Your Honor—"

"That's the problem. You've got no sense of honor, Mr. Larsen. This Professor Braden character, for all I know he's screwing monkeys in the Biology Department. I don't care. I don't want you spying on him."

Carmody tried to help, his voice bending into a whine, "But, sir, we have reason to believe that Mr. Braden is involved in an international terrorist cell. We don't know whether he's a perpetrator or a possible victim. We believe that the cell is aiming to assassinate a world leader."

Henrik's eyes widened. "Who? The president?"

"I don't know," Carmody admitted.

"The pope?"

"I don't know."

"The queen of England?"

"We just don't know," Carmody admitted sheepishly.

"And yet you expect me to trample on a man's rights to protect either a president, a pope, or a queen? No, sir. No way. Petition denied."

Ten miles north of the courthouse, Francis Braden lay half-conscious in the trunk of an Audi speeding to a mosque in Yonkers. They tossed his coat onto the Westside Highway, where the radial snow tires of a thousand drivers shredded it into woolen fibers, along with a few red transmitter wires from the FBI that would never again feel an electrical pulse.

Larsen and Carmody didn't talk to each other as they trudged down the spiral staircase.

"We have no choice, then, do we?" Carmody finally said, outside in the cold again "All we can do is circle the known locations and wait for someone to step out."

"Fuck that," Larsen said. "You have no choice. I'm retiring. You know what that means?" Larsen had a nasty gleam in his eye. "I don't give a shit what Judge Birdbrain says."

"You could lose everything."

"What? My good looks?"

"Your pension."

Larsen put his hand on Carmody's shoulder. Probably the first time they had ever touched other than to shove the other out of the way. "I got taken care of thirty years ago, did some favors. Open and shut. Long gone. Statute of Limitations. I've got my fuck-you million waiting for me to turn sixty-five. That gives me just nine months."

Carmody was not surprised. He had heard rumors that guys of Larsen's generation did some deals back in the '60s when Hoover was too busy snooping on the Kennedy's and Johnson to watch his own underlings.

Then Larsen unveiled the shocker: "You know how I'm going to spend the first ten minutes of the next nine months? Turning the switch on the fucking wiretaps!"

Carmody's heart split between elation and dread and the fear of jail time.

Within minutes they were in Larsen's hotel room at the Hyatt at Grand Central. The bed was unmade and Larsen's dirty underwear was hanging from a bedpost.

"Here goes," Larsen announced. He flipped a switch on Carmody's laptop while Carmody shielded his eyes from the sin of countermanding a federal judge. A flat redline raced across the screen. There was no signal. Larsen fiddled with buttons for a few minutes. Carmody reluctantly walked over to the computer and tried a few tricks. But the red line stayed flat. The bug on Braden's coat was not sending any sounds or even impulses.

"Shit," Larsen said. "Some payoff."

"Wait, I've got an idea," Carmody said. "The bug's not transmitting now, but maybe I can tap into the signals it sent before it went dead. He was back at the keyboard. Larsen looked over his shoulder and saw buttons and icons emerge with terms like "retrotrieve," and "time-dashed." Then a hum. The red line vibrated like a snake beginning to stir.

"I don't hear anything," Larsen said. "Turn the fucker up."

Carmody cranked up the volume, unleashing an atonal symphony. The tiny speakers sounded like they were broadcasting from inside a washing machine. Carmody's fingers glided over the keys and massaged the icons for bass, reverb, and treble. Then a long series of sounds. Words started spilling out, first garbled, then clearer as Carmody worked the gears of his machine:

"Your father, the son of Castro, is our hostage. He is safe. I hit him only three or four times. Proceed to Las Vegas as you were originally commanded. You are an emissary of Tremont. Don't forget that. You are to meet the leader of Cuba on the evening of December 31, just as originally planned. If you fail to show up and fail to follow your original commands, nothing will happen to you. But I'm afraid your father will suffer more. Much more."

Another voice interjected: "Wait! Who is this? I want to speak to Tremont. I've got something he wants." It was Luke Braden.

"Holy shit," Carmody said. "The Bradens are Castros? And Castro's the target? This is, like, exploding in my brain. We've got to bring this recording back to Henriks! Here's the proof he demanded."

"Are you fuckin' nuts! This is the proof we broke his ruling!" Larsen yelled. "You wanna get laid in Rikers Island!"

"Then what are we gonna do?"

"We gotta grab your boy Ryan at Tremont and squeeze him till he squeals. We can't go direct to Tremont. And after you nab Ryan, we got to face up to a bigger problem."

"What's that?"

"Figure out how to get to Castro."

CHAPTER 84

Tremont had just enjoyed a manicure, and Tiffany's had just delivered his new Baume & Mercier wristwatch. After the scare over Sonny's drowning, his plans were coming together nicely. He was confident that Luke would pass the Fidel Test, even though he would be doing it under duress. Luke had no choice but to be a good soldier. His father's life depended on it, and he had no other options. Playa had swiped the playbook, and Luke hadn't a clue what to do with it anyway. Likewise, Castro would agree to meet briefly with Luke, or else Tremont would expose him as the father of a bastard American son.

In just a few days, chaos would surround the island of Cuba, and Tremont would be the perfect white knight to cross the Caribbean and save the Cuban people from turmoil. He had done his homework for the past forty years. Who else could wear the peace prizes, medallions, and ribbons to assure the U.S. government and the UN that he had only the noblest intentions? Who else had conquered Wall Street and would have the financial savvy to bring prosperity and a market economy to that isle of huts and hovels? Who else could promise to work with Miami to turn decades of tears into a flood of foreign aid and entrepreneurial activity? Havana would be buzzing, and Yanqui dollars would be flying. Into Paul Tremont's pockets.

Today was the day to put the playbook into action. Tremont stood in his office, arms folded, in front of his new acquisition from Sotheby's. A Salvador Dali abstract of fifty cubes that looked like heads of Lenin or maybe the massive head of a Bengal tiger. He called Ryan into his office.

Ryan looked nervous. Now Tremont's time had come. He was about to move the world. He began to bark instructions like a submarine commander launching torpedoes. The net asset value of Tremont Capital was $90 billion. That was huge. Less than Fidelity and Vanguard mutual funds, but those were owned by millions of people. Tremont's capital owners could share a plate of oysters in a booth at Le Bernadin. Normally, the Tremont funds would be leveraged 4 to 1. That meant Tremont advisers borrowed an additional $270 billion from the banks, thereby controlling $360 billion in their portfolio. Three hundred sixty billion was slightly less than the Pentagon budget, but Tremont wasn't buying tanks—he was buying bonds, stocks, piles of nickel, gold, and Japanese yen.

"Ryan, we're ramping up. First, I want to quadruple leverage. 16 to 1."

"You're kidding, right?" Ryan knew he wasn't. "That's almost $1.5 trillion."

"Yeah, about 15 percent of the size of the U.S. economy. But it's a global economy now, and $1.5 isn't too high. I'm sure Citi and Morgan and all the others will be happy to lend us the funds. We're their biggest source of commissions, right? We borrow more, they make more."

"Yes, sir." Ryan started taking notes. "But what if things blow up, if the trades start moving against us? We'd be like some welfare queen hooked on a stack of credit cards."

"Nonsense. When Long Term Capital blew up in the '90s, they ramped up leverage to 100 to 1."

"And almost brought down the entire world with them. Russia, Brazil, and the Pacific Rim all went belly up."

"A bunch of idiot Nobel Laureate economists. We're smarter than they are."

Tremont unfurled his copy of the "playbook for prosperity" on the conference table and smiled malevolently. He ordered Ryan to execute the trades. It was a strange combination. They would buy up a big portion of Carnival Cruises; sell Altria, formerly Philip Morris; sell Archer Daniels Midland, which made corn syrup; buy calls on the S&P 500; sell Italian bonds in favor of U.S. Treasuries; and dump euros in favor of U.S. dollars. It made no sense to Ryan. Had Tremont gone nuts at last?

Tremont paced around his oval office like a cougar in a cage. Ryan was feeling delirious. He looked at the Dali and then at Tremont. For a moment his eyes played a trick and it appeared that Tremont had grown fangs.

"When Castro goes, it'll be like the opposite of the Kennedy assassination and the Bay of Pigs. The markets will march in the exact reverse direction. We will be there. Big time."

This was prehistoric history to Ryan. In a twenty-four-hour global marketplace, this morning's breakfast is ancient history.

"Ryan, do these now. And then we're taking leverage up further to 50 to 1. By eight o'clock P.M. tomorrow, I want to be at 100 to 1."

Ryan's face lost its color.

"Our risk management software will blow up when I feed in these numbers. What do I tell the SEC and the New York Fed when they call?"

"Tell them to mind their own damn business. This is a democracy, right?"

It couldn't work. Ryan knew it wouldn't. Maybe 16 to 1, maybe even 20 to 1, but 100 to 1 meant that Tremont would be controlling the levers of a machine the size of the entire U.S. economy or all of Europe combined. The system couldn't take it. Where would the money come from? What would Tremont do if he could pull this off? Tremont's plan was like asking a Corvette to race around the track until the wheels burned off and the engine exploded. Who was going to be sitting in the driver's seat when the flames ignited?

As Tremont raved, Ryan scribbled a name on his order sheet. "James Carmody."

CHAPTER 85

Luke faked his way through the meeting in McLean. He grabbed a folder as he waited in the lobby, tucked it under his injured arm, and kept pointing to it, as if it held Tremont's playbook. The ten members of the secret committee gave him a half hour to make his case against Tremont as he begged for their financial assistance in offsetting the positions described in Tremont's playbook. He wanted to persuade them to buy whatever Tremont was selling and sell whatever Tremont was buying. That would send Tremont's portfolio into a tailspin. Unfortunately, Luke could not point the committee to any concrete examples. They were hardened veterans, suspicious and guarded. A woman named Veronica, fortyish in a houndstooth suit and the charm of a lizard, kept pushing him to reveal the contents of the playbook.

"The playbook is coded," Luke told her. "Of course, I've got the key, so it's no trouble," he lied to them. "I just need your go-ahead."

"I'm afraid that's impossible," Houndstooth answered for her team. "I'm sorry you bothered to come down here. Furthermore, Mr. Braden, please don't tell anyone about this meeting." She tapped her finger on the telephone pad in the center of the table.

Luke was stuck, literally. He'd failed at his one hope of a counterpunch, and he didn't even have cab fare to Dulles airport. By the time he walked or hitchhiked to the airport, his father could be dead. And where was Cori?

He was done in New York, done in McLean. He needed to be in Vegas right away. Veronica's driver dropped him at Dulles. Luke was broke, and his credit cards would not work at the ticket counters. Feeling defeated, he scrambled to find his membership card for American Airline's Admiral's Club. Once inside, he found a cubicle office there and tried to keep his eyes open so he could organize his next move. The door closed behind him and he thought of one of his father's books, a play by Sartre, *No Exit*. Did he ever actually read any of his father's books? Would his father ever read another book? Luke's eyelids felt heavy and his shoulders were drooping when he was startled by a loud knock.

The Club attendant opened the door and flung a first-class ticket on the small table. "Courtesy of Paul Tremont."

CHAPTER 86

Carmody was screaming at the cab driver, who apparently came from some country where they hadn't yet invented traffic lights. "Faster! Don't stop for that jerk pulling the pretzel cart!" Carmody was late. He thought a taxi would be faster than waiting for an official FBI car.

Ryan Fleet had told his stunned staff that he was sneaking out for a quick sandwich, even though they could see that Tremont's leverage was climbing and turbocharging the markets. CNBC was all over the story trying to track down the fund that was creating chaos in trading pits from Chicago to Sri Lanka. But Ryan sneaked out anyway. He dodged a stream of taxis, tore through the lobby at the Hudson Hotel, and raced into a gay bar off Fifty-seventh and Ninth. He had ten minutes before people at Tremont would talk, before Tremont himself might notice that Ryan had gone some place other than the bathroom.

Following his instructions to Carmody, he jumped into the back booth of the Wisteria Bar. The lights were dim and the place smelled of cockroach spray. He looked at his watch. Carmody had four minutes left to show up. Ryan ordered a complicated drink, hoping it would keep the bartender away. Three minutes to go.

Carmody was pounding on the Plexiglas as they crossed Thirty-third, and his driver felt the vibrations against his Sikh turban. "Sorry, man. Eighth is bitch. I try Tenth."

Carmody looked at his watch. How much longer would Ryan wait? They turned the corner onto Tenth and saw a nightmare. Bumper to bumper traffic.

"Sorry, man. *Lingcahn* Tunnel traffic."

Carmody wanted to explode. He brushed his hands through his hair and expected a clump to come out. He needed to burn twenty blocks in two minutes. That meant sixty miles an hour. He couldn't run that fast.

In the bar, Ryan looked at his watch. One more minute to spare. Maybe ninety seconds if he stretched it to the danger point. His back was to the door. He didn't see a young man with a backpack stride into the bar, refusing to make eye contact with the bartender who liked to touch all his patrons. The young Arabic man slid into the seat next to Ryan.

Ryan jumped up. "Who the hell are—?"

The man ripped a long knife from his backpack and plunged it between Ryan's ribs, aiming upward toward his heart. Before Ryan could scream, the man flew out the back door onto Fifty-eighth Street and hopped on a bus back to Yonkers.

The bartender approached Ryan's booth seconds later to deliver the drink. Ryan was gasping, bleeding onto the floor.

"My, God!" the bartender shouted.

Ryan whispered something to the man, just as the brakes of Carmody's taxi burned rubber in front of the bar.

Carmody found the bartender holding his head in shock and immediately knew he was too late. The pints of blood cascading down the booth's cushion told Carmody that mouth-to-mouth resuscitation was useless, but he tried anyway. When the ambulance arrived, Carmody let go of Ryan's hand and asked the bartender, "Did Mr. Fleet say anything?"

"Yes," the bartender said, "something about the mayor."

"The mayor?"

"He said 'Bloomberg.'"

Carmody couldn't imagine what Mayor Bloomberg had anything to do with this mess. But there was one man who might know. He hailed another cab, picked up Larsen, and told the driver to floor it to JFK. They had to find Luke Braden. He was taking orders from Tremont. And that meant Vegas.

CHAPTER 87

Carmody and Larsen called their counterparts in Vegas and alerted them to Luke Braden's arrival. Larsen remembered the tape of Cori Leopard in front of the Mandalay Bay and figured that it was Tremont's favorite spot, the hotel where he'd put up Braden. The agents set up a stakeout near the big birdcage across from the check-in counter.

When Luke arrived at the hotel, he looked like hell, needed a shave, and his clothes were dirty and wrinkled. He walked up to the counter, wearing sunglasses and shifting his eyes left and right, hoping to see no one other than tourists. FBI Agent Malone, wearing the badge of a hotel manager, greeted him warmly and escorted him to a suite on the twenty-fifth floor. When they got to the room, Malone grabbed Luke by the arm and flashed his FBI ID.

"What do you want?" Luke asked. He thought about divulging information about his father's kidnapping. But Tremont's men would kill his father instantly if he brought in the FBI.

Agent Malone handed a phone to Luke. It was Carmody and he sounded shaken, nervous. "Braden, we know they've got your father."

"You're lying," Luke said.

"We're coming out to Vegas 'cause we think this goes beyond your father."

Do they know about Castro?

"Ryan Fleet is dead. Murdered. I need to ask you something," Carmody said breathlessly. "His last words. He said something about Mayor Bloomberg. I need to know if that means anything to you."

Luke thought. He pictured his tense encounter with Ryan after Sonny died at the spa. He had been angered by Ryan's reaction. Protecting Tremont. Denying that Tremont did anything wrong, even though it was obvious he'd murdered the woman. Ryan was a mercenary without a conscience. But now Luke was playing back the sequence in his mind. True, Ryan dismissively said to Luke, "No worries." But his face had looked pained. The worries were deep. Then a strange thought struck.

Ryan had left open the vault, knowing I was nearby. That's it! Ryan *wanted* me to steal the playbook, wanted me to have some leverage. But Ryan didn't have the courage to wield it himself. He let me take it.

But the playbook was encoded and useless. Now, though, in his last breath, Ryan had given Luke the clue he needed. Bloomberg! That was it. He'd broken the code! All those unreadable letters and numbers must refer to the arcane, idiosyncratic codes of the Bloomberg machine! When the playbook said "BTP2.5," it meant that Tremont would sell 2.5 billion euros in Italian bonds. NKR1B meant selling 1 billion Norwegian Krone. All the others would fall into place. But should he reveal this to the FBI? Wouldn't it place his father in deeper jeopardy?

He returned to Carmody on the phone. "It means nothing to me." He handed the phone back to the Vegas agent.

Luke felt elated until he confronted another obstacle: When he took the train to D.C., he found the playbook useless without the code. Now he had the code, but he didn't have the playbook. Or did he?

Agent Malone left Luke's room to pick up Carmody and Larsen at the airport. He didn't yet have the authority to put Luke under house arrest. Luke stood at the window and looked at the garish hotels: New York–New York, Caesar's Palace, the Luxor pyramid, and the Venetian. The whole world on one Strip. A strip show of mankind. Where da Vinci meets da Mob.

His phone rang. It was Dr. Stuart Burns. He had a simple message. "Stick to the plan. Ryan Fleet had an accident. Your father is safe at the moment. Stick to the plan." Burns hung up. But how do I stick to the plan? Dress up in a tuxedo and casually walk up to Fidel Castro and tell him that Tremont is a big fan? I'm supposed to do this while my father has been beaten half to death? Because if I don't, they'll finish him off?

The phone rang. Burns again. "Stick to the plan. Cori Leopard is safe with Mr. Tremont." And then he added a brutal three-word phrase: "*At the moment.*"

Luke flung his fist against the armoire so hard that the door flew off. His father was strong, too. If they beat him, he might be able to take it. But Cori. What was she, one hundred fifteen pounds? And what do they do to women hostages? What had Tremont done to Sonny? Luke closed his eyes, trying to erase the image of rape.

Luke's shirt was frayed. He yanked the BlackBerry device out of his pocket and thought about hurling it through the plate glass window and seeing whether he could crack the Luxor pyramid with it. The damn thing was useless when he tried to figure out the playbook codes. On the Amtrak train to D.C., he'd plugged in all the playbook trades but couldn't manage to decipher any of them.

Wait! The memory! The BlackBerry would remember which keys I stroked. Now I just have to hit the reverse key again and again. It'll give me the original list of trades from the playbook. Then I just have to go to the Bloomberg Web portal.

The counterpunch was emerging again. Luke tapped key after key and jotted notes. In a few minutes, he had downloaded the trades and translated them into Bloomberg-speak. He now knew which trades Tremont would make to cash in on the destruction of Fidel Castro.

What could he do? He could take the opposite positions in the market and bankrupt Tremont. If Castro survived, Tremont would lose his fortune. Luke needed to ruin Tremont.

Where would Luke get the money? He immediately called up Houndstooth in McLean, she who led the investment committee and controlled the money. Billions to spare in the pension fund. He acted contrite, apologizing for being so secretive about the playbook. He began disclosing some of the plays. The woman was intrigued; he could hear it in her voice. She was taking notes. A few moments later she was downright eager to ruin Tremont.

The playbook clearly revealed where Tremont was placing his bets. Killing Castro would bring profits to cruise companies visiting Havana. Tremont was counting on Castro dying and the U.S. lifting the trade embargo. So under Tremont's plan, Cuba would export tons of sugar, driving down sugar prices. Tremont was betting against Archer Daniel Midlands because a dead Castro would let Tremont open up the sugar plantations, which would hurt ADM's corn syrup business. Tremont's playbook was convinced that Castro's death would propel U.S. stocks and bonds higher.

All these positions could erupt against Tremont, if Castro survived. Tremont would be forced to reverse his bets in a violent market environment. No one, no institution can fight its way out of a hugely leveraged and hugely wrong portfolio. In two hours either Tremont or Luke would be pummeled.

And so, with his father beaten and Cori in Tremont's clutches, Luke had no alternative but to launch a treacherous, high-stakes game of financial roulette. Tremont would have been proud.

CHAPTER 88

"Follow the plan." Those were the deadly instructions. Luke dressed in the tuxedo delivered by the Mandalay concierge and slicked back his hair. Houndstooth started sending to his BlackBerry a stream of bold-faced, red stock quotes. The financial bets were on. He vomited twice, thinking about his father and Cori, but he could see no exit, no hope for them, unless he went through with Tremont's meeting plan. He checked the markets. CNBC still couldn't figure out who had driven the market to extremes, nor who had pushed the markets in the opposite direction. They blamed Chinese speculators.

At seven o'clock Luke walked to the elevator. His finger twitched and he had trouble pushing "L" for Lobby. Eventually he got it right, and walked slowly through the casino and the restaurant plaza and to the Convention Center where the Cuban amateur delegation would be taking on NCAA champions. Security guards were everywhere, and under-cover cops probably manned every craps table and coffee shop in the hotel village. It was New Year's Eve, but in Vegas time doesn't matter. It's always nighttime. Strippers and ball gowns mingle like in a Weimar cabaret. Luke showed his ID four times and was frisked three times. His telephone breezed through the metal detector. A security agent wearing a Cuban flag lapel pin patted Luke down on the testicles so hard he gasped.

They don't take chances with their "ruler for life." His grandfather. Luke wondered what Castro would think if he knew his son had been beaten and was writhing or retching or dying? Or that his grandson was being manipulated like a marionette? Was Castro so cold that he would smirk? Or would he try to stop the murders? Luke didn't know. No one really knew what Castro would do, whether his blood ran hot or cold.

If I don't know who Castro is, I can't have a clue who I am. All those years playing hooky from school, boxing at the gym, sneering at my father. What was the point? I spent my life rebelling against my father, but—my God!—Francis Braden was the rebel. He was the gutsy one. He was the one breaking free and trying to protect me. Luke entered the enormous room: 11,400 empty seats surrounding an empty boxing ring festooned with flags of Cuba and the United States. He felt the instinctive urge to move his arms, but his suit felt tight on his biceps and his chest. The collar pinched. He felt caged, defanged. He didn't belong here anymore. But where did he belong? With his father's books? On the trading floor of a hedge fund? The only place he ever felt right was in Cori's arms. And she was with Tremont now. He needed to erase that image right now.

The Cuban guard who patted him so roughly grabbed him by the shoulder and pushed him up a ramp. Luke wanted to resist, but he knew the only way to keep his father and Cori alive was to "stick to the plan."

As he reached the top of the ramp he saw a steel door, draped in the Cuban flag. He smelled cigar smoke. The guard pushed open the door for him and said, *"Paredon."* "To the wall." Luke knew this phrase. It was the cry of Castro's minions when they dragged their enemies to the firing squad.

CHAPTER 89

Luke followed the guard. He found himself staring into the blue eyes of Paul Tremont, blue like the fire of a blowtorch. His hair was mussed and his perfectly tailored jacket was hanging off one shoulder. Luke had never seen him disheveled, even after he'd killed Sonny's in the Grotto. The Cuban guard grabbed Luke from behind and jammed his elbows together. Tremont took two steps toward Luke and smashed a fist into Luke's face. Luke winced and twisted his body.

Tremont lifted Luke's face by his chin. "Do you know what you've done? Do you have any idea who you have screwed with, what plans you have destroyed? You useless piece of Communist shit. I groomed you, I brought you up from the stinking level of a washed-up athlete. You were stuck on the ground floor of an office doing what? Do you fucking remember? Checking packages, handing out hallway passes like a pathetic $40,000-a-year teacher? Within a few weeks, I let you put your ignorant hands on the joystick of Wall Street. And what have you done? You've taken the joystick and fucked yourself with it! You've driven us into the ground."

Luke watched Tremont's lips, spittle flying. He felt the Cuban yanking back harder and harder, maybe trying to snap his arms. But two faces kept passing him: his father and Cori. Tremont raged on, and each bitter word sounded like a shovel plunging into gravel. He imagined the gravel being dumped on graves.

Tremont hit him again.

CHAPTER 90

Larsen was desperate. He had to get to Castro. Warn him. The thought made him sick. When he took his FBI oath, he swore to protect Americans not communist dictators. But he had no time to deliberate. As Carmody watched nervously, Larsen picked up the phone and called the State Department. They kept redirecting his calls to the Latin research desk, as if he were looking for a grant. Useless.

"Godammit, his life's at stake!" Larsen screamed.

"Have your supervisor file a report," came the reply.

Larsen knew what he had to do. He had no choice but to jump far above his rank and command something so ballsy that it would destroy his career. It might even destroy U.S. foreign policy for the next fifty years. He called Agent Malone in Vegas.

"Where's Castro's plane?"

"On the runway. It's an Airbus A320."

"Impound it," Larsen ordered.

"Are you nuts? Where do you get off impounding the plane of a sovereign leader?"

"Malone, forty years on the force gives me that power. I'll take the fall. Now go out there and show your badge."

"No."

"Are you going to back me up if this blows up?"

"Malone, if this blows up, we'll both be in Guantanamo. Just do it."

Malone marched out to the runway and dared to use the word "impound."

The Cubans reacted badly, cursing and threatening retaliation. "You think we're drug dealers?" asked the pilot angrily.

But Larsen's gambit had a more immediate effect. The pilot radioed the Mandalay Bay. Suddenly, the elevators of the Mandalay Bay stopped and security guards poured into Fidel Castro's suite. The security force escorted Castro and his staff down a special elevator. They fled the hotel and raced in Bentleys to the airport. During the brief and tense ride, Castro's aide arranged for Air Canada to grant them use of a Bombardier jet to return to Cuba.

Castro was gone. Tremont's symphony, hat trick, and knockout punch had fizzled. Paul Tremont was sinking into an abyss.

Tremont exploded at the news. He knew what this meant. He had put chips equal to the whole U.S. economy on black. And the dice came up red. Communist red. Ryan's assistants tried to add up the damage, but their spreadsheets could not accommodate losses in the trillions. Citi and Morgan and Mitsubishi called in their loans and panic selling hit all of Tremont's longs and buying buried his shorts. The chairman of the Federal Reserve Board took unprecedented action, calling a bank holiday. But the blood was pouring out onto Wall Street. Tremont's funding collapsed. Tremont himself was literally roaring. His first call was not to his lawyers or bankers. He called Yonkers: "Kill Braden."

The Middle Eastern men who held Professor Braden had little to do. They tied a vacuum hose to the tailpipe of the car where they were keeping him, and directed it into the trunk. Within minutes, the professor was dead. They dumped him in the Hudson and caught a Greyhound to Cincinnati.

CHAPTER 91

"Where is my father? Where is Cori?" Luke managed to ask as his lower lip swelled up.

Tremont refused to answer. He hit Luke again and seemed to take pleasure in watching his handiwork. "Playa!" he screamed.

Into the room came Christian Playa. Luke immediately recognized the man, the one who had swiped his bag and stabbed him on the Metro. While Tremont appeared frenzied, his cheekbones quivering with rage, Playa look composed. The Face. Creased like it was raked. Thick, bushy eyebrows. He had thick clumps of hair crawling up the back of his neck.

"I believe you have met," Tremont said. "Mr. Playa, this is the man who has decided to sustain Fidel Castro's regime. That makes him the accessory to murder, rape, and repression, correct Mr. Playa?"

Playa nodded his head.

"But you did not act alone, did you, Luke?"

Luke didn't know how to respond. Castro meant nothing to him until a few days ago. Did he really care about his grandfather, now? No. He longed for his father and Cori. And they were hostages of Tremont, not the Cuban government.

"Bring her in, Playa."

A surge of hope burst inside Luke. Cori is alive. He would see her. And then he would try to figure a way out.

But it was not Cori who slowly limped into the room. Luke had no idea who the elderly woman was. She was thin and dressed in a black dress. Long white gloves covered up her arms. Her lips were bright with red lipstick. Her cheekbones were high, drawing Luke into her remarkably clear eyes.

"Do you know this old woman?"

Luke shook his head. Was she a friend of Tremont or another hostage? He couldn't tell. Tremont pointed to a chair, but the woman was too proud to sit. She would stand. And then she spoke.

"Luke," she said softly. "I tried to warn—"

It was the voice of the woman who had sent the disk.

Luke interrupted her. "You know my father? You talked about him."

Tremont snickered. "Of course she knows your father. This is your father's mother."

She nodded.

"And you know who your father's father is? Castro."

"This is the bitch of Fidel Castro. Oriana." Tremont grimaced.

Oriana neither blinked nor blushed. She was beyond that, forty years beyond embarrassment. She held her sharp tongue. She knew the good news. Tremont was destroyed and Castro was safe. She had won. Even if Tremont appeared to be holding the cards, the only thing he held was a delusion about who was in charge.

Luke was confused, devastated. Why should he care about these relics, Castro and this women, this Oriana? It was just DNA that linked them together. He would gladly kill Paul Tremont, Fidel Castro, and even this Oriana, if that would save the ones he cared about.

Luke finally spoke up. "Why are you doing this? I didn't need your nightmare."

Tremont smiled. "But I needed you. You were my tool for defeating Castro, for avenging what men like Playa and me lost, what JFK lost."

Oriana leaned against a chair, and then grasped it with her long fingers. She looked as though she might stumble. Playa reached out a hand to steady her, and for a moment his hand rested on hers.

Then Tremont launched the missile aimed at Luke. "Of course, you will now lose too, Luke. I'm so terribly sad to report that your father is dead. Pity. I hated to place that trade, I mean order." Tremont refused to blink.

The Cuban guard's arms tightened, but adrenalin, driven by blind fury surged through Luke. He bent his knees and lifted himself up by his powerful thighs, loosening the Cuban guard's grasp. Luke withdrew his right arm and jammed his elbow into the man's groin. The man doubled over, and like lightning bolts, Luke smashed a left, a right, and another left into the man's jaw. The man's eyes rolled up. Luke took his head and jammed it down on his knee. The Cuban collapsed.

Tremont backed up, looking for Playa to intervene.

"Playa, take care of him!" Tremont suddenly looked shorter than six-foot-three, his blazing eyes turning grayer, cloudier. Playa did not move.

Luke leapt across the room at Tremont and grabbed him by his collar. "I'll kill you! *I will kill you!*"

Tremont took one more chance to screw with his mind. "So now I'm Perez, am I?"

Luke smashed his forearms into the sides of Tremont's neck and brought Tremont's head down to his chest, immobilizing him. With one hand on the top of Tremont's head and the other underneath his chin, Luke knew he could twist and snap this man's neck. He yearned to do it. And then he pictured Perez.

"Go ahead, Luke," Oriana said firmly.

Playa was fiddling with a phone or gun or something else that was electronic.

Luke began to twist Tremont's neck, but the older man's moans made Luke hesitate. Tremont feigned a collapse and dropped a few inches, escaping from Luke's death grip. Then he threw his arms around Luke's shoulders and squeezed.

Luke felt a buzz, a ring, a vibration. His body began to shudder, as from an electrical shock. He felt Tremont's body shudder as well. Then Tremont's arms quivered and he collapsed to the floor, his chest heaving uncontrollably.

Luke himself was trembling, his chest seizing up. He looked at Playa, who was still fiddling with the metal object. What was it?

Playa had activated the taser in Luke's phone. Luke shucked his suit jacket, and the electrical charge stopped.

Tremont lay flat on the floor, his head twisting, his breath labored, his face without color.

He managed a gasp. "Oriana, tell him about November 1963."

She shook her head slowly but defiantly. She was still leaning against the chair, fragile and old. "No, I will not." She closed her eyes.

"Then I will," Tremont rasped. "Do you know why they haven't to this day figured out who killed Jack Kennedy? Jack was not the target in

Dallas. The Mob wasn't trying to wipe him out. Not the Russians either. Jack got in the way of a jealous woman. Fucked with the wrong girl. A crazy dame who was in love with Fidel Castro."

"You're insane," Oriana snapped, her eyes suddenly opening wide, staring down at Tremont on the floor.

"Am I?" Tremont said. He paused, as his chest heaved, searching for some breath. "Luke, you believe what you want. But I'm telling you that Oriana, your grandmother, paid for a hit in Dallas. But the president wasn't supposed to die in that motorcade."

Tremont's eyelids fluttered, but he continued to mumble. Luke put his face closer to Tremont's. "People say Oswald was a sharpshooter. He wasn't that great a shot," Tremont whispered. "He missed."

His last breath brought forth into the world, for the first time, these startling words: *"Oswald was hired to kill Jackie."* Tremont tilted his head toward Oriana. "Tell your grandson." He didn't utter another word. His eyes closed.

Luke froze. But Playa did not. While Tremont was whispering his dying words, Playa had picked up Luke's jacket and gently, protectively draped it over Oriana's shoulders. Her body shuddered, and then she fell to the ground. She did not move again.

Playa dashed out the door and slipped into the neon-lit streets of Las Vegas.

CHAPTER 92

Seconds later the police rushed into the skybox where Tremont and Oriana lay dead. Luke slipped out into the convention hall, desperate for air that did not stink from forty years of brutal scheming. And then he saw her. Cori. Luke ran to her and they hugged tightly. A few steps behind was Senator Harold Leopard.

"I thought Tremont had you," Luke said, his eyes welling up with tears.

"No, Senate Security held me in my father's office. I guess I was their hostage, but that wasn't so bad. Tremont never got near me. He must've been bluffing."

What else might Tremont have been bluffing about? Luke asked himself. *Oriana and Jacqueline Kennedy?* Was that why the Warren Commission and all the others had fumbled? They didn't have the wrong shooter; they had the wrong target. My father's mother, my own grandmother, hired Lee Harvey Oswald to murder Jackie Kennedy in Dallas? *What in the world does that make me?*

"Luke," Cori whispered quietly, "they killed your father." She began to weep, and while he brushed away her tears, his eyes overflowed, too. He drew her near again, and tried to make up for the times he had not hugged his father.

"All these years," Luke said softly, "maybe my father was just trying to protect me from this."

Senator Leopard kept the police away from Cori and Luke. They silently walked out of the convention hall and into the desert night as streams of gamblers, tourists, and shoppers passed by. Finally, Cori asked a question. "How did you convince the CIA to bet against Tremont in the markets?"

"It wasn't the CIA," Luke said slyly.

"But you went to McLean. Everyone in Washington knows that 'McLean' means the CIA. Even the road maps tell you the CIA is in McLean."

"So is the Mars Company, and they didn't care much for Paul Tremont."

They heard a roar overhead and looked up to see an Air Canada jet take off into the starry skies, heading east, ninety miles beyond Miami.

EPILOGUE

"Buzz the Strip," the gravelly voice ordered.

The pilot grabbed the throttle of the Bombardier and thrust his arm forward. The jet quickly banked to the right, down the Vegas Strip, roaring past the fake Chrysler Building and within a few hundred feet of the Eiffel Tower. A crowd at the Venetian Hotel stared up, wondering who had the audacity to interrupt the gondoliers.

Fidel Castro leaned back into the leather chair and looked out the window, down at the swirling lights, the pink neon, the strippers, and the stripped. The glory of capitalism.

He pulled from his breast pocket a slim wallet. He didn't carry cash. He opened the soft cowhide and withdrew a piece of paper. He read his handwriting, a date, "January 1959." The month he marched into Havana. He wasn't a wistful man. Eighty ruthless years on earth. But while old age can dry one's skin to parchment, it can also play tricks and bring tears to your eyes.

Fidel's bodyguards looked away from the raging prophet, who suddenly looked like an old man.

Fidel took the paper in his leathery hands and slowly turned it over. He stared down at the faded image. The Caribbean-colored eyes of a dark-haired beauty peered at him. He wondered what had become of Oriana.

ACKNOWLEDGMENTS

I must admit to being amazed by the author who blows kisses and hurls thank yous to the thousands of individuals who helped him write his book. Anyone who has time to engage in serious conversations with thousands of people while writing a book, must be plagiarizing it. Hemingway had it right. All you need is ink, a bottle of booze, and a view of the surf. Nowadays, a laptop helps too.

Of course, I had all those tools in Solana Beach, California, but more important a loving family that forgave those moments when I snuck into my office to bang out a line of dialogue. My wonderful wife Debby, General Manager of the La Jolla Playhouse, encouraged me with her warm, loving smile, while insisting I get out to enjoy other people's fiction. My extraordinary daughters Victoria, Katherine, and Alexia gave me hugs, cookies, and the confidence that Daddy could do anything. Victoria still insists a better title for this book would be *The Fidel Test*. So if *The Castro Gene* sells a billion copies, it would have sold a billion plus one with the "right" title. Several times each day, our dog Amaretto would drop a tennis ball at my feet, hoping that I would play catch with her. No doubt, she was concerned about my cardiovascular health.

Thanks also to my enthusiastic agent Susan Ginsburg and the energetic team at Oceanview, Susan Greger, Pat and Bob Gussin.

Teachers are important. I've been waiting for the right opportunity to thank my high school English teacher, Martin Meszaros, who knows more about the Lost Generation than anyone I know and over the years helped thousands of teenagers find their way. Julian Robertson, the legendary (and charming) hedge fund king, taught me that the most successful financiers can have the highest ethics.

I thank my mother, Joan, a wonderful storyteller and teacher, for reading drafts of this book. My grandparents passed away some time ago, but I thought of them often. My paternal grandfather, Robert Buchholz, was quite the athlete as a young man, winning the New York City tennis championship and boxing under the name Buck Roberts, a name that appears in this book. My father, Alvin, would have relished the boxing scenes too.

My maternal grandparents, Samuel and Pauline Lewis, frequently visited Cuba in the days before Castro, including their honeymoon in 1929. In my office, I have vintage photographs of them at the legendary Sloppy Joe's nightclub in Havana, lifting their glasses, adorned Gatsby-like in fur, pearls, and tuxedo. That photo appears below. My grandparents are the handsome couple on the left.

How long did it take to write this book? I guess it started in 1929, long before I showed up on the scene.

SLOPPY JOE'S NIGHTCLUB

HAVANA, 1929